TENDRILS OF PASSION
The Possession Chronicles #3

By
Carrie Dalby

For Joyce Scarbrough,
who loaned me my first Gothic romance,
and
James McAvoy, for being awesome

One

As much as Magdalene disliked dressing up and being
fussed over by Mrs. Melling during her birthday trip to Pensacola, it
was easier to handle thinking it a one-time event. Upon their return
to Seacliff Cottage, it grew to weekly and then bi-weekly trips.
Luncheons and teas at the Grand Hotel in Point Clear where the
society women chattered about everyone's business but their own.
Magdalene wished the trips were because Mrs. Melling was ready to
return to her previous lifestyle, but she went to find out if anyone
had gossip about her husband—not that the ladies would discuss
someone's husband with her at the table. Magdalene previously
entertained visions of cozying up the carriage house as a newlywed
with Douglas. Now she realized staying with the Melling family
wasn't in their best interest.

"Magdalene," Mrs. Melling said as she sat with her in the
backseat of the automobile on the way home from the Thursday tea
at the hotel, "did you hear the way Mrs. Inge spoke about her
children's governess? It was most unbecoming. If the lady is that
obnoxious, she needs to be released."

"I'm sure." Magdalene adjusted the veil over her wide-
brimmed hat that had blown askew in the breeze coming off Mobile
Bay. She'd heard snatches of the story from Mrs. Inge's booming
voice, but Magdalene was placed at a different table full of
debutantes.

"You need to speak up more, Magdalene. Some of the ladies
asked about you when you went to the powder room. They think you
are unwell because you are quiet and often looked pained at the
table."

It was painful for her to sit through the events—and not just because of the tight corset. Magdalene much preferred being a companion to a recluse than a socialite, but she felt it time for a little honesty. She removed her gloves and opened her reticule. After retrieving her engagement ring and placing it on her finger, she tucked the gloves inside and snapped it shut.

"I find these parties very uncomfortable to attend."

"Oh, my dear, I loathe most of the ladies and some of the topics are as droll as dry toast. But we must suffer through."

"While some of the topics are dull, others I find infuriating and sometimes even lewd." Magdalene's fists tightened but she didn't want to mention details about the young women's plots to take turns visiting the break area where the drivers waited. It wasn't Mrs. Melling's business that the ladies relied on the drivers to instruct them on certain techniques to aid their quest to win a man. "I'm not used to it nor do I wish to become desensitized to conversations like that."

Mrs. Melling ran a hand over her duster. "You are being most theatrical, Magdalene. Do explain yourself."

"For one thing, why can't I wear my ring at these events? Why must I hide my engagement? You're happy for me, aren't you?"

"Of course I am happy for you, but I do it for your own good. A lady's companion is a respectable job—often occupied by a distant relation whose family is on hard times. You look so lovely when dressed for society, you pass as one of us at first inspection and turn heads, as I have mentioned before. If it were to get out that you are engaged to the chauffeur, the ladies would immediately look down on you, making things much more uncomfortable than they could ever be now."

Magdalene turned red under her veil, noticing that Douglas seemed to be straining to follow their conversation over the sound of the wind. "I've had enough of society's double standards. Those ladies at my table today were comparing their drivers like pieces of meat in a butcher's shop. The things they said about Douglas—"

"Be flattered, my dear. Every woman enjoys seeing a handsome man, no matter his profession. I could have told you our Douglas is the filet mignon of the whole lot."

"But they were planning things no lady should discuss." From the conversations she'd witnessed in the last four weeks, she understood how Eliza Melling could have fallen into transgression with Claudio—she just hoped for the deacon's sake he was her only conquest.

Mrs. Melling laughed. "The men live their double lives, and we accept that. Most of the girls get that out of their system before they marry and gain experience so they need not fear their wedding night."

Magdalene's face paled, making her blotchy. "No one should be exposed to that. Let me drive us next time so Douglas isn't subjected to those ogling women."

"Do not make a fool of yourself, Magdalene. Whatever comes to pass, you will end up with his name."

Magdalene bit her tongue the rest of the ride home. When Douglas exited the automobile, the lady of the house gave his backside an appreciative glance and then turned to Magdalene to make her point.

The indignity rising within her had Magdalene boiling with rage by the time Douglas returned from walking Mrs. Melling to the gate. She sat in the backseat, arms crossed.

He climbed in next to her, taking her hand. "Let it go, Maggie."

"But you don't know what it's like!" She gripped his hand so hard he had to loosen it with his other.

"Aye, I do. What do you think the chauffeurs talk about while you ladies are dining? They all want to know about the fresh face that's with the Mellings this season and if I've…well, that's not fit for your ears." He winked at her, but followed it with a sweet kiss on her bare hand. "I field their questions, but make it clear that you're mine."

"I can't do that because she's banned me from speaking your name when I'm in public! She thinks my 'country wife' tendencies will show. Did you hear all that's transpired?"

"Most of it, but it doesn't change us."

"If my aunt ever responds for my father, maybe we can move beyond this stifling existence. I do think she's taking her time to torture me. And even if she replies, I'll never know if it's what my father truly said or not. We need to make our own plans. We can't stay here."

"I know." Douglas folded the riding veil over her hat so he could kiss her. "I'm working on preparing Uncle Simon. He's no longer fit for full labor, so we'll need to take him with us. This has been his home for decades and he isn't one that accepts change readily."

"He's been most kind to me. I wouldn't turn him out." Magdalene ran her hand over Douglas's cheek, enjoying the sensation of the prickly shadow of a beard on her palm. "We need to be together."

"I'll figure it out, Maggie. And even though you don't like it, you do pull off the fashionable look nicely." He gently touched the lace on her cuff and trailed his fingers up to her high neckline before bringing his lips to hers.

"Magdalene!" Mrs. Melling's voice carried across the yard. "Come quickly, Magdalene!"

In her rush, she went for the open car door, stumbling over Douglas's lap in the process. With a hand atop her head to keep her large hat from flying away, she dashed across the lane and through the gate to the front porch.

Mrs. Melling waved a telegram in the doorway and smiled like Magdalene had never seen.

"Is there news from my family?" Magdalene asked, though she knew her aunt wouldn't spend money on a telegram.

"Your family? Of course not. It's from Alex! He's engaged to Beatrice Kirkpatrick and they'll be here in a month. Oh, the glories of royal ties and the striking beauty of good breeding are mine!" She retreated to the parlor and poured drinks for herself and Magdalene, then Rosemary and Leroy, who she called in to tell the news, though they'd already heard her shouting about it.

The parlor reminded Magdalene of when she arrived five months ago. The dark drapes were shut to keep out the summer heat and it blanketed the red and mahogany room in a dreary hue. After the Wattses returned to work and Mrs. Melling settled down—the wine helping her relax—Magdalene fished for answers to her pressing questions.

"Who all will be coming in September?"

"Alex, Beatrice, and a chaperone—most likely her aunt Polly. She is often mentioned in the columns about her. Edith says Polly is very respectable. She's widowed and childless. At only thirty-two, she is still spry enough to stay up late to keep watch over her niece's virtue."

She'll need that with Alexander around. "Will they stay at the hotel or here?"

"Here, of course. Though I suppose we will need to be in the city as well."

"Where will they sleep?"

"We shall put her aunt in the small guest room and Beatrice will naturally have yours."

"Wouldn't it be advisable if Douglas and I marry before they return? That way you'll have more room for your guests and I'll be out of the way."

"You must not marry before Alex. I simply will not have time to plan anything until after his wedding."

"We don't want a fuss made. We have no extended relations that would come to fill the pews at a church, nor do we know many people beyond those who live and work here. You've done so much already that I don't wish to put you out over anything."

"It is no trouble, my dear. I shall tuck you away in the attic. It is hot up there this time of year, but with the windows open it should be tolerable."

Magdalene paled at the mention of the attic. "Will you excuse me?"

Mrs. Melling waved her away and closed her eyes, a smile of contentment on her face.

Magdalene wrapped her arms around herself to stop her hands from trembling. She climbed the front stairs, the temperature rising several degrees with each step. By the time she reached her room, she was sweating under all the layers of ruffles and corsets. She ripped the hat from her head, the pins pulling her hair and the veil tangling around her hand before she threw it on the floor. Struggling with the buttons down her back, she managed to shimmy out of the tea gown. After unlacing her corset and unbuttoning the wretched white boots, she yanked off her stockings and fell on her bed in tears.

A quarter of an hour later, someone knocked at her door. Magdalene made no move to answer it. She lay curled on her side in her chemise and petticoat, bare feet poking out from the bottom ruffles while praying Rosemary would leave her alone.

When she gave no response, the door creaked open.

"Maggie?" Douglas's warm voice pulled her from despair.

She sat up, eyes wide in surprise. Douglas followed the trail of clothing across the floor and then stared at her several seconds before covering his eyes with an envelope.

"I'm sorry. I didn't think…" He stepped back toward the door but placed his boot square on her hat. "Sorry!" He instinctively made eye contact with the apology—turning red and looking away.

Magdalene laughed, the residue of dried tears cracking on her cheeks. "What are you doing here?"

"I drove to the post office." He focused his attention on the closed window. "Mrs. Melling appears to have toasted herself into a nap. Since there was something for you, Rosemary said it was fine for me to bring it up. I'm sure she didn't expect you to be undressed any more than I did. But it's hot in here."

"Could you shut the door and open the windows?"

Relief filled his face and he tucked the envelope into his pocket. "Right away, Maggie. I'd hate for someone to stick their head in and see you…and me…" The door clicked shut and then he saw to the window.

The curtains billowed in the late afternoon breeze, reminding Magdalene of what caused her tears. She shivered in spite of the torrid heat of the August afternoon.

"Sit with me?" she asked as she patted the bed beside her.

"Your clothes?" He motioned to the mess on the floor.

"I'm not putting those back on. And besides, you've seen me in nightgowns and my bathing suit. Those show more than my underclothes."

Douglas cleared his throat and pointed to his chest. "Not up here they don't."

"Well, I'm sick of caring about propriety." Magdalene stood and kicked one of the boots across the room. "If Mrs. Melling wasn't being a controlling fiend, we'd be married. Go ahead and get a good look, because at the rate she's going, I'll be lucky to be married by the time I'm thirty."

"Maggie, it can't be that bad."

"You didn't hear all she said to me!"

They met in the middle of the room and embraced, Magdalene resting her head on his shoulder, crinkling the envelope.

"Take the mail, it might have good news."

Magdalene pulled the letter out of his shirt pocket. "It's from Aunt Agnes, but I'm too upset to see straight. Would you read it to me?"

"Not until I hear about what has you so distressed. Don't tell me you're pining over Alexander getting married." She looked at him quizzically. "Rosemary told me. I thought those ties had long been exorcised."

"I feel nothing for him but there'll be a house full of people here. With Mrs. Melling traveling back and forth across the bay with wedding preparations, I remarked that it would be good for us to get married before Alexander returns so there'd be more room in the house and I wouldn't be in the way." Magdalene spoke so fast she had to catch her breath to continue. Her chest heaved, and then her cheeks colored upon noticing Douglas's gaze. "She insisted on us not being married before Alexander because she wouldn't be able to focus preparations for both and that she would tuck me away in the attic for safe keepings. The attic! You know all that's happened there."

Douglas nodded and rubbed his hands over her arms because she'd broken out in gooseflesh.

"The mention of the attic brought back memories I hadn't thought of in months. Before Claudio completely cleansed the house, I had a reoccurring nightmare involving the attic and Alexander."

Douglas stopped moving, his hands resting just above her elbows. "And?"

"You don't need to know the sordid details, but the setup was an engagement party for Alexander and I was staying in the attic." Magdalene began pacing and the letter fluttered from her grasp to the floor. "Don't you see? The dream was while I was affected by the demon. Claudio told me demons have knowledge of things unknown to us. What if it was a premonition? What if Alexander will defile me while I'm up there?"

Douglas folded her into his arms and nestled into her tousled hair. "We'll change the course of events and not allow that to happen. I'll scale the wall and climb into the window each night to guard you if needed. Or, if all else fails, we'll run away together before anything could happen. But first, the letter." He picked it off the floor. "Do you still wish me to read it?"

"Yes, please."

Dear Magdalene,

> *If you haven't already run off with that beau of yours, I hope this letter finds you well. It has taken me so long to reply because I've been busy seeing to the affairs of your family. If you are still employed with the Mellings, you will be happy to know*

Though his voice broke several times in the last paragraph, Douglas continued reading until he finished, cradling a sobbing Magdalene in one arm. He dropped the paper and folded her into his chest with his full embrace.

"Maggie, such cruelty your aunt displayed. I'm sorry about your father."

She sucked in her tears long enough to speak. "I no longer have an aunt—she's dead to me."

Ten minutes later, her crying slowed as she clung to her betrothed. Her sobbing soaked Douglas's shirt and ran down her décolletage, but she made no effort to move.

"Maggie, you need to think about getting dressed. It's close to suppertime and Rosemary's likely to be sent to find you if you don't arrive."

She turned her wet face to him. "Kiss me."

Douglas leaned in and planted a gentle one on her lips.

"Kiss me as if this was our last day on earth!" She pulled out of his arms. "Breathe into my soul with your passion. I need to feel alive, because it feels as though part of me is dead."

He briefly closed his eyes, as if weighing his options, then swept her off her feet. Showing devotion, fervor, and compassion with his enduring caresses and absolute attention, Douglas brought them to the edge of ecstasy before setting her down.

"Thank you." Magdalene, weakened from the range of emotions she'd felt in the last hour, stayed beside him but ran a hand over her hair. "I'm sure I tasted like tears and look a mess."

"A beautiful mess." Douglas kissed her neck, lingering for a moment at her collarbone before straightening. "Now for your clothes. If someone were to walk in right now, they'd think I'd—"

"I'm sorry for keeping you here so long. It isn't fair to put you in jeopardy."

"We're in this together, never forget that. From now until forever, we're a team." He kissed her once more, and then escorted her to the wardrobe, where she pulled out a black skirt and a simple white shirtwaist. "Do you want your corset?" He pointed to it on the floor near the bed.

"No, I still feel the lines on me."

"She had it tight?"

"Ever since my birthday dinner in Pensacola she's been preening me like a doll. She's dressed me herself whenever there's a social function. It's disgusting and I hate that corset and those silly white boots the most."

"Why hadn't you told me? I knew she'd been buying you clothes but I didn't realize she controlled you like that. I'll get you out of here soon, Maggie." His hands massaged her waist through her chemise. "And she's crazy if she thinks you need to be bound into these dresses. You're perfect the way you are."

A lone tear dripped out of her eye, falling upon Douglas's bowed head as he tenderly kissed the base of her neck. No matter that she was parentless, Magdalene knew she'd never be alone. She slipped her arms into her shirt and allowed Douglas to button it closed, his hands trembling as he passed over her chest.

"You're too sweet for words," she whispered. "I love you."

"And I love you, Maggie. It has to be love for me to be torturing myself like this." He finished with her shirt and nuzzled into her neck. Douglas nibbled his way to each earlobe, causing her to squirm and giggle. With a calming touch to her cheek, he stopped. "Sorry. I'm sure you're not in the mood for frivolity."

She wrapped him in a firm hug. "Your attention does wonders for me. Never apologize for bringing me pleasure. I'm sure we'll need all the joy we can get in the days ahead."

Two

Now that she had news to brag about, Mrs. Melling increased her outings, going so far as to take the morning ferry to Mobile for a day of shopping on a Tuesday at the end of August. Magdalene felt like a melting confection in her tiers of pastel lace. By the time they exited the ferry and secured a horse-drawn cab, sweat pooled between her breasts. She used her oriental fan with the hand-painted cranes on it to cool her face.

They first stopped at the bank around the corner from Mr. Melling's office. Magdalene sat in the canopied carriage while Mrs. Melling went in. A young clerk ran out of the bank and disappeared in the direction of the law firm. A few minutes later, the clerk returned at a leisurely stroll, followed by Mr. Melling.

Magdalene tried to hide her face behind the dainty fan but it didn't work.

"Good morning, Miss Jones. You're looking particularly lovely this summer's day." He smiled like a wolf.

"Thank you, Mr. Melling." She folded her fan and let it dangle from her wrist.

He flipped the driver a quarter and held up the fingers on one hand. The driver tipped his cap and hopped out to take a break.

Magdalene shifted uneasily on the padded bench.

"I understand Captain Walker delivered your crates last Friday. It took a pretty penny to fetch those things from Seven Hills and ship them to Seacliff Cottage." He leaned against the side of the carriage, the pale blue sleeve of his seersucker suit hanging inside as his hand inched closer to Magdalene.

"I appreciate your generosity, but feel free to dock my pay to reimburse the expense. I don't wish to be beholden to you."

"But I'm so easy to repay, Miss Jones. No money need be exchanged." He reached for her knee, only to be smacked by Magdalene's fan.

"I see the stable boy has yet to train the stubbornness from you. That means there's still a chance for me, especially since I see no ring on your finger."

"Thank you for your concern, but I have a ring, though I am instructed to leave it off when accompanying Mrs. Melling."

He laughed. "I think that's one for the record books—Ruth has you cowed before I could do the honors."

Nausea filled her from the truth Mr. Melling spoke. *Why didn't I refuse to remove my ring on my birthday? If I had been firm in denying the first request, I wouldn't have a sickening feeling each time it leaves my finger because I would never be removing it. Nor would I be parading around Mobile looking like an Easter basket with flounces and a flowered hat.*

"George, you did not need to come out." Mrs. Melling touched his arm. "I was going to stop in the office to see if you would take dinner with us."

"And miss a chance to see you looking as lovely as ever? The rumors have reached the city about the stunning companion you bring to every luncheon and tea on the Eastern Shore, and the fact that this season has you looking more radiant than ever yourself. I must admit the stories are true. That blue is perfection on you, Ruth."

They twittered back and forth, small talk about clothing needed for the wedding parties and the Mobilians frequenting the other side of the bay. After the driver returned, Mrs. Melling asked about the midday meal.

"I have a noon meeting I cannot miss." He looked sideways at Magdalene and winked. He helped his wife into the carriage and gave her a quick kiss on the cheek. "Next time you come, give me a day's notice and I'll clear my schedule. Keep looking like you do and I'll force you to come home to me."

"Soon enough, George. Alex and Beatrice will be here within the month and we will spend time at both houses with the wedding being held at the cathedral. But I do not want to see that maid at the mansion."

"That flighty thing I thought would work out here?" Mr. Melling adjusted his suspenders. "I sent her off months ago. City life didn't agree with her."

"She was always disagreeable to me. I am glad she is gone. It will make coming home easier."

"Come to me before Alexander returns if you wish. I would look forward to it."

Mrs. Melling pursed her lips. "Write to me and talk me into it."

When they pulled away from the curb, Mrs. Melling whispered to Magdalene, "Quick, turn around and see if he looks after us."

Reluctantly, Magdalene glanced over her shoulder and saw Mr. Melling staring at her. He raised a hand in farewell. She turned back. "Yes, he's watching and waved."

Mrs. Melling clapped. "So he does still care. Maybe we should pay him a visit, to check on the state of the house before company arrives."

Magdalene was too busy worrying about being forced into accompanying Mrs. Melling to the Government Street mansion to enjoy any of the delights of shopping. She blindly followed Mrs. Melling through various sections of Gayfer's Department Store, touching fabrics when asked and sniffing perfumes when pressed to do so. Several packages were bought, wrapped, and sent on to Mr. Melling's office until Captain Walker collected them Friday. Magdalene thought at least one of the dresses was for her, but she could not be sure, so far had her mind slipped into darkness.

The hired driver took them to a boutique that specialized in Parisian clothing. The gorgeous display of opened-neck silk gowns in the window awakened Magdalene as they entered the shop. The sales matron, Mademoiselle Bisset, wearing a black dress with European lines, came out to greet them.

"Mrs. Melling, so good to see you here. It has been over a year since the last time, when you were shopping with—"

"That's quite enough of a trip down memory lane. Today, we are looking for gowns appropriate for an evening engagement party. My son, Alexander, is to be wed to Beatrice Kirkpatrick of *the* Kirkpatricks of New York. You might have read about it in the society column." Mrs. Melling's chin was high and her hands clasped before her.

"Of course, Mrs. Melling. We will be most happy to dress you and…"

"Miss Magdalene Jones, my companion."

"Yes, Miss Jones. I heard about your pretty complexion from a group last week after they returned from Point Clear. Now, when will the party be held?"

"The end of September. It will be the occasion of the season."

"I've heard you've thrown some splendid parties over the years, especially the one you held in your new home two Christmases ago. With your party being in autumn, we can go with deeper colors for more of a dramatic impact. Since it is often still hot, many ladies tend to keep with their summer gowns, so you'd stand out even more with a richer hue. Let me check your colors..." Mademoiselle Bisset held a few swatches of fabric in varying shades against each woman's cheek. "All of our gowns are the only ones of their kind in the entire southeast. We pay extra to be the exclusive dealer in the area for many of the Parisian designers, but we feel that those who walk into our doors want the best, something no one else will show up with at an event. You won't find these dresses in Atlanta or New Orleans. You'll be sure to turn heads no matter what you choose."

"That is exactly why we are here," Mrs. Melling replied. "We want people to notice us when we walk into a room."

Magdalene tapped her folded fan against the opposite palm in frustration until Mrs. Melling gave her the look that said "act like a lady, not a country girl."

"We have a lovely russet gown in silk and taffeta that I think would be perfect for you, Mrs. Melling. Just one moment." She went to the curtain and gave orders to someone in the back room. "And you, Miss Jones, I have just the thing. We received it last week and I've shown it to no one."

Mrs. Melling's gown came out, draped over the arm of a fresh-faced shop girl. The bronze color evoked crisp evenings and harvest moons.

"It just might do. I shall try it, but what of Magdalene? I do not want to stand around waiting for each other. We must be dressed simultaneously so we can make our dinner reservation."

"Of course, Mrs. Melling. I'll fetch it myself. I've arranged it on a mannequin as I was thinking of using it for our window display next week, but it will look better on Miss Jones than in the window. It's a Jeanne Hallée done in midnight blue silk."

When Mademoiselle Bisset carried out the mannequin, Magdalene gasped.

Taking her exclamation for excitement, Mrs. Melling was quick to agree. "You would be exquisite, Magdalene! You must try it on."

"No, I couldn't." Magdalene stood transfixed before the gown from her nightmare. "It's much too...much too fine for me."

Mrs. Melling came up beside her and tried to play off Magdalene's stammering with a smile. "She will try it at once."

Mademoiselle Bisset helped Mrs. Melling and the fair-headed young woman who'd brought out the russet dress pulled the striped curtains closed in Magdalene's dressing room.

"I'd rather dress alone, please," she whispered.

"It's policy, ma'am."

Having never been in a shop with such valuable gowns, Magdalene had not thought of the workers having to safeguard their inventory from damage.

"Very well. I suppose an extra hand with these buttons would be useful." Magdalene unpinned her obnoxious hat, setting it on the chair, and turned her back so the clerk could undo the row of buttons on her dress.

"This blue is a much better choice for you, Miss. You'll look lovely in it, I'm sure. All us girls fawned over it when it arrived. Usually, we're allowed to try on things, but not this one. You'll be the first one it ever touches."

"Anything is better than this thing." Magdalene stepped out of the dress after it had been lowered. "Shall I remove my boots?"

"No, the heel is a good height to mimic evening slippers and we'll need to judge the length of the gown." She tucked a thin hairnet around Magdalene's head to keep hairs from catching on the dress. "Would you like me to adjust your corset before we proceed?"

"Only if you loosen it."

The clerk giggled. "Not for this dress, but I'll loosen it for you afterward."

"Thank you. I was beginning to wonder how I'd be able to eat dinner when I barely have room enough to breathe."

The corset did more than keep her breath shallow—it managed to hold her stomach together while nausea swept her when the cool softness of the gown slid over her netted head. Just as in her dream, the sleeves were barely there, so fine was the ruffle of lace at the shoulders. The sweetheart neckline plunged as low as her chemise and the sales girl suggested a new corset.

"It will create an even smoother silhouette, Miss," she said as she buttoned the bodice up her back and removed the hair net. "But it looks perfect—no alternations needed that I can see. It looks like it was made especially for you. I'll tell them you're ready." She slipped out of the dressing room.

Magdalene, still reeling from the manifestation of the gown from her dream, fingered the silk and the sections of lace overlay as she stood in front of the slim mirror on the back wall. She touched the expanse of her chest that had never been on display before. The deep shade of blue did look as glorious against her skin as the dream showed her. If she could only wear this for Douglas, she would be in love with it, but she knew that a private viewing was not an option—unless it was for Alexander. A tear escaped her eye as the clerk returned.

"Water on silk isn't a good thing, Miss, but I'm sure you'll move a special someone to tears when you're seen. Come to the large mirror. Mrs. Melling is already there."

Mrs. Melling caught her breath when she saw Magdalene's reflection approaching in the three-sided mirror. "I thought I looked beautiful, but you, Magdalene! Princes would fall at your feet."

She escorted her into the mirror and commanded her to twirl. Mrs. Melling and the sales women chattered. There was mention of her using a strapless bustier instead of a corset. Magdalene could not follow the words because a growing darkness surrounded her. Several more items were boxed and purchased while Magdalene changed into her tiered dress.

With their day in the city over, Magdalene sat beside Mrs. Melling on the ferry as they steamed south from Daphne to their stop in Montrose.

"You have been most quiet this afternoon, my dear. Are you feeling all right?"

"I am a little peaked. Between the heat and this corset—"

"Hush now, someone might hear."

She decided to ask one of the questions burning within her. "Where is the engagement party to be held?"

"Seacliff Cottage, of course."

Magdalene's stomach muscles tightened. "Is that the proper setup? It's lovely, and perfect for entertaining small gatherings, but wouldn't the cottage be rather tight once you get more than a dozen people in the common rooms?"

"Very true, though I do want to show off the cottage to guests. It has been so long since there was a proper party." She clapped her hands. "We can serve pre-dinner drinks, and then ferry people from our pier to Point Clear for a party in the ballroom at the hotel!"

"But the logistics…"

"You need not worry about that. I'll see to it all. Besides, I thought having secured a gown like yours, you would be in raptures."

"It's much too grand for me, Mrs. Melling. What if it's better than Miss Kirkpatrick's? We can't have me outshining her, can we?"

Her laughter was uncontained and brought the attention of several others sitting under the canopy. "What a vain thought, my dear. Surely Beatrice will have an equally fine dress, but you do not have her breeding and refinement—those far outweigh any flashy gown. But I need to be sure at least one party goer besides me will be as fashionable as her East Coast friends. We cannot have her thinking Mobilians lack style."

Magdalene, red in the face and sicker than ever at being Mrs. Melling's pawn, went to the railing to watch as the tree-lined cliffs of Montrose grew closer. Waiting at the end of the pier was a lone figure in a crisp white shirt. The worries that besieged Magdalene all day began to melt in the resurgence of love she felt for Douglas. No matter what happened, they had each other.

Three

Magdalene sat in the sand the next afternoon with Claudio and Douglas. Both of the men had their shirtsleeves and pants rolled up, and she wore her lightest weight calico dress without the hindrance of corset or stockings. Mrs. Melling was deep in conversation with Rosemary, planning the menus for when Alexander and his fiancée arrived, and Leroy and Mr. Campbell were discussing fishing further back in the shade of the cypress grove. Wanting to tell Claudio and Douglas about the engagement party plans Mrs. Melling worked on—as well as the dress she'd purchased—Magdalene waited until Priscilla scampered past in pursuit of a crab.

Upon hearing about the dress, Claudio turned pale. "Are you sure it is exact?"

"Right down to the lace trim. The sales girl said it looked like it had been made for me."

"We can't let evil infest the house with Maggie still there." Douglas took her hand and kissed her finger wearing his ring.

"I think we should run away," Magdalene said.

"Patience, *signorina*. You might run away from evil and straight into another temptation. I receive my *sacri ordines* in Mass the day after the party. I may marry you as early as that Monday, but if you both wish to elope, I will understand."

"I need this last month to secure our livelihood. There are a few options for employment and housing, but I am researching and praying over what would be best for us and my uncle." Douglas squeezed Magdalene's shoulder. "I know you take the brunt of the difficulty with your position, but I'd bear that burden for you if I could."

Mr. Campbell and Leroy joined them and Priscilla returned with a crab dangling from the end of a stick it pinched.

"The bay's so still and the wind is from the east." Leroy looked across the water. "I wouldn't be surprised if there's a jubilee tonight."

Claudio brightened. "There was one last summer when I stayed here. Alex, Eliza, and I filled a washtub with crabs and three buckets with flounder with the help of the Watts family. Rosemary cooked everything perfectly."

"A jubilee?" Douglas asked.

"*Sí*, just as in the holy Bible when God provides for the people. Everything washes ashore for a bounteous harvest. These shores are blessed with this miracle each year, sometimes more than once, I am told."

"Do you think you could stay over, in case there's another one?" Magdalene asked.

"All play and no work is not good for me at this time, *signorina*. My spirit is preparing for the transition into the full priesthood." He pointed to his cassock hanging from a nearby tree. "I feel incomplete without it already. I need to focus on my studies and prayers. I will most likely have to forgo my Saturday visits here as well."

Magdalene crossed her arms and pouted. "Everything is changing."

"Besides, *Signora* Melling already told me you have a Saturday supper reservation at the hotel, so you will not miss me."

"Supper? She'll dress me up even more for an evening out." She leaned her head against Douglas and closed her eyes.

"Magdalene!" Mrs. Melling called out. "Do not get too familiar over there."

She opened her eyes and shifted forward, and Douglas rubbed his hand along her back.

"Better yet," she called, "join us over here. We could use your opinion on soups."

Magdalene sighed and both Claudio and Douglas stood, each taking one of her hands to help her up. She shook the sand from her dress and dug her bare toes into the shifting ground. Claudio kissed the hand he'd held before letting go and Douglas kissed her decorously on the cheek.

When Magdalene took a seat in an empty folding chair, Mrs. Melling started in on her.

"Those two spoil you like nothing I have ever seen! I do not think it proper for you to continue to spend such idle hours with them. I am sure their attention is flattering, but have you had a change of heart over Douglas? There have been so many young men showing interest in you the past few weeks, and supper Saturday could be followed by dancing. If you are tired of the driver, I could easily send him on his way."

"I'm here to discuss soup, Mrs. Melling, not the affairs of my heart, which, by the way, remains steadfast in its commitment to my betrothed." She stared at her employer, challenging her to speak ill of Douglas again.

Rosemary remained mute, pen poised over her booklet between the two women.

"Very well, though I fail to see your objection for me wishing you to have more in this life."

"Nothing is more warranted than true love and happiness." Magdalene gazed beyond Mrs. Melling to the shoreline. Douglas and Claudio waded in the water and talked animatedly. She wished she were with them rather than stuck in a chair.

"Ma'am?" Leroy approached the group. "The bay is showing signs of a jubilee. Would it be okay if my family stays on the beach tonight so I can keep watch? I'll bring a bell and be part of the watchmen. I'm sure I'm not the only one seeing the signs. Y'all can hear the signal at the house and join us."

"You predicted the last jubilee, so I am sure you are correct this time. Last year, we had more hands to help gather." Mrs. Melling sighed as one acquainted with loss, then turned to Magdalene. "If you hear the bell, you may accompany Mr. Campbell and Douglas down to the beach and then stay within sight of Rosemary once you are there and accompany her home. If Mr. Campbell is already gone, you will have to stay put. Is that clear?"

"Yes, Mrs. Melling." Magdalene hid her smile, knowing Douglas and his uncle would never leave her.

"And you agree to be her guardian on the beach?" she asked Rosemary.

"Yes, ma'am."

"Good. Now let's decide on the soup course for Alex's first night home."

***

"Maggie."

Magdalene rolled to her side and covered her face with an arm against the low burning gaslights.

"Come on, Maggie, the jubilee's started." Douglas ran a hand down the sleeve of the cotton dress she still wore. She'd slept on top of her made bed so she'd be ready to go when the signal rang.

"I hear no bells. What time is it?" She blindly reached for his hand resting on her shoulder and squeezed.

"Three thirty in the morning, and the bells have been ringing up and down the coast for the past fifteen minutes. Are you coming?"

She waited until she felt the mattress give under his weight and then slowly stretched as she rolled toward him. Her back arched and her bare legs reached beyond the hem of her work dress that had ridden up to her knees as she slept.

He placed his hands on either side of her head and bent over her. "I think you tempt me on purpose."

"Maybe I want to make sure I'm worth waiting for."

"Of course you are." He kissed her on the lips and then pulled her upright, arms going around her. "It's the jubilee that won't wait and the others need our help. Uncle Simon is waiting for us on the porch."

"Go on, I'll be down in a minute." She covered a yawn.

He raised an eyebrow at her. "Promise me you won't lie back down?"

"I promise." She traced his mouth with a fingertip.

He jumped up from the edge of the bed and lifted an eyebrow at her. "You don't know what you do to me, Maggie."

She stood, a devious smile on her face. "I'll mind my manners."

"You'd best. See you out back in no more than two minutes."

She stopped in the bathroom before going out the kitchen door. The air was clear but muggy, the moon a tiny slip of an arch like the top of a horseshoe hung over the bay for good luck.

Mr. Campbell had a walking stick in one hand and the lantern in the other. Douglas motioned him ahead and took Magdalene's hand as they followed him down the path to the beach, often pausing to kiss because they could. They stopped at the picnic site near the trees, which the Watts family had turned into a camp, complete with a fire to help keep bugs away. Priscilla ran up to them as Magdalene sat in one of the folding chairs to remove her boots.

"Mama told me to stick with you, Miss Maggie, and show you what to do." She pulled at the ruffled hem of her checkered play dress. "Papa wants your help with the crabs, Mr. Douglas, and he said Mr. Campbell is on flounder duty with Mama."

"You betcha, little lassie." Mr. Campbell lifted his walking stick and removed a cork from the bottom, revealing a six-inch spike. Then he set off for the shore with almost a kick in his step.

Douglas kissed Magdalene goodbye before heading for the shore, and Priscilla handed Magdalene a pail. They walked hand in hand to the section of shoreline that had already been cleared of crabs and flounder. Shrimp duty had them crouching low along the compact sand, following the trail the others had cleared as they headed north. Priscilla taught Magdalene how to hunt the shrimp in the dim light and soon Magdalene's metal pail was almost as full as the girl's. There were a few instances of accidentally grabbing an eel or almost stepping on a stringray in the shallows, but Magdalene enjoyed the labor.

At four thirty, Priscilla slowed, nearing exhaustion. The lantern lights further north along the beach were making their way steadily closer as people from Montrose made their way south, following the bounty of the jubilee. Magdalene carried Priscilla to her mother's side and gently laid her in one of the chairs, tucking a towel under her head for a pillow and using her father's shirt for a blanket.

Magdalene, back sore from all the bending, walked halfway to the shoreline and sat in the sand. She watched over the three men, all shirtless with their pants rolled above their knees. One dark, lean, and strong. Another hunched and pallid. The third with tanned, capable arms and a pale, muscular torso who she watched the longest. She pulled her knees up under her dress, tucked the hem around her feet, and rested her chin on her knees. The rhythm of Douglas scooping with the poled net, Leroy retrieving the crabs and dropping them into the collection tub, Mr. Campbell jabbing with his stick—*poke, poke, poke*—and then sliding the flounder into the waiting bucket lulled her into a state of rest.

Before she knew it, a warm arm went around her shoulders.

"Morning, Maggie."

Opening her eyes, she was greeted with a lavender sky over a deep turquoise bay. Half a dozen men and women in rolled-up work clothes combed the Mellings' section of beach, clearing the leftovers and anything newly washed ashore.

Magdalene smiled and put her head on Douglas's shoulder. "I enjoy being woken up by you."

"Soon, it will be every day." He lifted her chin and kissed her softly. "I've sent Uncle Simon up with a pail of flounder. I told him to wash and get in bed for a few hours. Leroy and Rosemary will be back for another load soon. I'll need to help him with the largest tubs."

Magdalene's first load was carrying a sleeping Priscilla to the house. She laid the child on a pallet of blankets Rosemary made across from the swing in the gazebo and then returned to the beach with the cook to fetch a few more pails. After all tubs and buckets were brought to the back porch, Leroy and Rosemary began dividing the harvest to share because it was too much for the household. A bundle for Claudio, Father Angelo, and the others at the Catholic church, and another grouping for the Watts family's friends at Little Bethel.

Douglas and Leroy carefully loaded the pails onto the floorboard of the backseat and set off for Daphne while Magdalene assisted Rosemary in prepping for a crab boil. The men returned the next hour with fresh corn, potatoes, onions, and green beans. Magdalene sat on the swing, shucking corn and snapping green beans with Douglas until it was time to see to Mrs. Melling. Then the day was filled with cooking, eating, and laughing. For the time being, Magdalene was able to forget the threat of being controlled by the Mellings.

Four

Friday afternoon was like Christmas when Captain Walker arrived with the delivery. The groceries as well as the money—accompanied by a letter—were brought first. Mrs. Melling smiled and sighed when she read the note. Magdalene sat quietly, smoothing the skirt of her lace-filled tea gown and watched as the deckhands piled load after load of boxes and crates into the front hall. After several minutes, Magdalene had to remark on the mass of goods.

"I don't recall us going into that many shops."

"Oh, some of these were extras from my orders last week."

When everything was in the house, Leroy showed Captain Walker into the parlor and Zora brought in lemonade for the two ladies and the captain. Mrs. Melling chattered more than usual and Magdalene sipped her drink on the settee, wishing she could skip the next several weeks of her life.

Half an hour later, Mrs. Melling asked Magdalene to see Captain Walker to the door.

"Are you well?" he asked once they were in the hall.

"Well enough. It's just that now that the end of my stay here is in sight, everything seems to be collapsing on me."

"How much longer do you have?"

"Four weeks, but I haven't made it officially to the family yet."

"Let me know if you need anything, either before or after you move on. I told Douglas the same. I wish you both well and told him I'd hire him in an instant if he's interested. That's how I got my start, being hired on as a deckhand for Claire's father."

"Thank you, Captain."

As soon as Magdalene returned to the parlor, Mrs. Melling was ready to sort the boxes. "First, we need to find your gown. It needs to be hung so it can air for twenty-four hours before you wear it to supper tomorrow."

"I thought it was for the engagement party."

"You shall use it then too, but I thought it best for you to wear it first somewhere else so Beatrice does not think we are trying to outshine her. It can be known that you had already worn it and it was not something especially for that one event."

A smug satisfaction that no matter what Mrs. Melling had said about her being too full of herself, she did think it possible for her to outshine the beloved Beatrice Kirkpatrick. "But what if I spill something on it?"

"Pray you do not, but there would be time enough to have it sent to Mobile for cleaning. Now fetch Leroy, and maybe even Douglas if he is not too busy, to help us unpack."

Relief that the gown wouldn't be worn for the first time in the presence of Alexander allowed Magdalene enough security to smile as she delivered her message. But by six o'clock Saturday evening, her stomach knotted. The Wattses were already gone for the day, having left at two since they didn't need to prepare supper. Magdalene spent an anxious afternoon in the stuffy parlor with Mrs. Melling. Freshly showered, she sat at her dressing table in new black silk stockings and short drawers, awaiting Mrs. Melling to come tie the ridged bustier to her satisfaction. Magdalene had it tied loosely while she waited, thankful for her last minutes of freedom. Being completely sleeveless was a new experience and she gazed often at her expanse of chest and shoulders in the mirror.

Mrs. Melling waltzed through the open door in a golden gown recycled from last year's wardrobe and commanded Magdalene to stand. "Hold in your breath."

Magdalene did not pull in her belly as far as she could, hoping to leave enough room to swallow a bit of food without too much discomfort. But Mrs. Melling knew every trick when it came to avoiding the tightest fit for waist definition, and Magdalene soon blinked back tears.

"Do make an effort to speak to people tonight, my dear. I can assure you we will be highly sought after this evening. Forget your obligations and try to enjoy yourself." She turned Magdalene around and spritzed a dash of rose water at her décolletage. "Check with me after you do your hair before going downstairs so I can be sure it is suitable. And go ahead and remove your ring. You do not need to try slipping it off and on in the automobile tonight."

"Yes, ma'am." She shut the door behind Mrs. Melling and choked back a sob.

Like an obedient subject, she placed her engagement ring in the top drawer of her dressing table and brushed through her hair. She pulled her gown over her head and got her arms through the fluttery lace cap sleeves, but could not secure all the buttons on the back with her bustier constricting her movements. Reluctantly, she went down the hall for help.

After buttoning her in, Mrs. Melling stood watch while Magdalene twisted and piled her coiffure. It took three tries for the lady of the house to be satisfied, then she decided they needed to leave fifteen minutes early so Douglas could drive slower to reduce any damage from the wind.

Still needing her shoes, Magdalene returned to her room while Mrs. Melling went downstairs. She paused before her dressing table mirror and gazed at the stranger she saw in the reflection. In this finery, she very well could pass for a cousin of the family, like Mrs. Melling allowed to happen more often than not so the society ladies would be more welcoming to the companion from Seven Hills.

She unwrapped the silver beaded slippers from the protective tissues and slipped her feet into the pointy-toed shoes, yet another item to bind her uncomfortably. Taking the kitchen stairs, Magdalene peered out the window. The Great Arrow had been pulled to the front gate to collect the inhabitants like a respectable household.

Douglas waited on the front porch, dressed in a proper chauffeur's uniform with a black tie and suit jacket. When he saw her through the screen, his eyes went wide and he stepped to the door.

"Maggie, even the words of Shakespeare can't do you justice." He leaned his forehead against the screen.

She smiled. "Do I need to try to tempt you now?"

"I'm unworthy to touch such elegance."

"Then open the door for me if it's safe."

"You're safe from me, but I don't think the world is ready for Miss Magdalene Jones."

"Soon-to-be Mrs. Magdalene Campbell." She spun around slowly, happy to show off for Douglas without being asked.

"As long as I'm the only man to kiss you in that gown." He stepped aside and watched to be sure her gown cleared the screen before closing it. Then he took her hand in his—the other at the small of her back—and kissed her in full display of Mrs. Melling waiting in the automobile.

"That is quite enough!" she shouted across the yard. "Bring her to me at once!"

"But what if I want to run away with her?" he whispered in reply, still inclined toward Magdalene.

"I wouldn't get far in these shoes."

"We'd only have to get to Claudio in Daphne."

"If you so much as wrinkle that gown…" Mrs. Melling blustered.

Magdalene tugged his hand. "I don't want her any madder at you than she is now."

"It was worth it, Maggie." Douglas straightened and offered his arm so he could escort her to the vehicle.

Mr. Campbell waited at the front corner of the fence to catch a glimpse of her. Magdalene broke free from Douglas and hurried to the old man.

"You look beautiful, Maggie."

"Thank you, Mr. Campbell."

"I think it's time you begin calling me Uncle Simon."

She kissed his cheek and whispered. "I'd rather be sitting on the porch with your nephew than dressed like this going into the lion's den."

"You'll do fine. Now go on before Mrs. Melling gets angry at me for getting a kiss from you."

Once Douglas brought her to the car, he helped her into her beige duster, sneaking caresses along her arms in the process.

"I hope these coats do not crush the gowns," Mrs. Melling said. "Maybe we should take the carriage instead."

"The coats are light," Magdalene replied as she sat down. She pulled a head scarf from the pocket of the duster and tied it loosely around her hair.

"The carriage would save our hairstyles, too."

"I take care of my ladies." Douglas stepped onto the running board and reached on top of the canopy, pulling down a black canvas that he'd rolled and tied to the canopy frame in half a dozen spots. He took the toggles along the sides and bottom and quickly secured them to the automobile before hurrying to the other side to do the same, only leaving the front driver side loose so he could get in and secure it from the inside. He turned around, his smile melting Magdalene's heart.

"I must say that is most ingenious, though I do wish I had asked you to shave. You look quite rough by the end of the week."

"No!" Magdalene shifted forward, running a hand down his jawline. "It's perfect."

"Really, Magdalene, you are behaving most inappropriately this evening."

"Inappropriate because I accept a kiss from my soon-to-be husband and greet his uncle before leaving?"

"You know what I mean, Magdalene. Do not try to make me sound ridiculous."

"Very well, then stop trying to control everyone around you. You dressed and arranged me to your satisfaction from head to toe. You've forced a uniform on Douglas, which you said was too pretentious for this side of the bay, and now you're attempting to tell him how to wear his hair. No, Mrs. Melling, I don't think I need to try to make you sound ridiculous."

"Things are different now that society has their eyes on us, especially for supper at the hotel. We cannot go in looking like a ragtag group of locals. After all, it is the premiere resort along the entire Gulf Coast."

"And I'll be sure to behave myself while we're there." Magdalene sat back and crossed her arms.

"No, dear, the ruffles. Please keep your arms at your side." Mrs. Melling tapped Douglas on the shoulder. "I appreciate your thoughtfulness in providing the protection, but could you please stop a safe distance from the hotel to remove the canvas so we can arrive in style?"

"Of course, Mrs. Melling," he said as he started down the lane.

A short while later, Douglas drove the Great Arrow—sides open as usual—into the hotel's turnabout. One of the debutantes Magdalene recognized from their luncheons exited the automobile in front of them with her mother, their chauffeur helping them out of their coats. The blonde was the one who had been the most vulgar in her opinions about Douglas. No matter how Mrs. Melling tried to play down the chatter of the young women, Magdalene wasn't one to forgive or forget.

While they waited their turn, Mrs. Melling removed their head scarves and set into place the wayward hairs. Their dusters were already on the seat beside Douglas as she had him help remove them after he'd secured the side panels so they wouldn't need the awkward disrobing in front of the hotel.

"Just remember to smile and be gracious, Magdalene."

"Yes, ma'am."

When Douglas exited the car, Magdalene saw the young woman turn to follow his movements, a wistful gaze on her face.

He helped Mrs. Melling out, her golden dress catching the electric lights with a warm glow. With all eyes looking their way, Magdalene slid across the leather seat and accepted Douglas's hand. With his back to the others, no one noticed when he murmured his love to her as she stepped out of the automobile. The crowd only witnessed her smile that caught him—and everyone else—in its radiance, along with the rich blue of the silk gown against her glowing complexion.

"Thank you, Douglas. We will send for you when we are ready." Mrs. Melling started for the entrance with Magdalene securely by her side.

The blonde tried to link her arm with Magdalene to squirrel her away with the younger set, but Mrs. Melling wanted to be the one to enter the dining room with Magdalene.

"Stop by after we are seated, Grace Anne. We need to be sure to make our reservation before settling in for small talk."

Magdalene followed Mrs. Melling through the lobby to the main restaurant and they were seated by the maître d' in a prominent position in the chandelier-filled space.

"So, this Grace Anne," Magdalene said, knowing Mrs. Melling loved to gossip. "What's her family like?"

"The Marley family attends the cathedral and is in lumber, new money. He did not hit it big until the Spanish-American War, so they have less than a decade with any proper ties. Her mother and I are in a ladies' society together in the city. Grace Anne is twenty-one now. She was in the social group Eliza was often with until she withdrew into her art." She sighed. "But enough of that. We must only speak of pleasant things tonight."

She sipped her champagne and waved like a queen to a lady across the room. Magdalene did her best not to shift uncomfortably as she picked up her own glass and one of the ridges of the bustier jabbed into her side.

A plain man wearing a white tuxedo and black tie stopped between their two chairs. "Mrs. Melling, it's wonderful to see you. I heard the news about Alex and had to stop to give my congratulations."

"Thank you, Rupert. Have you had the pleasure of meeting Miss Magdalene Jones? She's been staying with me at Seacliff Cottage since Alex left. Magdalene, this is Rupert Lyons."

"The pleasure is all mine, Miss Jones." He took her hand and kissed the back of it with his thin lips.

Magdalene did her best not to grimace and smiled politely.

"Will you be staying for dancing after supper?" His stare seemed to go right down her cleavage to her toes.

"I don't believe that has been decided yet." Magdalene picked her glass up and held it nonchalantly as she adjusted to take away his view.

He blinked twice. "Well, if you do stay, I'd be honored if you'd save a dance for me."

"That would be lovely, wouldn't it, Magdalene?" Mrs. Melling sounded eager enough for the two of them.

"Yes, thank you, Mr. Lyons." She looked away and took a drink, the bubbles tickling her throat on the way down.

The parade of well-wishers stopped when their main course was served. Magdalene managed to eat a few pieces of shrimp and a spoonful of rice before asking to be excused.

"Just to the powder room and back," Mrs. Melling reminded her.

She felt the eyes on her as she passed between the tables. Once in the hallway, Grace Anne took her by the arm. She tried to get Magdalene to sit on the settee with her in the foyer of the ladies' room, but Magdalene pointed to her aching waist.

"You poor dear. Eliza always complained when her mother laced her in. Some of us would take turns loosening each other's cords on breaks during cotillions. If you need help, the attendant here is well versed in letting out corsets enough for the wearer to eat."

The thought of a stranger messing with her bustier wasn't pleasant. "No, thank you. I just need to stand for a few minutes."

Grace Anne fluffed her lacey pink skirt. "What about your driver? No one has ever seen him in a uniform before. The chatter at every table tonight has been about your dress or the way your driver fills out a uniform. He puts all the others to shame, that's for sure. What does Mr. Melling pay him? I'll ask Daddy to offer him double."

Mrs. Melling got what she wanted—her household being the talk of the room—but it appeared to have cost both her and Douglas their dignity.

Magdalene started pacing. "His name is Douglas and it's not my business what Mr. Melling pays him, nor is it yours."

"I'll forgive your rudeness because I know the pains it takes to look that good." Grace Anne checked herself in the mirror that covered the opposite wall from where she sat. She adjusted her corset and fixed a wayward hair. "I'm going to see what that driver is willing to teach me while my parents take their dessert."

Magdalene stopped pacing and looked down at her. "I believe he's engaged."

"That never stops them." Grace Anne twirled to the mirror, kissing her own reflection.

Five

When Grace Anne flounced away, Magdalene had to rest a hand on the side table to steady the room from spinning. While she trusted Douglas implicitly, she couldn't stand the thought of women like Grace Anne lusting after what was hers. Nor did she appreciate being gawked over by strangers named Rupert or any of the other dozen men who stopped at the table with an excuse to greet Mrs. Melling. It was all a game to them but it sickened Magdalene. Desperate for relief, she sought out the attendant in the inner chamber and had her adjust her laces in one of the private rooms before returning to Mrs. Melling.

Out of the corner of her eye, she kept watch over Grace Anne's table. When their supper dishes were cleared, Rupert happened by Magdalene.

"Excuse me, Mr. Lyons."

"Yes, Miss Jones." He placed a hand on the back of her chair and leaned close, affording Magdalene a close-up of his nose that looked like it had been broken at some point in his life while he had a full view of her décolletage.

"I heard Miss Grace Anne wanted to go to the ballroom while her parents finished dessert. Would you be so kind as to escort her?"

"Anything for you, Miss Jones. I hope to see you in there soon as well."

"Are you up to something, Magdalene?" Mrs. Melling asked over the rim of her glass.

"Only helping two people who deserve each other get together."

"Do not be too quick to toss Rupert away. He has a bright future and political ties in his family. Tonight, he is yours for the picking."

Magdalene pointed to her empty ring finger. "I have already chosen the one I want to spend the rest of my life with, even if you refuse to recognize it. I don't feel like dessert. May we go home now?"

"Not until after ten. I need my coffee and cake. Give yourself thirty minutes and see if you do not enjoy yourself. Take that dance with Rupert. I am sure he would share the story at the engagement party of how he danced with the stunning Miss Jones in that exact dress first."

Seeing her way out, Magdalene agreed to go.

Grace Anne came down the hall, a smile on her face. She hooked Magdalene's arm and pulled her into the sitting area of the powder room once again.

"Rupert Lyons escorted me to the ballroom! He's never given me so much as a second glance but he gave me his first dance. This might be my lucky night, but should I waste it on a driver when I might get more dances with men who could be a marriage match? I think Dr. John Woodslow is here and he's a fine specimen."

Magdalene took the spot next to her in front of the mirror and pretended to care about the state of her hair. "Why don't you show me how this driver meeting works and I'll give it a try?"

"No, you can't possibly! Eliza told us her mother had a special sense and could tell when impure thoughts happened within anyone in the family."

Magdalene nearly burst out laughing, but bit the inside of her cheek instead.

"I'd hate for you to risk getting caught by her. I bet she's a tyrant."

"She doesn't scare me."

"And I told the girls you weren't the type after the way you looked at the luncheon the other day when we talked about it."

Magdalene shrugged. "Might as well try it once and see what it's like."

"Well, it's better not to do anything with your own chauffeur because that's just awkward, but I don't see how anyone would mind the extra attention from *him*. You said his name is Douglas?"

"Yes."

"Come on, then."

The two ladies strolled down the hall, slowing as they neared a side door shadowed by a potted palm. When the hallway cleared, Grace Anne slipped out, holding the door open for Magdalene to follow. They took a dimly lit path around a few crepe myrtle trees, their branches hanging low with the weight of the fuchsia blossoms, to a parking lot. All the chauffeured cars were backed in on either side of the narrow lane, a group of drivers stood to one side, smoking cigarettes and joking, while others lounged in the automobiles or leaned against the hood.

The Great Arrow was three cars up, and no other drivers were between the women and Douglas. Grace Anne motioned for Magdalene to stay behind the first automobile while she approached. A few of the men standing against the building opposite whistled.

"Whatcha wanna learn this time, sweetie?"

"Don't you know enough to reel in a rich one yet?"

Other such vulgarities were called out to Grace Anne, but she drank in the attention, lifting the skirt of her gown enough to show her ankles and a bit of her calf. She got right up next to Douglas's door. He remained slouched in the driver's seat, arms crossed, eyes closed.

"Not interested," he said without looking.

"But I need—"

"Hasn't the word gotten 'round that I'm not available for the type of lessons you women are looking for?" His brogue was thick and Magdalene could hear the anger behind his voice.

How many times has he been propositioned?

Grace Anne put her hands on the top of the door. "Douglas, isn't it?"

Magdalene could see his eyebrow rise, but he didn't turn to her.

"Douglas, it's for my friend, not me. She's a bit shy and way too proper to ask for herself. And if the lady she's with finds out, she'll get in a lot of trouble and you'll probably lose your job."

Douglas snorted. "If you're trying to pitch this to me, you're going about it all wrong."

"Well, I hardly know Miss Jones so—"

"Miss Jones?" He sat up and looked around for the first time.

Magdalene stepped out, a shy smile on her lips.

"Miss Jones is the only exception I'll ever make." Still not looking at Grace Anne, he climbed across the front seat and out the door on the passenger side. Douglas ran to Magdalene and offered his arm, which she accepted without making eye contact.

"The Scottish lad got himself the looker!" a driver called.

"Guess women like men with an accent."

"Get back inside, Miss," he told Grace Anne. "I know which door to bring her to. I won't keep her long this first time."

Grace Anne blushed and then ran for the door. Douglas took a step back and looked through the branches of the trees to see that she safely got inside the hotel. Then he made a show of removing his suit jacket, tossing it on the front seat and opening the rear door.

"And what would you like to learn?" he asked.

With a hand on his shoulder, she leaned in and whispered, "I've already learned everything I need to know about this place and I want to go home."

He motioned her into the backseat and stepped up after her, accompanied by whistles and hoots. Taking her into his arms, Douglas kissed her before either of them could speak.

"We're the talk of the dining room, you and I."

"You, obviously, but why me?"

Magdalene ran his tie through her fingers. "It seems the world wants to know why Mrs. Melling put you in uniform after all this time and the women are marveling over how well you 'fill it out.'"

"These people are something else." He leaned against the back of the seat.

"Mrs. Melling's infuriating. She's practically throwing me at one man and wants me to dance with him. He's only interested is seeking a better view of this." She motioned to her chest. "I don't think he's looked me in the eye for more than two seconds."

Douglas trailed his fingers from one lacey shoulder to the other, following the low sweep of her gown, stirring Magdalene's yearnings. "While this is a glorious sight, your true beauty is within those brilliant brown eyes—the windows to your soul."

She fell upon him, wanting to taste the words while they were still on his lips. Her hands played across his beard and he caressed her bare arms. When she moved to climb into his lap, he stilled her.

"That's enough of a show, Maggie."

She kissed him again, her cheeks flushed, lips plump from use. He touched his thumb to her mouth.

"Now you're even more alluring. If you get on the dance floor, you won't be able to leave without causing a brawl between the men fighting for your hand."

Magdalene linked her fingers through his. "I already have the man I want and I've given him my heart." She brought his hand to her chest, setting it just above the ruffled hem at her left bosom. "Only for you."

He trembled in the moment of intimacy and then breathed into her several more stirring kisses that left her body craving more. Douglas opened the door and stood, taking her by the hand as he exited.

"And the mighty Scot conquered the blushing beauty!" one of the men shouted.

"He wasn't lying when he said she was his girl," another remarked.

Douglas led her back to the hotel before she could hear the rest of the comments. They stopped in the shadows of the blooming crepe myrtles and embraced until the door swung open. Two giggling young women stumbled out. They'd obviously had too much champagne. Magdalene couldn't stand the thought of them fumbling through the parking lot to be groped and taunted. She looked to Douglas and he seemed to understand her concern.

"Could you two help me find the ballroom? I'm supposed to meet someone there."

The lady in pale blue looked over Douglas. "Looks like you already met someone."

"Yes, and he counts for a lot, trust fund or not," the one in a white gown added.

Magdalene ignored their remarks. "I need to get back to my chaperone before she misses me. You know how that is." They started moving around her, but she stopped them with an arm. "How would you like a dance with Rupert Lyons?"

The one in white sobered. "Rupert, not his younger brother, Daniel?"

"Yes, Rupert. Older and sophisticated Rupert." She played along, though she'd never laid eyes on his brother.

"Only if we get to dance with him first. There's no point in dancing with a man tonight after you've been in his arms." The one in blue looked Douglas over and sighed. "Dancing or anything else."

They both giggled and linked arms on either side of Magdalene. She hushed them before Douglas opened the door but they made a spectacle on the way to the ballroom. Magdalene managed to disconnect from them so she entered the room alone, a stunning blue shimmer in the otherwise light-colored space. Rupert found her at once and attached himself to her elbow.

"I met these two ladies in the hall and they were nervous about coming in, afraid they'd never be asked to dance." Magdalene ever so slightly angled toward him as she spoke. "Would you be a dear and take a dance with each of them before we have ours?"

"Only if you promise to save your first dance for me."

"Nothing would give me more pleasure." She smiled, relieved to have an excuse to refuse to dance with the dozens of men who asked while she waited for Rupert to waltz the other two ladies around the room.

Just before the second dance ended, Mrs. Melling came into the ballroom. Magdalene looked back at her as Rupert took her by the hand and saw the calculating smile spread across her face.

"I would gladly dance with three more of your friends for the chance of another one with you," he told her as they waltzed to a Vivaldi concerto played by a string quartet.

"That won't be necessary, Mr. Lyons, but thank you for the offer. If you could return me to Mrs. Melling when we're finished, I'd be most appreciative."

A blessedly short minute and a half later, he led her through the crowd.

"Here you are, Miss Jones, safe and sound." His other hand lingered on her back after she'd dropped his arm.

"Thank you for your assistance this evening, Mr. Lyons." Magdalene smiled in relief when his hands were no longer touching her.

"Yes, we are grateful for your attentiveness, Rupert." Mrs. Melling had his hand in hers. "We must repay you soon, but I am afraid it is time for us to head home. I am just not up to things like I used to be since Eliza's accident."

"Of course, Mrs. Melling. But if Miss Jones would like to stay, I'd be happy to see her home." The gleam in his eyes could not be overlooked. "My family's chauffeur is at your disposal."

Magdalene's heart seized when she saw the calculating look in Mrs. Melling's eyes, a sinister match for Rupert's. *Oh, no, she wouldn't…but she would!*

"Perhaps another time, Rupert, but we appreciate the offer."

"Thank you for not leaving me with him," Magdalene told her when they were on their way through the lobby.

"We cannot give him everything he wants on the first day, but have no doubt, I will send you with him another time."

Six

So ill with worry over Mrs. Melling's threat of pushing her together with Rupert, Magdalene stayed home sick on Sunday. She claimed stomach pains and a headache—which she did have. Mrs. Melling left Mr. Campbell to watch over Magdalene, and Douglas drove her to Sacred Heart Church near the hotel where many of the summer guests attended. Magdalene stayed in bed until she heard the automobile drive away. Outfitted in a cotton work dress, she ran for the stable.

Magdalene's trousseau crates from Seven Hills had arrived over a week ago, but Mrs. Melling had not given her the chance to go through them. The lady of the house was limiting her off-time with Douglas on purpose. No more driving lessons or outings "just because." Everything they did circulated around social events, whether the event itself or shopping for it, with the focus on Alexander's return and his coming wedding to Beatrice Kirkpatrick.

Mr. Campbell groomed Janus in the center of the stable as Magdalene went through on her way to the ladder.

"Mornin', Maggie."

She smiled in spite of her pains, happy he had picked up Douglas's nickname for her. Only those she loved, and those who loved her, called her Maggie. "Uncle Simon, I'd like to go through my boxes."

"They're not up there."

"But—"

Seeing the panicked look on her face, he spoke quickly. "They're in Douglas's room."

She sighed with relief. "I heard Mrs. Melling tell him to put them in the stable loft."

"That she did, but he doesn't do everything she bids him, now does he?" He winked.

"No, he doesn't. And I need to stop obeying all her hideous instructions as well." She kicked at a clump of dirt on the ground. "Do you mind if I go through my things?"

"My home is your home. There are a few biscuits leftover from breakfast and fixings for tea. Help yourself to whatever you wish."

"Thank you, Uncle Simon." She kissed his cheek and gave Janus a scratch behind his ear.

It had been weeks since she'd been inside the carriage house. Upon passing through the rickety screen door, she felt the quiet peace of home. It wasn't until the calming spirit surrounded her that Magdalene realized evil was creeping into Seacliff Cottage once again. A shiver went down her back though it pushed ninety degrees.

Since she had skipped breakfast, Magdalene set water to boil before climbing the ladder to Douglas's loft. Seeing his made bed, she thought back through the months to when she'd hung her shirt on his headboard as a way to get his attention and laughed, remembering how carefree they were then despite the threat of demonic influence. Compared to what she now faced with Mrs. Melling, it seemed much easier to deal with a demon she couldn't see than one of flesh and blood.

Four crates were stacked in the opposite corner from the bed, two large and two small. They were all stenciled with MAGDALENE JONES – SEACLIFF in bold black letters and nailed shut. After collecting a crowbar from Uncle Simon, Magdalene stopped to eat before returning to the loft.

Once she had a small crate opened, she sat beside it and began to dig through the straw. She found her mother's six-piece tea service, white china hand-painted with forget-me-nots. Magdalene teared up over seeing the familiar pattern. When she pulled the envelope from the teapot, she marveled at the bulk. A hundred dollars filled it in varying bills, as well as her parents' wedding rings. At least it seemed her aunt had been honest with paying the percentage. Magdalene knew her father's blacksmithing tools would have fetched a hefty price.

"Thank you, Papa," she whispered. "Thank you for all your hard work. I'm sorry I wasn't there in the end. Though, looking back now, Aunt Agnes might have been easier to deal with than Mrs. Melling turned out to be. I should have been there for you, Papa."

Her mother's gold wedding band fit snugly against her engagement ring. She placed her father's ring on her thumb so she would be sure to show Douglas when he returned, hoping he'd agree to let them use the rings for their own. With a smile, she cradled one of the cups in her hands, remembering the face her father had made the day after her mother passed and Magdalene attempted fixing him coffee the first—and only—time. They were both broken hearted, but his look of utter revulsion caused her to giggle, which made him laugh to see her so tickled. They'd spent the next fifteen minutes holding each other while a mixture of tears and laughter erupted from their broken hearts.

Magdalene wiped the moisture from her face and carefully packaged the tea set back into the crate. The other small box housed the few books they'd owned—their family Bible, a dictionary, her father's tattered copy of *The Pilgrim's Progress*, and her mother's *Little Women*—as well as the two cast iron skillets and a kettle. She repacked everything and pushed the crates to the side so Douglas could nail them closed later.

The larger crates were more difficult to open, but after levering the lid for several minutes, she finally got one loose. Inside were linens for both kitchen and bath from her parents' home and the unused items she'd collected while previously engaged. William had favored the color green. Douglas liked blue, which brought his eyes even more to prominence when he was around it. She took the white tea towel and fingered the blue hydrangeas her mother had embroidered on it. Fantasizing about the way Douglas held her in the back of the automobile the night before, she remembered his gentle hands and warm lips.

The screen door slammed below, rattling her from her daydream. "I'm going to start cooking, Maggie. Maybe you could take dinner or supper with us today."

She went to the top of the ladder. "I'd like that very much, Uncle Simon, but I'm not sure if I'd be allowed to."

"Sundays are supposed to be your time off, away from the Mellings. She's kept you around long enough without a break, I insist on you taking a meal with us today. I'll talk to the old battle axe myself."

Magdalene hurried down the ladder and embraced the old man. "And to think I was scared of you when I first arrived."

He chuckled. "There, there, Maggie. No need to cry."

"But I've made a mess of things." She wiped her nose with Douglas's handkerchief she always kept in her pocket. "No matter what I try to do there will be a Melling to stop me."

"You and Douglas have a bright future ahead."

"Only if we can get away from here. And we aren't going anywhere without you."

He patted her shoulder. "Don't worry about these old bones. Dry your face and finish looking through your things while I cook."

Magdalene nodded and climbed back to the loft. She repacked the linen crate and turned her attention to the last one. Struggling with the stubborn nails, sweat ran down her back as the sun reached midday. Through the open windows, she heard the Great Arrow pull into the yard. She stopped to watch out the dormer window as Douglas—dressed in his Sunday tartan vest, crisp white shirt, and navy pants—helped Mrs. Melling out of the car, her mint green dress ruffling in the breeze. It felt like a storm was blowing in from the gulf and it would be a welcomed relief from the heat.

With Mrs. Melling through the gate, Douglas returned to the automobile, covering it with the tarp. Magdalene called and waved from the window. He looked around, and upon seeing her in his room, ran for the house.

"Welcome home." She spread her arms for a hug. "Sorry I made a mess."

"You feel like I usually do, damp with sweat." He kissed her cheek. "I hope you didn't overexert yourself."

"It feels good to do something I wanted to do for a change, as well as be barefoot with my hair braided and not a corset to be seen."

Douglas caressed her waist as they kissed. "And you've never looked, felt, or tasted better."

She helped him remove his vest and she fell into him as their lips met, fingers trailing across his bearded jawline as she wrapped her arms around his neck. Magdalene pulled back to look at him. "It's Sunday and you didn't shave."

He cocked an eyebrow. "I figured since you liked the beard so much, I'd let it go until you think it gets out of hand."

"I do like it, but you might want to wait until the weather cools before you let it grow too long." She brought both hands to his face, pulling him in for another kiss. "A wild, red beard for our first Christmas together."

"Together…" His hands trailed her back then settled at her hips. "I like the way that sounds. You and I, together at last."

Magdalene opened the top buttons of his shirt and kissed his neck.

"My parents' rings were in one of the crates. See how the wedding band fits with your engagement ring?" She held up her left hand and pulled the ring off her thumb. "Here, try my father's ring."

It slid easily over his knuckles. "Might be a tad loose, but it fits well enough."

"Could we use them for our ceremony?" she asked.

"Aye, it would make it all the more special."

Mrs. Melling's shouts of "Magdalene!" interrupted their kissing.

With a sigh, she laid her head on Douglas's shoulder. "I'd forgotten her for a little while. It's a jolt back to reality."

"Just a few weeks to go, Maggie. Hold strong."

They went down the ladder, meeting Uncle Simon in the main room. "Maggie, you make yourself comfortable. It's your day off. Douglas, if you can keep an eye on the stove so nothing burns, I'll be back in a minute."

Magdalene settled in the rocker by the unlit fireplace, nervously moving the chair since she couldn't pace. The old man straightened his belt and went out the door to confront Mrs. Melling in the stable yard.

"What have you done with my girl?" She sounded like a yapping dog.

"Magdalene is visiting with me. As you recall, household staff traditionally get the Sabbath off until supper, yet you've been working her day and night for months. Today, and every Sunday from now on, she'll be taking her time off here, under my watch."

"You have no authority over her or what arrangements we've made as to her position here."

"On the contrary. I'm the closest relative to both her and her soon-to-be husband. She has every right to be here with me chaperoning the two of 'em during her time off. The question is, would you like her to take dinner or supper with us?"

Magdalene looked across the room at Douglas in the silence. He smiled reassuringly and put a finger to his lips.

"I suppose dinner, since it smells like you are already fixing it, but that will leave me alone for hours."

"Don't you usually nap Sunday afternoons?" His voice stabbed through the air.

"Well, yes, but should I need assistance—"

"And haven't you said before that Sundays are the days you feel the best?"

"Mr. Campbell," her voice rose with each syllable, "I fail to see how any of this matters to the situation at hand."

"It matters deeply. You've been overworking the girl and she aims to take her time off with her soon-to-be family. Don't look for her on the Sabbath until supper time, as you informed her when she was hired."

"Of all the insufferable…will you allow me to speak with her?"

"Let me check with her." He stepped into the house and looked over at Magdalene, knowing she'd heard every word. She nodded to him, so he let Mrs. Melling in the door.

She looked around the room, turning her nose up at the shabbiness of it. "I have not had reason to step foot into this shack for years and I am sorry I had reason to enter today." Setting her eyes on Magdalene, she smiled in a calculating way that reminded Magdalene of Alexander. "I just wanted to let you know I saw Rupert Lyons at church this morning. I invited him to take tea with us on Wednesday."

"But that's our picnic day with Claudio and everyone."

"Yes," Mrs. Melling looked at Douglas in the kitchen for a second and then turned her back on him, "and I am afraid it will have to be cancelled indefinitely. Now that there is high interest in my family, I cannot have word getting out that we frolic with the servants."

"Am I not a servant as well?"

"You are a ladies' companion—my companion. That is much different."

"But I'm paid every Friday like the rest of them."

"It is completely different, and as Mr. Campbell so aptly pointed out, you are without family. You need me to shepherd you along to your best possible prospects."

"I'm finding my way quite nicely, thank you." Magdalene sat back in the rocking chair, arms crossed.

"My dear, last night you dined in a fine hotel and danced with the most eligible bachelor in Mobile while wearing a Parisian gown. I can get you so much more out of life than you'll ever find within these walls if you just let me."

Magdalene shook her head, a tear rolling down her cheek. "I don't want it. I choose to be myself and I choose true love. It was good enough for my parents and it's good enough for me."

"And what did it get them? They're both in early graves."

Magdalene stood, anger and pain flaring in her eyes like fire in a forge. "And what did the double standards of the high and mighty social class get your daughter, Mrs. Melling? The only thing it gave Eliza was the opportunity for her to be murdered!"

Douglas rushed across the room, placing calming hands on Magdalene's trembling arms.

Mr. Campbell took Mrs. Melling's elbow. "I think it's time you got back to Seacliff Cottage, ma'am."

She shook his hand off. "Eliza had an accident. Everyone said so. What does Magdalene know? She was not even here!"

Douglas pressed his forehead against Magdalene's, hoping to get through her anger to the humanity of her soul. "Don't do it, Maggie. It's not worth it."

But Magdalene had been wounded one too many times. She pushed him aside and crossed the room to Mrs. Melling. Glaring at her eye to eye, she spewed the words sure to wound the most. "Your husband knowingly harbored the murderess and laid with her after knowing the truth of what caused the *accident* that killed your beloved daughter. Mr. Melling cared more for his disgusting fetishes than for his family or even justice. Now tell me why I'd want to impress anyone in the type of society that holds a man like that in high regard?"

"Who?" Mrs. Melling's voice trembled. "Who was responsible?"

Douglas pulled Magdalene—white-knuckled and red-faced—away from Mrs. Melling.

She fought for control and spoke all the bolder over the distance between them. "The one you never cared for, probably because you saw the way your husband looked upon her from the moment he saw her at the hotel."

Mrs. Melling's hand went to her mouth and her knees gave out. Mr. Campbell took her by the arm and walked her out the door, the air rumbling with approaching thunder.

Douglas rushed to the bathroom and came back with a damp cloth. Washing Magdalene's face with gentle strokes, he kissed her cheeks and forehead at intervals. She began sobbing, making it impossible for him to try to cool or clean her face. He dropped the cloth on the floor and pulled her into the rocking chair, holding her as she cried.

"Get it all out, Maggie," he murmured. "I'll still be here when you're done."

She wept until they both were wet with her tears. Then, needing to feel something other than the anguish racking her soul, she unbuttoned his damp shirt and kissed him hungrily.

"This isn't what you need," he said as she pulled his shirt off one shoulder. "Maggie, you don't need me, you need to find peace within yourself."

With one hand on his exposed biceps and the other on his chest, she stared at him as if she couldn't remember who he was. "Douglas?"

"Aye, Maggie."

"I think I'm going to be sick." She ran for the door.

Seven

Magdalene staggered to the tree line between the house and the stable and dry heaved, wishing the bile would come but it never did. Douglas pushed the loose hair away from her face and supported her.

When her gagging subsided, he carried her back to the little house and laid her on his uncle's bed. The smell of burned cornbread and overcooked turnip greens permeated the space. Uncle Simon came back from seeing Mrs. Melling home and set to work salvaging the food. Sitting on the edge of the bed, Douglas cooled Magdalene's face and neck with a fresh cloth, wiping away the trace of tears in the process.

"She'll never forgive me," she said, despair painted on her sallow face.

"It'll blow over like all storms do," Douglas assured her.

"This one's a hurricane with casualities, and I'll be the first victim." She touched his face with a searching hand. "Or maybe you because she knows that would hurt me more."

"Hush, Maggie. Don't worry about what you can't control."

"She'll keep pushing me together with that man, I know she will. And she'll keep pulling me away from you!"

Douglas smoothed her flyaway tendrils, tucking them behind her ear. "Give it time. There are only three weeks until Claudio receives his holy orders. We can make it."

"Claudio said he'd understand if we don't wait for him." Her voice rose with hysterics.

"We still need a place to live after I secure a job. We need to budget and—"

"The money!" She scrambled off the bed and stumbled for the loft.

"Maggie, you need to slow down and rest!" He followed behind, one hand on her back in case she lost her grip on the ladder.

At the top, she tackled the envelope, collapsing on the bed. "I feared it would no longer be here, that somehow she would have taken it away."

Douglas dropped to his knees on the bed next to her, a hand rubbing her back. "You're safe here."

She shook her head. "No, even if I stay in this house, she'll find a way to control me. We have to leave!" She thrust the envelope at him. "A hundred dollars from my father's estate. Use it to rent a house, a room, a shack in the woods. I don't care as long as it's away from the Mellings!"

"Maggie, that's for you, I can't take it." He slid it across the bedspread to her.

"Use it in your plans to get me away from here! I have no need to buy trinkets or dresses with the money. When we're married, what's mine is yours. Take it now to help plan for us."

"But—"

"Take it and get us away!"

"I've got it, Maggie." He lifted her chin and planted a healing kiss on her lips. "And I'll do the best I can."

When they were called down to eat, Douglas took Magdalene's hand. The three ate in relative silence, picking around the burned edges on the cornbread and skipping the mushy vegetables. Uncle Simon insisted on cleaning up, so Magdalene and Douglas retreated to the loft to go through the final crate.

Anticipation over the contents enlivened Magdalene's senses. She watched Douglas with eagerness as he used his weight to lever the crowbar under the lid to loosen the nails.

"I'm amazed you got these others open without help," he said as a bead of sweat ran from his temple down the side of his face. "I suppose that's how you got sick—all the exertion in this heat."

The nails squealed in protest as the first corner ripped free from the wood. Douglas stopped to wipe his brow and catch his breath.

"I can think of better ways to exert ourselves." Her brown eyes were luminous as the room darkened in the gathering storm. Below them, the sound of clanking pots and running water assured his uncle still worked. Magdalene led Douglas to his bed.

"Maggie…"

She caressed his back and shoulders as she wrapped herself around him, trying to get him to lie down—or even sit. The thunder rolled closer and Douglas let his guard down. They were on the bed,

Magdalene holding him to her. He could barely maneuver an arm to prop himself so his weight wouldn't crush her. In a flash of lightning, rain began to pound on the roof. The door to the passion Douglas usually kept locked burst open.

Magdalene, heart thrumming as quickly as the drops beating the roof, moved with him as his hands traced her clothes over parts of her he'd never touched.

"If you won't marry me yet," Magdalene whispered with panting breath, "at least take me so no one else can claim that privilege. I'd rather die than it not be with you."

"Oh, Maggie." He dropped his head to her chest. "Forgive me."

She ran her hands through his hair. "I know you truly love me and will be gentle."

"It's because I love you that we can't do this!" He rolled off and lay beside her, body warm and fingering the ring on his hand. "But you're right. We can't wait for Claudio, and especially not the Mellings. I'll talk to Father Angelo and Claudio when I pick him up Wednesday."

"But the tea—"

His finger went to her lips. "She said no servants. Claudio is a servant of the Lord, not this house. There's respectability to men of the cloth, even in their humbleness. She should have no objection to Claudio still coming because she's hosted him in the parlor for tea many times. You just have to sell it as it being a good idea for her as a hostess to include him."

Magdalene curled into Douglas's side and propped a leg over his. "I might be able to do that."

"I know you'll be able to. And if you don't, I'll come in and guard you myself." He kissed her forehead and hugged her closer. "Tell me what you found in the crates."

Magdalene smiled, enjoying her time in his arms as the rain continued and a cool breeze wafted through the dormer window. "My mother's tea set, cookware, books, and oodles of linens. It brought back such memories to see everything."

"Now, let's check what's in the last crate." He sat up, bringing her with him—the bed springs squeaking from the movement.

Magdalene watched as he struggled to open the lid the rest of the way. Once free, she joined him to look within. "My old everyday dresses! I've actually missed them, rough fabric and all." She laughed, pulling out a button-down, powder blue dress with tiny navy flowers, holding it to herself.

"Just the thing for Mrs. Campbell. You'll be fetching in that, and anything else you wear." He pulled a short-sleeved summer nightgown out next. "Like this here."

She snatched it away and he laughed.

"Are you forgetting I've already seen you in a nightgown, more than once I believe? And in your underclothes and bathing suit."

Magdalene giggled and threw the gown onto his head. "Keep it. I can model it for you soon."

Underneath her clothes were the two dresses of her mother's that her father had hung on to: her second best Sunday dress—she was buried in her best—and her wedding gown. The pale pink Sunday dress felt stiff and dated, but the bone-colored silk and lace two-piece suit had classic lines. Though rumpled, it was in good condition. She fingered the pleated lace overlay on the bust.

"Your mother's wedding set?" he asked.

She nodded.

"Would you like to wear it when our time comes?"

She knew he wouldn't mind, but she had to ask. "You wouldn't think it too old-fashioned of me, especially after seeing me in the latest Parisian gown?"

"I'd think it's a sentimental gesture, another way besides the rings that you can include the memory of your parents at our union." He kissed the tear that trailed her smooth cheek. "But I'd marry you even if you wore a potato sack."

She fell against him, a mixture of laughter and tears.

"I'll go downstairs and check on Uncle Simon so you can try it on."

The suit needed a good laundering to soften it and a few hems reinforced, but it would fit well enough, even with the bustle long gone. Magdalene called to Douglas once she changed back into her calico and pointed out her concerns.

"I don't know what to do. I'm scared to bring it into the house for fear Mrs. Melling will take it from me."

He hugged her. "I'll see to it for you and I promise it will be ready when we are."

The bottom of the crate housed smaller boxes of dishes and silverware, so she didn't bother to unpack each one. "It looks like we have a wonderful start to a household. I'm pleased Aunt Agnes saved so much for me, and after living with Mrs. Melling, I know my aunt is not the worst person in the world. Still, I don't want to be around either one."

"We'll be out of here soon."

"If we're going to steal away at some point, how are we going to get out with these boxes?" Magdalene asked.

"I think Claudio would keep them for us. I could bring over a few at a time when I fetch him." He took her hands. "We've done enough busy work, and settled a few ideas. Now it's time to relax for the final hour of your time off."

The rain had stopped, but the cool breeze stayed. They sat on the front stoop, just wide enough for them to sit snug against each other. Magdalene rested her head on Douglas's shoulder and Uncle Simon sat in the rocking chair behind them smoking his pipe. Conversation wasn't necessary as they watched the shimmering raindrops drip from the branches and the birds return to the yard from their hiding places.

At four thirty, she said goodbye to Uncle Simon and thanked him for fighting for her day of freedom. Douglas walked her to the kitchen door. He kissed her on the cheek, returned the wedding ring to her that he'd been wearing, and watched Magdalene through the screen until she disappeared into the stairwell.

Magdalene placed the wedding rings into one of the dressing table drawers and, feeling chilled, dressed in the blue Sunday outfit she'd brought with her rather than one of the finer ones Mrs. Melling had provided for her. She arranged her hair into the Melling-approved pompadour and laced on her shiniest black boots before going down the front stairs.

Mrs. Melling fretted by the fire in the parlor with a pile of newspaper clippings in her lap. "I am glad you can return punctually from your frivolous time with the help."

"I'm still here for you, Mrs. Melling, even after a few hours off." She folded her hands in her lap and sat in the wingchair across the fireplace from the lady of the house. "Do you need help with those?"

Mrs. Melling clutched the papers. "I spent my alone hours going through the newspapers from the last month, clipping all mentions of Alex and Beatrice from the New York and Mobile papers. I will arrange it into a scrapbook to present to them when they arrive."

"What a lovely idea." Magdalene looked at her with humbleness in her eyes. "And I'm sorry, Mrs. Melling, for what I said. I wasn't myself today."

"You most certainly were not. Those Campbells are a bad influence on you with their foreign ways and work hardened hands." She looked sharply at her. "He keeps his hands off you, does he not?"

"Yes, ma'am, he's a perfect gentleman." *Even when I don't wish him to be.* "Now that my mind is clearer, I look forward to tea on Wednesday. And it is a stroke of genius for you to have Claudio here along with Mr. Lyons so Claudio can see to you and Mr. Lyons can focus his attentions on me."

A slow smile spread across Mrs. Melling's face. "Yes, it will be most cozy that way. But what shall we dress you in?"

Eight

After a minuscule dinner on Wednesday, the lady of the house followed Magdalene into her bedroom. With trepidation, she undressed to her underclothes and awaited her employer's pronouncement.

"The embroidered lace tea gown is your lowest cut day dress, and I believe Rupert was emboldened by your lovely complexion and the view the Parisian gown afforded him. Men think they are smooth, but they are as obvious as a strutting peacock. That gown is very sheer. Change into the new pink chemise and I shall secure the coordinating corset. Be sure to button up your white boots before I lace you in."

Mrs. Melling refused to give up corsets under tea gowns though they were styled for comfort with the express purpose to be worn without binding shapewear. Magdalene fought back tears as the laces pulled tighter and her bust squeezed together to create an ample display. Only thinking of Douglas getting the chance to speak with Claudio and Father Angelo kept Magdalene from striking her employer.

"Now," Mrs. Melling simpered, "you be on your best behavior and be as meek as possible. Today, Rupert Lyons is the most charming man and can do no wrong. You shall utter nary a complaint. Do you understand?"

"Yes, ma'am." Magdalene sighed shallowly, for she could not get much breath.

Mrs. Melling tied Magdalene's petticoat around her abnormally small waist. Once dressed and Magdalene's hair arranged, she exclaimed, "You're the pink of perfection!"

Looking in the mirror, Magdalene agreed that she looked like a lady off the pages of *McCall's Magazine*, but she wasn't happy.

"Smile, Magdalene. Let your radiance shine and he will not only want you, he will need you."

A shiver worked its way from Magdalene's head to toes as she recalled the demonic words Alexander had spoken as he'd seduced her all those months ago.

There is no want, only need.

Her hand went to her heart in an impulsive movement and she bit her lip to keep from crying out as the voice sounded larger than life in her head.

"You stay here until Leroy comes for you. I want you to have a grand entrance."

With the click of the door, Magdalene knew she wasn't alone. The tentacles were back, spiraling around her limbs and gripping her torso tighter than the corset. Unable to sit comfortably, she paced the room and fought the urge to give in.

Minutes later, she heard the Great Arrow start up. She rushed to the open window and watched Douglas pull away, one of her large crates in the backseat. If he had looked up, she would have cried to him to deliver her from the evil threatening to tear down her resolve against Mrs. Melling's plans.

The minutes ticked by as Magdalene rubbed the wooden rosary bracelet she'd pulled out from her drawer holding her engagement ring. Finally, the rumble of a motor coming up the lane sounded through the cloudy afternoon. Hiding behind her curtain, she watched Claudio and Douglas exit the automobile, laughing. Resentment that they could be joyous while she battled demons took root. While she knew it illogical—and against her nature to hold grudges against either of the men—she couldn't stop the bitterness from clouding her judgement and slinking behind the curtain when they looked toward her window.

Not long after Claudio disappeared into Seacliff Cottage, Douglas returned from his house with one of the smaller crates and tucked it on the floorboard of the backseat. Then he came back with the other small box and placed it in as well. Magdalene tried to find comfort in knowing their wedding plans must be moving forward if Claudio agreed to keep their things safe, but no joy reached her soul.

She stayed hidden and watched as Douglas covered the automobile in case the cloudy afternoon turned to thunderstorms as it often did during the summer. She no longer felt the need to call to him for help, but she fought the compulsion to call out for other reasons.

Rupert Lyons arrived in a two-seater automobile, a driving cap covering his brown hair and goggles protecting his eyes. He shook out his hair after removing his cap and placed the goggles and hat in the front seat. His body lacked definition—being neither fat nor thin—and his boring face, slightly crooked nose, and nondescript dark eyes were plain next to Douglas's handsome features.

Douglas was kind enough to help him snap his car's canopy closed and loaned him a tarp to protect his shiny automobile from the possible weather. How Douglas could help the man who threatened her peace bewildered Magdalene. If she'd seen Douglas so much as lift a bag for Grace Anne, she would have beaten her off by whatever means necessary.

When Rupert walked away after a handshake, Magdalene turned from the window. She took her last few moments of peace studying her form in the mirror and trying to breathe.

Leroy knocked on her door. "It's time, Miss Maggie."

With shoulders back and chin high, Magdalene descended the front staircase, the gown trailing behind her in a scallop of lace. Upon entering the parlor, both Mr. Lyons and Claudio stood. Claudio stepped away from the chair by the fire and came to her in the doorway, muttering something in Italian before speaking to her.

"*Signorina*, your beauty grows each day." He kissed both cheeks and whispered. "The infestation is back. I can feel it."

He did the sign of the cross over both of them. "Father Angelo sends his blessings," he said before bringing her to the settee where Rupert Lyons waited expectantly.

Magdalene, taking Claudio's message to be one of agreeing to her and Douglas's coming nuptials, smiled from the heart. Being the one she faced, Mr. Lyons fell victim to her glow.

"Miss Jones, it's a pleasure to see you again."

"Mr. Lyons, the pleasure is mine." She curtsied deep enough to give him plenty to look at.

"Please, call me Rupert as Mrs. Melling does. I'm an old family friend." He turned to Mrs. Melling after Magdalene settled herself. "I read in the paper that the wedding is scheduled for noon at Cathedral of the Immaculate Conception on October second. I hope to receive an invitation."

"Of course, Rupert, and to the engagement party this month on the twenty-second. We'll be meeting here for pre-dinner drinks before being ferried over to the hotel for dinner and dancing. Invitations go out next week. They are being printed in Mobile as we speak. I know what good friends you and Alex were when you were away at the university."

"We were like brothers while studying law." He turned on the settee to face Magdalene, his knee brushing hers in the process, which caused him to wink. "I hope to see you at the party, and if so, may I have a dance?"

"Yes, I'll be there." She forced a smile.

Mrs. Melling cleared her throat.

"And I'd be happy to dance with you, Rupert." She folded her hands in her lap and gazed at him with false adoration.

Magdalene, having had enough of the games, glanced at Claudio in time to see him frown. The chatter continued, mostly led by Mrs. Melling about the wedding. When Rosemary brought in the tea tray, Mrs. Melling asked Magdalene to serve so she had to politely ask everyone how they wanted their tea and what cakes they were interested in trying. By the time she brought Rupert his plate of food, his flirting escalated to brazenly touching her hand as he took the dish from her.

When she brought Claudio his plate, she whispered, "She's making me be kind."

"Speak up, Magdalene. There must be no secrets between you and the deacon."

She straightened, and returned to the table to collect her own plate. "Sorry, Mrs. Melling. I was only wishing him luck on his approaching holy orders."

"Yes," he said, "I hope you are all able to be there, even though it is a busy weekend."

"When is that?" Mrs. Melling sipped her tea.

"The twenty-third." The annoyance trumpeted from Magdalene's voice, and for that Mrs. Melling gave her a harsh stare.

"It is difficult to keep anything but the wedding straight, my dear. Forgive me."

"There's nothing to forgive." Magdalene hid her frown behind a napkin.

"I am sure you understand, Claudio, with all the company and the engagement party the night before, we might not make it."

"I'll make it, even if I have to walk," Magdalene assured him.

"Really, Magdalene! You will have Rupert thinking I keep you locked away. If it means so much to you to see Claudio's ordination, I'll be sure you have the driver." Upon realizing what she'd said, Mrs. Melling hastily added. "Or the carriage at least. The driver might be busy assisting with after party business."

Upon finishing her teacake, Mrs. Melling looked across to Claudio. "I would like you to bring me to the mausoleum for prayer, if you do not mind."

"I would be happy to, *signora*. A walk after eating is always agreeable."

"Good, then it is settled." As she stood, both the men got to their feet. She waved Rupert back down. "You and Magdalene stay and chat. We will be back soon enough, no need to trouble yourselves."

Panic struck Magdalene and she clutched a hand to her tight stomach.

"Perhaps a walk would be good for everyone," Claudio offered, a look of concern on his face.

"No, I believe Magdalene looks peaked. She might need a drink to perk her up. Rupert, drinks are in the corner. I trust you to look after my girl." Mrs. Melling took Claudio's arm. "Come along."

When the front door shut, Rupert poured two glasses without hesitation. He swallowed one shot of brandy before pouring more and bringing the second for Magdalene.

"Are you all right?" He offered her the glass, which she took with no intention of drinking.

"I'm having trouble breathing," she answered truthfully. She stood, hoping to relieve some of the pressure on her abdomen.

Rupert downed his second shot and stood beside her, a hand at the small of her back. "How may I be of assistance?"

As much as she didn't want to admit it, the touch of his hand aroused her awareness of her femininity. She placed a hand at her waist, emphasizing her serpentine curves, and looked at him over the top of her brandy glass. She hadn't had that particular drink since Alexander left, and the combination of the smell and the renewed evil in the air made her knees weak and her body ache for touch.

"Do they teach one to appreciate this foul drink at the university?" she asked.

"What do you mean?" Rupert scratched at his hairline, a confused look on his bland face.

"I mean," she said as she paced, "you're the second college graduate to try to get me drunk with brandy."

"It's what my father drank after supper and I assumed it my right to do the same when I reached adulthood." Rupert stumbled over his words as though unsure of himself.

If he didn't get some confidence, she'd walk out the door and find a real man. "Are you one that prides himself on having all the rights and privileges afforded to those of your station?"

"Naturally." He adjusted his tie. Then, as if he decided she played him, he turned the tables on her. "Since I'm not the first to offer you brandy, may I know who was?"

"Only if you ask politely." She ran her fingers over the arm of the settee as she passed.

"Who, Miss Jones—or may I call you Magdalene?"

"I prefer to keep things formal, thank you."

That caused him to stop, but his eyes never left her moving form. "Very well, *Miss Jones*, who was the first to offer you brandy?"

She clasped her hands behind her. "Your dear friend Alexander, of course."

"I thought you came here after he left."

"Oh, no." Magdalene returned to circling the room. "Mrs. Melling just likes people to think that. I came three days before Alexander left."

"Three days?"

"And nights," she whispered from behind him. Then she swallowed all the brandy in her glass without coughing and set the glass on the side table.

A lecherous smile crept upon his face and he licked his thin lips. The next time she passed him, a hand grabbed her forearm. "Enough of the coy games, Miss Jones. Alex and I were like brothers, and, as brothers, we always shared."

"You misunderstand me, Rupert. Alexander Melling is not at all my type."

"Oh, Miss Jones, but you are exactly his type. Not the type to bring home to the parents, but the type to play with." He brought a hand to her other wrist. "And I taught him everything he knows, though he never learned to get over the feelings of guilt afterward."

"If one can judge a teacher by his student, I can already say I'm not impressed." She wrenched her arms free and stood defiantly, while still remaining playful.

"But I'm impressed with you, Miss Jones, and that's what matters most. You haven't seen anything yet." The intensity in his eyes was toxic, causing Magdalene to draw back. His right hand skimmed around her throat to her neck, his fingers caressing the bare skin of her upper back. "Don't be scared, I'm well versed in love making."

"In the parlor in the middle of the afternoon while Mrs. Melling has momentarily stepped out with a deacon?"

"No, but soon." He trailed his fingers across her throat. "I have the feeling Mrs. Melling will grant me any audience I seek with you. Somewhere in that muddled mind of hers she seems to think you're marriageable material for someone of my status. You've been playing me since the hotel when you made me dance with all the others first, and I don't appreciate that."

He rested his thumb in the hollow between her collarbones. Magdalene felt her pulse throbbing against it as the rest of his hand slipped down her front.

"Aren't you supposed to wait until after you get what you want to drop the romantic act?"

"Typically, I do, but I don't usually pursue women who aim to play me." He brought his face within inches of hers so she felt his hot, brandied breath with each word. "But you're special, Magdalene. Has anyone ever told you that?"

"Yes, and it's Miss Jones." She felt her breath mix with his. "And you're not what I expected. I wondered how you got any woman at all with Alexander in the room, but now I know what you lack in physical charms you make up for with boldness."

"You like bold, Magdalene?" He stepped forward so his body brushed against hers. "Tell me what else you like."

Magdalene was on the verge of showing him when the front door opened. She dropped into place on the settee, ankles crossed and hands in her lap.

Nine

Claudio saw Mrs. Melling to her chair, and then crossed the room to Magdalene. He offered his hand to her, palm down. She took it and immediately recoiled. Turning his hand, he showed her the crucifix and shook his head mournfully. "I tried, *signorina*."

Head swimming amid lusts, Magdalene patted the spot next to her for Rupert to sit back down.

"I was contemplating taking you for a walk, Miss Jones."

"The forest is lovely on the way to the mausoleum," Mrs. Melling said.

"She still does not look well, *signora*." Claudio motioned to Magdalene's flushed cheeks. "She should rest."

"Nonsense," Mrs. Melling retorted. "The air might do her good."

"It is not fresh," Claudio insisted. "It is so damp the air might rain without the use of clouds, though they are coming steadily on."

"At any rate," Rupert said with authority, "I should like to pay my respects to Eliza, and I invite Miss Jones to show me the way. That is, if Mrs. Melling can spare her."

"Of course. Take your time."

"No, hurry back," Claudio said. "The rain is coming."

"Then have the driver bring you home, Claudio. That way you will be back at the church before the storm."

Claudio's eyes widened and he gripped his cross as Mrs. Melling rang for Leroy to escort him out. "Remember to pray, *signorina!*" he called over his shoulder.

"What a strange fellow, but I assume it takes a special sort of man to enter the priesthood these days." Rupert extended his hand to Magdalene. "Shall we?"

Her smile shone like the sun on a spring morning though her eyes were cloudy. Upon exiting the house, Magdalene paused on the porch as though she'd forgotten where she was going.

"I'll allow you to lead me, Magdalene." Rupert's voice soothed her ruffled state. "You lead me there, and then I will lead you to heaven."

"You think very highly of yourself." She brought them around the far side of the house, holding her trailing skirt up and to the side so her shiny white boots paraded in front of her.

"I have much experience to draw from." The sound of gravel spraying behind automobile tires filled the heavy air. "Your driver needs to learn some restraint. He'll wear out the tires if he keeps that up, not to mention mar the finish on the body."

A smile crossed her lips, much different than anything Rupert had seen. "I'm glad to hear it. In my experience, the driver has been too restrained."

"You have experience with the driver?"

"He taught me how to drive."

Rupert looked sideways at her.

"With Mrs. Melling in the backseat the whole time." She knocked him on the shoulder with her fist. "What type of girl do you think I am?"

"I'm going to find out soon enough." His smile made her skin feel like there were roaches crawling over her flesh and she was unable to brush them away. "But you're at least the type to venture into the woods with a man who declared he is going to take you."

She tilted her head at him, slowing her pace. "You said what? When?"

"Always the tease." They were far enough into the woods as not to be seen from the house. Rupert pulled her into his arms and forced a kiss on her lips. "You don't need to play anymore, but if it helps you feel better, by all means, keep at it."

Magdalene jerked free. With each step away from Seacliff Cottage, the fog in her mind lifted and the horror of her predicament overtook her. Not knowing what else to do, she stalled for time. She led Rupert off the path and north of the intended site. If she were not in the stupid boots, she would have run for the carriage house and the safety of Uncle Simon until Douglas returned. The brandy churned in her stomach and she knew Rupert would not be the type to hold her hair off her face or wipe her mouth if she became sick.

Stumbling through the woods, the sky grew darker and thunder rumbled as though nearly on top of them.

"Let's get to the sepulcher, Magdalene. The rain won't be good for your dress."

Unable to prolong the inevitable with the rain beating upon them, she turned back. When the shimmering white walls of Eliza's resting place came into view, Rupert ran for the shelter. Magdalene trudged through the downpour. A streak of lightning illuminated the clearing, making her appear more ghostly than human in her pale, dripping gown.

"Come on!" he yelled to her above the boom of thunder. When she reached the bottom step, Rupert yanked her into the structure. "You're out of your mind! You could have been struck by lightning!"

"I was clearing my head."

"You're as crazy as Mrs. Melling, but much better looking." He pulled her closer, looking down her body inch by inch.

The tea gown was soaked and completely transparent. Magdalene might as well have been standing in her underclothes with each ribbed seam on her corset and every ruffle of petticoat as plain as her rosy lips.

His eyes focused on her gown's neckline, sagging low with the weight of the rainwater. "You picked the perfect outfit for a stroll in the rain."

"I didn't pick this dress."

He fingered the laces of her corset through the back of the gown. "I should have recognized Mrs. Melling's work. The only one I've seen come close to your form was Eliza." He laid a hand on her name on the wall, marking her place in the tomb. "She was such a flirt, but Eddie and Sean got a piece of her at least."

Magdalene slapped him across the face so forcefully the red imprint immediately showed on his cheek and her hand tingled.

"You really think you're one of them, don't you?"

She couldn't say she'd slapped him not for the Mellings' sake, but for Claudio's, so she stayed silent.

He took both her wrists in one hand and held them above her head against the marble wall, causing her breath to catch at the frigid surface against her skin. His other hand fingered her bare neck. She trembled in her cold, frightened state, trying to recall what the deacon had told her before he went away. Out the open door, the storm raged. Three days ago, she enjoyed an afternoon storm in

Douglas's arms, now she struggled to get out of the grasp of a stranger handpicked for her by Mrs. Melling.

"You'll never be one of them, Magdalene."

"I don't want to be one of them or here with you!"

"You came with me knowing my full intentions." He pushed her fully against the wall with his body. "It's not the ideal location, but it's the coolest place around."

"Enjoy it while you can because you'll burn in hell!"

"I expected wit and games, but anger and a self-righteous attitude are fun, too." His hand dropped from her neck to where she wished no man to be except Douglas.

Magdalene stomped her heeled boot against the top of his thin loafer. Rupert hollered like a wildcat and reached for his foot as she rushed for the door. He recovered quickly and grabbed her dress before she could run out. Pulling her to the floor, he struggled to remove her boots while pinning her down, unknowingly doing her a favor by removing the things that posed the greatest risk to her flight. She fought Rupert enough for him to believe he was doing something wrong.

When her boots were off, Rupert flung them out the open door and then closed it, plunging them into semi-darkness as the stained glass window on the wall opposite the door had no sunlight to illuminate it. Magdalene used the few seconds to stand, preferring to meet her situation in battle rather than lying down as prey.

Pray!

Claudio told her to pray, though she didn't know if it would work against someone like Rupert, still set on evil without being in the demonic house. On his way back to her, he dropped his wet jacket on the floor and threw his belt over his shoulder.

"Our Father which art in heaven, Hallowed be thy—"

He pressed his forearm against her throat, crushing her option to do anything but try to breathe as he pinned her against the wall.

"You really need to stop hanging around that deacon." He turned her to face the marble and put a knee into her back while bringing both arms behind her.

Remembering the belt he'd removed, Magdalene protested. "Please don't tie my arms. I'll stop fighting."

Rupert laughed, his foul breath coming out like the vapors from the burning lilies. He kissed her ear when he leaned close to wrap the belt around her wrists. "I wouldn't like you half as much if you stopped struggling. Your fight is part of what thrills me."

Once her hands were secure, he undid the buttons on her gown that ran from the low scooped back to just below her waist. Then he turned her around and slid the dress off her shoulders, but he could not remove it all the way because her bound hands prevented it.

Magdalene looked at the red handprint on his face and the frustration in his eyes as he realized what he'd done. Before she could say anything, his mouth was on her face and his hands groped across the top of her corset. She managed to knee him in the groin once as she tried to squirm out of his reach.

"I still have control of the situation." He observed the muddy state of her tea gown. "That dress is a lost cause now. We'll just have to think up a nice story to tell Mrs. Melling when we get back."

Both hands at her chest, Rupert easily ripped the thin lace down her front. Magdalene pushed firmly into the wall to stay upright, though it meant smashing her own arms in the process.

"Please," she begged. "It would be sacrilegious for you to do this here. Bring me into the forest or anywhere else."

"Enough with the self-righteous chatter. If you are what I think you are, this building in the perfect spot for you to get what you've been asking for, parading around like a flirtatious society woman."

Rupert lowered her to the hard floor. Her arms bent behind her so she could not lie flat, so he turned her face down and undid the belt.

As he turned her back, he said, "I'll trust you not to—"

She gouged at his face, a finger scratched against a yielding moist eye and another hooked a nostril. Then his elbow smashed down on her face, causing her to momentarily lose sight from the blow to her nose. As the pain subsided, she felt the warm blood run toward her lips. He kept an arm mashed against her face as he wrestled her with his other hand to secure her flailing hands.

"I'm no longer amused, Magdalene. Now you're just making a mess of things."

Her nose, swollen and dripping blood, seemed minor to her throbbing head. When he removed his arm, she made no effort to attack. He took both her hands over her head, pressed her arms to the ground, and tied them together at the wrists with his belt once more.

"This is a first in more ways than one." He ran his hands down the length of her body, removing her wet stockings in the process. "You've made this more memorable than I could have imagined."

Magdalene's teeth chattered as the chill of the marble seeped into her bones. He straddled her at the waist while her body tremored. She gasped for breath with her mouth barely open to keep blood from getting into it. He took a stocking and wiped it across her face a few times, clearing away the worst of the blood.

"I suppose you want this off next." He stared at her heaving chest. "I've never had the pleasure of undoing Mrs. Melling's handiwork."

Her teeth were chattering too much for her to speak. Magdalene wanted to spit in his face, but her body wouldn't cooperate for that either. She was a shivering mass of skin and bones when Rupert pulled her off the floor. Her bound hands fell in front of her as he turned her to get at the laces. He fumbled with the small knots and she twisted her wrists in an attempt to free them.

"I'll warm you up in no time, *Miss Jones*."

Just as the corset straps gave way, Magdalene loosened one loop of the belt enough that she thought she'd be able to pull free. Forcing herself to stay her position so she could wait for the best possible moment, she gritted her chattering teeth as Rupert weaseled his hands under the back of the corset and around to her ribs, causing the shapewear to fall to the blood-splattered floor as he molested her. She prayed for deliverance and yanked one hand free as she grabbed for his arm. In the struggle, the belt slid off her other wrist, the buckle clattering to the ground as she slammed against the wall with enough force to knock the wind out of her and start her nose bleeding again.

"You're not as smart as you think you are," he said.

With the corset gone, she recovered from the blow quicker, though she couldn't stop the warm life from pouring down her face. Magdalene struggled to position herself between Rupert and the door, but his strength overtook hers. Seconds later, he had her on the ground. Her teeth were back to chattering as she lay on the marble, but she had to keep fighting.

Ten

Just as Magdalene slipped into permanent despair, the
sepulcher door flew open and a flash of lightning backlit Douglas. He
immediately seized Rupert off Magdalene and flung him against the
marble. When Rupert went for Douglas, he found himself pinned to
the wall with Douglas's hands around his neck. Magdalene curled
into a ball like an armadillo for protection. She covered her ears
against the sounds of the fight, scared to know who would win and
what the state of the loser would be. Twice someone fell over her.
What seemed an eternity later, Magdalene was scooped off the floor
in Douglas's familiar arms.

"God forgive me, Maggie. I came as fast as I could." His
voice cracked as he stepped over Rupert's lifeless form.

Though the rain had stopped, the trees still dripped and
thunder continued to rumble in the distance as he carried her home.

"Maggie," he asked as they approached the clearing behind
the house, "do you need a doctor?"

She stayed mute and buried her bloodied face against his
chest.

He hollered for his uncle, and sent him into Seacliff Cottage
for Rosemary and Leroy. The three rushed from the kitchen door
moments later.

"She's frozen and scared to death." Douglas held her close.
"Rosemary, could you draw a bath and help clean her?"

"I'll do all I can." She turned toward the main house.

"I'd rather her not go in there."

"The washroom in the carriage house ain't fit for two grown
people, not to mention it would take an hour to heat enough water to
fill the tub. Bring her up the back stairs to her bathroom. It will be
easy to see to her in there and the taps run hot."

He nodded and she rushed inside.

"Uncle Simon, I'm going to need Claudio. Maybe even Father Angelo as well. Claudio transferred to the first wagon on its way to Daphne we came across. Take the carriage and bring them here as quick as possible."

Uncle Simon paused to kiss her forehead. "Dear Maggie, you're in good hands now."

"Leroy, I'm afraid I need to ask you to see to Mrs. Melling's guest. I left him in the mausoleum."

Motioning to Douglas's bloodied knuckles clutched around Magdalene, Leroy stated the obvious. "I'd say he got what he had coming to him. I'll help him get back here, but I'll be none too kind about it myself."

With instructions given, Douglas carried Magdalene toward the house. She didn't speak, but her eyes remained opened and senses sharp.

"I need your help, Prissy," Douglas called to the girl crying on the gazebo swing.

She sniffled and wiped her nose on her sleeve. "Is Miss Maggie dead?"

"No, Prissy, she's just badly hurt. Could you hold the door open so I can get her inside?"

"Mama said to stay out of the way and not to move from this spot."

"Your mama won't mind if you help Miss Maggie for two seconds. But if she gets upset, I'll let her know it was my doing, not yours."

She dashed across the porch, bare feet pounding the boards before she opened the screen. Douglas started for the back stairs but Mrs. Melling called from the hallway.

"Rosemary! I've been ringing for Leroy but he's not coming." She pushed into the kitchen from the front hall and stopped short upon seeing Douglas with Magdalene in his arms. "What on earth have you done to her?"

"What have *I* done?" Magdalene could feel the anger rolling across his body and felt for sure, if he had not been holding her, his hands would have been around Mrs. Melling's throat as they had been around Rupert's earlier. "I had to save my fiancée from the hands of your so-called *gentleman* friend."

Mrs. Melling waved her had to dismiss his perceived overreaction. "They were on a stroll to Eliza's mausoleum to pay their respects."

"The man has not one ounce of respect in him! Look at her!" His arms trembled as he stepped closer to Mrs. Melling. "He had torn her clothes off and was upon her when I found them."

"You know what a flirt she—"

"This isn't her doing! She was defending herself to the end. He had strike marks upon him and he'd bound her arms and beat her face. Look at her! Is this what a young woman is supposed to look like after an innocent walk, bloodstained and battered in her underclothes?"

As if seeing her for the first time, Mrs. Melling gasped and leaned over her. "Magdalene, what happened?"

Magdalene recoiled and buried her face in Douglas's shirt.

Mrs. Melling reached a hand toward Magdalene's arm, but Douglas stepped away. "Don't touch her. You're never going to touch her again. You or any of your kind!"

Rosemary pushed into the kitchen from the stairs. "It's ready, Douglas."

"And where is Leroy?" Mrs. Melling demanded.

"He's seeing to your guest. They'll be back soon enough." Rosemary followed Douglas upstairs. She'd placed the wicker seat next to the tub and Douglas lowered Magdalene to the chair.

He dropped to his knees before her, gently supporting her arms so she wouldn't tumble sideways. "Maggie, I'll never forgive myself for discrediting Claudio's fear. If you can't forgive me for not coming sooner, I'll understand."

"Hush now, Douglas." Rosemary shooed him "Let me get her cleaned up. She's still shaking with cold."

He paused to test the bathwater. "I'm not leaving this house without you, Maggie. Rosemary will take good care of you and I'll be in the hall."

As soon as he left, Rosemary took control. "Now, Miss Maggie, I'm going to take what's left of your clothes and help you into the tub. You tell me if you want me to stop or if anything hurts too bad, okay?"

Magdalene nodded, grateful for the care of her friend. Rosemary eased the chemise top over Magdalene's head and then helped her stand and step out of her ruffle-trimmed drawers. Upon seeing the corset marks on her torso, Rosemary gasped. "She's mistreated you terribly."

Rosemary helped Magdalene step into the tub. Once situated in the warm water, the cook filled the sink with soapy water to wash the blood from Magdalene's face without soiling the bath water.

Back and forth she went, wiping and rinsing until nothing remained on her face except a lump on her forehead where she struck the wall and her slightly swollen nose. "Now, do you want to lay back, Miss Maggie, and let me wash your hair?"

Magdalene nodded and sat still as Rosemary undid her hair. Then she slipped under the water and stayed until Rosemary took her by her armpits to drag her up.

"You feel dirty, don't ya?"

Magdalene nodded, her wet hair plastered to her neck and chest.

"Like you want to up and die from the pain it caused you?"

Again, she nodded, accompanied by a lone tear running down her already wet cheek.

"Don't you die, Miss Maggie. You've got a lot to live for. That man out there in the hall is as fine as any that's ever walked the earth and he loves you about more than anything I've ever seen. Now the way I see it, he blames himself for not being here because he was out doing his job and you blame yourself for doing what Mrs. Melling told you to do, but neither of y'all are blaming the ones truly responsible. The devil himself and that smooth-talking man with the fast automobile."

Magdalene stared at Rosemary, trying to absorb what she said, but after several seconds, she allowed herself to go limp and sink under the water. Rosemary caught her and brought her immediately to the surface.

"Do you want me to get Douglas in here to hold you up while I bathe you?"

With large eyes, Magdalene shook her head.

"Then get ahold of yourself." Rosemary washed Magdalene's hair, working the suds down to her ends. "You feeling any cleaner yet?"

Magdalene's head went back and forth.

"It'll take time. That man had his hands all over you, didn't he?"

She nodded.

"Taking off your clothes like he had no business doing, poor child." Rosemary fussed over her though only a few years separated them in age. "And your wrists! Men like him have no business in polite society."

Rosemary finished with Magdalene's hair, and then cleaned her face once more with fresh water from the sink. Starting from her neck, she washed and remarked out loud over each bruise, bump, or mark. When she got to her torso, she shook her head.

"Besides the ridge lines, I don't know which are from the corset and which are from the man. Was he all up in here?"

Magdalene nodded and began to sob.

Rosemary put down the cloth and let her cry for a minute. "That Douglas of yours will be pounding on the door if you keep that up, thinking I've hurt you. Now, do you want to me to keep washing or you take over?"

She held out her hand to take the cloth from Rosemary and used enough soap to cloud the water.

"I'm not being nosy, but I have to ask, Miss Maggie. Did that man get inside your clothes?"

Magdalene's lower lips began trembling and her breath came in raspy gasps as she tried to hold her composure. "He…he…" she stuttered. "He just put his hand…under…when Douglas got there."

"So he did save you, though he thinks he failed." Rosemary looked her in the eye. "I know it's rough and what you went through was awful enough."

Magdalene didn't move or acknowledge that she'd heard anything.

"As much as it seems the evil one is bearing down on you, you've been saved on more than one occasion, haven't you?" Still no response. "God's mercy allowed you to escape similar situations within these walls. Now tell me that's not true."

"It's true," she whispered.

"Now, I'm not saying what happened to you wasn't horrific. It'll take time to overcome the fears, but don't think for an instant that shutting out Douglas or anyone else who loves you will help. Trust me when I say it would only make things worse." Rosemary took Magdalene's hands out of the water and held them. "I've been there, Miss Maggie, and love and grace are the only ways to pull through."

Magdalene nodded. "I'll try."

"If you want to soak one more time, I'll refill the tub for you."

She sat wrapped in towels as Rosemary drained, rinsed, and refilled the tub. Rosemary stuck her head out the door to let Douglas know they'd be a bit longer. When she got out of the bath the second time, the marks from the corset were much improved and the fresh bruises were darkening. Rosemary wrapped Magdalene in her robe with a dry towel around her shoulders for extra warmth. When the door opened, Douglas immediately straightened from leaning against the opposite wall. His lip was split and he had a blackening eye, which pained Magdalene to see. He reached a hand out and she accepted it.

Rosemary allowed Douglas to lead her to her bedroom and she followed behind them. "Take her to the dressing table," Rosemary instructed him. "There's much to report to you."

"Father Angelo and Claudio are in the parlor with Mrs. Melling. I'd rather Magdalene only have to tell her story once, if that would make it easier." He looked to her and she nodded her agreement. "I'll wait for you in the hallway."

Rosemary helped Magdalene into a simple black skirt and ruffled shirtwaist that camouflaged the fact that she wore no shapeware. She brushed her hair to save her the strain, but Magdalene insisted on braiding it herself.

"Thank you, Rosemary. You've been very kind."

"It's no trouble," she replied as she opened the door.

"There's my Maggie." Douglas offered his arm. "Do you mind if we make one stop before going to the parlor? There's a certain little girl who is very concerned about you."

Magdalene nodded and Douglas helped her down the back stairs and out to the porch.

Priscilla jumped off the swing and ran over, throwing her arms around Magdalene's legs. "Are you all better, Miss Maggie?"

"Not all the way, but improved." She patted her head. "You helped me a lot by holding the door for Douglas. Thank you."

After a stern reminder for Priscilla from her mother to keep on the porch, the three adults were back in the house and entered the parlor.

Claudio jumped up to bless her. Gently cradling her face, he kissed her softly on each cheek. "I feared for you, *signorina*, because of the evil within the house and the look in that man's eyes. I had Douglas set me on the first wagon headed north and made him come back for you." His hands stayed on her face as if he were afraid to let go of her.

"Thank you, Claudio. He got to me in time."

"I did?" Douglas's eyes implored to know the truth.

Claudio released his hold and she turned to her fiancé. "Yes, thank you."

Mrs. Melling sat perfectly straight, her hands folded on her lap, and Father Angelo across from her in the opposite wing chair. "If you have not noticed, I am still missing my guest, though more people have arrived to accuse him of wrong doing. Should we wait until he returns so we may have both sides of the story at once or begin this ridiculous inquiry now?"

Father Angelo motioned for Claudio to sit. The deacon took Magdalene's hand and set her snug between himself and Douglas on the settee. Douglas took her right hand and Magdalene, surrounded with peace as she had not felt in weeks, was reminded what it felt like to be truly loved, further displacing the lingering chill from the sepulcher.

"Father Angelo," Mrs. Melling said, "do you not see how freely she touches these men? She is most shameful in her physical displays of affection. Surely she teases men along and then gets upset when one makes advances on her."

"*Signora* Melling," Father Angelo said as he shook his head, "if at your age you cannot recognize the love between friends and the pure love of righteous admiration, I fear there is no hope for you."

Rosemary stayed in the room, though Mrs. Melling never offered her a seat. She stood beside the settee, and as Magdalene told her story of what happened in the mausoleum, she interjected information about the accompanying wounds she'd witnessed on Magdalene's body, including, at the end, telling about her corset marks.

"Really, Rosemary! Mentioning something like that in this company is inexcusable."

"No, Mrs. Melling," Douglas rose from his seat as he spoke, "you treating Magdalene as a toy to parade around for attention is inexcusable. Her employment is over, and I'm removing her from this house."

"You cannot!" Mrs. Melling cried out. "I need her. As much as you make me sound cruel and aloof, she has been good for me. Everyone says I am much improved since she came, even my husband."

"Let's not bring him into this," Father Angelo counseled. "He is a whole different matter of concern. We blessed the house while we waited and there was evil within these walls to be driven out. It was my understanding that the man of the house has not been here for months. That leads me to believe you are the new source of mischief."

"This is a misunderstanding," Mrs. Melling argued. "The workings in society are different on my level. All women wear corsets until they hurt and all will flirt to catch the best beau."

The front door opened and heavy footsteps came down the hall. Everyone in the parlor turned to the doorway. Leroy brought in a staggering Rupert Lyons and Claudio jumped to stand in front of the couple.

Magdalene leaned against Douglas, hoping to go undetected by her predator, but Rupert could not stand on his own, nor could he see, as both eyes were swollen shut.

"I am most sorry, Rupert. Leroy, give him my chair. Shall I send for a doctor?" Mrs. Melling asked as she stood.

Rupert eased into the chair, wincing as he sat, making it appear that he had a cracked rib or two. "I only wish to get back to my family's house in Point Clear."

Mrs. Melling placed a hand on Rupert's arm. "I'll have my driver—"

Rupert jerked to attention, sucking in his breath to keep from crying out in pain. "I don't want that driver of yours. He's the one who did this to me. You should send for the police and have him sent back to his country."

Mrs. Melling looked to Father Angelo sheepishly. "The fact is, Rupert, the driver brought Magdalene home and they had an unflattering tale to tell about you. I'd like to hear your side, if you don't mind."

"*Sí*, we would like to hear from you what you have done," Claudio said. "Confession is good for the soul."

Rupert turned to the voice. "I thought we were rid of you for the day, Deacon De Fiore. My confession to you would be to no avail as you are not yet a priest."

"But Father Angelo is here as well."

"He is not my priest," he said quickly. "But tell me, how many people are in the room?"

"Enough to stand as witness against you at the judgement day." Claudio clasped his hands behind his back and began to pace.

"Be seated, Claudio," Mrs. Melling hissed. "This is not a criminal inquest."

"I'll say I made some poor judgements, but she went with me of her own will, even after I'd spoken to her in this very room about wanting her."

"Did she change her mind about being with you once she was outside?" Claudio asked.

"By then I was in the moment and—"

"Seacliff Cottage has been affected by evil spirits several times this year. It is because of the demonic influence within this room that Magdalene led you on, but under no circumstance is it proper for a man to continue his advances when a woman wishes to be left alone." Claudio's voice grew louder with each sentence. "And to restrain and injure a daughter of God in attempt to take that which is most precious is a grievous sin by which you shall be judged accordingly!"

Father Angelo spoke to Claudio in their native tongue, and Claudio—looking much calmer—returned to his seat. Magdalene took his hand back into her own.

"Is she here?" Rupert asked.

When Magdalene didn't answer, Mrs. Melling did. "Yes, she is here, cleaned up from the altercation." She lowered her voice. "I must say, she was quite roughed up. Not on the level that you are, but still…I am shocked."

"Since they're claiming evil spirits made Miss Jones tease me, can I not claim the same for my poor judgement?"

"No," Claudio said, "it would have left you when you exited the house if you were affected by it. The evil within you runs much deeper."

Rupert stood, a hand on the chair to steady himself. "I'm sorry this gathering had to happen over such a minor misunderstanding, but I would like to leave now. Is there not someone else who can take me home?"

"Rosemary, see that Mr. Campbell has the carriage ready while Leroy helps him out."

The Wattses went into action while Mrs. Melling fluttered around Rupert.

"I do hope you heal quickly. It would be a shame for you to be battered for the engagement party."

"I'll have to lie low for a few days, but I needed a rest." He stopped halfway across the room, leaning heavily on Leroy. "May I have a word with Miss Jones before I leave?"

Douglas stood. "I will follow you out of the house and then you can tell me what you wish her to know."

Rupert shrank back as if struck as he recognized the lilting voice. "What gives you the right to speak on her behalf when Mrs. Melling is here?"

"No!" Mrs. Melling moved forward, not wanting the truth to be known.

"Magdalene and I are engaged. Everything you say or do in regards to her concerns me."

Rupert paled behind the bruising. "I…I…I had no idea. I would not have come today had I known she was spoken for. Mrs. Melling, why did you not let it be known? They do make a charming couple now that I think of it."

Leroy escorted him out, leaving all eyes on Mrs. Melling.

"Now," Father Angelo said to the lady of the house, "it is your turn to admit your folly contributed to this unfortunate event."

Eleven

Magdalene settled into her temporary life with as much agreeability as possible for someone in her situation. Under the watchful eyes of Claudio and Father Angelo, Magdalene lived as a guest in the Melling house, free to come and go as she pleased and to take her meals with either Mrs. Melling or the Campbells. She spent most of her waking hours in the carriage house, quietly sitting with Douglas or Uncle Simon. Either Father Angelo or Claudio came each day to exorcise the house and bless both Magdalene and Mrs. Melling. The invitation to be married by Father Angelo was open, but Magdalene was no longer ready. Each night she woke with nightmares of either Alexander or Rupert coming for her.

On the Saturday night before Alexander was expected, Magdalene woke from the reoccurring nightmare in a cold sweat. The air sweltered though it was mid-September. The stuffy heat with no breeze through the open window left her unable to calm down. Just after one, she went barefoot down the back stairs and across the yard to the carriage house under the light of a sliver of moon and star-filled sky.

Magdalene opened the screen door so it wouldn't squeak and slowly shut it behind her. She crept up the ladder and straight to Douglas's bed. He lay on top the bedspread in only his under trousers, a misting of sweat across his bare chest.

"Douglas," she whispered.

He sat up swinging a right hook, causing Magdalene to jump back.

"Maggie, I'm sorry." He stood and embraced her, their damp bodies leaving traces of moisture on each other.

"I guess I'm not the only one having nightmares."

"Aye." He ran his hand over the top of her head to smooth the loose hairs. "I'll fight for you awake or asleep, always remember that. I love you."

"I love you, too." She trailed a hand down his chest. "Will you sit with me on the swing and pray for a breeze?"

"Anything for you, Maggie."

He pulled on a pair of work pants and a short-sleeved shirt, which he left unbuttoned. They exited the little house and walked hand in hand to the gazebo on the back porch of Seacliff Cottage. On the swing, she tucked her legs beneath her nightgown and nestled under his arm despite the heat. His shirt kept her from sticking to his skin where she rested against him, but she hugged her arm snug around his bare waist.

"I'm tired of waking scared and alone," she whispered.

"Aye, Maggie. It's no life for you." He hugged her tighter against him and kissed the top of her head.

"Could you talk to Father Angelo tomorrow and see if he can marry us before Wednesday?"

"Are you sure?"

"I'm ready to move on and be with you always."

He tilted her chin up with the gentle touch of his finger, and kissed her firmly on the lips. "Mrs. Melling goes to Sacred Heart in the morning, but I'll find Father Angelo tomorrow afternoon if he doesn't come himself. Of that you can be sure."

Moments later, a breeze filtered through the wisteria vines, bringing relief to the weary couple. Douglas pushed the swing with his foot, and held Magdalene close. She fell asleep on his shoulder and awoke with the dawn, his head atop hers and both of his arms around her.

Magdalene did not wish to disturb him, but her folded legs and arms needed to be stretched. She ran her fingers up his torso to his shoulder.

"Oh, Maggie." He exhaled deeply and pulled her tighter to him. Then, as if he realized she really was there, he lifted his head to gaze down at her. "Good morning, my soon-to-be bride. That wasn't a dream, was it? You told me to talk with Father Angelo today."

"Yes." She stretched her legs out in front of her and kissed his cheek. "Before Wednesday is the key. That's the day Alexander and Beatrice are expected."

"Sit right there, I'll be back in a jiffy." Douglas ran for the carriage house, buttoning his shirt as he went.

Magdalene used the time to stretch and arrange herself. She wondered if she should go in for her robe, but decided against it as she'd already spent the night without the benefit of a cover. Douglas walked through the yard and the closer he came, the prettier the item he fetched looked.

His face alight with joy, he placed her mother's wedding suit in her lap. "It's been ready for weeks, but I didn't want to pressure you, especially after—"

"It's like new!" Magdalene ran her hand over the silk and lace, softened with washing and the seams mended. "Thank you, Douglas. It means the world to me, just as you do."

"Zora did it all, happy for the extra work because she's saving for her own wedding next month."

"I'll be sure to thank her when I see her." She stood, holding the outfit to her chest. "Would you mind if I went up to try it on?"

"Nothing would make me happier, except seeing you in it." For the first time in nearly two weeks, their kissing grew heated, his hands roamed her waist and she played with his unruly morning hair. With a groan he pulled away and leaned his forehead against hers. "Days away! I've waited this long, I can wait a day or two more."

"If they married people on the Sabbath, I'd walk to church with you right now." She kissed him deeply. "I've missed this, but I—"

"I know, Maggie." He hugged her so tight she momentarily thought Mrs. Melling had corseted her. "I'd wait forever for you if needed, but I can't tell you how happy I am right now."

"Your smile says it all." She kissed him once again, his red beard tickling her chin. "I'll see you after breakfast."

Feeling refreshed for the first time since Rupert accosted her, she ran up the back stairs. To get the proper shape for the old-fashioned lines, she tied on her mother's whale bone corset to help her posture—but not enough to cause pain. Pleased with her reflection in all of the mirrors in her bedroom, she forced herself to change into her pale blue Sunday dress, though she remained barefoot.

In the kitchen, she found herself humming while she buttered her bread and boiled water for tea. Mrs. Melling came in from the front hall wearing her pink Sunday finery with a giant hat to match.

"I'm glad you are sounding cheerful, Magdalene. I do miss your smiling face, my dear."

"Thank you, Mrs. Melling. There's plenty of water for me to make you a cup of tea."

"I would hate to put you out, but maybe for old time's sake. Thank you, dear. Would you bring it to the dining room? There's something I need to discuss with you."

"Certainly. Would you care for biscuits or bread?"

"Biscuits, please."

Magdalene felt ready to share the love she had bursting inside. Happily, she filled a tray with a tea service for two, her buttered bread, and the biscuits and jam Mrs. Melling preferred.

Mrs. Melling sat stiffly at the foot of the table. Magdalene played along, serving the tea and biscuits as if she were employed. As soon as Magdalene sat, Mrs. Melling got to the point.

"Zora and a friend of hers will be here the next few days to set the house to rights, including your current room. I shall need you moved to the attic today so they can get started first thing in the morning. If you need Douglas here this afternoon to help you move your luggage, that is fine, but you need to be out of the guest room by supper."

"Could you give me one more day? Douglas is speaking with Father Angelo this afternoon about marrying us within the next few days." Mrs. Melling frowned but held her tongue. "If I have at least one more night, I might be able to move straight into the carriage house."

"I am sure you understand my predicament, Magdalene. I do not want them to rush the job, and I do not want to force you to move, but we are down to the last three days."

"Perhaps I can just move into the carriage house. I'd hate to have Douglas drag everything up in this heat and then back down in a few days' time. Or maybe just send the bulk of my things there, and take what I need from the carriage house on a day to day basis."

"Magdalene, you know I love you like a daughter." She took Magdalene's hands into her own. "We do not see eye to eye on everything, but on this I must insist. When you are married, you must not spend your wedding night in the carriage house. Stay in the attic room an extra day and use that space to get acquainted with your husband, not some rundown house by the stable. Eliza, whether she knew it or not, created a sumptuous room full of texture and colors. I see no better way to use the space one final time than as a honeymoon suite."

Magdalene knew just how well the space enticed even the most well-intentioned people, but she also knew she'd be happy in the hayloft with Douglas.

"May I speak with Douglas first?"

"Of course, dear. Let me know this afternoon." Mrs. Melling took a long drink of tea.

"But what do you mean by one final time?"

"We will tear it out to make it over into a nursery, of course. There are sure to be little Mellings before long."

Magdalene shuddered at the thought of babies with ice blue eyes and leering smiles and couldn't wait until her time within those walls was over.

***

Douglas polished the Great Arrow while Magdalene told him about Eliza's old room after breakfast.

"Do you really want our first night together to be connected with Seacliff Cottage?" he asked.

"The Mellings own the carriage house too, and we can't very well take a room at a hotel with you needing to be on duty first thing in the morning and no transportation of our own."

"True on both accounts." He flipped his uniform necktie behind him as he bent over the grill.

Magdalene took a seat behind the wheel and pretended to shift the gears. "I'm sorry I took so long. It makes planning difficult."

Douglas slid onto the passenger seat and squeezed her hand like he used to do before they set off on lessons. Then he fingered the engagement ring. "I miss our driving time. I miss the fresh air, the world going by but us side by side without a care in the world."

"Except whether or not I'd keep this thing on the road."

He touched her cheek. "You're a swell driver, Maggie. And don't think you're causing trouble, because you're not. Uncle Simon already told me he'd sleep in the stable to give us the house to ourselves the first night."

"I couldn't send him to the stable." Magdalene gripped the wheel and pretended to swerve.

"I don't like it either." He sighed and pointed to the dormer windows at the back of the big house. "That room has seen its share of sin, but with all the blessings the house has gone through…I'm still not sure. Do you mind if I ask Claudio about it?"

"That's a good idea. I'll pack while you're gone because I need to move my things out no matter where I go. It's awful to be homeless."

Douglas brought her hand to his heart. "You'll always be home in here and in my arms."

Magdalene soon set to work by emptying the contents of the desk into her small travel bag. In went the items from the dressing table, though she left the mantilla and perfumes Mrs. Melling had bestowed upon her. Her parents' wedding rings she placed in her reticule in the top of the bag, along with her brush and other items she knew she'd need daily.

Then she set upon the wardrobe. She pulled all the dresses and hanging gowns and laid them over the backs of the chairs, sorting out which she would take and which she would leave. Mrs. Melling had already informed her that everything she bought for her was hers to keep, but some of the dresses she had no taste for. Those she laid upon the bed and would have Douglas bring up to the attic room so they would be out of the way of the future Mrs. Alexander Melling. She divided the remaining dresses into two piles—those to keep and use soon, and those to keep and pack away. The clothes in the drawers were done the same way. When she finished with sorting, she retreated to the carriage house. There she sat in the front room and dozed in the rocking chair beside Uncle Simon napping in his own chair.

Douglas roused her with a kiss when he returned. "I'm glad you were able to rest," he said when she opened her eyes. "I know your sleep has been troubled of late."

She allowed him to pull her to her feet and they embraced. "I need a crate or trunk to pack a few more things away that I won't need until we're moved. Do you have anything?"

He nodded and led her to the stable, where he climbed the ladder. "Are you coming?" he called over his shoulder.

She waited until he reached the top and looked down at her. "I think it's safer for me to stay here today. Last time I went up with you, things got serious."

Douglas laughed. "Fair enough. What size do you need?"

"Something a tad bigger than the smaller crates from Aunt Agnes."

He carried down a crate and set it at her feet. Then he climbed back for another. "I'll need a few for myself and Uncle Simon."

"But where did they come from? I don't remember crates when I was last up there."

"Every week, Captain Walker picks up the empty crates from the previous delivery. The last two months, when I've seen ones that are a good size, I've bought them off him and stashed them away for us."

Magdalene turned to Douglas, bringing him into an embrace. "You've been planning and preparing for us all along. I'm sorry for making you wait."

"I told ya, Maggie," he said, his Scottish brogue thick, "I'd wait forever if needed. Even if it left us with one day together as husband and wife, it would be worth it."

After a series of roaming kisses, he smiled contentedly and picked up two of the crates to bring to the house. "How did the wedding suit work?"

"Wonderfully!" Magdalene picked up the last crate and walked with Douglas. "It's completely perfect. What are you to wear? Not that uniform, I hope, though you look handsome in it."

"So I've heard." He winked at her and set the crates for himself and his uncle on the front stoop and relieved Magdalene of the one she carried. "It's a surprise, Maggie. Is that all right?"

"I trust you."

"As I do you." He leaned in for a kiss, holding the box to the side. "I trust you with my heart."

"Dinner in thirty minutes," Uncle Simon called out from the kitchen. "There's plenty for Mrs. Melling, if you'd like to ask her to share."

"I'll see how she is," Magdalene said.

Douglas waited in Magdalene's room while she knocked on the sitting room door.

"Mrs. Melling?" she called.

"Come in, dear."

Magdalene hadn't been in Mrs. Melling's chambers since the incident. Shocked to see all the surfaces covered with newspaper clippings and photographs, Magdalene gasped. The lady sat at the little table in front of the closed window in the stuffy room.

"We'd like to invite you to share our dinner with us today."

"I simply must finish the scrapbook so Zora can clean in here. It's proving a larger task than I expected." Mrs. Melling looked to her with begging eyes, but Magdalene had enough of her own things to see to.

"Surely you must eat."

"I had those biscuits this morning, Magdalene."

"But it's so stale in here. You need fresh air."

"The breeze from the window ruffles the papers, but you may leave the hall door open."

"Very well." Magdalene turned to go.

"Are you decided on the room?" Mrs. Melling asked.

"Not yet. I'll let you know soon."

Back in Magdalene's chamber, Douglas marveled over the piles of dresses.

"I'm not taking them all. The pile on the bed I have no use for. I figured we could bring them to Eliza's old wardrobe in the attic and Mrs. Melling can deal with them later."

"Let's start with those, then."

Magdalene gathered the smaller items and opened the stair door. The room was stifling, so she set to opening all four windows, moving the easel to get at one. With the cross currents, the attic quickly aired and the hanging silks shimmered in the breeze.

Douglas set the pile of clothes on the nearest bolster and walked about the space as Magdalene placed the bustier and other things into a nearly empty dresser drawer. He came up behind her, nuzzling against her back and whispering in her ear. "I've only been in here with Claudio when he exorcised the house, which had a much different feel to it, especially knowing his history with Eliza. This is a sensual place, perfect for two people exploring each other."

He left a nibbling kiss on the back of her neck, which caused her to gasp. She turned to him and they took advantage of the privacy until Douglas pulled away.

"We need to stop, but soon we won't have to." He kissed her once more before turning to the Parisian gown on the top of the pile. "I wouldn't mind seeing you in that one more time, but I'll be selfish and say just for me and not a room full of people."

"I'm only for you, no matter what."

Twelve

Claudio arrived with the Watts family at three and joined Douglas and Magdalene in the gazebo. When Douglas informed him of needing to speak with Father Angelo about marrying them, their friend looked near tears.

"I am only happy for you," he assured Magdalene. "I am not sad for not being the one to do it."

"We want you to witness," she told him. "Just you, Uncle Simon, and the Watts family are to attend. Zora, if it's convenient for her, as well. It will depend on the time and location."

"I would be happy to, *signorina*, you know that."

"There's one other matter," Douglas said. "Magdalene has to move out of her room today and Mrs. Melling wants to put her in the attic."

A look passed over Claudio's face that Magdalene could not read. Longing? Remorse?

Magdalene continued the conversation. "And she wants Douglas and me to stay in the room after we're married, but we're not sure it's a good idea."

Claudio closed his eyes and steepled his fingers below his chin. When he opened his mouth, it was in his most authoritative voice that he spoke. "The sins committed there have been atoned for and the house is clean. As long as you are both moved out before Mr. Melling arrives, I do not foresee an issue. Now, come. Let me pray over you on this most happy occasion."

Claudio blessed both of them, and then went inside to see to Mrs. Melling and the house. He had Douglas and Magdalene accompany him to the attic as he blessed the room and even the bed. Douglas, eager to speak with the priest, received permission from Mrs. Melling to drive Claudio back to Daphne. The two men sat in the front of the automobile, the back loaded with the crates they'd filled that afternoon.

Magdalene busied herself in the kitchen helping Rosemary chop vegetables for supper to keep her mind off Douglas's return.

"It'll be different when you move on," the cook said. "You'll be back to doing your own laundry, plus that of two men. Not to mention cooking and housekeeping."

"I kept house for my father for nearly a decade before coming here, so I'm used to the work. Uncle Simon won't be employed, and he enjoys cooking when he's up to it, so I expect he'll be a help."

"And that man of yours," Rosemary leaned close so Priscilla's little ears couldn't hear. "I think he'd do anything for you, especially after a little attention."

Magdalene blushed. "I'm sure he'll be more than helpful to me when he isn't working. He has that sort of personality."

"I'm sure, Miss Maggie. He's the true-blue sort." She leaned in again. "I know you've been without a mother a long while, but if you have any questions about the way things work, you let me know. I'm not one to shy away from giving you a talking to about it."

She thought of the talk she'd heard from the society girls over tea and some of the things the drivers had joked about in the back parking lot of the hotel. That, coupled with her foray into art books and her own sensations she'd felt aroused, she was certain she had a good idea what to expect on her wedding night.

"Thank you, but I'm okay." Not wanting any further tidbits of information, Magdalene excused herself after she finished cutting the carrots and retreated to the carriage house where she paced the front room.

"Anxious, Maggie?" Uncle Simon asked from his rocking chair on the front stoop.

Magdalene came to the screen door. "Just about Douglas getting back with news."

He lit his pipe and puffed out swirls of smoke. "You know he'll be gentle with you, so you don't need to worry on that account."

"Yes, I know." *Can I not escape* the talk *wherever I go?*

"I only mention it because after going through what you have, I'd think it normal for a young woman to be concerned about that."

"Thank you, Uncle Simon." She turned back to pace the floor, alone with her thoughts.

When Douglas returned, he jumped out of the Great Arrow and Magdalene met him in the yard. Sweeping her into his arms, he spun around with her. "Tuesday afternoon, Maggie!"

Dizzy with the spinning and the reality of the approaching day, Magdalene closed her eyes and rested her head on his shoulder.

"Claudio is going to borrow a wagon from one of the parishioners to bring Father Angelo here and back, so I won't need to leave you after the ceremony. How's that for thoughtful?" He pulled her up and kissed her hard on the mouth. "Let's go speak to Mrs. Melling and see if I can't clear that afternoon and evening from responsibilities."

Her hand in his, she led the way through the yard to the kitchen, where they told Rosemary and Leroy the news.

"She'll be clucking like a mad hen that afternoon with her boy and that woman coming the next day," Rosemary said. "But I'll be there with or without leave, mind you."

"Is she still in the sitting room?" Magdalene asked.

"Yes, and I don't envy Zora for the work she'll have the next few days. Mrs. Melling's made a royal mess."

On the way up the back stairs, Douglas placed a hand on Magdalene's hip. She felt each sway as she climbed, and by the time they reached the top, both his hands were on her. Magdalene turned to Douglas in the hall, his hands trailing the waist of her Sunday dress. Their mouths played hungrily against each other as they pressed together.

"I think we'll need to see a little less of each other the next few days," she whispered into his ear as she ran her hands over his shoulders.

He dipped her back and kissed her neck before righting her. "It might be safer that way, though not nearly as enjoyable."

They held hands down the hall, Magdalene stopping outside the open sitting room door. "Mrs. Melling, may we have a moment?"

She sighed, but stood from her seat at the table. "I needed a break and am sure I shall need glasses by the time I am done with this. All this newsprint is rough on my eyes."

The only place to sit was at the table Mrs. Melling had just vacated, so Magdalene and Douglas stood a few steps inside the cluttered room.

"I've arranged for Father Angelo to marry us on Tuesday afternoon," Douglas said. "I'm sorry for the short notice, but there are no plans for errands at that time. I would like the afternoon and evening off from work, please."

"Of course, Douglas." Mrs. Melling gazed between the couple. "I always said you two would make a striking pair. I am glad for you both, truly I am. Especially after the trouble a few weeks back. I am happy to see my Magdalene looking brighter than ever."

"I'm glad she's recovered as well."

"You should be able to remain free from service until you meet the ferry on Wednesday afternoon."

"Thank you, Mrs. Melling."

"Have you decided on the attic yet, Magdalene?"

"Yes, ma'am, I'll move in right now and we'd be happy to stay Tuesday night, if that's still fine with you. We'll take our meals and bathe in the other house, though."

"You may stay through Thursday if you'd like. Feel free to keep using your bathroom through Wednesday morning. I'll have Zora give it a good cleaning when she gets here that day so it's bright and shiny for Beatrice and her aunt. You two need a little luxury. Enjoy it while you can, though this project of mine…I fear I'll never finish. If I had another set of eyes checking dates of the printings, it would be much easier."

"I could help a bit this evening and maybe tomorrow, though I do need to see about buying a second traveling bag."

Mrs. Melling smiled like one who'd won her hand at cards. "That would be splendid. As for the travel bag, I believe there is an old one in the wardrobe of the small guest room. If so, it is yours. Now, clear yourself a seat—"

"Sorry, Mrs. Melling," Douglas said, "but Uncle Simon has supper ready for us. Magdalene can come back after she's eaten."

"Yes, and Rosemary should have yours ready as well. Be sure to eat, you need your strength and the fresh air," Magdalene said. "May we accompany you down?"

"No, I need to clean the newsprint off my hands first. But it's good to have you back."

Douglas led Magdalene to the small guest room. "You know you don't have to help her."

"I know, but she's being kind about the room and giving you the time off."

"Don't place too much trust in her, Maggie. You owe her nothing."

Magdalene opened the wardrobe in the corner of the green room and found a serviceable, if lightly worn, leather bag. "This is perfect for a few changes of everyday clothes to keep with me. Can you help me bring up the rest of my things before we go to supper?"

Douglas hurried them downstairs after bringing the last load to the attic so they wouldn't linger in the secluded room. They took their supper of cornbread and gumbo with Uncle Simon and then Douglas walked her to the back porch of Seacliff Cottage.

"Just two more nights of saying goodbye." He held her tight as the breeze rustled through the wisteria vines. "You holler out a window if you need me, and I'll be up there as quick as anything."

Magdalene breathed in his scent at his neck where he'd opened the top two buttons of his shirt. "But I do need you."

He indulged in a kiss that she didn't want to end, and melted against him.

"Come on, Maggie. Let's be strong these final hours. Go on and help Mrs. Melling, but don't allow her to control you in any way. Will I see you for breakfast?"

"Maybe after. I'm not sure how late I'll be up with that scrapbook mess. Don't wait for me in the morning."

And late she was kept in the sitting room. Magdalene sorted through the pages on the sofa and passed them to Mrs. Melling in the correct order for her to mount within her black album. It was well past eleven when the women turned down the lights and went their separate ways.

As she climbed the attic stairs, Magdalene remembered when Mr. Melling tried to accost her in the stairwell and shivered. She thought of all the threats to her chastity she'd experienced on the Mellings' property but received deliverance in one form or another. Mr. Melling, Rupert, Alexander, and even Douglas and Claudio had made advances on her—or she on them. Blessed she had escaped with her virginity, she was quite certain that come Tuesday afternoon, she would never again need fear for her purity. Once Douglas claimed her, no man would dare defile her, as she would be another man's wife.

Thirteen

Monday morning started late, with tea and biscuits
courtesy of Rosemary in the newly freed space in the sitting room.
Magdalene, dressed in a simple skirt and blouse, sat barefoot on the
velvet settee, riffling through the stack of pages after eating. She
came up with nothing. Then Mrs. Melling conveniently remembered
that was her pile to toss.

"I'm going to take a walk and see Douglas for a few
minutes," Magdalene announced before she could grow angry over
her wasted time.

From the kitchen window, she saw Douglas and his uncle
busy in the yard with all three of the horses and two strangers.

"What's going on out there?" she asked Rosemary.

"The family is selling the horses and the carriage and wagon."

"But why?"

"They don't want to be bothered with the upkeep, especially
with Mr. Campbell leaving and Mrs. Melling not being here full time.
Now that they have an automobile, there isn't any need to keep
horses and a new stable hand if the family will only be coming every
other weekend like they used to."

"But what of you and Leroy?"

"We check in on things and see that the house is tidy. They'll
send us word when to expect them and we're sure to be here.
Douglas is teaching Leroy to do basic maintenance on the
automobile and drive to the ferry and back so he can collect the
family when they come."

"But there's less than two weeks for him to learn! We head
out a week from Friday."

"He's been working with him for two weeks already, Miss
Maggie, and he's doing fine."

"I didn't realize…"

"You were in a muddle these past days but it ain't no reason for you to fret. Your Douglas is a fine teacher and my man's a good learner."

Magdalene watched as the horses where hitched up to the carriage for the last time on Melling property. "Tell Douglas I looked for him. I'll check back when I can."

Magdalene passed the afternoon in a flurry of work, determined to be done with Mrs. Melling so she could spend her wedding day on her own preparations. As she'd taken breakfast and dinner with the lady of the house, Magdalene excused herself at five o'clock.

"As I'll be so busy with plans for Alex, if I don't see you, much happiness with your union, my dear."

"Thank you, Mrs. Melling, and for your hospitality. You've been very kind."

"It is the least I can do. After much thought, I fear some of my actions placed you in harm's way, and for that I am sorry. You are leaving me, and Claudio soon will be, too. Sometimes it is too much to think of without sorrowing."

Magdalene's heart went out to the woman, but stronger was the pull to Douglas. She patted Mrs. Melling's hand in departure. "You'll be doubly blessed with family, remember that. Good night, Mrs. Melling."

After supper with the Campbells, Douglas retrieved a rose-printed box, much like a small hatbox, from the loft before escorting Magdalene out the door.

"What is it?" she asked as they walked toward the little fence separating the looming house from the stable yard.

"Your wedding present." He kissed her hand that he held, keeping the box tucked under his other arm. "I want you to open it tonight and decide how you want to use it."

"Here, at the gazebo?" she asked, the eagerness in her voice on the verge of taking over.

"No, when you get to your room. I don't trust myself to remain with you tonight." He nuzzled into her on the back porch. "Our last goodbye."

Magdalene began stroking his beard, grown shaggy in the past weeks, and pinned him against the back wall.

"Maggie," he said between kisses, "Maggie, just one more night." His free hand curled around one of her wrists and he pushed against her to get free, but it only made her more frenzied. "Maggie…please don't make this more difficult for me."

The soft, pleading tone of his voice struck a chord in her soul. She stepped back, blushing from her moment of weakness and the blatant reminder that she wasn't the same woman she was when she arrived at Seacliff Cottage six months before.

"I'm sorry, Douglas."

He kissed her quickly on the lips. "Don't be. Just save it for tomorrow. I love you, Maggie."

"And I love you." With the box now in her hands, she kissed him once more.

Alone in the attic, Magdalene settled onto one of the oversized cushions on the floor, the pink floral pattern of the box at odds with the jewel-toned room. She opened the lid and removed the protective tissue, revealing a silky slip of a nightgown of royal blue with bold white lace trim around the bottom hem. It was unlike anything she had ever seen. When she tried it on, it hit just above her knees length-wise and encompassed her exact chest measurements.

After studying herself in the mirror, she set to work tidying the room while wearing it, loving the sensual feeling of the silk shifting across her body as she unpacked her clothes and rearranged the floor cushions. She reached into her little bag and retrieved her sketchbook and pencil case. Then, digging under everything, she lifted the flat bottom piece of the bag meant to help hold its shape and slid a stack of folded papers out.

Settling on a pile of cushions with her pencils and book, she opened the pages and looked through the copies she'd made from Eliza's sketches. These fabric-draped walls, one with and one without the lounging form of Claudio and the close-up of Eliza and Claudio embracing. She sighed over the lines she had not been able to get quite right and then wadded them in her fist. It was time to move on from them and create her own images of herself and Douglas.

Magdalene removed the new nightgown and hung it from the wardrobe door. After tying on her robe, she placed her clean nightgown on her shoulder and shoved the sketches into the robe pocket. Stopping first in the kitchen, where she burned the drawings, she locked herself in the bathroom, taking a long soak and thoroughly washing each part of her body.

✳✳✳

In the morning, having had troubled dreams throughout the night, Magdalene opted to stay in the cocoon of the attic bed rather than fight the urge to rush to Douglas. When she arose, she aired the blankets by spreading the bedding around the room. She took another long bath, this time piling her hair atop her head to keep it dry, and dressed in a new chemise and drawers, wrapping her robe over them before exiting the bathroom.

"Morning, Miss Maggie." Priscilla, whom she had never seen upstairs, waited for her in the hall. "Mama said to tell you she'll bring a brunch tray to you in a few minutes."

Magdalene bent down and hugged the girl. "Tell her thank you for me."

She stopped in her old room to check the time. Half-past eleven. The space, void of emotions without her things scattered about, was fragrant with potpourri. Magdalene hurried to the window to chance a peek at Douglas, but he wasn't in sight. Back in the attic, she left the door open and removed her robe—not wanting to sweat under the extra layer—and set to work brushing her hair in preparation for her hairstyle. Rosemary came up with a tray of eggs, toast, and juice and set it on the low table in the center of the room.

"Thank you, Rosemary. It's most appreciated, but I'm not sure I can eat."

"Those nerves will be there, with or without food in your stomach. Unless you want to risk fainting during your wedding, I suggest you eat."

Magdalene tucked her loose hair behind her ears. "You make an excellent point."

"And besides, you'll need your strength for later. You'd be surprised how appetites grow when—"

"Yes, I understand."

Rosemary laughed. "Not talking about it doesn't hide the facts. I'm going to have a tray of fruits and cheese up here for you, and plenty to drink, so you won't need to worry none about coming down for supper tonight." She pointed to the nightgown hanging on the wardrobe. "He gave it to you early?"

"How did—"

"Don't be upset, but I helped. After Douglas saw the fine work Zora did on your mother's suit, he asked her to make you a nightgown. He picked out the fabric himself and I got your measurements off your garments when the laundry came back the other week. Did you try it on?"

"Yes, and it fits beautifully."

"You'll make that man happy, I'm sure." She winked. "Now eat, and I'll be up for the tray in a while and to see if you need anything else."

Magdalene, hungrier than she realized, cleaned the plate before she began braiding her hair. Sitting on a cushion before the floor-length mirror, she worked for an hour to get it to encircle her head. When she secured the final pin, Rosemary returned.

"That looks fine, Miss Maggie. Do you need any help? It's after one."

"No, thank you. You've done much already."

Rosemary pulled the sheers over the back dormers. "You stay away from the windows and I'll be up for you when they come."

Magdalene shut the door and brought out the whalebone corset, which she wrapped carefully around her middle. As the skirt had a built-in under layer, Magdalene forewent a petticoat and began buttoning the blouse. The lace overlay began at the puffed shoulders and came down to the V at the bottom of the shirt, further emphasizing her comely shape. The lace insert of the front of the skirt, surrounded by a slightly longer section that hung from her hips and around the back, mimicked a train without the fuss of too much length.

Pleased with her appearance in the mirror, Magdalene smiled and paced the room as she waited for Rosemary to return.

Fourteen

A short while later, Rosemary asked if Claudio could see her. Magdalene tucked the new nightgown into the wardrobe and Rosemary hollered down the stairwell to him.

"*Signorina*, I must not call you that after today, but there is already one *signora*." He kissed Magdalene on both cheeks and hugged her close. "I suppose to stay proper and remind myself of my place, I must call you Mrs. Campbell."

"Maggie will do, as it seems everyone else I love calls me that."

He tried it, and though endearing, it was awkward with his accent. "It does not roll from my tongue as easily as it does from Douglas's."

"It should come easy for him since I'm his." Magdalene turned up a shoulder and put a hand at her waist.

"There's no time for play," Rosemary reminded them.

"*Sí*, I only come to deliver Douglas's bag, collect the rings, and be able to tease him that I saw you first."

"Then take a good look so you may tell him all about me." She turned around, her skirt billowing out.

"*Sei bella*. You are beautiful, as always, Magdalene. Now, the rings."

Magdalene removed her parents' rings from her reticule and passed them to Claudio, folding his hand over them. "You've kept us safe these many months, and without you, today would not be happening. You've been a great blessing to Douglas and me." She kissed him on both cheeks and removed her hand from his, a tear glistening in the corner of her eye. "I'll see you both soon."

"Ten minutes!" Rosemary hollered to him as Claudio bounded down the stairs. Then, turning to Magdalene, she shook her head. "It's a good thing he's going away. You two are tender on each other."

"It's not like that." Magdalene thought of his exquisite lines and the times she'd wanted to touch him, to draw him. "Well, not usually."

"I know exactly what it is. You're true friends, but he's exotic and handsome and you remind him of Eliza."

"Eliza?" Magdalene's hand went to her chest.

"I'm no fool. There's been mischief within these walls before you came and I daresay there'll be more after you leave. 'Tis the way of the Mellings."

"But you stay on with them."

"They pay well and I go to my own home every night." Rosemary fluffed Magdalene's sleeves. "Everyone must do as they can to get by in this life. Now, are you ready?"

Magdalene nodded and followed Rosemary down the attic stairs. They stopped by the small guest room where Zora cleaned with her friend.

"It's time," Rosemary called. "You able to come?"

"No, Mrs. Melling insists she can't do without me for thirty minutes." Zora came to the door. "But you look right nice, Miss Maggie. Pretty as a picture."

"Thanks again for your work on the suit. And for what you made under Douglas's commission. It fits wonderfully."

Zora's smile was broad. She tucked a loose hair under her bandana. "I've got a job lined up sewing for hire out of one of the mercantile shops in Daphne. I'm pleased that my first professional work was for you and Douglas. You take good care of that man."

"I aim to."

Along with Priscilla, who they collected in the kitchen, they went out the back door. Priscilla led the way, dressed in her best white Swiss dot dress and clutching a bouquet of salmon-colored roses. Only then did Magdalene realize Rosemary wore her yellow Sunday dress and not one of her typical work outfits. While the other two wore their best boots, Magdalene followed last in line, barefoot, down the path to the beach.

The slight aroma of brackish water—more subtle than the tang of the gulf—blew across the sand when they reached the last curve in the path. Rosemary motioned for Magdalene to stay where she was while she let the others know they were ready. Priscilla handed the roses to Magdalene and then skipped ahead of her mother.

Anticipation over seeing Douglas and the long overdue ceremony pulsated through Magdalene. She gathered one side of her skirt when she began her final steps as a single woman, following Rosemary to the cypress grove, where Claudio took her arm and led her past the Watts family and Uncle Simon to Douglas. The groom stood before Father Angelo wearing his best white shirt, tartan vest, and matching kilt. Framing his smile was his red beard trimmed to a week's worth of growth. Magdalene felt like she would float away when Claudio put her hand in Douglas's. His touch—warm and strong—conveyed he would do all he could to love, honor, and protect her.

Father Angelo stumbled over some of the words in English, but he kept the ceremony brief and heartfelt. When it was time for the rings, Douglas reached into the pouch hanging at the front of his kilt. The rings were tied together with a strip of the same blue silk her nightgown was made from. Seeing it before the priest, Claudio, and everyone turned Magdalene's cheeks pink.

After they were pronounced married and blessed—first by Father Angelo and then by Claudio—Douglas and Magdalene shared a tender kiss. The others surrounded them for handshakes and hugs, wishing them well. After a few minutes of goodbyes and many thanks, the Wattses returned to Seacliff Cottage, followed by Claudio escorting Uncle Simon and Father Angelo up the path.

"Well, my wife, what should we do first?"

She ran her hands up his chest to his neck, undoing the top few buttons of his shirt in the process, and trailed kisses from his neck to his lips. "There's so much I want to do, but why don't we start with a walk on the beach. It's been a while since we've been able to do that."

He undid her top button in return. "I'm prepared for it, as are you."

He pointed down to their bare feet and Magdalene laughed.

"I stopped looking when I saw the kilt. I had no idea you had one."

"Don't you remember when Mrs. Melling asked me about it my first night and I told her I only wore it for special occasions?"

"I thought you were joking, but really, it's amazing. Much better than the chauffeur's uniform." She ran her hand over the navy-and-green plaid at his thigh. "Family traditions and heritage are important, no matter if we're separated from loved ones by oceans or death."

"If you want that walk, Maggie, you might want to keep to holding hands."

After a few more kisses and well-placed touches, he removed the pouch from his waist and they ran for the bay. Douglas, with his legs already bare from the knees down, took the lead and Magdalene followed. He took her skirt in one hand, and with his other hand on her back, pulled her against him.

"May I show you, Mrs. Campbell, what I wanted to do with you the first time we played on the shore together?"

Eyes wide with interest, she nodded.

"Do you mind if you get a little wet?"

"We do have swimsuits we can change—"

He kissed her. "Do you really think I'm going to let you out into the world when you change from this dress for the first time?"

She shook her head and smiled.

"The question is, do you mind getting a little wet to see what I've been wanting to do since that first week I arrived?"

"Show me."

"Remember how you kicked that water at me and then ran?"

She nodded in response.

"Do it!"

She did, and within half a dozen strides, he caught her from behind by the waist and pulled her against him with impassioned force. He kissed her neck and ran his hands over her chest as he turned her toward him. With hands holding her backside, he pressed against her in such a way that she felt every angle of his body touching hers—the way they'd fit together when they would finally be one. The pounding in his chest resonated in her own.

With parted lips and roaming tongue, he tasted her mouth and invited her to do the same. Her hands were in his hair, over his shoulders, and down his vest, echoing his own movements on her body. Ready to fall to the sand with him, Magdalene gasped for air.

"And that," he whispered as the bay lapped at their feet, "is a taste of what I've wanted all these months."

"Thank you for waiting." She kissed his neck. "Though part of me wishes you hadn't, I know it means even more that we have today and the rest of our lives together to express our love."

He caressed her cheek. "Maggie, may I take you home?"

"Yes, a thousand times, yes."

Hand in hand, they ran for the cypress grove, where Douglas hooked his pouch around his waist. "My trusty sporran."

"What all are you carrying in there, beside the rings?"

"My watch with a curl of my wife's hair in the locket, a knife, and a few handkerchiefs."

She ran her hands along the sides of his waist. "So it's a fancy pocket to show off your slim-fitting kilt."

"Aye." He turned it so it hung from his back and rubbed against her. "And it moves out of the way, unlike pockets, which make things awkward when you have something like a boxed ring in them."

Magdalene laughed and blushed. "Oh, I'd forgotten about that. I really thought…and then you were reaching down…" She smiled.

"Soon, Maggie." He scooped her into his arms and carried her up the path.

Douglas continued through the empty kitchen and then set her at the bottom of the back stairs. They made their way up slowly, as they touched and kissed like Magdalene had wanted to the night she tried to get her first non-possessed kiss from him.

At the top of the stairs, Magdalene slipped into the bathroom to wash her feet and freshen herself—making sure all her clothes were where they should be, even if the bottom few inches of her skirt were damp. Rather than wait for Douglas, she ran up the attic stairs and quickly checked the room. Both a pitcher of water and a bottle of wine were beside a fruit and cheese tray on the table. Magdalene pulled out the new nightgown from the teak wardrobe, placing it on the front like she had it earlier.

Douglas locked the door as soon as he arrived. He left his pouch on the dresser and turned to Magdalene. "You like the gown? I saw you blush when I brought the rings out."

"It's wonderful and feels good on me."

"Did you decide what you want to do with it?" He came up behind her and wrapped his arms around her waist.

"I want to wear it now, and you can help me change." She turned in his arms to face him. "Could you get the buttons for me?"

He went for a kiss while his hands went blindly up her front to the first fastened button amid the lace. When he had worked halfway down, he paused to run a finger along the ruffle of her chemise. With the top all the way opened, he helped her out of it and laid it carefully on a nearby cushion. Then he unfastened the back of her skirt and helped her step out of it before hanging it over the easel in the far corner so the hem could dry.

Magdalene had to teach him how to undo the corset, her hands over his as he loosened the cords. When it fell away, he took over in removing her final layer. Rather than falling into rapture and roaming her without restraint, he stayed slow, deliberate, and watched how each touch created a different response in her alert body. Just when she was about to insist on getting to him, he led her to the wardrobe and slipped the blue silk over her head, covering her most precious areas.

"You're perfection, Maggie." He kissed each of her shoulders, exposed by the sleeveless gown. "Will you let down your hair?"

They sat upon the jewel-toned cushions while she unpinned the braids. With the hairpins out, he untied the end of the braid and began untwisting it. Magdalene couldn't help but think of Alexander and the wild way he tore apart her hair and ran his fingers through it. While she wished Douglas was the first man to undo her hair, she found comfort in the fact that his way was far superior. He retrieved her brush from the dresser, sat behind her, and went through the soft brunette waves. When he wasn't brushing, he held her hair aside to kiss her neck or shoulders. He brought the brush through her hair a final time and began braiding it in a simple, loose form.

"It turned out better than some of my ropes." He took the tip of the braid and tickled her nose with it.

Magdalene laughed and turned around so she straddled his lap. "We can still joke together, I'm glad for that."

"Did you think that we would change when we were married?" He traced the low neckline of her gown. "It's still the same me and the same you, with the same desires, needs, and humor. Only now we don't have to bridle our passions as we used to."

"We've waited so long." She undid his vest and tossed it onto the pillow with her blouse.

With his shirt open, she tugged it free from the kilt. She tossed it aside like the vest and her turn to marvel arrived. Her soft hands stroked his muscled body, and when the sensations grew too strong, he pulled her up and danced her to the pallet bed amid the silken drapes. She helped him unbuckle his kilt and he removed her gown so nothing was between them when they lowered onto the purple sheets for the first time.

Feeling him completely against her, Magdalene gasped.

"Don't worry, Maggie." Propped above her, the palm of his hand found her cheek. His thumb caressed her lower lip as he gazed into her eyes. "I'll be as soft and easy with you as you want."

She ran her hands over his chest and around his back, pulling him to her. "I just want to feel you, and feel alive."

Fifteen

Magdalene awoke curled against Douglas, his fingers trailing her spine. She rubbed her hand through the hair at his chest, rousing him from his half-asleep state.

"Mm, ready for more?" He stretched, causing Magdalene to shift away.

The sky through the sheer window panels appeared lavender. "What time is it?"

Douglas removed his watch from his pouch on the dresser and set it on the center table, taking a grape from the tray. "It's nearly seven. Why don't we eat?"

Pausing to slip on her gown, she settled between his crossed legs on the cushions, the backs of her legs warm against his where they touched. She leaned on him for support, further enticing him with her body's simple contact.

"Good thing we don't have to make it through a full meal. You're much too appetizing."

They ate, touched, kissed, and drank, afterwards sharing a warm bath, and then they were back in the attic. Their night passed much like the afternoon—periods of intensity followed by rest, all connected by their shared physical attraction and deep-rooted love.

They awoke early to the sounds of birds chirping in the canopy of the forest, and Douglas immediately reached out to touch her.

"Good morning, Magdalene Campbell." He pulled her hand to his bare chest. "It beats for you, can you feel it?"

"Yes, and I want to feel the rhythm of our love."

Magdalene slid atop him, his hands going over her hips to position her. Breathless and tingling all over, she fell back on the pillows minutes later while Douglas worked for his release. Afterward, they retreated downstairs to shower, but they still returned to lie in each other's arms.

After ten, a knock sounded at the door. Magdalene tied on her robe and answered it. Rosemary stood at the top of the stairs with a breakfast tray, the smell of bacon filling the room.

"We owe you, Rosemary," Douglas called from the bed.

"Seeing this girl's smile is enough for me." She passed Magdalene the tray and pulled the door shut on her way down.

Douglas, wearing only his under drawers, set the old tray on the floor with their empty dishes and relieved Magdalene from the full tray. They sat side by side on the cushions and ate and laughed.

Toward the end of the meal, she asked the question she'd worried about for weeks. "Where are we going after next Friday?"

"Dauphin Island. I've signed on with Captain Walker."

"To be a wharf rat?"

"No, Maggie." He laughed. "He wants me as first mate."

"I didn't know you had water experience."

"I don't, but I didn't get seasick on my voyage to America and spent my free time asking the crew questions. Since the captain knows I'm good with automobiles and a solid worker, he's willing to train me as we go. And if all goes well, in a few years' time I'll get my own ship in his fleet."

"Captain Campbell?" She curled up next to him.

"I have lots of learning to do before that happens." He stroked her arm. "Just like with us finding what works best and what we enjoy, it'll take practice and time."

"And do we have time for more practice?" Magdalene gave him a probing kiss.

"Always."

***

"I wish you didn't have to go." Magdalene looked over Douglas's shoulder at his reflection in the mirror.

He knotted his uniform tie around his neck. "It's just a thirty-minute roundtrip to the ferry landing in Montrose and then I'm yours the rest of the day."

"Still, I wish you weren't leaving." Magdalene crept her hands toward his belt. "Though it might be fun to get you out of this uniform when you get back."

He turned and embraced her, his hands fingering her chemise. "I always knew you were fiery, but you're so much more than I imagined. I thought it hard to walk away from you before, but now that I know what I'm missing…"

After their caresses and kisses, Douglas had to straighten his uniform. "Finish getting dressed and you can wait with Uncle Simon. He's expecting us for supper, and then we'll be back here."

"Do you think we should go ahead and move to the carriage house now?"

"Why?" Seeing her concern, he took her hands into his.

"With Alexander coming home—"

"Maggie, he can't hurt you now." Douglas hugged her to his chest. "I'll be here with you. And even though we'll no longer be able to use the fancy bath, don't you want one more night with this privacy?"

Magdalene looked around with a smile. "It has been fun."

"And it will be again tonight."

She kissed him goodbye and dressed in a brown skirt and beige blouse. After braiding her hair, Magdalene ventured down the front stairs one final time and stopped in the parlor, where Mrs. Melling wrung her hands in her chair.

"I wanted to wish you well with the visit and the final plans."

Mrs. Melling looked up, eyes sharp and as cold as the men in her family. "How very kind, Magdalene, but I must remind you that though you may stay in the attic as long as you like, you must stay out of the common areas."

"Yes, ma'am, I'd never venture here but I knew you'd be alone one last time and I wanted to wish you well. We'll be out of the attic before anyone is up in the morning, so I won't be a bother to you anymore."

"Tomorrow morning?" Mrs. Melling's calculating gaze traveled over her in such a way that Magdalene felt immodest. "Well, it is clear that marriage agrees with you. Even in that drab outfit and simple hairstyle you have the glow of a true woman."

Flustered, Magdalene backed toward the hall, eager to get away from the lady of Seacliff Cottage.

"And, Magdalene, be sure to keep out of sight, even in the carriage house. I don't want to see you flirting with Alex or trying to catch his eye like you used to."

Indignant, Magdalene's hands went to her hips. "Unlike other married people in your household, I know how to behave myself."

"That remains to be seen."

Red with anger and frustration, Magdalene fumed through the kitchen and out the back door without a word to Rosemary. She paced the yard until she heard the automobile coming up the lane, then she ducked into the stable. Standing to the side, she watched from the shadow as Douglas and Alexander exited the vehicle parked in front of the main house. A shiver went down her spine seeing the two men together.

Alexander, though he'd gotten some sun in his months on the East Coast, looked pale next to Douglas. Her husband had at least three inches of height over him, and several inches of muscles with his work-hardened body. The heir to the Melling legacy helped a gorgeous brunette in a red ensemble out of the passenger side of the automobile and Douglas helped a pleasant-looking woman in a gray traveling suit from the other side. Both ladies held their heads high as if they were looking down their noses at everything. After holding the gate open for the group, Douglas returned to the automobile to retrieve two hand bags, which he carried to the house. Then he pulled the Great Arrow into the stable yard.

Magdalene stepped out of the shadows as he parked the automobile.

"Welcome home." She stood on the running board and leaned over the door to kiss Douglas. His jaw held tightness. "What's wrong?"

"Several things."

She stepped aside as he got out, and then waited for him to get the tarp, but instead he went for the carriage house.

"Aren't you going to cover it?"

"I have to go back out to fetch the luggage."

"I couldn't believe that group only had two bags. I'd think they would travel with trunks of clothing."

"And they do, but apparently there was a mix up at the train station. Their trunks for Mobile made it to the platform, and the Mellings' driver from their house collected them, but the ones marked for here were lumped with luggage going to the hotel in Point Clear. I'll have to collect them after supper."

They stopped on the front stoop. "That's not so bad. I could ride over with you."

Douglas smiled and kissed her cheek. "Of course you could. I didn't think of that. An evening drive would be nice."

Her fingers brushed over his short beard. "Then why doesn't the joy reach your eyes?"

He clutched her. "I knew who he was the moment he stepped off the ferry—he has his father's cold stare. When I saw his hand possessively on the arm of his fiancée, I could only think of his hands trying to get at you."

If he had known half of what Alexander's hands had done, what she herself had done! Magdalene suppressed another shiver.

"But he didn't conquer me." *Except in my dreams.* "And I'm yours and you walked away without giving him a bloody nose or black eye, which shows the threat is no longer there."

He caressed her back. "Yes, you're mine and I'm yours, but I wouldn't go so far as to say the threat is gone. I'll be keeping you close."

While they were eating, Leroy knocked on the screen door.

"No need for that, friend," Uncle Simon called. "Come in."

"Are they driving you crazy yet?" Douglas joked.

"Just about. I'm here with a message for you from Mrs. Melling." The way he spoke to Douglas made Magdalene's blood turn cold. "She said to remind you to retrieve the luggage at six thirty, in full uniform, and be sure you're back during the seven o'clock hour so I can help you carry them upstairs while the family is eating supper so they won't be disturbed."

Douglas wiped his mouth with a napkin and checked his pocket watch. "That's not a problem. We'll head over as soon as we're finished eating."

"And the final part of the message is that under no circumstance should Magdalene ever accompany you during your work assignments."

"What? Why would she say that?" Douglas asked.

Leroy shrugged. "Come to the kitchen when you get back and I'll help you with the luggage."

When the door shut, Magdalene turned to her husband. "I might have upset Mrs. Melling this afternoon."

"When did you see her?"

"While you were gone to the ferry, I stopped by the parlor to wish her well." Magdalene crossed her arms. "She reminded me to stay hidden and warned me not to try flirting with Alexander, so I kindly let her know that, unlike people in her family, I knew how married people were supposed to behave."

Uncle Simon choked back a laugh, but Douglas's face turned a reddish purple.

"I'm sorry!" Magdalene cried. "She just stared at me with that Melling gaze and spoke so condescendingly, I couldn't help but throw it back at her."

"I've warned you to stay clear of her, Maggie." He touched her hand. "I'm not mad at you, just upset that she's still pulling your strings. You either stay here with Uncle Simon or lock yourself in the attic while I'm gone, okay?"

She nodded and brought his hand holding hers to her lips for a kiss. "And the drive sounded lovely."

He leaned in for a real kiss. "Another time, Maggie. I'll be back before long."

After helping Uncle Simon clean the supper dishes, Magdalene stole across the yard and entered the kitchen. Rosemary worked the final supper preparations, the stress of the Kirkpatricks' first meal at Seacliff Cottage displayed on her usually tranquil face.

"Do you know if the upstairs hallway is clear?" she asked.

"They're all in the parlor for pre-supper drinks."

"Thanks, Rosemary. It smells wonderful. They're fools if they don't enjoy your cooking."

At the top of the back stairs, Magdalene eased the door open. Seeing no one about, she dashed for the attic stairs and locked herself in as Douglas suggested. Knowing he'd be back within the hour— and in his full uniform—she had the idea to wear the Parisian gown for him, like the time they met in the back parking lot of the hotel, he in his uniform and she dressed like a princess. But this time there would be no scandalous meeting or rude shouting from other drivers, only the opportunity to do as they wished in their private chamber.

Magdalene undressed and pulled the black bustier and silk bottoms from the drawer. It was difficult to situate alone, but after struggling for what seemed like half an hour, she had it tied on and all her cleavage in the right place. Fastening the back of the midnight blue gown proved just as difficult, but when she looked in the mirror, she realized her efforts were worth it. She did her hair into a loose pompadour, knowing it would be let down soon enough. Certain Douglas would be there any minute, she paced the room to await his knock.

When it came, she undid the lock and stepped away from the door so he would see her fully when he opened it. "Come in," she called.

The door swung inward, revealing Alexander in a gray suit. "Mother said I would find you here."

Sixteen

Alexander stepped into the attic, closing the door
behind him, and set his cool gaze on Magdalene. "I was curious
about why you weren't with Mother when we arrived. She said she
had to dismiss you, but was allowing you to stay until your affairs
could be settled."

"That's not the truth." Magdalene stepped back, distancing
herself from his advancing steps.

"You've changed, Magdalene, but that familiar passion is
beginning to stir within me." He undid a button on his jacket. "Do
you feel it?"

"You mean the evil that caused you to try to kill me, or have
you forgotten the vile things you did to me?" She kept her words
bold out of fear that speaking softly would lessen her resolve to stay
alert. And with the flutter in her stomach beginning, she could not
afford being weak.

"That's long past us. We're both new people, it would appear.
You, a luscious woman in full bloom, and I a not-yet-married man in
need of a final fling. We're meant for each other, at least for a little
while." In two quick steps he was within arm's reach. "Do you know
I have often dreamt of you in a dress like that, in this very room?"

Magdalene's hand went to the skin below her throat. "You've
dreamt of this?"

He reached a hand out to her. "Of you, this room, a low
neckline like I always wished to see you in. Yes, Magdalene, many
times in my dreams we have met and always the end is the same—in
consummation." He ran a finger across her cheek and lifted her chin,
making her look at his crisp blue eyes.

Magdalene wanted him to touch her more but knew it was
the demon tainting her desires. Drawing upon her stubbornness, she
fought to get him to speak the truth. "By what means did you
conquer me?"

Before she thought to move, he dropped his hand from her chin to her chest, running a finger along her décolletage. She jerked back and began pacing, trying to make her way to the door, but he always cut off her path.

"In my dream, you beguiled me first. I just had to make sure nothing was done to stop me from bringing you ultimate pleasure."

When he fingered his blue tie, Magdalene knew he'd been having the same dream, but it wasn't supposed to be like this—it was supposed to be on the party night, and she knew better than to wear this dress or be in this cursed house then. Today, on the evening after her marriage, she should have been safe. Mr. Melling wasn't there, but she hadn't foreseen the evil within Alexander. Even Claudio thought the demons originated with the sins of the father, not guessing the wayward behaviors of Alexander were just as strong.

"Unlike that dream—nightmare—you're not welcome here."

"But it's just like old times, Magdalene. Pacing, flirting, hoping for a touch or a taste. Yet you're different."

"Because I don't want you here! I'm not falling into one to your snares!"

He removed his tie and ran it between his fingers. "But you do, and you are, Miss Jones."

"I'm no longer Miss Jones! I'm married and I want you out of this room!" Alexander's eyes went wide. "Didn't your precious mother tell you, or was she too busy telling lies? I quit working because she tried to pair me off with one of your friends when I was already engaged. In her guilt, she allowed me to stay here until my wedding."

"Her guilt?"

"Her attempts to woo men from your society included sending me off unchaperoned so I had to fight off advances against my innocence."

His eyebrows went up. "One of my friends tried to best you?"

"Yes, now move!" She tried to shove him away from the door but he grabbed her wrist.

"Tell me who it was."

"Let go of me." She returned his fierce stare with her own.

He released her wrist but didn't move. "Tell me who."

"He said he was your old college friend and taught you everything you know, except he was never able to teach you to move beyond the feelings of guilt after a liaison."

"What nonsense! Who was it, Magdalene?"

"Rupert Lyons."

His eyes showcased pain before he gave a hollow laugh. "He's always jealous of who I have. My Lucy wore a dress much like yours to a Mardi Gras masquerade last year and he couldn't keep his hands off her either." Alexander looked at Magdalene with renewed interest. "Just how far did he get with you?"

She slapped his smug face and retreated to the other side of the table. "Get out of here!"

"I want to know who you're married to. And if you are married, why aren't you in his house or he here with you? What man leaves a woman dressed like this in someone else's house?"

"If your mother wanted you to know, she would have told you. Obviously, the truth would be too difficult for you to bear."

"Spare me the melodrama, Magdalene. He's either too weak to tame you or you're lying. At any rate, you're here waiting for me, which says plenty."

"I'm dressed like this for him, not you. He's more of a man than you'll ever be. Crawl back to your brandy in the parlor with your rich fiancée and leave me be."

Alexander's look of shock turned to a boastful smile. "I can still stir you to passionate speech, and you're as beautiful as ever when you're upset. At least now you rely on yourself rather than scriptures or crucifixes." He put a hand on the doorknob, looking back at her. "You know this isn't over."

As soon as he shut the door, Magdalene locked it and paced the room, trying to decide if what happened was real or part of the returning nightmare. If Douglas learned Alexander had come, he'd lose his job because he'd go after him. She made up her mind not to tell him because they couldn't afford to be homeless for over a week.

Several minutes later, a knock sounded on the door. Magdalene approached it with caution.

"Maggie? Are you there?" Douglas called after his second set of knocks went unanswered.

Only then did she turn the lock and step aside. "Come in!"

Her heart pounded with her previous fear and renewed enticement upon seeing her husband take in the sight of her with longing in his eyes.

"You remembered." He came to her, planting kisses along the sweep of her neckline.

"Will you teach me, driver?" she teased.

"Only you." Douglas stroked up her bare arms and went to her hair, gently undoing the loose style. "I missed you, Maggie."

"I missed you, too. Do you think we should go to the other house? Slip out while they're dining?"

"We already decided we'll go in the morning." He kissed her on the lips and then down to her chest.

Falling into the rhythm of the moment, Magdalene unbuttoned his jacket and ran her hands up to tug the sleeves off. "Did you lock the door?"

"Aye, but enough with worrying. Let's enjoy our last night here."

Magdalene needed to replace the nightmare and the real life visit from Alexander with intimate memories of Douglas and her in the attic with the Parisian gown. Kissing him deeply, she slid her hands down to his waist. Dropping to her knees, the gown billowed around her like an opening flower. She started unbuttoning his shirt from the bottom up, hands roaming as she rose to her feet with each undoing. Standing once more, she fumbled with the knot of his tie. When it and the button behind were opened, she hungrily tasted his neck.

"Easy, Maggie. I'm not going anywhere." He pulled her onto a pile of cushions, lay beside her, and slowly caressed her exposed skin. "We have all night and the rest of our lives."

"I can't help it if you stir my desires." She placed a leg over his and ran her hands over his torso.

Douglas reached for her leg, but found it buried under the layers of the gown. "The skirt is a bit cumbersome, but the top is handy."

"Would you like to remove it?"

Douglas answered by pulling her up so he could undo the fasteners on her back. He stepped to her front when they were opened and dropped the gauzy ruffles off her shoulders, exposing her bustier inch by inch until the gown dropped all the way off.

"I've never seen anything like it."

Magdalene stepped out of the dress and turned around. "It is the latest in lingerie from Paris."

Douglas felt his way from her chest to her waist until he grabbed her hips, his hands running along the black silk of her under drawers. "You make it perfect, Maggie."

When he kissed her softly on the lips, her hands went to his belt and she worked to undo the buckle. Once in his final layer, they retired to the bed to further explore. The visions of Magdalene's nightmare were replaced by euphoria.

A few hours later, a knock sounded on the door. Magdalene and Douglas startled and her heart began to pound.

"Ignore it," she whispered.

But Douglas crawled out of bed and slipped on his uniform pants. Magdalene, though she couldn't be seen from the doorway, pulled the silk sheet up to her chin to cover her nakedness. Never before had she felt so exposed, though Douglas stood between her and the evil.

"Does someone need assistance?" Douglas asked, his brogue thick, as he opened the door halfway.

Alexander scoffed. "If I'd have known she was telling the truth, I wouldn't have guessed it was you."

"Excuse me?" Douglas's knuckles went white around the doorknob.

"Didn't Magdalene tell you I stopped by while you were out this evening? We had a nice chat, catching up on what I missed these past months. Since Mother forgot to inform me Magdalene was married, I thought she might have told me that to slow me down." Alexander's voice changed tones, egging him on. "But seeing you in your natural state, Mr. Campbell, I see just how you'd be her type. She always thought me too weak, until I started dominating in her bedroom. Then she saw where my real strength lies."

As Douglas tossed the door open to get Alexander in his full sight, Magdalene lunged across the room, holding the sheet around her. "No, Douglas, he's not worth it!"

She caught his arm when he'd pulled it back to get a full strike and stumbled against him, the sheet slipping off her shoulder. Douglas, seeing her state of undress, moved his arm to nudge her behind him.

"Listen to her if you want to keep your job, but if not, I can always hire Magdalene to model. She looks divine in purple silk."

Magdalene, hoping she'd be able to keep the sheet up with one hand, reached around Douglas's stomach and hugged him as a reminder to stay back.

"My notice is already in and I'd be more than willing to shave off a few days for the satisfaction of teaching you not to speak about my wife." Douglas raised his hand and Alexander gripped the hand rail, scurrying back from whence he came.

Magdalene relaxed her arm around Douglas and breathed normally for the first time since the knock.

Douglas turned to her, anger burning in his stare. "Why didn't you tell me he came?"

"Nothing happened and I didn't want to upset you, afraid you might go after him."

"Do you want to protect him, Maggie? Do you have feelings for Alexander?"

"No! I was afraid we'd all be homeless for the week." She reached for his hand, but he brushed her away, crossing his arms over his broad chest. "I was worried for you, for us. I didn't think it through. I should have told you."

"What else should you have told me about?" His lips set between a frown and a scowl.

"What do you want to know? Ask me and I'll tell you all, just please don't be mad." She hugged the sheet around herself.

The pleading in her voice appeared to soften him. His eyes lost their harshness. "How far do I need to go back with you to understand this relationship you had with Alexander Melling?"

"It wasn't a relationship. It was one weekend in March, the one before you came. The demons were pulling our strings, just as they were the times I got you and Claudio fighting—it wasn't really me."

"But you had real feelings for me, and part of that behavior is really him. Like Rupert, location won't stop him because he's carrying evil." He ran his hand over his beard. "Is that why you asked to go to the carriage house when I returned, because he found you here?"

"I no longer feel safe, except in your arms." She looked up at him with pleading eyes.

"Were you wearing that gown when he came?"

She nodded.

"So your dream came true." The bitterness in his voice showed his pain.

"Not completely, but he did tell me he'd dreamed of me up here. And it appears the ending of his dream was the same as mine. Won't you forgive my mistake and protect me?"

"Aye, Maggie, of course I will, but you need to be honest with me about what you're facing." He folded her into his arms and she dropped her hold on the sheet to hug him in return, her head resting on his chest. "Did you feel anything when he was here?"

Slowly she nodded and then looked up. "Just the slightest pull."

He stroked her hair, running his hand from the top of her head all the way to her waist. "Those blessings Father Angelo and Claudio gave us yesterday won't last forever. I have to get you out of here."

Seventeen

Magdalene and Douglas dressed and readied their few bags before heading across the yard. Feeling watched, she turned back to Seacliff Cottage. Alexander stood in his gaping window. He raised a hand to her and she could feel the demonic tentacles reaching through the darkness. Shuddering, she pressed closer to Douglas on their journey.

In the carriage house, Douglas lit two oil lamps. He left one on the kitchen table and had Magdalene wait while he carried the other up the ladder. Once back down, he went to Uncle Simon's room to let him know they were there. Magdalene climbed the ladder with her smaller bag and set it beside the dresser. Her breezy summer nightgown she'd given Douglas the day they went through the crates was carefully laid across the bed. Touched that he'd planned for her to wear it her first night there, she hastily changed.

She sat on the bed waiting for Douglas, but he didn't come. Kitchen sounds found their way to the loft as the aroma of coffee wafted up. Then she heard him on the ladder. He stopped at waist level with the floor and placed two bags in the loft. Magdalene hurried over to get them so they'd be out of the way.

He smiled, though sadly, when he saw her nightgown. "You look sweet, Maggie. Would you care for any tea?"

"Just half a cup would be good, thank you. I'll be down."

"Not like that you won't, tie your robe on first."

Magdalene sat across from Douglas at the table, mesmerized by how the light of the oil lamp softened his tense lines to a gentle gaze. He added sugar to his coffee, which made her smile and blush. It took him a minute of both of them drinking to catch on.

"Oh, yes. The mysterious matter of how one takes coffee," Douglas said. "I suppose now that we're married and you aren't hiding anything from me, you'll be able to tell me."

Magdalene took a sip of her tea. "Lydia claimed how a man takes his coffee shows how he likes things in bed. Cream is smooth and rhythmic. Black is rough—"

"Aye, I understand." He gazed at her across the table and took her hand, making circular motions over her knuckles. Magdalene stretched her legs under the table, her robe falling to the sides as her toe skimmed the outside of his leg. "And you, Maggie…I think you'd take coffee with red pepper if you drank it."

She rounded the table, leaned over his back with her hands about his shoulders, and kissed the side of his mouth. "As long as it's with you, I'll take it all."

Standing, he turned and held her tight. "I'm sorry I got angry," he murmured into her hair as he stroked her back. "I'm not mad at you, Maggie. I'm frustrated with this place and all the temptations we must combat."

"It's all been worth it because now we're together as husband and wife."

His lips were soft against hers and his arms firm. With a trailing touch as he let go, he kissed her again before pulling away. "Let me clean the dishes and I'll meet you upstairs."

Magdalene stopped in the humble bathroom, and then hung her robe on a hook in the loft before curling onto her side in the middle of the bed. When Douglas joined her, she watched him undress, marveling over his form that she wanted to touch and draw and taste.

Seeing the yearning in her eyes, Douglas hesitated before extinguishing the lamp. "It's dark up here at night. Should I leave it on so you can see?"

"No, just come to me."

In the seconds after the lamp extinguished, she lay in complete darkness listening to the creaking of the floorboards as Douglas crossed the loft. Her heart began throbbing from a mixture of fear and anticipation. Last night, they'd kept the gaslights burning low in the attic room as they were unfamiliar with the space and each other. Here, she was the stranger in Douglas's room, though now acquainted with his body.

The bed squeaked when he sat on the edge and Magdalene tilted slightly to the side as the mattress gave way under his movements. His hand found her leg and his touch pursued the curve of it up to her hip and on until it rested on her pounding chest.

"Don't be scared of the dark, Maggie." He nuzzled her. "Do you know how many nights I lay awake on this bed, dreaming about holding you?"

"I'm not scared when you're with me."

***

A few hours later, Magdalene jerked awake. Terror gripped her throat so she couldn't scream. She reached across the bed for Douglas but found an empty mattress. Recalling the nightmare—a new one—she sat up and, with trembling limbs, waited for her eyes to adjust to the darkness. Moments later, her eyes settled on her husband sitting at the edge of the loft, watchful, as though he expected something to happen.

Still unable to speak and not trusting her legs to stand, Magdalene tapped on the brass headboard with her rings. Douglas crossed the loft before she could fall back on the pillows.

"What is it, Maggie?" He pulled her onto his lap. "You're shaking like a wet cat."

She tried to talk, but it sounded like she had a frog in her throat.

"I'm sorry I left you alone. I woke up a few minutes ago, feeling like something bad was about to happen. I sat by the ladder to keep an eye on things."

"Evil did come," she croaked, "in my sleep."

He smoothed her hair away from her face and kissed her cheek, his short beard tickling her skin. "You'll have to rely on the Lord to safeguard your mind and soul as I can only protect you bodily. Would you like me to pray?"

She nodded. Douglas hugged her closer as he prayed for healing and peace, his breath warm and sweet across her face. "Now, tell me what troubled your mind and then it will have no power over you."

Magdalene took a deep breath. "I was in the dark, lying expectantly in the bed because I heard you coming to me. Your hands roamed my body, and I knew they were yours though I couldn't see." She took a hand in hers and pulled it to her lips. "They're big and strong, with slight callouses. But then the touches changed to Alexander. He was upon me and I screamed for help but you didn't come. And then when I woke, you were gone."

"Maggie, I'll never leave you alone in the dark again." He stroked her arms, bare under the short sleeves of the nightgown. "Tell me, though, how did you know it was Alexander if it was so dark?"

She thought to say his blond hair was light enough to see but realized the truth must be out. "I know his touch and tainted ways from my first weekend here. We had several encounters, but I escaped from them with that which I was able to give to you our wedding night."

"If by encounters you mean similar to what Rupert did to you—"

"No, not like that, except the last night when he tried to…"

"Tried to what, Maggie?" He gripped her hands.

"He, or the demon rather, tried to kill me. And when that didn't work, he grew forceful."

Douglas's arms tremored. "I knew I should have belted him when he exited the ferry."

Magdalene curled into his chest. "He apologized the next morning—the only time he ever admitted wrong doing—and said he was going to his priest for confession. When he left, he wrote Claudio, asking him to help me and his mother."

"He comes to you now with no good intentions." Douglas kissed her forehead and shifted her out of his lap so they could lie beside each other, an arm wrapped around her protectively.

"The saving graces were that the oppression seemed to flow between us, so we weren't both frenzied simultaneously."

"Were you instigator often?"

"Often enough, I'm ashamed to say, but it fell away when he…began to dominate, as he said. Then I began fighting for freedom and always won. Those moments I was myself, the other times, it wasn't fully me."

He propped on his side, a gentle touch trailing from her shoulder to her hand. "But what attraction was at the base of it, and are those feelings still there?"

"No attraction beyond he's pleasing to look at. I couldn't stand the man when I was outside of the house. Men like him have never been my type and I let him know, as he told you when he came to the attic. And Mrs. Melling informed me before she sent him away that I wasn't his taste, that he preferred blondes."

Beside her, Douglas clenched his fists. "His mother sent him away? Just how obvious was your relationship? And he came back with a brunette, one that pales in comparison to you."

She turned to Douglas and felt for his face in the dark. She held his cheeks and kissed his lips. "There was no relationship. Just a bit of flirting and then stolen moments of…demonic lust."

"That doesn't make me feel better."

Magdalene gave an exasperated sigh. "I caved under my weaknesses. It knew the strings to pull to lure me in and I fell hard—for the sensations, not Alexander. It was the same whether it was you or Claudio, but with you…always with you, my attraction is constant, within or without the house. I wanted you for myself the moment I saw you in the stable."

He found her hand and held it. "What sensations and weaknesses?"

"You have this." She pulled his hand to her breast and swallowed a sob. "Must I expose myself emotionally before you as I gave you myself physically? By knowing my flaws, you will hold everything you need to destroy me."

In the dark, his fingers brushed her wet cheek. He kissed her tears and stroked her neck. "I'd never hurt you, Maggie. And never in a millennium would I ever wish to destroy you."

"Even if I no longer fulfill your needs?"

"You, Magdalene Renee Jones Campbell, are everything to me. I did not bridle my natural man for half a year only to toss you aside at some future point." He climbed atop her and leaned his forehead against hers. "I want to come home to you every day. I want you to have my children. I want you by my side as this red beard turns to gray. I want to sit on the front porch and rock away my old age with a house full of grandchildren while holding your hand."

She arched into him and kissed him fully. "Show me, Douglas. Make love to me that will span our lifetime together. Show me that you want me forever."

And he did.

***

While Douglas dozed contently, Magdalene lay awake in the pre-dawn darkness. Though spooned in the arms of her husband, she felt vulnerable. Empty. Douglas's charming phrases professing his devotion fulfilled her in the night, but now—alone with her thoughts—they did not satisfy her. She had heard similar things from William and that trust broke. Would Douglas keep loving her? Would he understand? Dare she attempt to explain to him the toll her broken engagement had on her all these years later? Doubt was a terrible thing to keep company with in the dark.

Magdalene, still awake when the first rays of morning light peeked through the dormer window, turned to face Douglas and ran both hands over his chest.

"Mm, mornin', Maggie," he murmured as he blindly reached for her roaming hands. When he found them, he followed her arms up to her shoulders and then down her sides to her hips, which he used to pull her closer. "I love you more today than yesterday."

They kissed and she ran her fingers through his hair as she moved against him. "Show me how much you love me."

He brought his hands to her face and studied her eyes. "I thought we came to that agreement during the night."

"It's a new day." She kissed down his neck and wrapped a leg over him.

His hand reached her face, fingering her cheek. "What is it, Maggie? Surely all this isn't normal."

"Wanting your spouse is completely healthy." She managed a smile.

"Aye, but tell me what's bothering you."

She slipped into the warm spot alongside him, stopping the tears from falling as she gathered her breath. "It's difficult for me to feel loved unless given physical attention that only someone who truly wants me can give. Words can be hollow and feelings might change. I need more than words."

"These past two days, have we not fulfilled all the physical actions associated with our vows?" He sat up and studied her face in the dim light. "Who wounded you, Maggie? You've carried this longer than your time here."

Feeling her heart laid bare, Magdalene curled into herself. "His name was William Johnston and I was engaged to him when I was eighteen. He filled my head with romantic notions, and as I'd kept house for my father four years, I knew I could handle the responsibilities of a wife quite easily. Things were proper between us, holding hands and a chaste kiss good night after an outing. Nothing more. Even the few times we found ourselves alone, I held his stupid hat to keep my hands from roaming. I did everything right, but the week of my nineteenth birthday—the week before we were to be married—he ran off to New Orleans for a more exciting life than what he could have in Seven Hills."

"He was a fool, Maggie. You were a sweet, tender young thing." He ran the palm of his hand along her shoulder. "But bless him for not following through because the Lord knew I needed you."

"So I suffered that heartache so we could be here together?" Her eyes narrowed, searching his countenance for the answer.

"The Lord works in mysterious ways." He kissed her deeply. "You have me now, always and forever. I won't leave you, Maggie. I've waited too long for this, for you. I crossed an ocean to find you—my one true love."

His hands caressed the length of her and she turned to him and whispered, "I always thought if I had given William more, he would've stayed. When I came to Seacliff Cottage, Alexander was more than willing to physically show how much he wanted me. I was eager to explore what I thought was true devotion—that of the flesh." Douglas stopped caressing when she mentioned Alexander. "But the feelings were fleeting and he was soon gone. Then I met you and began learning what love really is. While my head and heart were converted, my body was obstinate in its need for what it saw as fulfillment of true desire. That's what temptations have plagued me. And that's why I need you to show me—my body still doesn't trust the feelings of my heart."

His hands were back to traveling her figure. "Oh, Maggie. You'll wear me out when I'm working full time, but I'll do what I can to help you completely understand my love."

Eighteen

Magdalene threw herself into the role of woman of the home, going so far as to kick Uncle Simon out of the kitchen he'd cooked in for himself for more than three decades. Though she was out of practice and not used to the contrariness of that particular wood burning stove, her meals were edible. Douglas worked on the automobile and prepped the stable to be turned into a garage for the Great Arrow between his driving duties.

Friday afternoon brought Captain Walker and the weekly delivery. As Douglas was out with the family for yet another tea at the hotel, the captain spoke with Magdalene about the arrangements for the following week.

"I'll aim to arrive between noon and one, and after the Mellings' delivery is made, the three of you load up what you have here and then we'll steam to Daphne to collect your crates Douglas said you have stored with the deacon. If he can have a wagon waiting for us at the dock, that would help us get to the island before sunset. I've secured the lease of a two-bedroom house for you, though I'm afraid there isn't running water like you're used to here. An outhouse and pump are what you'll have to work with."

"I survived with that all my growing up years. Thank you for everything, Captain Walker."

Magdalene didn't have time to talk with Douglas when he brought the family back from tea because he left to collect Mr. Melling from the ferry. Magdalene kept herself busy in the kitchen the rest of the day.

On Saturday, Douglas roused Magdalene just before dawn and told her to dress in something she wouldn't mind getting dirty. Wearing one of her calico dresses and he in old trousers and shirt, they ran barefoot down the path to the beach and frolicked in the water. Often, they ended up on the sand with the tide lapping over them as they embraced.

Both soaking wet, Douglas scooped her into his arms and carried her up the path as the sun rose over the cliffs. "Let's dry off in the stable so we don't drip across the house," Douglas suggested.

Before they were through the stable door, Magdalene had his shirt half unbuttoned. He paused just inside so he could concentrate on their kisses, which led to more touching and opened buttons.

"Maggie…" Douglas pinned her against the ladder as they continued to feel each other. "In the loft?"

Though she didn't want to lose his touch, she turned to climb. At the top, Magdalene removed her dress while Douglas spread a blanket over what was left of the hay pile. They hung their outer clothes from rafters near the open window and then tumbled together onto the blanket.

"Didn't I always say that my house girl would come to mischief in the stable?" Mr. Melling's voice carried to the loft, turning Magdalene's damp skin ice cold.

Douglas, hovered over her, witnessed the fear in her eyes. "I'll take care of him," he whispered. He stood and wrapped the blanket around her shivering form in damp underclothes before adjusting the waist of his own.

Standing at the edge of the loft, Douglas spoke down to Mr. Melling. "She's no longer employed by your family. I don't see how this concerns you."

"But you're employed here, and if you're molesting young women in my stable, it is very much my business. Send her down to me and I'll see that she's sent on her way properly."

"If you think I'm going to send my wife to you, you're sorely mistaken."

"Your wife?"

"Yes, and *your* wife knows all about our nuptials but keeps the information to herself. Why don't you ask her why she hasn't wanted to share our glad tidings with your clan?"

"Just what are you implying about Ruth?"

"Nothing whatsoever, Mr. Melling." Douglas turned back to Magdalene, still huddled in the blanket.

"Just what are you two doing in my stable at this hour?" he hollered up.

"We went to the beach for an early swim and stopped in to dry off." Douglas went back to the edge and looked down. "We'll return to our house soon and I'll be on call at eight as usual."

Mr. Melling grunted. "Don't rush yourself. It'll be a late night and I doubt anyone in the house will be clamoring to go anywhere before ten. And, Magdalene," he called louder, "congratulations on your wedding. I do hope to wish you well in person sometime."

"I don't foresee that happening," Douglas informed him, "but thank you for the gesture."

Watching Mr. Melling exit the stable before returning to Magdalene, Douglas knelt beside her on the hay and brushed her wet hair off her face. "He's gone, and with it the perfect mood. We'll have to try this again another time."

"I'd like that, but let's go home now."

***

Douglas rested after the midday dinner while Magdalene watched from the carriage house windows to the commotion around Seacliff Cottage in preparation for the evening's engagement party. When she saw Rosemary crossing the yard, she stepped out to meet her.

"We've got Zora and her friend helping to rearrange the whole downstairs but a few of the furniture pieces are too much for us. Do you think Douglas could help Leroy right quick before Mrs. Melling starts yelling about the girls' shortcomings?"

"Of course. Is there anything I can do for you from here?"

"Would you mind entertaining Prissy? I'm afraid all day at the kitchen table isn't very appealing to her."

"I'd be happy to take her down to the shore for a walk."

"She'll love that. Thanks, Maggie."

Magdalene climbed the ladder and roused Douglas from sleep. "Leroy needs your help moving a few things inside Seacliff Cottage."

He moaned and stretched before sitting on the edge of the bed. "How long have I been down?"

"Less than an hour."

He pulled her toward him and rested his head against her white shirtwaist as his hands roamed up her back. "And when I get back, you'll lie down with me?"

Wishing she could, she sighed. "Sorry, but I agreed to watch Priscilla the rest of the day. I'm going to take her to the beach for a while."

"Not alone, you aren't. Take Uncle Simon."

Magdalene and Priscilla collected Uncle Simon from his job pulling nails from stable boards and they spent an hour on the shore gathering assorted shells and rocks while the old man dozed under the cypress trees.

When they returned, Douglas waited for them in the rocking chair on the front stoop. He took Priscilla on his lap and listened as she told him about their adventure.

"That pretty pink one there." He pointed to broken shell in her tin bucket. "I bet there's a story to how you found it."

He watched with genuine interest and a smile curled on his lips as Priscilla proceeded to tell him about the shell, as well as each and every other item she'd collected. Magdalene stood on the bottom step, transfixed by the scene before her. Having never seen a man show such tenderness to a child that wasn't his own, her heart swelled knowing she'd made the right choice for her future.

As if he felt her stare, he looked up. With a shimmer of love in his blue eyes, he cocked an eyebrow at her and mouthed, "What?"

Magdalene went for the door, a lump heavy in her throat. She paused to touch his shoulder. "You'll be an amazing father," she whispered to him before opening the screen.

Catching her hand on his shoulder, he intertwined his fingers in hers and looked up from his seat. "Where do you think you're going?"

"To prepare an early supper so you'll have time to eat before the Mellings demand your services for the evening."

He stood and kissed Magdalene. "What have I done to deserve this devotion and care?"

"You've loved me unconditionally." Her hand trailed down the front of his shirt. "Send Prissy in when she's done showing you her collection."

He pulled her in for a hug and whispered. "Will you have something to show me, too?"

Magdalene giggled. "*Much* later."

She cooked and baked with a light heart, which steadily grew heavy as the afternoon progressed. Douglas dressed for work in the loft as the sun slipped below the trees and the dread of being home without him in the dark struck hardest. Leaving Priscilla in the front room with Uncle Simon, Magdalene rushed up the ladder and nearly tripped on her long skirt.

Douglas had her in his arms at the top. "What's it, Maggie?"

"Why do they have to go by car when the rest of the party is going by boat?" she asked, referring to Alexander, his fiancée, and their chaperone going to and from the hotel in the Great Arrow while the rest of the party ferried from the Mellings' dock to Point Clear.

"It's the whole 'grand entrance,' I suppose." He caressed her back.

"But you'll be stuck for hours in that dark parking lot with all that vile talk and—"

He kissed her on the lips. "I'll be thinking of you the whole time, don't you worry."

"And all those propositions."

He kissed her nose. "You're my one student, Maggie."

"Not true. I've heard you've taught Leroy how to drive."

Laughing, Douglas hugged her tighter. "Maggie, I love you. I'll sit in the car and nap if I can, all the while dreaming of you and your voracious desires, which I'll be pleased to see to on my return, no matter the hour."

Her smile was twofold. "But we have Claudio's ordination to get to in the morning. We'll need time to prepare for that. Mrs. Melling promised me the car or carriage to attend. Since there's no longer a carriage, it looks like you'll be my driver."

"It will be our day as much as possible. Let's hope the rest of the family is sleeping in the morning so we can go alone." He ran his thumb over her lips then kissed her. "I'll return as soon as I can."

For the next hour and a half, Douglas parked the guests' automobiles who'd driven themselves and Leroy directed the coachmen of those arriving by carriage and the chauffeurs to where they could rest before going on to the hotel to await their owners. Uncle Simon and Priscilla sat on the front stoop, the little girl hoping for a glimpse of the guests in their "princess" dresses while Magdalene paced within the house.

When the arrivals slowed, Uncle Simon was ready to come in but Priscilla refused.

"Come out and sit with her, Maggie. I need to lie down for a spell."

Reluctant, Magdalene went onto the porch. It was shadowed from the yard because all their lights were off in the house and it stood along the forest. She felt secure enough, knowing no prying eyes from Seacliff Cottage could easily spy her under the tiny slip of a waxing moon.

"What do you think Mama's doing in there?" the girl asked in a whisper.

"She's doing a wonderful job going between the guests, smiling and serving drinks."

Priscilla leaned against Magdalene's legs and quieted. As the noises of the party centered more inside Seacliff Cottage than without, the hum of the evening settled around the little house. Magdalene saw Douglas retrieve a bag of cloths from the stable and go down the row of vehicles parked along the lane, removing the layer of dust the carriages had kicked up. At least the night was clear so he didn't need to worry about rain with the open cars to care for.

At Magdalene's feet, Priscilla began breathing steadily, so she pulled the girl into her arms and cradled her while she slept. No longer having a clear view of Douglas, she allowed her eyes to wander toward the main house. Within the fenced yard, two men in white tuxedos came through the back gate toward the stable, stopping to look over the automobiles, a cloud of cigarette smoke hanging over them.

"Have you seen your mother's companion since you got back?"

Magdalene's stomach churned upon hearing Rupert Lyon's voice for the first time since the day of his attack.

"Yes, and she's looking well. Why do you ask?" Alexander replied.

"She promised me a dance tonight, but I assume that's no longer going to happen."

"Why wouldn't it?" Alexander ran his hand over the grill of a roadster, and then exhaled a ring of smoke.

"She's not here, for one thing. And…"

"Yes?" Alexander tilted his head, daring his friend to speak the truth.

"Things didn't go so well our last time together." Rupert blew his smoke into a tighter ring, as if trying to outdo the other. "So close, though I doubt I'll get another try with her."

"I don't know about that. From what I understand, you're bolder than ever, and she *is* here."

"She is? In that luscious blue gown?"

Alexander took a drag on his cigarette. "Doubtful, as she's not attending the party, but she does fill that out nicely, doesn't she?"

"Where is she, then?" Rupert looked around, causing Magdalene to shrink in the rocking chair.

As she did so, she noticed Douglas coming up the row of automobiles, slow and deliberate. She wondered if the men's voices carried his way as they did hers.

"She's staying at the carriage house. Handy, isn't it?"

Rupert snorted. "And what does Beatrice think of that?"

"She hasn't laid eyes on Magdalene. I keep her hidden away for my own enjoyment."

"What about that chauffeur?" Rupert's voice sounded a little shaky and he ran a finger over his eyebrow. "He was quite forceful the last time I encountered him."

"He'll be stuck at the hotel all night, waiting on Beatrice and me." Alexander threw an arm around Rupert, pointing him toward the little house. "She'll be in there, alone except an old man who'd probably sleep through a train crashing through the wall."

"So you wouldn't mind?"

"I'm not making you draw lots, am I?" Alexander's laugh was harsh to Magdalene's ears.

"I bet she's superior to Twila but a few notches below Lucy."

"Don't ever speak her name. But you're welcome to—"

"She's not yours to give away!" Douglas tackled them both.

Magdalene stifled a scream.

"Prissy, wake up!" She stood the girl on the ground, a firm grip on her shoulders. "Run to the house and get your daddy, quick! It's an emergency!"

Magdalene hesitated on the steps, not sure if she should involve Uncle Simon or not. Fearing for his safety, she instead ran to where Alexander currently held Douglas's arms behind his back for Rupert to punch him unhindered. Douglas slammed his head backward, striking his skull atop Alexander's, who quickly released him. Rupert, already in motion and unable to stop the swing that Douglas ducked, took a punch in his own gut instead.

Seeing her coming, Douglas yelled, "Maggie, stay back!"

The other two men turned to her, keeping one eye on the man who'd simultaneously taken them down. Magdalene didn't stop until she was in the middle of the triangle, tears in her eyes.

"If anyone should be striking someone, it should be me!" She turned on Alexander. "I'd slap you so hard you'd return to your fiancée with a red hand of shame on your pretty face."

"You wouldn't dare." His stare was as icy as his voice.

"Don't tempt me!" Her shaking hand pointed at Rupert. "And you, if I wore my boots, would receive a kick to the shin to remind you with each step to keep your filthy hands and leering eyes off me!"

"I've already apologized for that, Miss Jones." He glanced over at Douglas. "And I believe I've paid my dues."

Douglas came up behind her. Because of the way she faced, she thought it might have been Alexander coming after her. She lunged at him before she realized who it was.

Alexander laughed. "You haven't tamed her yet?"

Douglas folded her into his arms. "She's not an animal to be broken, you wretch!"

Leroy ran out to them, surveying for any causalities. Seeing the standoff, he stayed to the side.

"Go back to the house," Douglas whispered in her ear. "I'll be there in a minute."

Magdalene crossed the yard, looking behind her at Douglas every few feet. He'd gone to Rupert and had his tuxedo jacket in his fist while he said something to him. Alexander moved to defend his friend but held back when Leroy stepped in. With the tense exchange over, Leroy dusted the two men off and walked with them back to Seacliff Cottage. Douglas ran for Magdalene on the front steps.

"What did you say to him?" she asked.

"Nothing for your ears, Maggie." He walked her in the door and set her at the kitchen table while he put water on for tea.

"Did you hear what they were talking about before you jumped them?"

"Yes," he said matter-of-factly. "Did you?"

She began to tremble and then sob. "Don't leave me here tonight!"

He took her back into his arms, a soothing hand caressing her hair. "I'm not going to leave you unprotected. The Wattses will stay with you until I return."

She continued to cry.

"Six more nights and then we're gone from here forever, Maggie. The family goes back to the city on Monday, so it's just two more nights with them. We can survive that long."

But to one in her situation, it didn't feel possible.

While Maggie sipped her tea, Zora came running to the house. "It's time for the automobile," she told Douglas. "I'm going to stay with her until the others are done with the house."

"Wake my uncle if you need to," he told the maid. After kissing Magdalene on the lips, he took her hand. "I'll see you later."

On the front step, he leaned back in the door. "And, Zora, talk with her about what we planned the other day."

Magdalene wiped her eye with one of Douglas's handkerchiefs. "What was that about?"

"Your Douglas has given me another sewing job, but as he doesn't know much about what style you'd like, he wants me to get your input."

"Another nightgown?"

Zora laughed. "It's something more practical this time. An apron."

"He makes fun of me for tying a towel on, but it helps protect my clothes and gives me a handy place to wipe my hands." Magdalene smiled. "He's thoughtful, isn't he?"

"The sweetest guy around, next to my own man. Ain't nobody sweeter than that," Zora said. "The only thing he did was buy the fabric, and I have plenty for two. Do you want sleeves? Ruffles? Pockets?"

Magdalene felt better at having something fun to think about and she knew that was her husband's parting gift—happiness. She drew a few design ideas on pages from her sketchbook and passed them to Zora while they ate cookies. They used the rest of the kettle of water for more tea as the sounds of the party faded to the shore and the call of the boat's horn sounded through the night.

Leroy, carrying a sleeping Priscilla, came to the door. Magdalene folded a quilt into the corner by the unlit fireplace for her to sleep on. Before he left, Magdalene stopped him.

"Douglas said you all would stay with me until he returns, is that right?"

He nodded. "We're likely to be working until then, but we'll be here."

"Rotate places with me whenever someone needs a break," Zora told him.

Magdalene touched his sleeve. "Did you hear what Douglas said to Mr. Lyons?"

The butler nodded.

"What?"

"That he'd kill him the next time the man tried to get his hands on you."

Magdalene's hand went to her throat.

"It's not that shocking, Miss Maggie. Douglas came close to doing just that when he found you in the sepulcher. You might not have noticed outside, but in the gaslights you could tell Mr. Lyons had a bit of paint on his skin to mask the bruising that's still on his face. Remember how his eyes were swollen shut?"

Magdalene shuddered. "I try not to think of that day."

"Of course." Leroy went to the door. "Let me get back to work."

The hours passed with Rosemary and Zora taking turns resting in the front room with Magdalene. When Saturday turned to Sunday, they finally finished everything except moving the furniture pieces Leroy needed Douglas's help with. Magdalene cooked eggs and toasted bread for a midnight meal. Not long after the group settled in the various chairs, the horn of the boat sounded below the cliffs, followed by people, and then automobiles starting.

Anxiously, Magdalene sat at the kitchen table waiting for Douglas. After an agonizing five minutes, she got up and poached a few more eggs so he'd have something to eat when he got back. She put the lid on the skillet to keep it warm before hearing the distinct sound of the Great Arrow outside.

Having already dropped his passengers at the front of the house, Douglas rushed into the house.

"Everything okay?" He spoke into her hair as he enveloped her in a massive hug.

When she assured him it was, he invited the others to stay, but they insisted on returning to Daphne so they could get a few hours of sleep in their own beds. After eating, Douglas checked on his uncle, who'd slept through the whole night. Then he locked the front door and followed Magdalene to the loft.

As she undid his uniform tie, he ran his hands over her hips. "You'll never guess who came knocking on my door in the parking lot."

Magdalene's fingers fumbled with the knot at his neck and she narrowed her eyes at him in the dim light produced by the oil lamp. "Who?"

"Your friend, Grace Anne." His hands continued to caress her.

"And what did she want you to teach her?" Magdalene yanked a button open on his shirt.

"She came to learn…" Douglas ran his hands up her sides, pulling her against his body as he kissed her cheek. "She came to learn what happened to you because she didn't trust Mrs. Melling's story about having to let you go."

Magdalene gasped. "And what did you tell her?"

"I told her how we'd been engaged for months, but Mrs. Melling kept parading you around and you finally had enough." He undid the buttons down the back of her blouse, kissing her skin as it became exposed. "I told her we were finally married this week and she wished us well and told me she'd tell the other ladies to leave me alone. It appears there are society people capable of good intentions left in this world."

"That's refreshing to know." Facing him, she pulled his shirt off and went for his waistband.

Douglas gently removed her blouse as she yanked off his belt. "Maggie, don't you need some sleep?"

"We have less than five hours before we need to get up in the morning. Do you really want to spend it all sleeping?"

Nineteen

Upon checking her pompadour in the mirror beside the highboy dresser, Magdalene stamped her booted foot.

"What is it?" Douglas looked up from fastening his Sunday shoes. "Still thinking I should wear my kilt for Claudio's special day?"

"I left the mantilla Mrs. Melling gave me in my old room. I wanted as little to remember her by as possible and left it in the dressing table with the perfumes. Now what do I do?"

Douglas stood and smoothed the crease on his black slacks. "Maggie, you know you couldn't wear that even if you still had it, right?"

She turned to him with a frown. "Why not?"

"What color mantilla does Mrs. Melling wear?"

"Black."

"Why do you think that is?" He took her hand and played with her rings.

"Because she's in mourning."

"No one explained to you in your months in a Catholic household and your time with Claudio?"

"No, what is it?"

"You are no longer allowed to wear a white mantilla in the church because you're married." He tweaked her nose and leaned to her ear. "White is for virgins."

"So I'm supposed to walk in the church advertising that—"

His belly laugh was as big as his grin.

She slapped at his arm. "Stop laughing!"

"Maggie, we've been married five days. I'm sure everyone knows what we've been doing."

"That doesn't make it right!" She folded her arms and huffed.

He kissed her cheek and laughed again. "Wear a scarf or a hat. Something that doesn't advertise what you have or have not been doing."

She stamped her foot again. "Why didn't anyone tell me?"

"What, that you were an untouched woman going to worship the Lord and that now you have become one flesh with your husband?" He reached around the waist of her dress to caress her and got an elbow in his ribs.

"I'm not in the mood."

"Now that's a first!" He tugged her to the bed and they both laughed, which turned to kissing and touching.

"No, we can't be late!" She rolled off him and went back to the mirror. "And now I need to redo my hair."

"You look fine. Just park a hat up there and all will be well."

"But I left all the fancy ones in Seacliff Cottage."

"Get the straw one you like to wear at the beach. No one will care, especially God. He doesn't judge us by our appearance."

"Fine." Magdalene snatched the straw hat off the hook and clambered down the ladder in her best black boots. She grabbed an apple out of the bowl on the cutting block and pushed out the screen door to wait by the automobile.

She leaned against the grill, chomping the apple in her frustration, when she heard the yard gate spring shut behind her. Refusing to be moved or bothered by anyone—including a Melling— she held her position.

"And what is this?" a feminine voice with a sharp edge asked.

"This, dear Beatrice, is Magdalene. She was Mother's companion while I was gone and now she's the chauffeur's wife. Magdalene, is everything all right?"

Momentarily freezing, Magdalene speedily chewed the remainder of her too-large mouthful and tried to pick what felt like a piece of apple skin stuck between her two front teeth without the use of her hands. She straightened and turned with a tight-lipped smile.

"Quite all right, Alexander, thank you." Her eyes swept over him and landed on the famed Beatrice Kirkpatrick of New York, fashionably dressed in a tiered black dress with the coveted white mantilla upon her sophisticated up-do. "And my congratulations to you, Miss Kirkpatrick."

"At least you're able to mind your manners enough to address *me* properly." Beatrice adjusted her white gloves.

"Sorry to disappoint you, but Alexander and I go way back. He'll be the first to say I'm nothing more than a naïve country girl." No longer caring what the two from the house thought of her, Magdalene took a slow bite from the red apple. She caught

Alexander's eye and he smirked, which created a warm sensation in the pit of her belly.

Beatrice placed a hand on her heart and looked repulsed. "Alexander," she hissed, "get rid of her!"

He merely shook his head as if to say he had no control.

"Maggie!" Douglas ran out of the carriage house. "You forgot your duster!" When he saw Alexander and his fiancée at the automobile with her, he slowed to a walk. "Morning, Master Melling, Miss Kirkpatrick."

"There seems to be a rush for the Great Arrow today," Alexander remarked.

"Aye," Douglas said as he helped Magdalene on with her driving coat. "I didn't expect anyone from the house to be up this early with the party going so late, but Mrs. Melling promised Magdalene several weeks back that she could have use of the automobile this morning to attend Claudio's ordination."

Beatrice scoffed. "Calling people by their first names and promising the automobile to servants? How do people live in Alabama?"

Alexander patted her hand. "It's been a trying year for Mother. From what I understand, Magdalene has been a great help to her these past months, and Magdalene, in turn, has become close friends with Claudio."

Magdalene, still chewing, nodded.

"And don't forget Claudio is a friend of mine. That's where we're heading as well," he told Magdalene before turning back to Beatrice. "As we have a married couple to escort us to church, we can save dear Aunt Polly from having to finish making herself presentable for at least a few more hours. Why don't you let her know she can rest for the morning?"

With a backward glare in Magdalene's direction, Beatrice clipped her way to the house.

"Talk about needing to train a woman." Magdalene rolled her eyes. "Have fun with that one, Alexander."

Douglas choked on a laugh.

Alexander smiled and stepped closer, causing Douglas to stand between him and Magdalene. "Since you're acting as chaperone on this trip, would you like to sit between us in the back?"

"That wouldn't be proper. The men must sit on the same bench." Magdalene opened the driver's door and climbed behind the wheel. "And I call front for the ladies."

She pulled out her goggles from the pocket and adjusted them on her face, followed by her head scarf to secure her hat and then gloves.

"You can't be serious!" Alexander slapped his knee. "Mother really let you learn?"

"She did." Magdalene threw her apple core into the forest and wiped her hand on a rag left on the front seat. "But it's been several weeks. I might be a bit rusty."

Douglas leaned in and checked a few gauges. "It'll be a good test to see what you retained, but I'm sure you'll do well."

Feeling emboldened by being behind the wheel while Douglas leaned over the door, Magdalene ran her fingers up his beard and guided his lips to hers. They kissed deeply, despite the watchful eyes of nearby Alexander.

When Douglas stepped away with a smile, Magdalene threw a bold look at Alexander to let him know she knew he wanted her kiss, too. Alexander flashed his impish grin, then waited for Beatrice by the gate.

"Maggie, I see that gleam in your eye. You're going to behave yourself this morning, aren't you?"

She started the automobile. "Of course."

Douglas stepped onto the running board and held onto the canopy's support bar as Magdalene began rolling forward to turn around. "Then why do I get the feeling that kiss was more for Alexander's benefit than mine?"

Magdalene hit the brakes and leisurely drank him in as she raised her eyes to his face. "Have no fear of that ever happening, Mr. Campbell."

"Nevertheless, you'll be getting a blessing from the new priest before the morning is over."

***

Claudio waited in front of Church of the Assumption and ran to the automobile when it pulled into the parking area.

"Alexander, welcome home!" He embraced his friend when he emerged from the backseat and kissed both cheeks. "It means much to me that you came."

While they made introductions on the passenger side, Douglas helped Magdalene out of the driver's seat. With her driving accessories removed, he took her coat. "You did well, Maggie, just as I expected."

Douglas reached in the automobile to get her hat that fell off when she untied her scarf, but Claudio came to them before he could hand it to Magdalene.

"*Sig*—no, Mrs. Campbell!" The deacon hugged her tight before kissing her cheeks. With his hands holding her arms, he studied her face. "You are well, no? Marriage appears to agree with you. And I have a small gift."

He reached into his cassock and removed a folded square of black lace which he shook out and laid atop her head.

She looked to her husband. "Did you plan this?"

Douglas laughed. "No, but I wish I had."

Claudio looked between the two. "Is it not good? One of the sisters makes them."

"It's most appropriate, Claudio." Douglas put an arm around his friend's shoulder and whispered to him.

Knowing what he shared with the deacon, Magdalene blushed.

Claudio came back to her side with a smile. "Poor *posseduta*, not in the mood. Most unfortunate, and all because of a mantilla."

Magdalene elbowed him in the side, but laughed. Her smile faded when she looked across the Great Arrow and saw Alexander and Beatrice watching. While his fiancée looked annoyed, Alexander had a knowing smirk that unsettled her mood.

"She's Methodist," Alexander told Beatrice, as if that explained her behavior in being overly friendly—and forceful—with the deacon.

Claudio adjusted the lace on her head and offered his arm. "Come, all of you. I will find you good seats. Bishop Allen is here from Mobile so it is crowded today."

Hearing of the bishop, Magdalene noticed Alexander pause and wondered how his visit had gone when he went in search of repentance in the spring. Claudio led Magdalene into the chapel, followed by Douglas, and then Alexander and Beatrice. They found seats near the front, and Douglas slid onto the pew first, followed by Magdalene. Claudio motioned Beatrice in next, but Alexander jumped ahead.

"I know how you prefer the aisle, Beatrice."

The deacon frowned and Douglas stood to switch seats with Magdalene, but she motioned him to sit. Magdalene crossed her ankles and tucked them under the bench beneath her. Once her husband was seated, she put her arm around him and rested against his side, leaning away from Alexander on her left. Douglas rested his hand on her far knee, letting Alexander know who had possession of Magdalene.

"Do not leave without me greeting you," the deacon said before he made his way to his seat.

Father Angelo conducted some of the service in Italian and Bishop Allen in English and Latin. When those advancing to the priesthood were brought forth, Douglas passed Magdalene a fresh handkerchief. So absorbed in the ceremony, she flinched when a gentle tapping on her boot jolted her. Then a shoe rubbed up the left side until it reached her stockings.

Douglas looked at her and patted her knee. She squeezed his hand to let him know she was fine, and then she ever so slightly turned her head toward Alexander. In her peripheral vision, his mischievous grin curled at the corner of his mouth. The flood of memories of his last full day in Seacliff Cottage in March washed over her. The foot nudges under the dining room table, the lustful groping, passionate kisses, and the attempted undoing of her virtue and life. A day of longings turned nightmare.

As soon as the service ended, Magdalene pushed past Alexander and Beatrice. She rushed up the aisle to the door, one hand holding the mantilla to her head as she flew. Once outside, she ripped the lace covering off her head and dropped it on the front seat beside her duster. Not being able to sit still, she started down the road on foot.

"Maggie!" Douglas called from the steps of the church, but she didn't stop. He had to run to catch up with her and took her by the hand. "What happened?"

She fell into his arms and caught a sob in her throat. "He's not watching, is he?"

"Alexander was stopped by Bishop Allen's people, so he's still inside with Beatrice." He lifted her chin to look her in the eyes. "What did he do to you? I saw nothing."

"He only rubbed his foot against mine, but it triggered memories that I'd rather not recall." Magdalene shivered in the midmorning sun. "I must stay away from him. I don't trust myself."

Knowing what she needed to regain her focus and realign her loyalties, Douglas led her into the shade of the nearest oak and pulled her close. "We're together 'til the end, Maggie, and he'll be gone in the morning," he whispered in her ear. "The next chapter of our lives is about to begin—don't be stuck on the old pages."

His fingers traced her lips and then he fit his mouth to hers in a way that reminded her that they were truly one.

Breathless, she tugged on his Sunday tie. "Can we go home now?"

"Aye, but let's find Claudio first."

Claudio waited for them at the automobile in his new robes and stole. "Are you all right, *signorina?*"

She fell against his chest face first. "Bless me, Father, for I have sinned."

"Not funny, Maggie." Douglas pulled her off their friend. "But she does need a blessing. It's not going well at Seacliff with everyone home, but the family heads to Mobile on the morning ferry."

While Claudio anointed her forehead with oil, Alexander and Beatrice arrived.

"I thought you said she was Methodist," Beatrice remarked.

"Blessings are universal, as are prayers from all believers," Claudio responded. Looking at Alexander, he handed Magdalene off to Douglas. "And everyone needs help when dealing with temptations. I heard Bishop Allen requested to speak with you."

"He wanted to come by Seacliff Cottage this afternoon, but I had to turn him down as it's not a good day with everyone recuperating from the party and preparing for the city in the morning." Alexander looked across the yard. "I suggested he stop in at Government Street once we're in Mobile."

Before they left, Douglas invited Claudio for a visit that week and reminded him of needing the use of a wagon Friday to transport their crates to the dock.

"*Sí,* friends, I will see you Wednesday and we can discuss the plans further. Magdalene," he took her hand and whispered, "be stubborn and strong, and all will be well."

"Thank you, Father De Fiore." She smiled at him. "You'll do great things."

Douglas opened the back door on the driver's side of the Great Arrow for Magdalene. "You look much too exhausted to be behind the wheel."

He tucked her duster around her like a blanket. Once the others were in, Douglas drove them home.

***

The tension from the exchanges with Alexander lasted well into the evening. Magdalene wanted nothing more than to curl up with Douglas in the loft, but he spent the afternoon nursing his uncle, who was in bed with a fever. Rosemary brought them chicken stock at supper, and with the cornbread Magdalene made, the three ate a light meal. Once Uncle Simon slept, Douglas came to the loft, dropping on the bed fully clothed.

"I'm worried about him, Maggie. I think we should fetch a doctor tomorrow if he isn't improved."

She ran her hand through his beard. "You'll have the car available and no appointments to bring people to. You just have to finish converting the stable, right?"

"Yes, and Leroy's coming to help with that the next two days."

"Then it sounds like you need a full night's rest." Magdalene unbuttoned his shirt without the least hint of seduction.

"I do need sleep, Maggie. Thank you for understanding." He stood to remove his Sunday pants and hung them over the back of the chair. When he got into bed, his arms went around her. "I'll make it up to you soon."

While she enjoyed the comforts of her husband's arms, Magdalene didn't sleep well. Restless—but afraid to move lest she disturb him—she lay with her head cradled where his shoulder met his chest. She mentally battled the memories of past transgressions while surrounded by Douglas's warmth and goodness. Several times throughout the night a lone tear escaped an eye, but she hooked them with a finger before they could drip onto him.

When the sky outside the dormer window looked more purple than black, Magdalene crept from the bed and dressed conservatively in a green calico that she'd brought with her from Seven Hills. She rolled the sleeves up to her elbows and took pains to braid her hair neatly, tying the end with a piece of green velvet ribbon before going down the ladder.

She lit the oil lamp on the dining table and then brought it with her to Uncle Simon's room. His face was ashen and his blankets wet with perspiration. She began searching the dresser for fresh bedding.

Uncle Simon raised his head. "What's going on, Maggie?"

"I'm looking for clean bedding. Yours are soaked through with sweat."

"All the extras have been packed and hauled away with the crates."

"Then you'll need to sit in the living room while I launder these. Pray for a sunny morning so they'll be good by naptime."

Magdalene helped him collect fresh clothes and made sure he made it into the bathroom before she went back for the bedding. Once he settled in one of the rockers with her mother's old shawl around his shoulders and his jacket on his lap, she filled the washtub with suds and water at the pump in the stable yard. She cleaned the sheets first, knowing they'd dry the fastest, and draped them along the fence posts of the side yard where the horses used to roam.

She was up to her elbows rinsing the quilt when Mr. Melling came around.

"Such hard work to be doing at an hour like this, Magdalene. Surely you could wait until full light before tackling such drudgery."

"Uncle Simon needs his bedding dry before he'll be able to rest again."

"Campbell's unwell? I had no idea." His face showed a hint of compassion.

"His rheumatism has grown worse this summer, but he's run a fever the last day and a half. We'll probably need to send for a doctor."

"I came to remind Douglas that it will take two trips to get everyone and the luggage to the ferry this morning, so we need to start half an hour before usual." He held out an envelope. "And I was reminded your little group would be leaving Friday, so we won't be seeing you again. Here's the men's pay for the week."

"My hands are too wet to take it, but thank you. You can leave it on the driver's seat and I'll collect it when I'm done."

"I insist you take it from me so it won't be blown away or lost." He pulled out his billfold and retrieved a crisp ten dollar bill. "And take this for Campbell's doctor visit and any medicine he might need. He's put in decades of good service here and I hate to see him suffer."

His sincerity pricked her heart so that she stood and dried her hands on the towel about her waist. "Thank you, Mr. Melling. I'll be sure to tell Uncle Simon of your generosity."

With her hand outstretched, she stepped forward to take the envelope. Mr. Melling's cold hand took her wrist when she had hold of the money. "And, Magdalene, don't feel you need to be a stranger to the family. I'm sure I speak for all of us when I say we'd be happy to…entertain you should you be interested."

She jerked free from his icy grasp and hurried to the house to deliver the money and check on Uncle Simon.

Later, she hung the final blanket out and started breakfast. Douglas came down the ladder with his jacket and tie slung over his shoulder, but otherwise dressed. He kissed Magdalene's cheek before going to his uncle.

"It's good to see you up, but you aren't looking well."

"Maggie kicked me out of bed before the sun."

"What? Why?"

"She didn't like seeing me wrapped in sweaty sheets. She's already washed everything and hung them out to dry."

Douglas rushed back to the kitchen and took Magdalene in his arms. "Why the rush, Maggie?"

"I woke early and it appeared his fever broke during the night. I couldn't see leaving him in a damp bed. He said the extra bedding was boxed away, so I took everything out to the pump and cleaned them. I'm going to need you to dump the water, though. It's too heavy for me."

He kissed her head. "Maggie, you should have let me help."

"You'll have your chance soon enough." She handed him a plate with an omelet. "No time for toast, remember you've got two trips to make into Montrose. I'll have your coffee in a minute."

He rubbed her shoulder with his free hand. "I'll take it with cream and sugar today, please."

She bopped him on the backside with a wooden spoon.

"I didn't say pepper!"

Magdalene brought a cup of coffee to Uncle Simon and then took care of Douglas's.

"What's this?" He opened the envelope and picked up the ten dollar bill.

"Mr. Melling came by while I did the washing. The money in the envelope is this week's pay and the ten dollars is to go toward medical care for Uncle Simon."

Douglas arched his eyebrow so high his forehead wrinkled. "No strings attached?"

Magdalene shook her head. "I guess he has a heart somewhere in that cold, hard soul."

"He said I put in many decades of service and was sorry I've been poorly," Uncle Simon said from across the room.

Douglas ran a hand over his face and looked at Magdalene. "I should have been with you. Anything might have happened."

"I saw it all from here." Uncle Simon motioned to the front window. "He was only there a few minutes and the only time he was close to her was when she took the envelope."

"Thank the Lord," Douglas muttered.

Several minutes later, he brought his dishes over. "It was wonderful, Maggie. I'll see to the washtub when I get back, as well as anything else you need help with." He kissed her, followed by a wink and a smile, which caused her stomach to feel tingly.

After he pulled the Great Arrow around to the front of the house, she went out to flip the bedding before she saw to Uncle Simon's and her own breakfast. In the back of her mind, Magdalene thought Mrs. Melling would stop in to say goodbye. Though the last two months were unbearable in her company, she had spent several pleasant months with the woman. By the time Douglas returned from his two trips to Montrose, she'd had no visitors.

Feeling melancholy, Magdalene met him on the front step and half listened as Douglas told how Mr. Melling had given him directions to the nearest doctor and he'd left a note at his home requesting his services. "We'll need to stay close in case he's able to stop in today. If things aren't better and the doctor doesn't come, I'll take him there tomorrow."

"That's a solid plan." She paused. "Do you mind if I take a walk?"

"I don't want to go off and leave him, Maggie."

"I'll go alone." Seeing the look on his face, she continued, "There's no one left to hurt me. I'll stay on the drive, just to the main road and back."

He fingered the dark smudges below her eyes. "Did you sleep at all, Maggie?"

"I don't know," she whispered. "Maybe a bit after midnight, but I can't be sure."

"Why didn't you wake me, let me try to help you?" He kissed her forehead and lips.

"You were up almost all the night before—"

"Aye, so were you."

"But you were exhausted, I wasn't."

"But you are now." He squeezed her elbow. "If you want to walk, go. But I want to make sure you get a nap, so hurry back."

Magdalene ambled down the dirt road, seeing only a deserted lane and a mixed bag of memories—many she would rather forget. She made it as far as the front gate of Seacliff Cottage when her anger surged. Snatching a rock from the edge of the drive, she pulled back her arm to throw it at the house that had caused her such torment.

"Why can't all of the memories be gone?" she cried out as she pounded a fist on the fence. "Why only steal from me the one with Douglas and not the ones with Alexander? He's gone, take the memories of him! Leave me at peace with my husband!"

As though taunting her, the power within the house would not let her release the stone. Tentacles pulled her legs like puppet strings, drawing her into its diabolical plot. Magdalene hugged a porch column as though it was a long-lost friend. A gale blew, pulling at her dress, though none of the trees surrounding the yard moved. The doorknob rattled but she did not know if it was something trying to get out or the house wanting to open itself to her.

I will show you the way to the peace you seek. Come with me and make it yours.

She staggered to her feet. The wind ripped the breath from her chest and she dropped the rock. Rushing for the door, Magdalene grasped the cold metal with both hands. Accepting her destiny, she crossed the threshold with a contented sigh.

Welcome home.

Magdalene danced to the empty parlor, where she poured herself a drink of Douglas's favorite Scotch from the bottom cabinet. It had to be the Scotch and not the brandy because she needed to replace all the memories of Alexander with new ones of Douglas. Seacliff Cottage deserved a loving couple to make it whole again and she was compelled to turn the house from Melling to Campbell. Magdalene lounged contentedly on the settee, sipping the Scotch as she waited for the visitation she knew would come.

Twenty

A quarter of an hour later, Magdalene heard Douglas calling for her outside. Knowing he'd see the open front door, she refilled the glass so it'd be ready for him and settled in Mr. Melling's chair by the fireplace.

Douglas's shoes struck the parquet in the hall. "Maggie? Are you here?"

"In the parlor."

"Maggie, I don't think—" He did nothing except stare at her positioned with legs hanging off the arm of the chair and a glass of brandy in her lap.

"We've earned it, have we not?" She took a sip and stood, holding it to him. "Drink. It's not as good as it tasted from your mouth."

He accepted the glass but didn't bring it to his lips. "Maggie, we shouldn't be here."

She spun around, her lithe arms moving to an unheard song. "The Mellings are gone and you're not expecting Leroy until after dinner. We have all morning."

"But Uncle Simon—"

"He's resting and the doctor will have you last on his list for the day. Drink, I remember how much you said you enjoyed it." Magdalene circled him twice.

Douglas raised the tumbler. Magdalene ran her hands over his shoulders and then came in for a kiss. Testing his willingness, she allowed his mouth to lead. By the time his glass was empty, they were both half unbuttoned on the settee.

She raked her fingers through his hair and kissed him just below his jaw. "We were meant to be together here."

His hands went under her skirt, caressing the length of her legs. "It feels like I waited forever for you, Maggie."

"Let's go somewhere more comfortable." She took his hand. "Come with me, we can make it ours."

"Back to the attic?" He kissed down her neck to the exposed edge of the chemise.

She tugged the rest of his shirt open, running her hand down his abdomen. "Carry me up the front stairs."

Douglas took her in his arms, and after a few false starts that ended with them once again necking on the settee, he successfully carried her to the second story. He set her down before the door to the attic, but she rushed for her old room. The bright space smelled too strongly of perfume. No longer feeling that it was hers, Magdalene gave chase and Douglas followed. He caught her around the waist and pressed her against the wall in the alcove.

"How many times was I in this room with you, wanting to do this?" He trailed his hand down her front. "Maggie, my love, you're all I need."

Magdalene focused on the sensation of her husband beneath her hands and lips, attempting to cling to the present. She urged him to her old bed and they sank on to the coverlet in a tangle of passion. She gasped over his zealous touching. "I need you, Douglas."

"Not here, Magdalene." His mouth came to hers for an enticing kiss.

If it wasn't to be in her old room, she needed to locate where. With panting breath, she broke from his arms and stumbled into the hall. The wind swept past her and blew open the door two rooms down. The curtained window and the dark paneling held onto the night like a familiar friend. Backing up to one of the posters at the foot of the bed, Magdalene arched against it as Douglas pulled her dress to the floor. To drown out the smell of the sandalwood, she tasted the vanilla flavor of his kisses and inhaled his fiery scent as he brought them to a fervor they'd never before reached. After he exhausted himself, Magdalene lay beside Douglas as she stared at the ornate mahogany canopy with a satisfied smile.

***

The chimes of a clock striking ten echoed in the hall. Jerking awake, Douglas jumped up. He stumbled for the window and yanked open the curtains before turning back to the bed.

"Where are—" Upon looking around the room, his face twisted with agony. "Dear God, what have we done?"

Magdalene, who stayed awake after their love making, smiled dreamily. "We made it ours."

Her grabbed her bare shoulders and shook. "No! You've made us his!"

"I'm more fully yours than ever before." She got to her knees and reached for him. He brushed her hand back and stepped away from the bed. "I had to fill this house with you and me rather than the shameful things from that weekend. There'll be no more regrets for having been swayed, no more longings. I'm yours completely!"

"Not in Alexander's bed! Did you smell him as I touched you? Where you thinking of him as we were one?" A solitary tear fell from his right eye and disappeared into his beard.

"No, it was all for you! I only thought of you!"

Douglas snatched his clothes off the floor and locked himself in her old bathroom. Sounds of the shower running made her realize he tried to scrub the feeling of filth off his skin like she did after Rupert's assault. Only then did she comprehend what she had done by bringing him to another man's bed. Even if it was a bed she herself had never been in, Alexander had slept on those very sheets just hours before.

I'm not fit to live!

With a wailing sob, Magdalene ran up the attic stairs, intent on stopping the evil within her. There she took the Parisian gown from the wardrobe and pulled it on, not bothering to fasten it. She ran to the nearest dormer window, but her plans to escape her horror were struck down because she would not fit through the small opening.

We tried to kill you.

Seeing the truth of the demon's words, Magdalene began shaking. She remembered thinking at one point that she'd never be able to harm herself like Alexander had done by clawing at his skin, but she'd been ready to throw herself from a third-story window just to clear her head.

Accept that I've won you.

The familiar sensation of a tentacle slid up her leg, wrapping her body and throat in its clasp. Screaming out her pain, she collapsed on the floor and pounded one of the emerald pillows. "Be done with me! Kill me now before I hurt him more!"

You taste like fear.

"I'm not scared of you! You've taken what was most precious to me—my husband's trust. Now I'm destitute and fear nothing for I have nothing to lose. Let me die!"

She thrashed about on the cushions then jumped to her feet, almost tripping down the stairs in the gown as the ruffled sleeves slipped off her shoulders.

"Let me die!" she screamed as she ran toward the kitchen stairs.

The bathroom door opened and Douglas, only half dressed, sought to understand the commotion she made. She glanced back before the stair door swung shut. The look of terror in her eyes spoke louder than her screams.

"Maggie!" He followed her down the stairs. "Stop, Maggie!"

She turned to him only when the prep counter was between them. "No, it's too late. I was wrong to think no one was left to harm me. The demon has finally bested me by playing me against myself."

"No, Maggie!"

"It's over. I'm as good as dead to you." She pulled one of Rosemary's knives from the drawer. "Shall I do it here or without the house? Maybe spilling my blood elsewhere would give me a slight victory."

"Maggie, no! I love you, I do! I know you didn't mean it. I realized it wasn't your choice. I was coming for you to bring you out of these cursed walls."

"I wounded you most grievously and you'll never want me again. Just let me go. Let me slip quietly away, then tuck me into a sepulcher by the sea like Eliza." She raised the knife over her heart, the chest line of the gown hanging dangerously low in its unfastened state.

"The Lord is my shepherd; I shall not want." Douglas's voice was calm and low as he prayed.

Magdalene's hand holding the knife wavered as he continued the Psalm.

Her hand stayed up as Douglas inched closer. She could see the moisture of tears on his countenance through the blurry wetness of her gaze.

"Surely goodness and mercy shall follow me all the days of my life: and I will dwell in the house of the Lord forever." He was beside her, staring into her petrified brown eyes, when he finished. "Maggie, don't do this to me, please. We've walked through the shadows, but together we'll find the sun. I need you. I need your love."

Tremors wracked her arm that held the blade, but that didn't stop Douglas from grabbing for it. She lurched away from him and brought the edge across his forearm, the blood immediately trickling onto the wood countertop.

Magdalene screamed and threw the knife across the room. "It wants sin! It wants blood! It wants my life!"

He pulled her to his bare chest, pinning her arms behind her while he lifted his other hand above her, blood dripping off his elbow as he did so. "In the name of the Father, and of the Son, and of the Holy Spirit. Blessed is our God at all times now and always and forever. Amen."

***

Magdalene awoke in Douglas's bed in the loft, dressed in her summer nightgown and covered to her chin with the blue bedspread. From downstairs, she heard voices but couldn't make them out. Recalling what she had done to herself and Douglas, her lower lip began to quake. Her hand that cut her husband lay upon her stomach in a benign way. She knew what it was capable of and wanted it removed.

"Take it from me! Cut it off!" Her voice rang through the little house.

Claudio, in his new robe, surplice, and purple stole, ascended into the space, seeming larger than life under the sloping roof. He came directly to the bed and sat beside her.

"Do not be troubled, Magdalene. I am here." Leaning over her, he kissed each cheek as he had always done and then did the sign of the cross over her. "You are delivered once again."

"I'm no longer worth saving." Unable to look upon the chiseled lines of his handsome face, she curled into a ball under the covers.

His weight shifted on the bed and his shoes dropped to the floor with two *thunks*. Settling himself cross-legged on the foot of the bed, he began reciting scriptures in his native tongue. For half an hour he spoke with no response from the one hiding. Then Magdalene thought she heard the rhythm of a familiar verse.

She pulled out from the blankets and recited it in English. "But they that wait upon the Lord shall renew their strength; they shall mount up with wings as eagles; they shall run, and not be weary; and they shall walk, and not faint."

"*Sí*, Magdalene. Do not be weary of your trials. The Lord will lift you up if you let him. There are those who would carry you until you have the strength to walk for yourself."

"Not anymore. I've driven Douglas away by my actions. You're all I have and yet you leave me soon as well."

"By what means do you think I am here? As soon as Leroy arrived, Douglas sent him in the automobile to fetch me. And coming here, I can tell you, was the scariest ride of my life! The man is not yet fit for driving in town."

The smile did not quite reach her mouth, but it tugged at the corner of her lips.

"And you know, *posseduta*, if you wanted to see me today, you could have invited me to supper rather than go through all this."

Magdalene's short laugh broke into a sob and she stretched her legs under the blanket to kick at Claudio.

"Come, *amico!*" he called. "The fight once again runs through her soul."

Douglas was immediately up the ladder, like he had been pacing the floor below. Dropping to his knees beside the bed, he reached for her hand.

"Forgive me for my weakness, Maggie." Their fingertips touched but Magdalene began to pull away. "I should have taken you out of that house as soon as I found you. I should have known something wasn't right, but I was swayed."

"But it was because of me you entered the house and ended up in that bed. What you accused me of doing wasn't the truth, though I can now understand why you thought that." She intertwined her fingers through his.

"Forgive my harsh words. I was scared and angry at the situation. I wasn't thinking clearly." Gently, he touched her cheek. "I'm sorry for hurting you. I'm as devoted to you as ever. To know my words caused you such pain as to seek death—" His strength broke and he collapsed against the side of the bed.

Magdalene noticed the intricately wrapped bandage around his right forearm. She dropped into his lap, her arms around his broad shoulders.

"It wasn't you. The demon had its hold on me and that was the only way out I could see. I would never forsake you like that, Douglas. Never." She kissed him and ran her fingers through his beard and over his chest before nestling under his chin. "I'm here, and if we can both forgive each other and ourselves, we'll be fine, won't we?"

He kissed her in return and roamed his hands over her nightgown. "Aye, Maggie. We can make it."

Claudio unfolded his legs and stretched his feet to find his shoes. "I can see you have things under control. I will see you downstairs at some point. Do not rush."

Douglas reached a hand out to him, holding Magdalene close with the other. "Thank you, Claudio. I knew you'd be able to reach her."

"*Sí*, but I must say with you both married and I with my *sacri ordines*, we should put a stop to meeting in bedrooms with Magdalene in her night clothes. It is not appropriate." He stared down at them for several seconds before the smile broke across his face.

Then Magdalene was on her feet, though somewhat dizzily, and knocked him on the arm with a loose fist. "Does that mean you'll stop calling me *posseduta*? That's probably not an appropriate name for a priest to call his friend."

"I am sworn to speak the truth. And keeping with that, I have to say that is my favorite of your night dresses." Claudio fingered the eyelet at her shoulder.

Magdalene playfully slapped his hand away. "That's because you haven't seen my blue one."

"Nor will he." Douglas stood with the others.

"I shall give you two some space and see you downstairs in the near future." He took them each by one hand. "Your love is being forged stronger by these trials. Cling to each other, as well as the Lord, and you will be able to conquer anything that is set before you."

Alone, Douglas and Magdalene sat on the bed, she with her head on his shoulder and him with his head upon hers, their hands clasped on his knee.

"How is Uncle Simon?" she asked.

"The doctor came a few hours back. He thinks he has an infection somewhere and suggested a tonic, but there's nothing more he can do for him with his age and the rheumatism. Rosemary is looking after him and cooking supper."

"Supper? How long was I asleep?"

"Going on seven hours. Do you feel better now?"

She nodded.

"Would you like to get dressed and come down to eat?"

"I'd like that." She stood and looked around the room. "What happened to what I was wearing…before?"

"I carried you here and changed you. When Leroy and Rosemary came, she brought the gown back to the house and collected the rest of our things. I was careless with your dress when I took it off you in Alexander's bedroom. It's a bit wrinkled, but if you'd like to put it back on—"

"I'll get something fresh."

"And don't worry, she cleaned up the blood and the doctor saw to my arm."

"I'm sorry for cutting you. I wasn't myself."

"I know, and neither was I. When I think back on my vehemence, I'm ashamed. I hope I wasn't too rough with you."

She kissed him softly on the lips and squeezed his knee. "Not at all."

Twenty-One

The visitors left after supper with the promise of Leroy coming back in the morning to help finish working on the stable, as well as bringing Claudio to check in with the couple's spiritual well-being.

"It is better for my soul to come announced than to be sent for in a flight of panic." He kissed Magdalene goodbye. "And you need to stay out of that house! Do not even go within the fence."

After Magdalene assured him she would stay away, the priest climbed into the back of the Watts's wagon. He sat next to Priscilla and waved with the girl until Magdalene could no longer see them.

"Are you ready to go inside?" Douglas wrapped his arms around her.

She shook her head and leaned into him.

"Well then, would you like to see what we've been doing in the stable to make room for the Great Arrow?"

Though it wasn't high on her list of priorities, Magdalene agreed. They held hands as they walked through the open barn doors. All the stalls except the two back ones had been removed. Hanging from the rafters on the right side was a simple swing made from an old plank and two pieces of rope.

"I know how you liked sitting on the gazebo swing, so I practiced some nautical knots to rig this up." He patted the seat. "Here, let's see how well I did."

Laughing, Magdalene stepped forward.

"I'm joking about the knots being iffy. I had Claudio try it first and it held, so you'll be fine. Leroy even took Rosemary and Prissy for a ride on it—at the same time."

"So my swing's been enjoyed by everyone but me? I'll have to remedy that."

Douglas held the board while she smoothed the back of her brown skirt to sit. Once on, he walked backward with the ropes, favoring his wounded arm.

She squealed when her bare feet left the ground. "Not too high!"

"Relax, Maggie. Be free." His hands pushed against her each time she swung toward him, causing her to swing higher on the next pass.

Not having swung on a single seater since childhood, Magdalene had to work at releasing her fear of immediate danger from a fall. As she trusted her husband more, her muscles loosened and her smile grew.

Douglas, unable to push her any higher, looped around to the front to watch. "I haven't seen you smile like that since our wedding day."

Feeling giddy, she stuck her tongue out at him.

"You're beautiful, Maggie. If I could draw, this is the moment I'd capture."

She stopped pumping her legs and her momentum slowed. When she felt secure enough, she jumped off mid-swing, and half-ran, half-fell into Douglas.

"Easy there." He took her by the arms and kissed her forehead. "Next time, let down your hair so you can feel the wind in it."

She laughed and began unraveling her braid. "Thank you for this."

"I'm going to check on Uncle Simon. Wait for me here?"

She nodded and watched him go into the deepening twilight. From her vantage point on the swing, the last of the season's lightning bugs were visible as they flickered across the stable yard. Rather than the excitement of her first ride, a quiet peace breezed around her as her loose hair lifted off her back and then swung into her face with each contradictory motion.

Douglas returned with one of the oil lamps from the house and set it on an upturned crate. "I should have lit a lantern before I left you here."

Magdalene let her feet go slack to slow herself. "I've been watching the lightning bugs. How is he?"

"Sleeping peacefully in bed." He raked his fingers through his dark hair, setting it on end. "It seems like days ago you were out washing his bedding. So much has happened, but we end the day together, and that's what counts."

He opened his arms to her and she jumped off the swing, allowing him to absorb the momentum of her dismount. She put her arms around his neck and stared into his blue eyes in the warm glow of the lamp.

"Will you always be here to catch my fall, put me to bed when I'm overcome, and forgive my trespasses?"

"Maggie, as long as there's breath in my body I'll do everything I can for you."

***

Tuesday morning saw Douglas, Leroy, and Claudio—unrobed with sleeves rolled up—rebuilding the stable door to widen it for the automobile to be driven in and out with ease. Sometimes Magdalene sat in the swing and watched, while more often she saw to Uncle Simon or worked in the kitchen. They finished the job just before noon and Magdalene fed them chicken and dumplings, prepared wearing one of her new blue gingham aprons.

"I'll be sure to let Rosemary know you can cook and for her not to worry after Douglas's well-being," Leroy said before leaving.

Magdalene laughed. "And thank Zora for her fine workmanship when you see her."

Claudio pulled his vestments back on and prayed over her. "You are looking better today, and that was a delicious meal."

Magdalene untied her apron and hung it on the back of one of the dining chairs. "I'm much better. Thank you for everything."

He turned to Douglas. "I will find a ride in the morning and you can bring me home after I see to everything, *amico.*"

"Yes, and thanks for your help today. The extra hands made for lighter work."

When Claudio and Leroy were gone, Douglas and Magdalene stood in the stable yard, staring at each other for several moments.

"My final job for the Melling family is to park the Great Arrow in the stable. After that, I'll be yours until midday Friday when Captain Walker comes for us." He raised an eyebrow at her. "Think we'll grow tired of each other by then?"

"Three whole days?"

His fingers played up the sleeve of her lace blouse. "Yes, Mrs. Campbell, three days and nights."

"I'm sure I can think of something to occupy your idle time." Her arms around his neck, she came in for a kiss. As he reached around her, his fingers caught on the buttons on the back of her blouse, reminding Magdalene of how he'd buttoned them that morning—with a kiss for each one.

"We can start by celebrating one week of marriage as soon as I get the car inside and dusted."

"May I have a ride, driver?" She did her best to look shy.

He took her by the shoulders and leaned his forehead to hers. "And have you all over me as a distraction when I'm driving indoors for the first time? It'll be the backseat for you."

Douglas offered his arm and walked her to the rear door of the automobile with a smile. After she was in, he ran to the house to check on his uncle and then he was back with an even bigger grin.

"Sleeping?" she asked.

He nodded and started the motor. Easing off the brakes, he let it coast into the stable as much as possible, turning the wheel to the left once they were through the doors to allow room for the use of the swing on the other side of the space. He turned off the motor and Magdalene tapped him on the shoulder.

"Aye?"

"Driver, I was wondering if you could show me how to kiss. I want to make sure my man is satisfied with my technique."

With a laugh, Douglas turned around so he knelt on his seat. "Maggie, the only unsatisfactory thing about your kissing is when it stops."

Aspiring to be part of his joy, she stole a quick kiss and leaned against the upholstered backrest with a smile that showed she wanted more.

"You'd be my undoing if we weren't already married." He climbed over his seat and onto the bench next to her. "I'm glad there are no horses to stare at us. I tend to think Janus would've been more vocal about what we're doing than the drivers behind the hotel."

Magdalene laughed and cuddled against Douglas. "He would, wouldn't he?"

"He liked your calming touch almost as much as me. He'd be jealous for sure." He tucked an arm around her shoulders and stretched his legs to the side.

She followed his lead and propped her feet on the back of the front seat. "I'm glad we have some private time, though I wish your uncle wasn't sick."

"It puts a damper on things."

"I'll do the best I can for him when you're out on the water. It'll be good for me to have someone to watch over and keep me busy when you're working. Life's better when there's someone relying on you for nourishment and care. It gives purpose to each day."

"Now there's a cry for motherhood if I ever heard one." He tickled her ribs, causing her to squirm. "It's good to know you understand the importance of food and care. I thought your main purpose each day this past week involved getting me undressed."

She grabbed his knee. "Isn't that part of caring for a husband?"

"Yes, Maggie, but it's not everything." He trailed his fingertip down the side of her face. "Moments like these, talking and laughing, are as important to our well-being as anything else."

Her hand shifted to his belt and she gave him a sultry stare. "But what if I'm here just to get you undressed?"

"Then I'd have to warn you that my brothers all turned ugly on their twenty-seventh birthdays, so you better enjoy what you see while you can. You've got a good six months with me, but after that it's questionable you'll even want to look at me again."

"I love you." She curled her fingers around his belt buckle and kissed him.

"We came to this union with such great camaraderie, I want to be sure we keep it. Don't just love me for my body, love me—"

"—for your wit and knotting skills. Yes, I do." She grinned up at him. "Lose your looks if you must, but don't lose your ability to make me smile."

***

Midafternoon, they returned to the house. Though Uncle Simon was still asleep, Douglas woke him to be sure he drank some tea and helped him to the bathroom. Then the three sat in the front room while Douglas and Magdalene took turns reading aloud from her mother's copy of *Little Women.*

As suppertime approached, Magdalene began preparations for their meal, sending Douglas to the main house to retrieve a few perishable items from the icebox Rosemary wanted them to use. He returned with the last of the milk as well as bacon.

"I was thinking it'd be fun to go fishing some time if you think Uncle Simon could make it to the beach," she said.

"We'll see how he is tomorrow, but that would be nice." He rubbed a hand along her back. "There are a few servings of syrup left in the jug we need to use up."

"Do you want pancakes?"

He nodded.

"Tonight?"

"Anytime, Maggie. And I'll help, just tell me what you want me to do."

She set him to work whisking eggs for the batter while she fried the bacon. Having sat up most of the afternoon, Uncle Simon was ready for bed immediately after supper.

"Meet me at the swing," she whispered to Douglas before he helped his uncle ready for bed.

Magdalene cleaned the kitchen and then dashed to the ladder. She stripped down and pulled on her wedding gift, enjoying the feeling of the silk against her skin. With her hair unbound and a feeling of complete inhibition, she ran out the front door.

The sky was inky blue with a smattering of stars mingled between the pale puffs of clouds. She paused in the middle of the yard to look at the heavens, all while imagining Douglas's face when he'd walk into the stable and see her swinging in her nightgown. It was all planned out in her head. She'd lay a towel on the seat of the swing so the rough wood wouldn't snag the silk. Her legs, bare from the knees down, would kick in the air and her hair would blow back in the breeze. It was a lovely vision—one that shattered when she noticed a rectangle of light burning from the half-opened curtains of Alexander's bedroom. Other lights were on inside Seacliff Cottage as well.

Through the open windows of the carriage house, she saw Douglas emerge from the back bedroom. Magdalene dashed into the stable so she'd be ready for him, hoping he'd see her before he had to inspect the main house on the off chance he'd left lights on when he went to get the food. She readied the swing with a cloth and ran it back a few steps before jumping on. Sailing higher, Magdalene closed her eyes, imagining that she looked as evocative as she felt with the air kissing her skin and her hair tickling across her bare arms.

She willed Douglas to come for her, but was met instead with Alexander's voice.

"Magdalene, you mystical creature. You never fail to surprise me."

Opening her eyes to meet the source of the words dripping with yearning, her body tensed to see him crossing to her.

"Don't come any closer!"

He slowed, but still advanced.

"Stop!" Douglas's voice thundered through the stable. "You need to respect her boundaries."

"And you need to stop leaving your wife unattended when she's dressed so provocatively." Alexander gave his full attention to Magdalene, grabbing the ropes to stop the swing, her knees bumping against him. Douglas rushed toward them, but Alexander held up a hand in warning, giving him pause. "Hear me out, driver."

"If you touch her, I'll—"

"Kill me. I heard your rousing speech when you gave it to Rupert, but there are two things you didn't account for when it comes to me." He spoke to Douglas but his eyes were on Magdalene, his head inches away from hers, and his hands on the rope level with her face. "One, I don't scare as easily. And two, I know the pleasure of touching your Maggie with mutual satisfaction, and I might find it worth dying for."

Douglas continued on his course and came behind the swing because he could not get between them without jostling Magdalene. Alexander raised his eyes to meet Douglas and set his square jaw.

"What are you doing here?" Douglas's stare was hard.

"You're as nosey as your uncle. I don't owe an explanation to you, but I will tell Magdalene." His hands dropped on the ropes until they were less than an inch above hers.

She felt her husband at her back, keeping Alexander in his full sight.

"The women are all in a tizzy with wedding preparations, with more coming into town tomorrow in the form of my future mother-in-law and Beatrice's chattering older sisters. I wanted to give them space to do their planning and save my sanity, so I told them I was coming back to Seacliff for some quiet reflection before the ceremony and I would see them all Saturday evening when I returned to the city."

"And you don't think it's rude to abandon your bride the week before the wedding with out-of-town guests arriving?" she asked.

He stood and pulled a gold-plated cigarette case from his pocket, lighting one. "With her entourage, she barely notices my absence at any time, much less a busy week like this."

Magdalene looked up at him. "I wouldn't be so sure about that. Your presence isn't background material."

He blew his smoke at Douglas and laughed. "How flattering. And you, Magdalene, you succulent thing. You've been naughty, haven't you?" He dropped to his knee before her, his cigarette dangling from his lip as he put one hand on the rope below hers. "Running around in that gown with every curve clearly on display beneath the silk."

"She's not on display for you, so keep your tongue in and your hands to yourself." Douglas's voice turned her cold with its fury.

Alexander blew more smoke at him, which also caught Magdalene in the vapors. "She may not be on display for me right now, but there was some sort of display in my room while I was gone. Imagine my shock when I walked into my room only to find it smelling of Magdalene and sex."

She began to shiver as his blond head angled closer, his piercing gaze threatening her existence.

"Did you come looking for me, Magdalene? Did you decide to taste of me once again? Or did you simply want to bed your husband where your true love last slept?"

She covered her face with her hands, trying to hide the tears.

"Come off yourself!" Douglas stepped around the swing and pushed Alexander back until he stumbled against the automobile. "That house suffers from infestations and you know it!"

Alexander took another drag from his cigarette and looked between the couple. "I'll leave the house unlocked and my bedroom door open, Magdalene. It's only a matter of time before you find your way home. While I wait, you've given me this vision of yourself to fuel my fantasies."

The chill of the Melling gaze set in, causing Magdalene to tremor.

Douglas, ignoring Alexander's parting remarks, pulled Magdalene into his arms. "Don't worry, Maggie. I won't let you out of my sight."

"I'm sorry."

"You did nothing wrong." Douglas removed his shirt and pulled it around her, swallowing her shoulders with its expanse.

"I wanted to give you a vision to always remember for our first week together. I thought we were alone. I never would have—"

"I know, Maggie. Let's get inside and I'll fix you some tea." He started walking her toward the stable door.

"What if I want coffee?" Her fingers trailed over his chest.

"Then I'll fix—no, you don't even like it."

Magdalene stopped before him and pulled open the shirt he'd put around her, pushing her silk clad torso against his skin. "I like the way it tastes on your lips."

She could see the yearning in his eyes as their bodies converged, but his smile was bittersweet. "We aren't doing anything until you relax for a little while. I love you too much to take advantage when you've been through an emotional moment."

"But I'm not emotional. I feel strong and beautiful." She shook back her loose hair as she clung to him.

"And you are, Maggie." He felt his way down her arms to her hands and took them into his own. "You don't need mine or any other man's attentions to make it so. That's what I think you crave. Validation. And that's most likely what the demon preys upon when you are within the house—your need for approval when you feel weak or unneeded."

As though she'd been slapped, she broke from his grip and turned her face away so he wouldn't see the tears.

"I'm not trying to be harsh, I'm trying to help." Douglas gently turned her back to him and held her to his chest. "You're too magnificent a woman to be more concerned with what others want from you than what you want for yourself. If you want to seduce me, I'm more than willing to oblige, but don't do it because you think you offended me and want to be sure I still desire you. You needn't worry about my yearnings for you. You're all I'll ever need."

At home, Magdalene accepted the chamomile tea Douglas prepared before bed. Sometime past midnight, the temperature grew warmer than it had been during the day. Magdalene began sweating and tried to wiggle out of Douglas's arms to make a trip to the bathroom. He tightened his hold around her from behind.

She kissed his arm that lay across her chest. "I'll be right back," she whispered.

He stretched, releasing her, and kicked the covers off before settling flat on his back.

After stopping in the washroom, Magdalene got a cup of water from the kitchen sink. She took the drink to the front door and peered out the screen before deciding to step out. The air was as oppressive as an August day, the night air eerily still. With a shiver brought on by the strange atmosphere, she turned back to the door, but not before noticing a pale figure in an upper window at Seacliff Cottage.

She stared across the yard, her head tilted toward Alexander. Naked from the waist up, he placed his hands on the frame on either side of the window.

"Magdalene!" He called her name with finality and it crashed against her chest with longing. "Please come to me."

Her body trembled and she tossed the remainder of her water off the porch, afraid it would slosh out of the quivering cup. Gaining control of herself, she acknowledged Alexander's prowess with an exaggerated curtsey. Magdalene went inside to rouse her husband because she couldn't handle the allure of Alexander alone.

"Maggie, it's too hot." Douglas nudged her off him. "Are the windows open?"

"Yes." She went for an earlobe. "I think there's a storm coming."

He rubbed his hand down her gown, not opening his eyes. "What time is it?"

"Half-past one."

"Have you slept any?" His hand went to her neck, fingering the tender places along the way, the white bandage on his bare arm a painful reminder of her mistakes.

"No." She placed a leg atop his. "I know it's hot, but let me try exhausting myself."

"Oh, Maggie, tell me what's going on in that beautiful head of yours." He sat up, pulling her with him. "Get your brush and let me fix your hair."

She returned to the bed and he took her by the hips, positioning her between his outstretched legs. He began brushing her hair at the bottom, working his way steadily higher as he smoothed the tangles.

"What happened when you went downstairs?"

Her first instinct was to say, "Nothing," but she needed to get past any shame the pull of Seacliff Cottage caused in her. She took a deep breath. "I used the facilities and then got a cup of water in the kitchen. I was so hot, I went to the front porch to get air. Alexander was at his window, watching. He beckoned me."

Douglas placed a hand tenderly on her shoulder. "I'm a fool for not getting up with you, especially after promising to never leave your sight."

"I wasn't swayed. I came for you, not him."

He gathered her hair into sections to braid. When he finished, her thick braid hung over her left shoulder, bound at the bottom with a white ribbon that matched the lace on the hem of her nightgown. "I'll do all I can to make you want to keep choosing me."

Twenty-Two

The couple slept past morning light, limbs draped over each other without a stitch of a blanket upon the bed. It wasn't until the kettle whistled that Douglas's blue eyes opened.

"Uncle Simon?" he called out. "Are you up?"

"Up and fixing something for us to eat," he shouted in reply. "I feel good for the time being and I want to give our Maggie a break this morning."

"Thank you!"

Magdalene, not trusting herself to answer, snuggled back against Douglas's chest. He embraced her and the movement overpowered her as the rush of feelings she'd felt in the night returned.

"I see that fire burning in your eyes," he whispered as his hands continued to roam over and under the silk gown. "I'm yours, but we need to keep quiet this time."

Remembering some of the passionate sounds they'd made in the dark caused Magdalene to blush and bite her lip.

"It's okay, Maggie," Douglas whispered as he touched her warm cheek. "There's a time for inhibitions, but when Uncle Simon is cooking isn't one of them."

She giggled and relaxed into his arms. "Perhaps we should wait until later. You know how I get."

His laughter vibrated through her like a wave of joy. "Aye, my love. We fare better with privacy any time of day."

They lay in each other's arms a few minutes more before dressing and going to the table.

"As the air changes, these old bones begin to ache." Uncle Simon massaged his knuckles. "When do you think the storm will blow in?"

"Hopefully not until after Claudio arrives." Magdalene spread butter on a piece of toast while Douglas poured her tea.

"How are we going to get him home?" Douglas mused. Then, looking to his uncle, he shared the news. "Alexander is back."

"Claudio's his friend, too. I doubt he'll let him walk home in the rain." Magdalene smoothed the napkin on her lap over the black skirt.

"You must have seen more kindness in him than I have," Douglas said.

Magdalene gazed into the past. "He has the potential for generosity and can be affectionate."

Douglas cleared his throat. "Enough of that topic. I'll see to the transportation issues when the time comes. Uncle, do you think fishing would be good today?"

He shook his head. "Not on the beach with a storm brewing in the gulf. You could go along Rock Creek for freshwater fish, though. I've had luck there in the past."

"We'll see what happens when Claudio gets here."

"What must I be the deciding factor of?" The priest stepped in the front door and dropped his black bag next to the wall.

"Fishing," Magdalene said as she went to him.

"I am a fisher of men." He greeted her as always, and then with a smile said, "You glow today, Magdalene. The heavens shine upon you as the clouds roll in. All is well, yes?"

As she nodded, Douglas spoke out. "No. Alexander is back."

Magdalene shrugged. "Well, except for that."

Uncle Simon slipped to his room to allow them privacy.

Claudio let loose a string of what Magdalene could only assume were obscenities in his native tongue, for which he apologized afterward. "I must go speak with him. Excuse me."

She watched him run across the yard until he disappeared into the house.

"Your eyes follow his every move, Maggie. They always have." Douglas slipped between her and the screen door so he could look her in the eye. "What do you see when you look at him?"

She smiled and kissed her husband's lips. "I see his fine lines and the man he is behind the cloth. I see his love for God and the passion he has for life. And when I see him driven with purpose like he is right now, I pretend he's running away with Eliza so he can hold it all."

"Oh, Maggie." He kissed tears off her face. "Not everyone is destined for a love like ours."

"But he had it. He had it and it was taken from him. Sometimes I think if I ever see Lydia again, I won't be able to control my rage over what she did. What Mr. Melling did by covering it up. What this whole, ridiculous family continues to do in the name of society and pretense!"

Douglas stroked her back, running his hand over her best summer blouse. "It's too hot to get worked up over things you can't control."

"But what of those things I can control?" She held him against the doorframe and kissed him until he returned the favor. "Sometimes control involves letting go."

The sky opened and large raindrops splattered on the roof and pock-marked the stable yard. Magdalene dashed out the door and into the middle of it. With hands thrown wide, she lifted her face to the crying sky and immersed herself in the sensation of being washed clean.

"Maggie!" Douglas called from the front steps before running to her.

When he reached her, she explored each line on his weathered face with her hands as the rain streamed down them. Unlike Alexander's porcelain complexion, Douglas had laugh lines around his mouth and eyes, as well as fine lines and color on his forehead and cheeks from years of outdoor living and work. He was ruggedly handsome in the most pleasing ways, and Magdalene let him know with her touches.

"Maggie, let's get inside!" he shouted to be heard over the pouring rain.

She took his hand and turned to the stable, but he scooped her into his arms and ran for the house. Under the canopy of the front stoop, he refused to let her go.

"We need to stay together. There's no telling how long the rain will last and I don't want us stuck in the stable with Uncle Simon here."

His gaze drove out any thoughts she had of running away. She would stand beside her husband no matter what. She laughed, gave him a wet kiss, and laughed more. "You can put me down now. I'm not going anywhere."

Lowering her feet to the floor, he looked at her soaked form, focusing on her white blouse. "Maggie, I can see right through your shirt and under things. Here." He unbuttoned his shirt and put the soaking thing over her chest.

"We're home, let me just go change rather than piling me with another wet layer." She tossed his shirt back to him and looked him over with a sigh. "You do have great lines, you know." She gently touched the outside corner of his eyes. "Especially these. You keep me smiling along with you."

Then his hands were cradling her oval face and he drank in her form, a gleam in his bright eyes. "If the others weren't here, I'd make love to you in the rain in a heartbeat." After an intense kiss, he opened the screen for her. "Go on and change before someone besides me sees you."

"You might as well come with me so we're dripping all over the place at the same time. It'll make clean up easier."

"Not this time, Maggie."

"Why?" She played with the latch on the screen he still held open.

"I don't want Claudio or, God forbid, Alexander walking in while we're in a state of undress."

"Don't be silly. It'll take you a minute to change." She tugged at his arm.

"Maggie, go on alone. If I see you fully right now, there'll be no stopping me, and Claudio could be here any minute. Go without me."

With a rosy blush reaching her cheeks, she leaned in for a kiss. "And you told me in marriage we wouldn't have to bridle our passions."

"I was wrong and you're tormenting me more than ever."

It might have been cruel, but she laughed all the way to the loft. She loved that she appealed to Douglas and it gave her a heady feeling to know the effect she still had on him after marriage. While undressing, she fantasized what it would be like to cleave together with rain drops twinkling across their bare skin. She found the image alluring and she promised herself it would happen one day.

Not wanting to possibly rain damage one of her nicer outfits, she dressed in her black-and-white striped wash dress. Then she dried the loft floor with an old shirt and brought the damp pile down to hang dry in the bathtub. Douglas was still standing shirtless on the porch, his arms crossed as he stared at Seacliff Cottage. Magdalene collected dry clothing from the loft for him, which she set beside the sink in the washroom.

She brought a towel with her and draped it around his shoulders. Douglas put a hand over hers where it rested on his arm.

"Thank you," he whispered.

"What are we looking at?" she asked in an equally soft voice.

"I thought I heard yelling."

"Do you think Claudio and Alexander are fighting? Should we go see?"

"*We?* No. You've been the goal in enough tussles in that house. I'm not dragging you into another. And I'm not level headed enough to stay neutral when it comes to that man. I'll give it another hour. If Claudio isn't back, I'll check on things."

"Then come get dry. I brought a change of clothes down so you don't have to drip up the ladder. You'll need to re-bandage your arm as well."

"Aye, Maggie, and you stay inside while I change."

Magdalene waited in the rocking chair closest to the front window. After a minute, a figure in what looked like a dark robe came up the muddied lane from the front of the house. As it drew closer, she could tell it wasn't Claudio. It wasn't until the person was in the stable yard that the revulsion of who it was set in.

Magdalene slammed out the screen door. "You have no right to be here! You're not welcome nor wanted!"

"Mags, please! I didn't know where else to go." Lydia stopped five feet from the porch, fresh rain dripping off her already soaking cloak. "I went to the house but I heard yelling. I was going to ask Mr. Campbell if I could rest here until the family calms down."

"There's no one from the Melling family except Alexander and he'll never calm down enough to speak to you!"

"Then I missed George? I meant to come Saturday when I knew he'd be here for the party, but I couldn't catch my ride to town in time." She shifted uneasily, seeming to pat a bundle under her cloak. "If the family is gone, why are you still here?"

"*My* family is here for two more days, then we move on from this cursed place. But temporary home or not, I won't let a murdering harlot like you into this house!"

"Maggie." Douglas came up beside her as he finished buttoning his blue shirt. "What's going—oh." He gave Lydia the once over and moved Magdalene aside.

"What are you doing?" Magdalene looked aghast as he opened the screen. "Don't let her inside this house!"

With an authoritative gaze, he turned on his wife. "It's for the sake of the child." He motioned Lydia up and removed her cloak, hanging it on the back of the porch rocker with a quick motion and nudging her inside before any moisture could drip on the baby swaddled to her.

"Thank you. I always thought you had a kind face, and a liking for Mags. I suppose I was right on both accounts."

Magdalene kept by the kitchen table and stomped her foot as Douglas led Lydia to the rocking chair she'd been sitting in.

"The babe must have been suffocating under that cloak in this heat. May I help you unwrap him or her?" Douglas held his arms out for the baby after Lydia took her seat.

"It's the only thing I had to keep the rain off us. Here," she said as she removed the baby from the swaddling, handing her child over in nothing but a diaper, "meet Georgiana."

Magdalene gasped, not from the shock of the child being named for her father, but from the delicate way Douglas took the infant into his hands. Softened to the situation—but not letting go of her anger—she paced between the kitchen table and the front door.

When Douglas finished looking at Georgiana, he held her to his clean shirt, his hand completely dwarfing her uncovered back. "She's beautiful and looks like she'll have her mother's curly hair and the striking eyes of her father's side. How old is she?"

"Ten days." Lydia pulled a well-used handkerchief from her pocket and wiped her nose.

"Then she has a few days' jump on me and Maggie's union." He shifted his weight from foot to foot, creating a gentle rocking motion for the infant.

"I'm sorry to bother you. I know it's upsetting, especially to Mags, who seems to know of my shame in regards to Eliza."

"*Shame?* Is that what you call murder?"

"It was an accident," she whispered.

"And how do you accidently sew burrs into a saddle pad?" Magdalene yelled.

Georgiana's little body tensed and her face reddened before she let loose a pathetic cry. Douglas passed her back so her mother could soothe her.

Uncle Simon opened his bedroom door and looked around. "I thought I heard a baby."

"We have visitors." Douglas walked his uncle to the nearest chair.

"It's the young woman who caused the most trouble for me in my entire career," he said as he settled into the rocker across from Lydia.

"His health's gone downhill since Eliza's death. Losing her horse was torture for him." Magdalene placed a hand on her hip and scowled.

"Neither of us were here then, Maggie. Let him speak for himself." Douglas reached for her arm, but she jerked away.

"I'm sorry I did it. I never meant to kill her, just give her a scare is all. When I realized she was stepping out with the deacon of all people, I was worried if someone found out about her, they'd find out about George and me. I didn't know her horse would throw her like that. I thought at the most she'd get bumped off and be sent back to Mobile to recuperate."

"There were enough burrs in there to get a grown man bucked across the bay," Uncle Simon said. "Flora was as gentle as they come, but sensitive."

Lydia openly sobbed, which caused Georgiana to wail as well.

Magdalene opened her mouth to speak, but Douglas took her by the arm and walked her into his uncle's room, closing the door behind them.

"What are you doing?"

"Saving you from doing or saying something you might regret later."

"There'll be only relief once I tell her everything that's going through my mind! She has no right—"

"Maggie, she's scared and alone. She had a child out of wed—"

"That's her own fault! I saw the way she was with Mr. Melling."

"And I've heard how Mr. Melling was with you on several occasions." Douglas tried to take her hand, but she pushed him away. "Maggie, do you not think it possible that a young woman who wasn't as stubborn and opinionated as yourself, upon receiving advances from a man like that, might romanticize the situation until she believed he loved her and would whisk her away some day?"

Magdalene's firm stare began to waver as she saw the truth in the situation, but anger coursed through her body until she ached for it to be released. She clenched her fists and paced the room.

"What will it do to Claudio to see her? What can she possibly hope to receive from Alexander now that she knows Mr. Melling isn't here?"

"I don't know, but we can't send her and the baby out in this storm. It would be the death of the child, Maggie. Georgiana isn't well and I refuse to be part of something that will lead to the loss of innocent life. If you're upset, and I know you are, take it out on me." He punched himself on the chest and held up his arms. "Come on, Maggie. I know you wanted to deck me when I opened the door to her and again when I sat her in your chair. You need to punch something because she got away with killing Eliza while Claudio suffered so much pain."

Magdalene lifted her fist, but instead of hitting, she fell against his chest. "Why do you have to be right? Why do you have to look so attractive holding a baby? How did you learn to hold one like that? How do you know so much?"

He wrapped his arms around her and sat on the edge of the bed. "Those older half-brothers from my father's first wife gave me plenty of education in the way of families. They were all having children of their own when I was barely twelve. I learned from watching and doing and it's unfortunate, but I saw more than one precious life go to an early grave due to illness. Lydia is carrying more guilt than is good for one soul. Do yourself a favor and don't add to it, she'll have more heartache soon enough."

Magdalene pulled one of Douglas's handkerchiefs from her pocket and wiped her eyes. "I'll do my best, but I won't promise anything. And if she calls me *Mags* one more time—"

He kissed her firmly on the lips. "If she does, you'll get over it because you have me to turn to and she has no one but a sickly child who depends on her for everything when she herself is destitute."

Magdalene drew back and punched him in the stomach.

"Feel better?" he asked, not even flinching.

"Just enough to walk back out there."

Douglas took the third seat in the living area while Magdalene paced the floor, anxiously watching out the door for Claudio. The rain was letting up and she hoped he would notice and return from Seacliff Cottage.

Lydia continued her story of shame. "George fired me as soon as it was obvious what grew within. I lost my job at the hotel when I went to Mobile, and when I stopped in to see if they would take me back, the matron turned me away immediately. I can't continue on with my relatives. I wanted to show George what a beautiful daughter we made, hoping he might have a change of heart about me or at least give us an allowance to live on, but I can't afford to travel to Mobile to see him."

"Now isn't a good time to do that." Everyone looked to Magdalene when she spoke. "Alexander's wedding is the talk of the city and Mrs. Melling would never forgive anyone who caused ripples in her carefully orchestrated event. Wait until after the wedding and then send a letter to him at his office."

"That's a solid plan, Maggie." Douglas smiled at her and nodded as though thanking her for trying to be kind.

Magdalene, feeling somewhat better for having shared her knowledge, turned back to the door. Claudio crossed the yard, mist rising around him from the cooling earth as he approached like a messenger of death.

Twenty-Three

Claudio passed through the drizzle and Magdalene stepped out to meet him on the stoop. She touched his face, turning it to either side. "Douglas heard shouting a while back and I feared the worst. Did you two not come to blows?"

He laughed and kissed her cheeks with a lingering quality. "That only happens when you are around, *posseduta*. We did have a disagreement, several over the course of the time I was there, but things are no worse than they were when I walked through the door. He likes to call me names and make fun of my clothes. And though he knows he is afflicted, he refuses to be helped. I am afraid he has become comfortable in his sinful ways and thinks they are a permanent part of him, but I will keep trying to reach him."

He grabbed for the handle of the screen but she blocked his path with a hip. "We had a visitor arrive while you were gone. I'm certain you won't be pleased."

"I will gladly meet any of your acquaintances. I love all mankind because I see them as God does."

Magdalene leaned in to whisper. "I hope so, because I was screaming mad. Douglas had to take me aside and lecture me about my attitude."

Claudio smiled and leaned closer. "And how did that work out?"

"I punched him in the stomach." She stepped aside for him to take the latch and entered the home with him laughing behind her.

"I do not know how you deal with her, *amico*. There must be sainthood for you in the future." Claudio's smile faded as his gaze settled on Lydia. His expression changed from shock to anger to fear to sadness and then finally settled on relief within a few seconds, pulling Magdalene's heart along with it. "I have been praying to see you before I leave."

Magdalene's mouth hung open as Claudio crossed the little room and dropped to his knees before the former maid. The kind way he looked at Lydia and took her free hand created a surge of jealousy, believing the woman did not warrant such affections—especially from one so wronged by her actions.

"I only meant to scare her. I'm sorry, Deacon De Fiore." She hung her head as new tears began to fall.

"I am Father De Fiore now and I insist you confess your sins and relieve yourself of the burdens you carry."

"There aren't enough hours in the day for that." She sniffled.

"You know I am but an imperfect man. Surely you can find the time to let me help you."

Douglas stood and escorted Uncle Simon to his room. Then he climbed to the loft and returned seconds later with one of his flannel shirts, which he held open to receive sleeping Georgiana. Lydia gave her over to Douglas, and then Claudio adjusted one of the vacant chairs in front of her.

"I don't know where to begin," she stuttered.

He laid a hand on her knee. "Start from where it hurts the most."

Douglas, with the baby tucked in one arm, guided Magdalene with his free hand, pointing to the kitchen table and then the loft, an eyebrow cocked, questioning where she wanted to go.

Magdalene climbed to the loft and marveled over the confident way Douglas maneuvered the ladder with one arm—a wounded one at that. When he reached the top, she couldn't stop herself from kissing him.

She looked at the baby in his arms. "Will she really die?"

"She doesn't breathe right and is too thin, a bad combination." He tucked the beige shirt further around Georgiana's tiny frame. "Would you hold her? Afford me a glimpse of your motherhood just as you yearn after my patriarchal glory?"

Magdalene stepped away. "Mine would be a scene of cold awkwardness whereas yours is all confidence and warmth."

"Come now, Maggie, just for a moment."

"I'll make her cry."

"Then you can learn to soothe her. I know you have a gentle hand when you want to."

"As opposed to my cold, stubborn one?"

"More like hot and sensual."

Magdalene smiled at him and shook her head, but held her arms out in the same moment. "Just one try, and only because Claudio isn't mad about Lydia. I still don't like her being here. You need to stay close and take Georgiana back if she hates me."

"Such little faith, Maggie."

She sat on the bed and held her arms straight out, causing Douglas to laugh. "What?"

"A little effort will go a long way." His smile brushed aside her annoyance. "Have you no experience?"

"I'm an only child and the youngest out of my few cousins. I think I've held a baby three times in my entire life and never one that small. The last time was before my mother died, when she hosted a quilting bee for her friends at our house."

"How sad for you. Their tiny bodies are miraculous. Were you never passed a newborn from down the pew during a church service by a proud parent wanting to show the baby off?"

"For some reason, people in my church don't like to see unattached young ladies holding babies. Maybe they think we'd catch unholy ideas about having one of our own."

He stood before her, bumping her knees between his own. "Rid yourself of the fear of holding one. You're no longer unattached and you love the act of procreation like I never thought possible. Babies are inevitably a step in our journey together."

His words called on something primitive within her, softening her resolve. She bent her elbows, mimicking Douglas's own stance in preparation to receive the child. "I'm ready."

Once Magdalene held the tiny wisp, her nerves settled.

"How does it feel?" Douglas asked.

"Not as terrible as I expected." Magdalene easily held the baby in the crook of one arm and with her free one nudged down the shirt to marvel over Georgiana's little hands. "And it's amazing that we started so small and grew into who we are now. I don't reflect on things like that often. It makes me want to draw."

"How long has it been since you have?"

"Weeks. I've had the urge several times, but not like I do now."

Douglas reached out to take the baby. "Don't let me stand in the way of expressing yourself."

Magdalene clutched the baby to her chest. "I've got her. I might as well keep her a few minutes more."

He brushed his finger over Magdalene's nose and laughed. Between Magdalene's jostling movement and Douglas's laughter, Georgiana began to fuss. Magdalene panicked and tried to shove the baby at him.

"No, Maggie. You're doing fine. Trying rocking a little, switching the weight from hip to hip. I know you are capable of all sorts of maneuvers with those hips." He moved in to use his hands to guide her.

"I'm quite capable, Douglas, remember?" But the baby's discomfort continued.

"Another trick is to hook your pinky and let the babe suck on the knuckle. It's supposed to work to soothe for a short while until the mother has time to nurse."

"Won't she get mad when nothing comes out?"

"I don't see how babies on this side of the ocean can be all different from those in Scotland." He nudged her hand. "There, and it has to be the little finger for one so small. She's got it. See, it does work."

"Are they all like this?" Magdalene felt a stirring within as the tiny upturned lips and tongue suckled her finger in search of nourishment. "Her little mouth is so perfect."

"Not as perfect as yours." Gazing at her with sincerity, he melted her soul. "And not as perfect as what we can create together."

Looking from Douglas to the baby and back again, a symphony of emotions collided somewhere in her chest that created an echo of longing below her naval.

"Take her, please," she whispered. "Take her and sit on the bed so I can draw."

"The look in your eyes says you want to do more than draw." He cradled Georgiana to his chest, her tiny head resting near his shoulder and her body scrunched beneath the cover.

Magdalene retrieved her sketchbook and pencil from her bag on the dresser. "I've had a certain image burned into my mind that's become a bit of an obsession to me since you spoke it."

"Interesting, because I now have a vision that I yearn to see fulfilled since I saw you holding this baby."

"I suppose we'll both have to wait." Magdalene pulled the chair a few feet away from the bed and turned to a clean page.

Her hand moved across the page with soft strokes of the lead, working the outlining shapes as she looked from Douglas to the page.

"Am I holding her right?" he asked.

Magdalene nodded, smiling to herself because he thought she drew Georgiana. A few minutes later, she was pleased with the sketch, right down to the questioning arch of his left brow. It wasn't as fine as Eliza's work, but she'd managed to capture her husband in a way she would always be happy to look upon. She sat beside him and held it for him to see.

"It looks nothing like Georgiana. I thought you had more skill than that."

"Douglas!" She gave him a hard look and snatched it from view.

He laughed softly, rocking the baby to keep her asleep. "Let me see it again now that the subject matter won't be a shock."

"I had to capture my heart on paper first." She held the book open for him.

"Not a bad looking bloke you got there, Maggie. But does my eyebrow really do that?"

She clutched the sketchbook to her chest. "Lord help me, it does, and gets me every time."

Magdalene sat back in her chair and drew Georgiana. She couldn't bring herself to draw her husband holding someone's illegitimate baby, so she focused on a close-up of the tiny fist beside her sleeping face. She took more time with it than she had with her portrait of Douglas, working the shading in by smudging her finger across the page to blend some of the lines—all while trying to ignore his exaggerated facial expressions as he attempted to make her laugh.

The picture was nearly finished when Claudio came up the ladder. "Are you both decent and finished playing *mamma e papà?*"

Magdalene snapped her book shut and turned to him. "Don't be crass, Claudio. I behaved myself respectfully in front of our little guest, though I was played at by my husband, first by his touch and then by his attempts at a smoldering gaze."

Claudio motioned to the book. "You are working?"

"Practicing. It's been a while, but I'm satisfied with my efforts today."

"*Buona!* Lydia is anxious to see her baby. She has never been without her and now that she has confessed to all, she needs the comfort of her child."

Douglas immediately went for the ladder, Georgiana tucked in his good arm. Magdalene placed her book on the dresser and looked at her smudged hands.

"I need to wash and see to dinner." When she turned to leave, she almost stepped on Claudio's foot. "Sorry."

His hands went to her shoulders. One rose to touch the pencil behind her ear. "Eliza often wore hers there."

As he lowered his hand, his fingertips trailed the side of her face, causing Magdalene's breath to catch in a small gasp. The tenderness he had with Eliza and the ache of spending time with the one responsible for her death must have cost him dearly.

But comfort like he appeared to need wasn't within her means to give. "Claudio, please let me pass."

"Of course." He clasped his hands behind his back and stepped to the side.

Magdalene continued to the ladder with an upward glance at Claudio, who stared at her like she was his answer to everything. When she stepped out of the bathroom after seeing to her hands, Douglas took her by the elbow and pulled her back into the room, closing the door behind them.

"And now for a moment of privacy with my wife." He hands roamed as he kissed her, but Magdalene didn't reciprocate. "What is it? Are you upset because I distracted you while you drew?"

"No." She kissed his cheek and squeezed his hand. "It's Claudio. He's not right. I think Lydia's burden was too much for him, coupled with spending the time in Seacliff Cottage. Priest or not, he's still human. Either experience could affect him, but coupled into the same hour…I fear for him."

"Did he say something to you after I left?"

She nodded. "But don't be mad at him. He touched the pencil behind my ear and said Eliza wore hers there."

"That's nothing but a memory," Douglas said.

"But then he caressed my cheek and the way he looked at me nearly broke my heart."

"Your heart belongs to me, Maggie. No other man should be able to break it." He kissed her lips gently and raised a hand to her face, finding the moisture of fresh tears. "What's going on?"

"I'm scared, but dinner won't fix itself. I need to figure out what to feed this group."

Douglas took her hand. "I'll help you."

"No, stay with the others. Keep an eye on Claudio as well as Lydia—I don't trust her."

***

The rain poured, along with the addition of an increased wind, as they ate. Uncle Simon declared it the outer bands of a hurricane and retired for a nap.

"I'm sorry, but I can't drive out in that to get either of you home," Douglas informed Lydia and Claudio. "Stay here for the night."

Lydia pulled her suckling child closer as she rocked. "I'll go to the barn so we won't be a bother."

"No," Douglas told her, "it wouldn't be safe."

Magdalene paced the room, her bare feet crossing the worn wood as the minutes ticked by. Claudio and Douglas played a game of chess at the kitchen table and Lydia dozed in the rocker holding Georgiana. Afraid the baby would fall out of her arms, Magdalene eased the infant from her mother's hold and snuggled her to her own chest.

While Douglas studied the game board, Claudio watched Magdalene walk the room with Georgiana. Conscious of his gaze, Magdalene smiled at him but immediately regretted doing so when she saw a gleam of yearning behind his returned smile. It was followed by a slew of Italian that sounded uncomfortably like a soulful confession.

"Your turn." Douglas nudged Claudio's arm to get his attention.

"My pardons. Magdalene is captivating with an infant, no? I could not help but watch."

"Aye, I look forward to seeing her mother our children." Douglas caught her eye and winked.

Just then, Lydia jumped up. "Georgiana!" Upon seeing Magdalene with the baby, she crossed the room to collect her. "Mags, I was so scared I dropped her. I must never hurt the dear."

"Lydia," Douglas spoke as she returned to the chair, "has Georgiana been baptized?"

She shook her head. "No, and it worries me. Sometimes I think we won't survive another day and I worry over her salvation."

Douglas nodded at Claudio.

"I have my supplies with me," Claudio said as he approached her. "I have holy water and would be happy to baptize the child."

"Here? By you?" Her tone was aghast.

"I am a servant of the Lord no matter my faults."

For every second Lydia did not speak, Magdalene's fists clenched tighter.

Douglas wrapped his arms around her shoulders from behind and whispered in her ear, "Maggie, it's not for you to decide. Not for you to judge."

Magdalene turned, buried her face in his neck, and pushed against him until he struck the stove. "How dare she refuse to deem Claudio worthy of blessing her illegitimate child!"

"It's not our burden. We can only afford her the opportunity to do right for the baby."

"But if she doesn't accept now, there might not be another chance."

Douglas nudged her until she was in the far corner of the kitchen. "Georgiana is her child, not yours. The sin is upon her if she does not see to the babe's welfare."

"But she doesn't—"

"Let it go," he said into the soft spot below her left ear. "Turn that anger to passion and take it out on me."

Her fists pummeled his chest before she slumped against his chest and let him hug her. Claudio found them in the corner of the kitchen, wrapped in each other's arms.

"She has agreed to the baptism and wishes to name you both godparents."

"But I'm not even Catholic." Magdalene sounded exasperated.

Claudio held his hands out to her and she reluctantly left Douglas's arms. "You are the only woman besides her for a mile. And if what Douglas fears is true, this might be the only chance the baby has. It is what we have to work with. God will provide the rest when we do our part, *sí*?"

Magdalene nodded.

"Then do your part. We need you, Magdalene."

She ripped her hand free and crossed her arms, turning away from Claudio and the tone that escaped him—sounding much too similar to Alexander for her comfort.

Douglas climbed the ladder and returned to the kitchen with the black mantilla Claudio had gifted Magdalene, placing it on her head with a smile.

"Is this necessary since we aren't in church?"

"No, but it makes you look Catholic." He kissed her cheek and pulled her into the front room.

She smiled despite her reluctance, thankful for her husband's humor to lighten the situation. Douglas opened the door to his uncle's room so he could listen to the baptismal sacrament as it was administered to Georgiana. Much to Lydia's dislike, Claudio officiated in Italian. She fretted over not knowing what he said, but he assured her she would understand if she listened with the spirit. Claudio looked more at peace than ever. His face unworried, his dark eyes bright with the joy that often shone from him when about the Lord's work. If he could stay actively engaged with the priesthood, Magdalene was sure he would have a joyful life, despite his heartaches.

As soon as the group said Amen, a thundering crash shook the house. Douglas ran to the front door and then to his uncle's bedroom to look out the back window.

"An oak went down in the woods! Its top branches are scraping the side of the house. I think we all better stay in the front room, away from the tree line, from now on. We can pull Uncle Simon's mattress in here for him and bring blankets from the loft when we need to."

Magdalene returned to pacing while the others settled near the unlit hearth, fussing over Uncle Simon and the baby. On her third pass by the door, she startled at seeing a dark-clad person on the front stoop. Not believing her eyes, she placed a hand on the screen and leaned toward the mesh for a better look. The pale hand of the outsider touched against hers, the tiny grid acting as a conductor to the electricity between them.

"Playing confession with the priest, are we?" Alexander asked, pointing to her head. "I bet he likes that."

Magdalene took her hand from the door and stuffed the mantilla into her pocket.

"In case you haven't noticed, there's a hurricane out here. Would you let me in?"

When she swung the screen open, all eyes turned toward her. As soon as the figure in a black trench coat and derby stepped into the room, Douglas crossed the space to take his wife by the hand.

"Talk about inviting the devil in, Maggie," he whispered fiercely. "He's worse for our sanity than Lydia and you know it."

"It looks like I interrupted a party of some sort. I heard the tree go down and more will likely follow. I came to invite you to ride out the storm in Seacliff Cottage with me. It'll be safer for you away from the forest." Alexander's eyes fell to Lydia in the rocking chair and hardened. "What's she doing here?"

"Hello, Alex—uh, Master Melling. I came looking for your father but was informed he's back in the city. The weather caught me unaware so I'm stranded for the time being." The baby began to fuss, causing Alexander's gaze to fall upon the infant. "I don't mean no trouble, I just wanted to give George the chance to do right."

"Like hell he owes you anything! You've been nothing but trouble since he hired you. You drove my poor mother to distraction. She wasn't the same after you came. Even Eliza was put off by you."

At the mention of Eliza, Lydia began to sob. "I didn't mean it. I didn't mean any of it."

Douglas swooped in and took Georgiana from Lydia. He brought her to Magdalene and positioned himself between her and Alexander.

Alexander turned to Magdalene. "And what's this child to you? Why does your husband protect it so?"

Douglas squared his shoulders. "We've been appointed godparents, if it's any of your concern."

He leered at Claudio. "Now that's rich! Is that why you came today, priest? To play havoc with my family's affairs. I assume she claims my father as the man responsible, as though she could prove it. She was at the hotel meeting who knows how many men as she saw to their chambers."

Lydia cried louder.

Claudio came to Alexander's side. "Look at the baby, Alexander."

Douglas barred the way to Magdalene, but Claudio waved him down and stepped forward with Alexander. Magdalene, holding her breath, pulled the shirt away from Georgiana's face. The movement stirred the baby and she opened her eyes, the color of blue hydrangeas.

"Dear God, she looks like Eliza," he gasped. "I remember the first time Mother placed her in my arms and told me to always protect her. I failed, like so many other relationships in my life."

He turned to the door, hands clasped behind his back as he stared through the driving rain at Seacliff Cottage.

"Here is a chance to redeem yourself," Claudio said. "Does the offer to shelter this house still stand, including everyone within these walls at the moment?"

Alexander removed his dripping hat and ran a hand over his hair to smooth it before turning around. "Yes. The lot of you can come, but I suggest us going in small groups so we can help those in need. I'll bring Magdalene with me first."

"Do you think me daft?" Douglas spat the words and clenched his fist. "We'll bring Lydia and Georgiana first."

"Georgiana?" Alexander looked repulsed by the name. "Mother will have a fit if she ever finds out."

Barefoot, Douglas rolled up his pants to his knees and Magdalene helped him button Georgiana into his driving coat, the long duster falling past his cuffed pants. Claudio helped Lydia into her cloak and the three men saw the first group to the door while Magdalene readied Uncle Simon in several outer layers of clothes and his old boots.

Douglas soon returned.

"Shall we all dash across together?" Claudio asked.

"No." Douglas gripped his arm. "I'm going to need to get Uncle Simon dry and settled and I don't want Maggie over there without me beside her. Nor do I wish her here alone. Stay with her until I come back."

"Of course, *amico*."

Douglas angled toward him. "You understand she's all that's precious to me in this life. Swear to me you'll protect her."

"I swear, before God and his host of angels, that I will watch over her."

But Claudio's oath didn't sit well with Magdalene. She paced the room when Douglas and Uncle Simon left, a wary eye on the priest.

After several minutes of both of them pacing like caged animals, she spoke. "Claudio, you didn't swear to protect me, only to watch over me. What can your eyes do if there is evil approaching?"

"You are clever, Magdalene. I could not promise to protect you because I myself may be a threat."

"So if Alexander walked in, you would watch as he tried to sway me?"

"I might be obliged to chase him off from what I myself want." He stepped closer, loosening his clerical collar. "Hearing Lydia confess has been an eye-opening experience. I feel the weight of Eliza's death no more because I forgave who was responsible. I now know it was not punishment from God, but a new opportunity for me. While my passion with Eliza was great, I was never at peace with her because of the anguish over my sin. But with you, Magdalene, I am never happier than when I am around you. *Posseduta* or not, you bring me joy." He reached for her hand but she slapped his away.

"You're mad, Claudio! It would be just as much sin—more so because I'm married and you have your holy orders. You're not thinking straight."

He circled around her, his words soft. "You have told me before that if Douglas abandoned you, I would be all you had left. You cannot tell me you do not care for me."

"No, because I do! You've been a great friend. And yes, I enjoy your company as well, but not in the way you imply."

"I have seen the way you often look upon me, like you are trying to see the lines Eliza drew beneath my clothes. I will let you see, let you feel for yourself if you wish."

The terrifying knowledge overpowered her of what she would be confronted with when she walked in the doors of Seacliff Cottage. If Claudio could be so affected after an hour within the walls that morning, how much more temptation and evil would lurk when she was trapped with a fallen woman, her illegitimate godchild, and two men who had tried to seduce her? Magdalene would rather take her chances in the forest with a hurricane.

Twenty-Four

Magdalene ran out the door and straight into Douglas on the front step.

He took her by the arm. "You aren't going without your coat, Maggie. The sky's darkening further though it still isn't nightfall. We need to move fast."

She nearly tripped on Claudio's black leather bag when she reached inside for her duster. Looking up at him, she pointed to it. "Don't forget your bag, Claudio."

The coldness in his eyes chilled her as he hoisted the bag like it weighed a hundred pounds. She did not know if was he capable of touching the holy tools, but she would keep the bag close for her own use if needed.

"Douglas, take the bag for him. He struggles."

He easily tucked it under his arm. "Come on, we need to hurry!" He saw Claudio out and running, then pulled the main door shut behind Magdalene when she exited.

She clung to his wet coat and shouted over the storm. "Please don't leave me with anyone! Stay with me always!"

"Come on, we'll talk inside!" With her hand in his, he dashed into the stinging rain.

Her tears of fright mingled with the droplets on her face. By the time they reached the kitchen porch, no one could tell she'd been crying.

She squeezed past Douglas through the door and he slung the bag atop the kitchen counter.

Going immediately for the clasp, Claudio stopped her. "There will be time for that later. Let us dry first." He pulled off his wet cassock. The shirt beneath clung to his torso in damp patches.

Magdalene turned away and began unfastening her long coat.

"Maggie, did you not hold your skirt when you ran?" Douglas asked.

She shook her head. "I forgot."

"You can't sit around in that. We'll have to go fetch something from the attic for you to wear."

"I vote for the blue gown," Alexander said as he strolled into the kitchen. "I don't think Claudio had the privilege of seeing that one."

"Now look here," Douglas shouted as he pointed at their host, "I'll stand for none of this! We appreciate your hospitality, but if you're going to try intimidating us the whole time, Maggie and I will go back to the carriage house."

"Yes, please, Douglas, let's go back home!" She took his hand and tugged toward the door.

Alexander put his hands in the air. "No, stay. Magdalene is free to wear anything she'd like. Any of you needing dry clothes are. Go, get comfortable. I'll bring tea into the parlor."

"Are you capable?" Magdalene couldn't help asking.

Alexander shrugged. "Claudio will help me."

Douglas placed Magdalene's coat over the back of one of the kitchen chairs before leading her up the back stairs. "Do you want to choose from your old things?" he asked.

"Yes, I'm not rifling through Mrs. Melling's wardrobe or anyone else's."

"One of the fancy dresses you despised?"

"As long as it covers me, I'll take any of them." She stepped into the upstairs hallway.

"Let me check in on Uncle Simon. He's in the little guest room, though upstairs in a storm isn't ideal. There's only one small window and I pushed the bed against the interior wall."

"Where's Lydia, then?"

"In the den with Georgiana. She said they'd sleep on the couch in there."

"I suppose she's used to the stench of it."

Magdalene locked herself in the bathroom and took her time washing up and towel drying her hair. When she finished, Douglas looked relieved. "I was about to break down the door. Is there no brush?"

Magdalene laughed as he pulled her into his arms. "No."

"Then I suppose it won't matter if we muss it even more." He ran up the attic stairs, pulling her along. Once they were in, he locked the door and began taking off his shirt.

"Douglas, now?"

"It might be our only chance without being obvious. I don't like the idea of Alexander being privy to our bedroom practices." He started unbuttoning her dress. "Besides, you need out of these wet clothes and that puts us halfway there. See, even your underclothes are wet. They must come off."

Magdalene was right there with him for all the sensations as the wind and rain beat upon the roof. Afterward, he held her in his arms for a few minutes, and then he went to the wardrobe in search of clothing. He removed a pink tea dress.

"Nothing white or pastel. If I get out in the rain—"

"Good point, but that doesn't leave many options. You might be stuck with the Parisian—"

"That's not even funny." She went to pass in front of him, but he caught her around the middle and they found themselves on a pile of cushions. "Let's just stay."

"I wish we could, but if the roof gets damaged, we don't want to be up here. Plus, we have Uncle Simon to watch. That's why I wanted to get our time in now." He trailed his hand over her.

She fingered around the bandage on his arm before pulling him to her, kissing him as they slipped off the pillows. "Just a little longer and my clothes might be dry."

He kissed her once more and pulled her up. "That dress needs a good scrubbing to remove the mud before you wear it. So it looks like it has to be the blue one or this black gown you wore for the mausoleum's dedication."

Having worn the gown twice, she knew the black lace overlay on top would provide coverage for her should she need to escape into the rain. "Bring it to me."

"No, not yet." Douglas went to the drawers and found where she'd stashed the Parisian lingerie.

"Are you expecting to get me undressed again later?" she teased.

"It's always good to be prepared. Here, let me help you fasten the back."

While Douglas clothed himself, she checked her reflection in the mirror. To her surprise, the new shapewear brought the gown fresh lines at the waist and bust. The flush of arousal glowed upon her skin and her lips were red from use. Her appearance coupled with the time they'd been gone would be all the clues the others would need to know what they'd been doing.

While Douglas checked on Uncle Simon, Magdalene hung her clothes in the bathroom. The lace mantilla fell out of the pocket of her dress and she hastily tucked it into the small pocket in the gown before braiding her hair. Then they went down the backstairs to the empty kitchen. Claudio's bag sat on the counter and Magdalene stopped in hopes of retrieving a talisman, but Douglas urged her out the door. She realized she'd neglected to tell him what Claudio had said when alone with her. Angry at herself for allowing the passion with Douglas to rule their time together, she knew she would regret not explaining things to him at some point.

"And the lovebirds finally see fit to join us, and you dressed for our hurricane party, Magdalene." Alexander sat most ungentlemanly in his father's wingback chair, legs sprawled before him and a modest fire in the hearth. "I'd offer you to sit by the fire but it appears you may have already had things hot enough today."

Douglas cracked his knuckles and stared at their host.

Claudio rose from the settee. "Why don't you warm more water and I'll see to Magdalene, *amico*."

No! Magdalene screamed in her head.

With a glare at Alexander, Douglas picked up the teapot and left the room. Claudio took Magdalene tenderly by the hand and brought her to the settee.

"Are you well?" he asked.

"Yes, thank you." She crossed her ankles and clasped her hands in her lap to keep still.

"I'm pouring drinks for all." Alexander stopped before her. "Would you like some wine or brandy?"

She met his gaze. "Scotch, please. That's the only thing I have a taste for anymore."

His laugh, deep and freeing, caused Magdalene to giggle. Only Claudio looked put off by her play on words.

Alexander leaned over Magdalene, his wide blue eyes pricking her nerves. "And did you have your Scot in my bed again?"

Claudio pushed him away. "Leave her be. Her married life is no concern to you."

"It is when she brings it into my bedroom." Claudio looked between Alexander and Magdalene, and then Alexander continued. "Did she not tell you? While I was in the city the other day, she and Douglas had their way with each other in my bed. Tell me, Claudio, is that not a cry for help? The action of one so unfulfilled with her lot in life that she must send a message to the man she truly wants?"

"Can this be, Magdalene?" Claudio asked.

"No! It's the demonic influence, you know it is! Both of you are being ridiculous."

"I think it's your influence, Magdalene." Alexander slipped onto the settee next to her, took her hand from her lap, and pressed it to his own knee. "I have been a gentleman within these walls. Never did I seek a conquest here because it was the sacred home of my memories with my first and last love affair. That all changed when you arrived."

"Oh, I'm sure you were an angel of a man before you met me." She sneered and jerked her hand free.

"She did call me an angel."

"Then it must be for your fair complexion, because it's certainly not for your kind ways."

"You wound me, Magdalene." He reached for her but she jumped into action before he could touch her. He raised his hand in triumph and turned to Claudio. "And so it begins! Our liaisons always start with her prowling the room like the tigress she is."

"Do not get excited, Alexander. She does that with everyone."

"So you've seen her at work?"

Claudio smiled. "Many times. And each one is a pleasure."

Alexander laughed. "Oh, this will be fun! I'm glad to have my friend back."

Magdalene pointed at the priest. "That is not Claudio!"

Claudio met her before the fire, tendrils of heat rising from either the hearth or his body, Magdalene could not be sure. "This, Magdalene, is the natural man who has always been inside me." His arms went around her waist, tugging her against him. "As the storm rages without, my desires fight to escape."

"Don't let her speak!" Alexander coached him. "She'll recite words that you don't wish to hear."

"Will you allow the demon take you today, *posseduta*? Just for an hour? Ten minutes?" His mouth moved steadily closer to hers until she had no choice but to be kissed or become violent.

"No! You would never forgive yourself, Father De Fiore! In the name of Je—"

Alexander lunged at her before she could finish, but she'd said enough to cause Claudio pause. Douglas came in with the teapot in time to see the two men grappling over Magdalene. The teapot barely stayed upright as he dropped it onto the table on his way to the fireplace. He flung Alexander out of the way and took her from Claudio. Douglas led Magdalene to the settee, where he immediately fixed her tea while ignoring the others.

Afraid to speak, Magdalene wondered if Douglas could tell Claudio had her in his grip and it was Alexander trying to snatch her away rather than the other way around. She waited to see if Alexander would brag over his fallen friend but he merely passed her with a smile on the way to the decanters while Claudio collapsed into Mrs. Melling's chair, his hands over his face.

"Tea, Claudio?" Douglas asked after Magdalene had her cup.

"No, thank you." He kept his head down.

"My friend doesn't need tea, he needs brandy!" Alexander delivered a tumbler to Claudio.

To Magdalene's surprise, he started on it straight away.

"You're next, Magdalene."

"Excuse me?" Douglas asked.

"Her drink, of course." Alexander laughed. "She placed an order while you were out, but with the rousing conversation it was momentarily forgotten."

Douglas looked at his wife, his eyebrow arched. "Are you okay?" he whispered.

She nodded, and then Alexander stood before her with a full tumbler. "Here's your Scotch. What was it you said when you asked for it? It was the only thing you had a taste for?"

"That's exactly right." She placed her teacup on the coffee table and accepted the glass from Alexander, not flinching under his fingering touch as the drink exchanged hands. Right under his nose, she placed her free hand on her husband's thigh and squeezed his muscled leg.

"Here, Maggie, lets show him how you like your Scotch." Douglas smirked as he took the glass from her and drank. After setting the half-empty tumbler on the table, he fell upon her lips, nudging her until she pressed against the backrest and he was in her lap, their bodies heaving together as the kiss deepened.

"Enough!" Claudio roared. "You mock your relationship with this public display! You of all people should realize you are not showcasing your love, but showing that Magdalene is nothing but a prize to be flaunted in front of others to provoke their own lust. Shame on you for inviting sin into the hearts of others!"

Dismayed, Douglas lowered his head and reached for Magdalene's hand. "I'm sorry," he muttered. Then he poured himself a cup of tea while Alexander laughed.

Claudio continued looking upon Magdalene. Not knowing what to do under his oppressive gaze, Magdalene took hold of the tumbler and drained the rest of the drink. Douglas gave her a sideways glance and hung his head once more. After a few sips of the tea, he put down the cup, leaned back in his seat, and draped an arm over his eyes.

He sighed. "God forgive me."

"I forgive you for causing me to have impure thoughts about your wife."

"Bugger off, Alexander."

He laughed and sat back in his father's chair to watch the next round unfold as Claudio approached Magdalene with outstretched hands.

"Come, let me get my bag and we will rid this house of all evil."

Claudio's voice, calm and secure, made Magdalene remember the righteous way he'd called out Douglas's wrongdoing. She trusted her friend was back to normal. With her hand on his arm, Claudio led her into the dining room.

"Let us begin here, *posseduta*." He stood before her, head tilted to the side as he studied her form.

She looked around. "But your bag is in the kitchen."

"*Sí*, but we are alone together. There is no evil here." He touched her cheek like he had earlier in the day. This time, it caused her to shiver.

Magdalene looked into his brown eyes and saw the passion she admired in him. Tentatively, she raised a hand toward his face.

"It is good to touch." His finger traced her lips, and when she still did not move the final inches to make contact, he leaned his cheek into her palm. "See, I am flesh and bone. These lines are real."

She brought her other hand to his olive face and felt his square jaw, strong brow, and Romanesque nose. "Your angles all complement each other."

"I believe they would complement you as well. My exquisite lines and your smooth curves are a perfect match." He trailed his hands down from her shoulders, focusing on the bare skin of her forearms, which he caressed with his fingertips. "We could do much good together."

A breeze churned through the room. Magdalene, afraid the window had blown open in the storm, looked around her and noticed the empty nail above the door.

"Where have the religious relics gone?"

"Alexander wished to safeguard them during the storm. They are tucked away. It is smart thinking on his behalf." His hand went to her neck, playing about her collar bones and the base of her scalp under her braid as his soothing words continued. "Magdalene, you can touch me. My vestments are gone. I am just a man."

"And I'm a woman." She put her shoulders back and circled the room to the far side of the dining set. She sat on the corner of the polished table and propped a foot on the armrest of the nearest chair. "Come to me, Claudio."

Twenty-Five

"What are you doing peeping in like that?" Lydia's shrill voice rang out from the hall.

There was a *shushing* followed by a scuffle and the dining room door swung open. Magdalene turned from her seat on the table and blinked at the sight of Lydia and Alexander.

Lydia ran off hollering. "Mr. Douglas! Mr. Douglas, come quick! The deacon's gone rogue again!"

"Blast that stupid wench!" Alexander stalked away, the door swinging shut behind him.

Magdalene turned back to Claudio, who had frozen at the interruption, hand on her knee under her skirt. His other hand at her neck—he had been about to go in for a kiss—and his body pressed against the sweep of the gown between her legs.

"What have I done?" His voice grew louder with each word until he screamed the last one. His hands released her and reached for his crucifix, but it wasn't around his neck. He went into his pocket but came out empty handed. "What did I do? I planned this, but when? How long have I been plagued?"

Magdalene stood and reached out to him. "It wasn't you."

Douglas stormed into the room. "That's quite enough!"

Claudio fell prostrate to the floor, muttering in his native tongue and seeming to plead in prayer. Magdalene bent to kneel down with him.

"Don't touch him, Maggie! What did he do to you? What did you do to him?" The pain and anger on his face was gut-wrenching to look upon.

"Nothing! Just a few touches, like I told you he'd brushed my cheek earlier."

Alexander came in the door. "It didn't look like nothing from this angle. It looked like they were ready to do all manner of fornication."

"And what does that make you, being one willing to watch such things?" Lydia entered the room. "I saw them after Alex tried to push me way. I don't know what he was doing on the other side of Mags's dress, but I always knew he was evil. I didn't want him blessing my baby."

Magdalene, bright red and shaking with indignation, came at the maid. "He's not evil! He was oppressed by whatever diabolic influence is housed within these walls, just as I'm sure all of us in this room have been at some time or another. It's not his fault and he did nothing more than touch my knee. Stop tormenting him! We didn't even kiss."

"Given another few seconds of privacy you would have." Alexander hooted. "He had everything set up from head to toe and things would have gone quickly if that wench hadn't interrupted."

Douglas turned to the young woman. "Thank you, Lydia."

"You *thank* her?" Magdalene turned her wrath on her husband. "This whole situation wouldn't be happening if it wasn't for her! She's the one who started the adultery in the house. She's the one who murdered Eliza. And she's the one who had to come crawling back here for a handout!"

"She killed my sister?" Alexander dropped into a dining chair by the sideboard and looked to Magdalene. "She killed my sister?"

"Yes," she hissed. "By her evil plotting and lust-driven ideas."

Lydia ran from the room.

"I want you out of this house!" Alexander roared.

"I told you to hold your tongue," Douglas said. "She's burdened enough."

"You want to protect her and nurture her child, but she makes me sick, as do you and your self-righteous chatter of forgiveness and waiting for marriage! If you had taken me when I first asked you to, we wouldn't still be stuck in this house!"

Douglas was open-mouthed and staring while Claudio withered on the floor in pain. Magdalene dropped beside him and took his hand.

"I'm here, Claudio. What do you need?"

He answered weakly in Italian and Magdalene looked up at Douglas. "Fetch his bag from the kitchen. We need the crucifixes and everything else to help him."

As soon as Douglas ran out, Alexander came closer to Magdalene. "Did you really offer yourself to that fool and he turned you down?"

"Now's not the time"

"But it is, Magdalene. Tonight's the perfect time for fireside stories, and I get the feeling yours are burning."

"You have no idea. Leave me!"

Alexander slunk to the corner and then out the door as Douglas ran back in. "The bag isn't in the kitchen."

"I can't think straight. I can't form the words." She grabbed Douglas's bandaged arm and pulled him to the floor, ignoring the blood that began seeping through the wrap. "Pray for him. You have the power of deliverance. Save him from himself and I'll search for the bag."

"Don't leave this room, Maggie." He stood to follow.

"Save him! I won't forgive you if you let him suffer in madness, especially after succoring Lydia. If you deny our friend, you deny me."

Douglas turned to Claudio and did the sign of the cross over him and began with, "Hail, Mary."

Magdalene, having a glint of an idea who moved the bag, ran to the front stairs. She stumbled into Alexander's bedroom, eyes searching the space for Claudio's bag.

"And the prodigal lover returns." Alexander, lounging on his bed, opened his arms to her.

"Where did you hide it?"

"Hide? I hide nothing here. This is a room that holds no secrets. It is a space to bare all, not shroud in darkness." Alexander moved to the edge of the bed, one arm still out in welcome. "But if that's your excuse for coming to me, by all means, search my bed for what you seek. You'll find no complaints from me."

"There's no time for games. I know the pain of awakening from the oppression of this demon. I know what horrors it can make you do to yourself to try to quiet the pain. I've felt it as I tried to jump from a window and plunge a knife into my breast. I've seen it in you, as you clawed at your skin to be free of the influence." She stood before him and placed a hand on his chest. "Do you not remember the agony of that night?"

"Yes." His hands went to unbutton his shirt, and she stepped back. "Every time I feel or see them, I think of you. Now tell me, how am I to explain this to Beatrice on our wedding night?"

He stood and opened his shirt, revealing a cluster of scars across his upper chest, his pale skin puckered and pink on his otherwise flawless torso. Magdalene gasped as the distress of sympathy swelled within her. She reached out, though she didn't wish to feel them. Alexander grabbed her wrist and pressed it to his tarnished chest, dragging her fingers across the angry lines.

"Do I tell her these are the marks from the one that got away? Or that there's a scar for every sin I've committed? What if it's from madness? I'm sure she'll be disgusted in any of those cases."

"I had no idea you still carried pain." Fresh tears rolled down her cheeks.

He laughed. "You probably don't think me capable, do you? Cold, hard Alexander Melling isn't capable of pain and suffering. You think I only wanted to take, not give. But let me tell you, Magdalene, I only wanted to give you pleasure." His voice and eyes turned soft, and he touched her lips with his fingertips. "I wanted to teach you what it is to love and crave another person, but you kept shutting me out when we grew close to total commitment."

"I'm sorry, Alexander."

"I couldn't please you. I wasn't good enough for you. I wasn't the right man to satisfy your needs. You left me broken and bleeding, just as I did to my Lucy." His eyes were sharp with the rawness of his lamentations.

Moved by his words and emotions, Magdalene wrapped her arms about his neck. "You did show me pleasure, Alexander. You taught me how to show affection and receive it. You helped me understand my desires and taught me how to act on them."

"And yet the man you chose to give what is most precious turned you down when you offered yourself to him. How ironic." His arms went around her waist. "Can we put each other out of our misery and see what it is we could have had so we don't keep dreaming about it?"

She hesitated in replying, giving Alexander the opening he needed. He snaked his hands up from her waist to her ribcage with a movement that stirred her body to response, but her mind wasn't ready. She stared into his luminous eyes and parted her lips in anticipation, until she remembered of the portrait of Eliza in the hall. And Georgiana. The Melling gaze.

She dropped her hold on him and sidestepped out of his arms.

"I need the bag, Alexander."

"And I need you." He took her wrist. "I can't let the priest get more action with you than I do."

"Do you want to end up like Claudio, on the floor in aguish?"

"I've been there before, Magdalene. Remember?" He pointed to his chest. "I remember it every day. You owe me something for the pain you caused me."

She broke free from his grip and circled toward the open door. "The bag."

"A kiss."

Magdalene froze, weighing the option of getting Claudio help verses immorality.

"The bag for a kiss, Magdalene. Surely you care for him enough to part with one kiss. After all, you were willing to give one to him minutes ago. How close do you think he is to clawing himself to shreds right now? What healing salve could your heavenly body impart to him by bearing the bag of holy objects?"

How long had she been inside Seacliff Cottage? The dark, unyielding skies told nothing of the hour and Alexander had no clock in his chamber. The sanctuary of his room was complete in its unadorned state, the focal point of the room his massive bed. She had lain there with her husband and now the master wanted a moment of her time to save her friend.

"Now it's a kiss and a touch. Wait any longer, Magdalene, and you'll have to give more."

"I must have the bag." It was already an afternoon of debauchery, so she stood before him, eyes closed.

"You'll have to do better than that, Magdalene. I want *you* to kiss *me*. And don't forget the touch."

"I—I don't think—"

"I'll start it for you." He hooked a hand behind her head and brought their lips together, the other hand on her neck, stroking her skin. Pulling a few inches from her face, he smiled. "Your turn, for the bag."

Not thinking, she plunged in, her desperation to help Claudio manifest in her display. She had Alexander against the hard paneling, practically gnawing off his lips in an attempt to appease his demands while a hand ran over his scars to remind herself who he was.

She broke away, breathless, but he tackled her to the bed. Pushing him off her, she struggled to keep an arm free from his appendages and gain her footing on the floor. "The bag! You promised the bag!"

"I changed my mind." He straddled her chest, pinning both hands above her head. "Haven't we been here before? Maybe it was in a dream."

She broke into a cold sweat, the urge to flee overpowering her will to fight. Deciding on screaming or not, she took a deep breath.

"No, you don't. Women always have a handkerchief or something handy." He slid down her, feeling for pockets. From the little one at her hip he retrieved the black mantilla. With a laugh, he shoved it into her mouth. "A dear gift from the priest put to good use. If you behave, I'll take it out so we can do other things with that mouth of yours."

"At least your father was polite enough to shut his door," Lydia said from the doorway. Magdalene had never been so glad to hear her voice. "I think you better help the lady up, Alex. Your mother would be most distressed to find out about this, and probably your fiancée, too."

He turned to her. "You wouldn't dare!"

"What do I have to lose? My job's long gone, along with my reputation. What's one more scandalous story to tell on my visit to Government Street?"

"Why you little—" He sprung for Lydia.

"My silence has a price," she spoke hastily.

Magdalene sat up and yanked the lace from her mouth, warily watching the exchange between Lydia and Alexander as the two people she distrusted most bartered over her situation.

He scoffed. "I should have known. Didn't I tell you not to trust this one, Magdalene? She's willing to sell your virtue for her own profit. How much, Lydia?"

"Twenty-five dollars a month, payable in cash on the first of the month. And Mags walks out of here with me. I'm not such a heartless creature. She did try to protect my virtue once."

Alexander snatched a pillow off the bed and threw it at Lydia. "And you're out of here as soon as the weather clears, never to approach another member of my family, nor claim that bastard child a Melling, nor speak of your relationship to the family or anything that transpired within these walls to a living soul as long as you live!"

"That'll cost a fiver right now to hold me over until the first." She held out her hand for the money, knowing Alexander would have to pay. "And if my payment's a day late, I'm on the next ferry to Mobile for a conference with the Melling ladies."

He cursed and raged while he dug through a dresser drawer. Magdalene, smoothing her gown, made her way to Lydia's side,

<hr>

hoping to absorb some of her bravado. When Alexander handed over the money, she spoke up.

"The bag, Alexander."

"I'm not letting you walk in there with it." Alexander shoved past the women and buttoned his shirt. He stomped down the hall to the backstairs where he scooped the bag off the bottom step of the kitchen stairwell and continued through the room.

Magdalene, who'd followed him to the stairs, turned back to Lydia. "Thank you for coming when you did, and for what you did for me."

"I knew you meant well that day and now we're even. I was sent to check on Mr. Campbell, so excuse me. You needn't trouble yourself with me again." Lydia went in the guest room.

Overwhelmed with questions, Magdalene rushed downstairs to try to salvage her standing with Douglas, knowing demonic anger could be just as harmful as tempting lust.

Twenty-Six

Magdalene stumbled into the parlor. Alexander sprawled in his father's seat like he'd been when she first arrived and Douglas, cradling Georgiana to his chest, was on the settee next to Claudio. The priest clutched his bag in his lap but all eyes were upon her, though no one spoke. She passed behind the men, pausing to place a comforting hand on Claudio's shoulder.

He flinched away. "Do not be familiar with me, Mrs. Campbell. I am not yet right with my Father."

She sucked in her breath and clasped her hands together as she continued to the far side of the settee, taking a seat in the armchair beside Douglas. Their knees almost bumped, but he leaned away from her as he shifted the baby to his blood-stained, bandaged arm.

"Do you need a respite? I can take her for you." She spoke softly, a hint of a pleasing smile upon her lips.

"No need to concern yourself with what offends you, Maggie." The arch of his brow was harsh. "Alexander found the bag you were looking for. Did you enlist his aide in your search? Perhaps he found in you what he was seeking."

"The bag"—Magdalene turned white as Alexander spoke— "for a kiss and a touch." The last word oozed off his tongue and into the room with sickening clarity.

Magdalene jumped out of her seat and paced the length of the room. "I did it to free Claudio from his suffering!"

"If you had stayed in the room with me like I told you to, you would have seen I was able to deliver him without the use of the tools." Douglas's voice was spiteful. "You entrusted me with that task, didn't you?"

"Yes, and I'm sorry I wasn't there to witness the miracle." She stopped on the other side of coffee table from her husband. "I was afflicted with the compulsion to seek the bag. It was a trap to snare me."

"If you had listened to me, you wouldn't have fallen victim."

Lydia came in and retrieved her infant from Douglas's tense arms. "Mr. Douglas, your uncle is fine. I can assure you Mags wasn't in Alex's room of her own will. A proper lady like her doesn't sign on to be gagged and—"

Douglas pushed Lydia and the baby into the side chair as he leapt across the room at the Melling. He forced Alexander's throat against the wingback chair in a grip that turned his face red as Douglas's fist pulled back in preparation to punch.

"Do it!" Alexander fought for breath. "Do it and every last one of you is out in the hurricane, from baby to shriveled old man."

A sound—part growl, part battle cry—erupted from Douglas. Lowering his hand from the other man's neck, he grabbed a fistful of shirt and pulled Alexander from his chair, ramming him against the fireplace wall. The impact caused several things to fall off the mantel.

Lydia put an arm over Georgiana and dashed from the room as though afraid a brawl would breakout. But Magdalene knew Alexander wasn't rash enough to challenge Douglas. She stood behind Mrs. Melling's chair and watched as her husband's anger held an unwavering threat over Alexander's ashen form.

"You claim you're not scared of me, but had you seen Rupert Lyons when I was done with him, you'd be as scared of me as he is. Did you notice how he wore face paint to your engagement party to cover the marks that still marred him weeks later? Did he tell you when you swapped stories of your conquests how his face was so swollen he was blind? How I beat him within an inch of his life because he dared try to defile my Maggie? Don't think yourself so special I wouldn't do the same to you."

"*Calmati, amico.* You have proved your point, now it is time to stand down." Claudio shifted the bag on his lap and undid the fastener. Taking a deep breath, he plunged his hand inside and removed one of the Saint Benedict crucifixes. "Bring this to your wife."

Relief over Claudio handling the talisman and Douglas releasing his hold on Alexander swept through Magdalene. Then apprehension about her own condition flooded her mind as Douglas approached with the icon.

"Are you mine once more, Maggie?" He held it out to her. "Or do you wish to wound me with your wrathful words?"

"I've been yours from the moment I saw you in the stable." She brought both hands to his outstretched one and fingered over his skin before placing her hand atop the crucifix. With an exhale of relief, she took the symbol of deliverance into her right fist and Douglas's hand into her left. "We made it through once again."

His touched her cheek with a gentle stroke. "But I'm afraid the day is far from over."

Claudio stood, motioning for the couple to take the settee. "Please sit, and accept my apologies for my conduct toward you, Mrs. Campbell."

"Claudio—"

He held up a hand. "Father De Fiore."

"Must you shut me out?" she asked as Douglas saw her to the corner of the settee furthest from the door.

"I am distancing myself to protect you during this sensitive time. None of us are safe here, but most of all you. The demon has marked you as the supreme acquisition since you first came. Through various channels it has sought to have you in sin as it tears down all good relationships in the process."

Magdalene was about to say the demon did have her but she realized that with Douglas—even though they were in Alexander's bed—it wasn't a sin because they were already married. The purpose of the morning of drinking Scotch and having their way with each other was to send them into despair over their own shocking behavior. And it worked, almost too well.

"Let me go back to the carriage house and save you the trouble."

"Don't be ridiculous. You're staying with me and I need to stay where it's safest for those in my care." Douglas put an arm around her. "But I've seen enough of your stubborn display today. Can you please listen to my thoughts, to reason?"

Alexander laughed. "She's a woman! What does she know of reason?"

The mantel clock struck the five o'clock hour and the four people in the room looked at each other. Alexander, who'd still been standing at the wall Douglas shoved him into, stepped forward and retrieved what had fallen from the shelf during the violence, including the portrait of Eliza.

Lydia returned with Georgiana. "I can't get her to nurse, but she's resting. I'd be happy to fix supper if someone would hold her."

Not trusting Alexander to help out, and knowing it would be too difficult for Claudio to look after the baby with Eliza's eyes, Magdalene placed the crucifix on the cushion and stood.

"I'll hold Georgiana." Seeing the reluctance in Lydia's face softened her. "I'm sorry for my harsh words. You can be sure I'll treat her well."

"You said nothing I didn't have coming to me. The truth shouldn't hurt, but it does sting." She passed Georgiana to Magdalene and kissed the babe's forehead. "You'll be safe with your godmother, dear one. Even though she doesn't care for me, she will care for you. Her husband will see that she does. Always remember I love you."

The words left an uneasiness in the pit of Magdalene's stomach. "Lydia, wait."

But she ran into the hall and then the front door opened with the roar of wind and rain.

"Stop her!" Magdalene shouted. "She's going to end her life!"

Claudio went out the door first, followed by Douglas, who hesitated on the porch.

"Go!" Magdalene called, upsetting Georgiana. "He might need your help to control her!"

With a look of dejected resolve, Douglas pulled the front door closed behind him. Magdalene paced the length of the hall to soothe Georgiana before thinking to go back for the Saint Benedict's crucifix she'd left on the settee. Instead of the crucifix, she found Alexander stretched across the seat.

"Looking for something?"

"That, Georgiana," she cooed, "is your obnoxious big brother. He likes to think himself very important but he's nothing without his last name and family's money."

"Very funny, Magdalene. Sit beside me and I'll tell her some stories about her fair godmother." He stayed stretched out but patted the edge of the settee.

Magdalene ignored him and visually swept the room as she roamed. Not seeing the cross, she went for Claudio's bag. Supporting Georgiana's head against her chest, she leaned over to grab the handles and set the bag in the corner chair by the potted palm—far enough away so Alexander could not easily snatch it from her. Digging into it, she felt around amid the bottles, aspergillum, and vestments. She pulled out the stole and wrapped the purple fabric around her neck like a scarf.

"Now there's a good look for a Methodist girl. Shall I fetch your mantilla to go with it? I think you left it on my bed. Perhaps we should look for it together."

She kept digging until her fingers closed around the familiar wood and metal piece. Pulling it out, she brandished it at Alexander, which made him laugh.

"It's not a weapon, Magdalene. It's a worthless symbol for those clinging to a dying religion."

"That's not the real you speaking." She tucked the cross between the baby's wrap and her dress and resumed her walk, glancing back to the settee. "I've seen Alexander drop in shame before a crucifix, pleading for forgiveness. I know Alexander looked for help from his priest when he grew ashamed of his actions. The real Alexander Melling might actually be a decent man if he chose to live honorably."

"You jest, and that is the true weapon with you—words. I've seen how you fling them at those you despise and even your husband when it suits your needs. Don't try to change me with your scraps of goodness. I know you, Magdalene, better than you know yourself."

"Possibly with some things, but there's a lot you have no idea about. We've shared a few tender moments, but that doesn't expose all." She stopped near his feet at the end of the settee. "If you learn to let love rather than appetites be your guide, with that angelic face of yours and the fact that you know plenty to keep a wife happy, you could have a fulfilling life while living uprightly before the Lord."

"I tried that once and failed miserably." His gloomy words turned to a rowdy laugh that made Georgiana cry. "But this advice comes from the woman who's been handled by two men other than her husband in one afternoon!"

Magdalene stuck her knuckle into the baby's mouth.

"Those moments with Claudio and then me came so soon after you and your husband had your time together. Up in the attic, was it, or did you visit someone else's bed this time? Maybe my father's?"

She struggled to keep her voice down, but the rumble in her chest still agitated Georgiana. "I'll never set foot in his rooms! After you left me, he—"

"What, Magdalene? Tell me. What did he do? Did he hurt you?"

"He tried several times, but there are just some things not even the great tempter can make appealing."

"Then there's yet hope. Some part of you desires me. Have pity, Magdalene. Lay the child aside and cling to me once more."

She backed toward the door, shaking her head.

"Infernal misery is what I've endured these months! Seeing these scars." He pulled at his shirt. "Remembering our moments of glory before the darkness descended and you sought your way out of my arms. And today, in the dark of the early morning through the opened windows, I had to listen to your cries of passion with another man. And again, this afternoon, knowing you were under the same roof with him. It's madness you seek to push me toward!"

Her defenses weakened against the enormous weight of Alexander's anguish and the passion rekindling within. "I'm sorry. I meant you no harm." A single tear slipped down her cheek and Alexander capitalized on it.

"And now I harm you. That sting of truth as Lydia said. But our story can have a happier ending. One shared occasion is all I ask to heal these scars." He rose before her in the doorway, a pale hand reaching for her cheek to brush away the tear.

The front door burst open and Douglas staggered into the hall. "Alexander, I need you, quick!"

"Where's Claudio? Lydia?" Magdalene asked, her voice rising over the wind and rain beyond the opened door.

"There's no time!" Douglas shouted.

The men raced out and Magdalene rushed to the kitchen, holding the baby to her chest. From the back window she saw Douglas leading Alexander into the forest, heads bent against the driving rain.

"God help them!" A sob cracked in her throat and then she hurried up the back stairs to her old room to see if she could see anything. Nothing except a gray mass of sky darkening to black and the waving canopy of the forest. Magdalene went to the next room to check on Uncle Simon.

"There's been more than a few raised voices this afternoon," he said. "What's going on out there?"

"I don't know!" she cried. "There've been some arguments, and I said some unkind words to Lydia earlier. She rushed out like she was going to end her life and Claudio followed. Douglas followed him and he just came and got Alexander for help. Now I'm stuck here helpless with the baby."

"Never helpless, Maggie." He shifted in the bed, working his way to a sitting position. "You are here, safe and well. When they come back, they'll all be wet through and needing dry clothes and something hot to eat and drink. Your helping hands could be the deciding factor of health or illness."

"How can I do anything burdened with the child?"

"A baby's no burden, Maggie. As you're unaccustomed to one, it would be unwise for you to try doing all that with one strapped to your side. Allow me to care for the wee thing. That I can do from here. Collect clothing and towels on your way down and then prop the back stair door open to listen out for me."

"But—"

"Go on, Maggie."

Remembering Douglas's plea for her to listen to other people's reasoning rather than being stubborn about her own ideas echoed in her mind. She passed Georgiana to him, the cross falling onto the bed in the process. Magdalene raced into Alexander's room next door, grabbing shirts and pants from the wardrobe, including his robe off the coat rack behind the door. She threw them down the front stairs and then grabbed a handful of towels from her old bathroom on the way to the kitchen. That pile she dropped at the foot of the back stairs and then set the kettle and two extra pots of water on the stove to heat.

Not knowing what else to do, she went to the pantry to look for food. She pulled out several soup cans and placed them on the table before pulling out more pots. Then she paced the triangle between the window and the pile of towels and the stove, waiting for the next wave of emotions to pass. Her chest was tight, her muscles weary. But worst of all was the aching sense of loss that she didn't know the source of. Would Eliza's sepulcher need space for one more?

Twenty-Seven

The kettle's whistle interrupted Magdalene's brooding. She turned down the heat on everything to keep the water warm. Uncle Simon called for a damp washcloth to see if he could get Georgiana to suck some moisture from it.

"It might just be my imagination, but she feels feverish."

Magdalene touched the delicate skin on the back of her neck and winced at the heat. "Oh, Georgiana, wait for your mother to get back before doing something rash."

"Thanks for bringing the cloth, but you must keep an eye out for the others."

She reheated and added more water to all the containers on the stove before she saw a human emerge from the darkness of the forest. She went to the back porch before thinking, catching the misty backlash from the blowing wind.

Alexander supporting Lydia around the waist lumbered across the yard. When they reached the porch, he shoved her at Magdalene and raced back into the trees.

"Lydia, you stupid thing! Why did you have to run out like that?"

Magdalene tugged at Lydia's wet garments, stripping her down to her worn underclothes. Then she pulled Alexander's robe around the other woman before forcing her into a chair and toweling her hair.

"Leave me be! I'm a wretched creature." Lydia dropped her head, wet curls cascading over her face. "I didn't mean for anyone to chase me. I'm not fit for saving!"

Magdalene took her hands. "What did you do? What happened?"

Lydia pushed her away. "There's too much blood on my hands. The heavens must hate me!"

Leaving the towel for her hair draped over Lydia's shoulder, Magdalene paced back to the window. She watched several minutes before two figures emerged supporting a third between them.

The men headed for the front, so she scooped a handful of towels and ran through the house to open the door. Douglas and Alexander each had one of Claudio's arms around their neck and a hand around his middle. The priest's head flopped lifeless toward his chest as they came into the house. They brought him to the settee and lowered him, placing a pillow behind his head.

Magdalene hastily undid his shirt. "Build up the fire, Alexander!"

She made fast work of pulling off his shirt and shoes, but Douglas placed a wet hand on her shoulder when she was at Claudio's belt. "Maggie, let me."

Freezing, she looked from where her hands were up to her husband. "I'm only trying…I didn't mean…I wasn't even thinking—"

"I know, Maggie, I know. You've done well."

He nudged her to the side and took over removing Claudio's pants.

Slowly backing out of the room, she bumped against a wet Alexander. He turned her around. "You made such quick work with Claudio, I'd be more than happy to let you help me with my clothes, Magdalene."

She slapped him across the face and ran for the kitchen. Lydia still cried, head on the table. Magdalene grabbed the rest of the towels off the floor and rushed back to the parlor. Douglas had Alexander by the collar.

"Leave him be and see to Claudio." Magdalene dropped the towels at their feet and went to the priest, tucking a towel around his chest. "There are dry clothes at the bottom of the stairs for everyone."

"Could you fetch a blanket for him?" Douglas asked.

She stumbled over the pile of clothes and up the stairs in her long gown, ripping the cover off Alexander's bed.

Back in the parlor, Alexander huffed when she entered. "First you dump the contents of my wardrobe at the foot of the stairs and then you steal my blanket. What next, Magdalene, the heart from my chest? You'll have to claw it out yourself this time."

Both Magdalene and Douglas turned to him. He stood before the fire in his under drawers.

"Get some clothes—" Douglas stopped abruptly. "What happened to you?"

Alexander pointed an accusing finger at Magdalene. "She happened! Rupert was a snake needing to be beat to stop what was inappropriate, but not me. I stopped myself by trying to release the evil within. This," he shouted as he clutched his scars, "is what I carry of my time with Magdalene! Every day my skin glares at me from the mirror, reminding me what a fool I was to rush things with sweet, stubborn, sensual Magdalene Jones of Seven Hills. Soon I'll have to lie beside my wife with these memories of Magdalene etched in my skin, unable to hide my dark past from the one who should revere me."

Douglas leaned away, a look between shock and pity playing across his face.

"I'm sure your Maggie painted me differently, but not even she understands what I've gone through for want of her touch." Alexander, gold towel draped over his shoulders, tilted his head to the side. "You, though, driver. I bet you understand, even if you're the strongest out of the lot of us to put aside carnal appetites for a season."

Wanting the subject changed, Magdalene nudged past Douglas with the blanket. She removed the damp towels from Claudio's body, naked to his under clothes like Alexander, and searched for a clue as to why he lay lifeless.

"What happened out there?" she asked as she pulled the cover up to his chin. "I see no wounds."

Alexander watched Magdalene's every move, still standing with his back to the fire, his pale form outlined in yellows and reds.

Douglas pulled off his wet clothes and brought a towel to his shaggy hair. "Lydia ran for the cliffs. Claudio was right behind, trying to stop her. With their head start, I had trouble keeping them in sight through the rain. In the clearing at the mausoleum, he caught her by the arm and struggled with her. A wall of wind came through and several of the younger trees fell, their roots not strong enough to cling to the saturated earth. Lydia, trying to pull away from him, was right below one that started to come down. Claudio leveraged his weight and swung her out of the way while he took her place."

"He would do that." Magdalene laid a hand on his shoulder.

"From where I stood, it looked like he caught the tree and lowered it to the ground, but when I got there, I saw it had pinned him. The back of his head was on the steps to the mausoleum. There wasn't blood, but there's an indentation where his head struck the edge of the marble. He's unconscious."

"Lydia thinks she's killed him. She's sobbing in the kitchen."

"We can't leave her alone, Maggie. Can you bring her in?"

Magdalene looked over at the state of his undress, and Alexander's as well. "Maybe in a minute."

"And Georgiana? Where is she?"

"With Uncle Simon. He wanted me free to help you all when you returned."

She went to Claudio's bag and found his personal crucifix in a side pocket. Kneeling beside him, she lowered the blanket and removed the purple stole from her neck and laid it across his upper chest, doubling it across from shoulder to shoulder. She gently placed his cross atop the stole so the coolness of the metal wouldn't bother his skin.

"Don't leave me, Claudio. There's still much good left for you to do in this world. I'm sure I'll need your deliverance before the night is over." After replacing the blanket, she leaned over him, kissing each cheek and then his lips.

Magdalene straightened and glanced toward the fireplace. Alexander had an arm before Douglas, barring his path. She was confused until she realized what she'd done.

"I'm sorry, Douglas. He's dear to me." She ran for the kitchen, wiping tears from her eyes. "Can you help me get coffee and tea, Lydia? Everyone needs a little warmth, but the soup will have to wait a few minutes."

"Where's Georgiana? I entrusted her to you."

Magdalene turned up the burners. "You left her to become a motherless child, and I'm grateful to see you back. She's resting with Uncle Simon, but as soon as we get this to the parlor, I'll fetch her for you."

"But I killed—"

"Claudio is sleeping on the settee and the men are changing into dry clothes. Come, help me with the tray. We might need two."

Lydia calmed with something to do, but still wasn't herself. When the coffee was ready, Magdalene left Lydia to finish with the tea as she carried the tray to the parlor. Alexander and Douglas sat in the chairs on either side of the fire, both leaned forward in conversation. They turned to her simultaneously, Alexander on the left with a smug expression and Douglas nursing concern.

"Coffee?" She stopped at Alexander's chair first and stood before him while he poured himself a cup, adding a dash of cream.

When she waited for Douglas to pour his, her hands began to tremor with apprehension, rattling the cup against its saucer.

"Are you okay, Magdalene?" He touched a hand to the tray to help steady it. "Sit, and I'll fix your tea."

"Lydia's coming with it any moment."

"I'd rather not see her," Alexander said.

"That can't be helped. She's suicidal and—"

"Claudio should have let her end her sorry life."

"And have you save twenty-five dollars a month?" Magdalene glared at him and then glanced about the room, feeling cold, like something was off. "Should we pull Claudio closer to the fire?"

Douglas stood and motioned for Alexander to help. Between Douglas and Alexander, they arranged all the seats—save the one by the palm with Claudio's bag—into a semi-circle around the fire. Magdalene hid a smile as she watched Douglas. He wore Alexander's pants, several inches too short and not buttoned at the waist. The shirt hung open and uncuffed because it would not go around his muscular build.

They resettled in the same chairs opposite the fire. Claudio's settee now stood next to Alexander, feet closest to the fire. Lydia came through the space between the next chair and the priest's head with the tray. She set it by Magdalene on the coffee table in the middle of the seating arrangement, then looked about, nervously eyeing Claudio's covered form.

Magdalene passed through the opening.

"Where are you going?" Douglas asked.

"To check on Uncle Simon and bring Georgiana down."

He placed his cup of black coffee on the mantel and joined her in the hall, a hand going to the small of her back. "You've given me much worry today," he whispered as they slowly climbed the front stairs. "Your behavior has been distressing."

"I'm sorry." She stopped at the top of the stairs, leaning her head to his shoulder. "It's troubling to be here with temptations stirred."

Douglas pulled her into Alexander's room, shutting the door behind them. "Did you not tell me when we were in here two days ago that there would be no more longings—that I was yours completely?"

She nodded, eyes wide.

"Then why these shameful displays and flirtations today, Magdalene? This is not the way for you—for us. Something must be done to stop it."

"Yes, we need to leave!"

He pressed her into the door, breath hot on her face. "The two in the next room will not survive a trip through the weather. The rain pounds with a million stinging drops and the wind rips the air right out of your lungs."

The length of his body against hers felt unwelcoming for the first time. "Douglas, please let me go."

"Not until you promise to behave. I can't have you stinging with words and ripping hearts from people's chests. It's tormenting me, Magdalene."

She brought a hand to his cheek. "I promise to try harder to fight the temptations."

"Those feelings aren't always easy to judge. Let me help you decide the rest of our time here." His hands went to her shoulders, then down until they were at her waist. "Stay with me always. I'll be your master."

Douglas's hands roamed as he kissed her with force. She moved along with him, hands within his opened shirt, but her unsettled emotions prevented her from enjoying it.

"The baby," she said between kisses.

"You're my concern." His mouth nibbled the base of her neck.

"I promised to bring Georgiana down, and we can't leave Lydia alone with Alexander."

She slipped from his grasp and opened the door, Douglas following.

"I was just going to call you," Uncle Simon said. "She's not doing well. Did her mother make it home?"

Magdalene nodded. "I'm going to heat some soup as soon as I bring her to Lydia. Would you like to come down to eat?"

"I'm afraid these old bones won't make it back up the stairs today."

Douglas's shirt around the baby was slightly damp. "She needs to be cleaned. Did Lydia have a bag with her?"

"I don't remember one." Douglas touched Georgiana's hand. "She's feverish. We can use a kitchen towel for her bottom and get a bigger towel or a new shirt for her wrap. Let me help my uncle to the washroom and then we'll go down."

"The baby needs her mother now," Uncle Simon said. "Let her take Georgiana."

"No. We stick together in all things."

"Magdalene is capable of taking the baby downstairs without you holding her hand."

Douglas leaned toward his uncle, taking Magdalene by her free hand. "There's evil everywhere."

"Of course there is. It's Seacliff Cottage," Uncle Simon replied.

Douglas's hand went to Magdalene's shoulder. "She stays with me."

Uncle Simon put his feet to the floor and stood, sizing up his nephew. "What's wrong with you?"

"I've conversed with the demon and understand how deep the wounds in this house are."

Magdalene gasped, knowing he must be referring to Alexander.

"Don't be a fool, Douglas." Uncle Simon stepped to the door. "The devil never unveils his plan."

Without comment, Magdalene rushed for the front stairs, clutching Georgiana to her chest. She heard Douglas behind her—felt his hand reaching to grab—but he wasn't fool enough to take hold of her on the stairs. Once at the bottom, his arm was about her waist and his breath on her cheek.

"Don't try to run from your husband." He nuzzled into her side and kissed her ear. "You're mine, Magdalene."

Fighting back tears, she did her best to walk without shaking. With Claudio still sleeping—or worse—there would be no one to deliver her when the evil was within Douglas.

Lydia took her child as soon as Magdalene entered the parlor.

"She needs fresh wraps," Magdalene informed her. "I'll find something."

She paused over Claudio, slipping a hand under the cover to feel for movement in his chest. Douglas took hold of the blanket, raising it to watch where she touched.

"Keep your hands off him in the future," Douglas said. "I'll tend to him from now on."

Magdalene jerked her hand away, her gaze briefly crossing Alexander's lounging form. He smirked and shook his head. She went for the kitchen, Douglas right on her heels. After bringing Lydia fresh towels and picking a new shirt from the pile by the stairs, Magdalene returned to the kitchen to prepare the soup.

"Would you please open the cans for me?" she asked Douglas while she cleaned her hands thoroughly at the sink, hoping to keep him busy.

"Of course."

Outside the window, the world was a coal-colored mass of wetness and the wind drove the rain under the covered porch, pelting the window with spray. Despite the layers of the gown, Magdalene began to feel chilled. Her bare forearms were gooseflesh as were her unstockinged legs.

"Douglas, could you ready two cups of tea? We need to bring one to your uncle and I never got mine."

"Turn the burners down and we'll get them together."

Douglas's arm was around her before they were in the hallway. Once they were in the parlor, he stepped ahead to collect the tea tray. Lydia worked at pinning the kitchen towel on her baby as a makeshift diaper, not making eye contact with the others. Douglas returned to Magdalene's side, one hand on her back, the other holding the tray.

"You'll chase her away acting like that, driver." Alexander sized them up. "She's not one to enjoy being smothered."

"You know nothing." Douglas pushed Magdalene ahead of him into the hall.

"I know she likes to be free to breathe hard and fast."

Magdalene grabbed the tray from Douglas before it clattered to the floor. He'd only taken a few steps back to the parlor when Alexander played the next card.

"Careful, driver. You left her alone. Don't turn your back on her."

Douglas stopped. It couldn't have been more controlling if he were a puppet and Alexander pulled the strings. Sickened with dread, Magdalene left with the tray.

"Quick, she leaves you!"

Magdalene had the tea service on the kitchen counter when Douglas caught her. "Stop this! He's got you worked into a tizzy over me for all the wrong reasons."

A hand went to her cheek, the other to her back, pulling her closer. "There's nothing wrong. We're married and you're mine." His blue eyes burned with intensity and his hands were hot as he rubbed against her. "Here, Magdalene. Now."

"Uncle Simon needs tea and everyone needs supper." He kept at her, going for the buttons on her back. "Douglas, anyone could walk in the kitchen. If you want to safeguard me, here's not the place."

"Forgive me." He took a step back, his lingering hand slowly releasing her arm. Then his left eyebrow arched and a smile curled his lips. "We'll continue after supper."

Twenty-Eight

Magdalene saw Uncle Simon tucked in the upstairs guest room for the night and joined the remainder of the group in the half-circle around the parlor fire. Claudio had still not woken and Georgiana fussed restlessly.

"May I take her to the den so she doesn't disturb anyone?" Lydia asked.

"Yes." Alexander took a rare glance at her. "Some quiet would be nice. And get out of my robe as soon as you can."

The wind and rain created more than enough noise as the hurricane increased. Alexander offered post-supper drinks, pouring the remainder of the Scotch for Douglas and Magdalene and bringing two glasses to the chairs opposite the fire from his own.

"No, thank you." Magdalene waved the glass away.

"Lose your taste for Scotch, did you?" Alexander poured one of the half-full tumblers into the other and passed the full glass to Douglas.

Magdalene looked up at Alexander's pale face, thankful his clean shirt was buttoned. "I don't want any drinks tonight. I need to keep my wits."

"A night like this is when you should let loose, not worry about anything except your immediate needs and survival. Am I right?"

Douglas took a swig and sighed. "Quite right."

"And what are your needs, driver?" he asked.

Magdalene sought distance from what would happen, resettling in the two-person settee Lydia vacated.

"My needs are to share my drink with my wife and see that she's properly satisfied."

Alexander grinned. "And I'm here to help."

Douglas drained the rest of his glass and joined Magdalene. With hands on either side of her face, he gently brought his lips to hers. She relaxed under his tender kisses. They turned harder and she tasted the Scotch from his tongue. His hands went down her body, groping against each curve as he adjusted himself from being beside her to a dominant position. Trying to get out from under him, Magdalene slid to the edge of the settee, but it only increased Douglas's reach around her back. Fearful of being squashed under her husband's oppressive needs, she tried to escape from the side. Magdalene caught a glimpse of Alexander standing over Douglas's shoulder. He held up his glass of brandy to her in a toast.

"Douglas, we're not alone."

He tugged her dress aside at the neck to kiss her shoulder. "We're never alone in this house, but that's never stopped us."

Instead of immediately fighting her intensifying terror, Magdalene played along so she could think how to escape Alexander's watchful eyes. But relaxing under her husband's touch wasn't a good idea. She responded to cravings of her own, arching into him as his hand found its way under the hem of her gown, dragging the dress up her bare legs as he danced his fingers from her ankle to the edge of her silk shorts.

Magdalene called for the one she most often turned to for deliverance. "Claudio, please wake up!"

"Are you going to let your wife cry out for another man?" Alexander asked.

Douglas moved a hand to the back of the settee to better look down at her. "Am I not the one to satisfy you today?"

The sadness in his blue eyes cut to her bones. "Always, Douglas, but not while someone watches. We need privacy."

A flicker of remembrance crossed his face and he smiled as his hand kneaded her thigh. "You're uninhibited and I love you for it, but if I'm not enough, there's another who would please you tonight."

"That's right. Keep her in control." Alexander circled them like a crow ready to snatch a shiny treasure.

Knowing what she needed to do, she ran her hands through Douglas's beard and brought them down his chest. "You're all I need. Let's go somewhere more comfortable."

She pulled him to her with all the motions of longing so she could get right to his ear without interference. "When we're alone, I can show you how I feel, but for now, let me tell you. Remember our marriage vows on the beach. We need no one but each other and God."

Douglas groaned and closed his eyes. Alexander, most likely thinking he'd reached some point of ecstasy, laughed and returned to his seat with his brandy. Douglas felt around Magdalene's upper leg and his eyes opened wide.

"Maggie?"

Her radiant smile shone through her previous fear. She kissed him and his body stilled.

"Was I cruel to you, Maggie?" he whispered as he shifted some of his weight off her. "You don't look to be in a comfortable position."

"Did you have your fill, driver? Are you ready for me to take over?"

Douglas's face paled. With shaking hands, he sat up and smoothed her dress around her legs. Then he pulled her off the settee and into his arms. "Maggie, what did I do?"

"Are you being stingy after our heart to heart earlier?" Alexander moved toward them, seemingly brave because of Douglas's pallid face and trembling limbs. "You promised to share."

"I don't believe that possible." He saw Maggie into Mrs. Melling's wingback chair beside the fire and stood before her.

Alexander laughed. "You don't remember anything, do you?"

"I remember you taking Claudio's bag to lure Maggie, her spiteful words, and going outside to get Lydia and Claudio back. And then…Magdalene kissing Claudio while he lay on the settee"—he looked around the room—"but it was over there."

"Let me refresh your memory." Alexander unbuttoned his shirt. "You asked me how I came about these beautiful scars and I told you it was self-inflicted from when I tried to stop the demon from harming Magdalene. It either sickened you or stirred your pity because after you saw her kiss the priest on the lips, you confided in me."

"I'd do no such thing!"

Alexander smiled. "Such is the way with demons. I promised to help you see that Magdalene was fully satisfied before the night was over so you wouldn't have to worry about her grabbing the closest man—conscious or not. Unsure of her devotion, you paraded her around like a dog on a leash to do the most mundane tasks."

Douglas's shaking slowed but all the muscles in his body tensed. "Maggie, I'm sorry." The words came as a whisper under his breath, and she wrapped her arms about him.

"Then came the fun part." Alexander rubbed his hands together. "After supper drinks, in which you were determined to share even though Magdalene declined, you climbed upon her, thrust your tongue into her mouth, and touched her all over. If you'd had use of the full settee rather than the two-person one, I'm sure the display would have been better, but as it was, you revealed much more of Magdalene's legs than I ever had the pleasure to enjoy."

"You're a loathsome beast!" Douglas shouted.

"I am what I was raised to become." He bowed. "Alexander Randolph Melling, at your service. If I'm not vile enough for your liking, give me another day within these walls to mature my demonic ways. I'm sure by tomorrow there'll be no remorse for having tried to have my way with your wife tonight. Several times, actually."

"You don't mean that, Alexander." Magdalene peeked around the side of Douglas, still clutching her husband's waist.

"I've wanted you many more times than what I've acted upon."

"I meant the guilt! It's trying to save you from yourself, and you need to listen. You aren't inherently bad, even if your father commits adultery and harbored a murderess."

He turned to the fireplace and snatched Eliza's picture from the mantel. "Do you mean the actions of that foul maid I had to drag in from the hurricane were known by my father?"

"Aye." Douglas stood stronger. "It was Magdalene who figured out why Eliza was thrown from the horse. My uncle approached your father with the information, thinking he'd like closure and knowledge of the truth. But Uncle Simon was berated for not following instructions that would have destroyed the tampered saddle pad."

Alexander screamed in anguish and rent his shirt. "First, I learn of his despicable actions toward Magdalene, and now this unforgiveable act. If I see that woman in my house one more time, I won't be accountable for what I do to her!"

Not even when Alexander had tried to kill her had Magdalene been so afraid of what he was capable of. In that moment, she feared for Lydia, though she'd wished her gone herself on other occasions.

Magdalene stood behind her husband and whispered, "I must warn her."

"Aren't you going to follow her, driver?" Alexander asked as she left the room.

"No, and I'm no longer your driver or anyone else's."

Magdalene knocked on the closed door to the den. She grew nervous when the three sets of knocks went unanswered and tried the knob. It turned beneath her grip, but Magdalene didn't wish to see inside.

Lydia sat on the chaise lounge, clutching Georgiana to her chest and sobbing. She looked up when the door swung open, and from the sorrow within Lydia's eyes, Magdalene knew Georgiana was gone.

"See to her remains for me. I must leave." Lydia thrust the lifeless bundle at Magdalene.

"No, Lydia, stay until the storm passes. You're welcome to stay as long as you keep out of Alexander's sight."

"There's no place for me here." She wiped her nose on the sleeve of the robe.

"You can't let Claudio's injuries be in vain."

"Georgiana gave me freedom when she gave up her life. I can leave and move on to a new town where people don't know my shame. I'll just have to live with my burdens, but at least they're invisible to others."

"You won't get far with the storm increasing. At least stay until the weather lessens."

"I won't promise anything and I owe you nothing." Lydia dashed out of the room and the click of the half-bathroom door echoed through the hall.

In the silence that followed, comprehension that she held death in her arms engulfed Magdalene. She had held her own mother's hand when she'd passed on, but the thought that she'd been cheated out of being with her father at his time of passing stung her anew. Loosening the white shirt that Georgiana was swaddled in, Magdalene exposed the innocent face. Her mouth was slightly open like she would have cooed a smile at any moment. Tears blurred Magdalene's vision and she hung her head over the infant.

A cool wind swept through the narrow room, calling Magdalene's attention to where she had settled. Someone sat beside her on the chaise. She gasped at it being Alexander. He had a hand on her arm that held Georgiana but she did not fear him. There was brokenness in his gaze, not malice.

"She's taken both my sisters from me." His voice made Magdalene shiver, and he responded by putting an arm around her. "She's taken all, but left me the gift of Magdalene in this tainted room."

He took Georgiana from her arms and swaddled the shirt around the infant's body. Standing, he rocked her in his arms a few times and then settled the quiet bundle on the couch opposite them. Magdalene couldn't remove her eyes from the dead baby and saw nothing of Alexander's movements until he crouched next to her, positioning her to lie back on the chaise.

"Relax, Magdalene. You look stressed."

Panic rose to her throat. "Where's Douglas? What have you done to him this time?"

He laughed as he eased her back by the shoulders. "His dear uncle was kind enough to have a coughing fit right after you left. He thinks you're succoring the wretched woman, but she's locked herself in the bathroom and I've locked us in here."

The ghostly breeze stirred the foul odors of cigar and musk in the room. Magdalene looked about in alarm.

Alexander's torn shirt hung open and the breeze caught it as he positioned himself over her. "Yes, Magdalene, I feel the wind. I always have. I used to think it was Eliza but now I know it to be my friends, the ones who teach me how to please you."

"The devil's no friend!"

"He is when he gives me what I desire." Alexander tenderly touched her face. "And in return I want to give you what you yearn for."

"Then let me out of this room. There's no pleasure within this space for me."

"Give me time and I will change that."

"No!" She sat up, pushing him to the end of the chaise. "Our time is long past, if it ever was to begin with. Focus your thoughts on Beatrice. Allow yourself to crave her touch, for mine is no longer available to you."

"I still wake in the night with that dream, my scars burning as I crave to make those images a reality. Have you no heart for what I've gone through for you, Magdalene?" His icy gaze melted, the frost running off in tears as he reached a hand toward her knee.

The wind massaged her skin and ruffled her skirt, stirring her memories of their moments together. Magdalene accepted Alexander's touch on her leg, her heart softening to his plight. Cautiously, she lifted her hand toward the scars, a yearning to heal the wounds compelling her toward them.

"I'm sorry I failed you, Alexander." She fingered his chest.

He took her hands and kissed her fingertips. "Will you make it up to me now?"

Magdalene closed her eyes, searching for the answer that evaded her. There was something shouting, "*No!*" but the emotions and memories assured her of Alexander's needs.

"You have the power to heal me, Magdalene. You always have. I suffered all summer for want of you. Bring my misery to an end."

Her smile was all Alexander needed.

Twenty-Nine

The knocking on the door caused him to halt, hands on the third button on the back of Magdalene's gown.

Sitting sideways on his lap, she caressed his smooth cheek. "It's our time. Ignore it."

He moved her loose hair further aside and kissed her neck, causing her to sigh contentedly. Pleasure was all Magdalene cared for.

The knocks were louder the second time.

"Go to hell, Lydia!" he shouted, and then his hands went back to work on the gown.

Instantly the knob wriggled and the knocking turned to pounding. "Maggie!" The door vibrated as though someone rammed into it. "Maggie!"

The man leaned his head against Magdalene's exposed upper back. "He's a regular good Samaritan like Frederick Davenport, but the door is stronger than him."

"Who is it?" She pulled his torn shirt the rest of the way off, dropping it on the floor.

"No one of importance." He undid another button, slid her gown off one shoulder, and caught his breath. "What are you wearing under there?"

Magdalene glanced down at the black bustier peeking out of the gown, trying to remember when she got dressed. The pounding on the door continued, making her turn. He kissed her neck to regain her attention.

"I think it's the latest in Parisian lingerie. But I don't remember."

"Parisian, like the blue gown? If I'd known this was underneath, I never would have left the attic that night." He hastened undoing her dress, pulling her arms out of the puffy sleeves to reveal the strapless expanse of her chest in the shapewear. His hands roamed while he marveled over every inch of her glowing skin as he laid her back on the chaise. "Oh, Magdalene, remember my gentle touch when this is over."

"Maggie, I'm coming!" The voice and pounding in the hall reached a crescendo and then fell silent.

"Who's coming?"

"Someone who should have kept a closer eye on me, but he'll have to take an ax to the door. Now, if that gorgeous thing is up top, what's hiding under all these layers of skirt?"

"Extremely short silk." She giggled. "But don't tell anyone."

"No, Magdalene, this is just for us." He kissed her on the mouth and started pulling up her skirt.

Studying his intent face as his smooth hands made their way up her legs, she felt a tug of memory. "Are you always this good to me?"

"I'm afraid I've made mistakes in the past. But this is why we're here, to mend them." His eyes were bright and sure in the gaslight.

"And you love me?"

"I love your touch." His hand reached the top of her leg and felt its way over the silk. "You're so soft, just like I imagined all these months."

The thought echoed through her mind. Soft. Soft hands. His hands were too soft. "What did you say your name was?"

"Are you in the habit of lying with men you don't know?" He tilted his head, blond strands falling over his forehead as he smirked.

"I know you, I just don't remember at the moment." She ran her hands down from his scars to the waist of his pants and leaned up to smell the spot below his ear. "But you feel familiar. And I know that sandalwood scent from somewhere."

"We aren't strangers, but it's time to get to know each other better. Surrender to me."

Shattering glass from something hard coming through the window crashed into the room. The heavy drapes absorbed most of the impact, but the rod fell along with a rocking chair from the back porch. A bearded man climbed through the broken glass accompanied by wind and rain that swirled around his enraged form. He crossed to them in a few hasty steps and punched the blond square in the face, throwing him to the floor between the chaise and the couch. Her lover grabbed his torn shirt off the ground and held it to his bleeding nose as he fumbled with the lock to escape.

"Maggie, I keep failing you." The rescuer smoothed the gown to cover her and gathered her into his arms.

Slowly, she raised her hand to his cheek, touching his ginger beard as she searched his countenance.

"Do you not know me?"

She shook her head. "But I want to. Touch me."

Cradling her face with one hand, he gently kissed her on the lips and trailed his calloused hand down her left arm.

"I know your touch, know it's you who loves me."

"Aye, Maggie, you own my heart. You're my wife." He hugged her and then raised his hand to do the sign of the cross over her before heading for the door. "May God heal your mind, body, and soul."

"Douglas!" She kissed him multiple times across his face until he stopped walking.

"We need to get out of here. The rain's coming in."

"Georgiana! Put me down and take her." Magdalene pointed to the couch.

Douglas set Magdalene's feet on the floor and opened the swaddled Georgiana to look upon her. After closing her eyes, he delicately drew a cross on her forehead with his fingertip. "What sort of evil is he? No man in his right mind would toss aside a dead infant to molest that which is not his. Half of me pities him, though the other half wants to slash him to shreds." Douglas carefully wrapped Georgiana back into the shirt and held her to his chest. "Where's Lydia?"

"She locked herself in the hall bathroom but she wants to run away. She asked me to see to Georgiana's burial."

Douglas cradled the baby to his chest. "Let's get you changed into something else and check on her."

Magdalene, clutching the gown to her body, went to the foot of the front stairs and rooted through the pile of Alexander's clothes while Douglas closed the den. She chose a pair of casual pants and a navy shirt. After slipping her arms into the shirt, she let the gown fall.

Douglas, standing a few feet away, shook his head. "Why did I ask you to wear that lingerie? It only gave Alexander more of you to see."

"And what a sight!" Alexander called from the top of the stairs as Magdalene buttoned the shirt over the bustier.

Magdalene continued dressing, only raising her face to look at Douglas. To her surprise, he stayed calm, his eyes resting upon her as she pulled on the gray trousers and folded down the waistband until they rested snugly on her hips.

"I always knew you wanted in my pants, Magdalene." Alexander, still shirtless, looked down from the banister railing. "I just didn't know you'd look so fine in them."

She shook her head in dismissal before stepping to Douglas's open arm. "Let me take the baby and you try talking to Lydia," she whispered.

Magdalene, holding the bundle that had been Georgiana, went into the parlor to check on Claudio. His breathing seemed stronger. She ran a finger across his forehead. "We need you. Come back to us soon."

She pulled one of the smaller chairs alongside the settee and sat facing Claudio with her feet tucked between his back and the cushion to warm her toes. His quiet form and the dead baby in her lap were constant reminders of the precarious situation she was in. She raked her fingers through her tangled hair and braided it. Having no tie, she left the end undone. It unraveled a few inches, unlike her nerves, which were all the way frayed.

Douglas's calming voice as he spoke to Lydia through the locked door in the hallway was comforting. He said something about meeting him in the kitchen to talk, which Magdalene hoped the maid would agree to. A door opened and then footsteps went down the hall.

"Claudio, we're making a mess of things without you. There's a body to bury and confessions to hear. Please wake up." She went so far as to poke his back with her toes, but he didn't respond.

"You keep strange company, Magdalene." Alexander passed behind her, trailing his fingers across her shoulders as he made his way to the fire. "Once again, your husband goes to someone he thinks needs him more than you. This time, you're left with the dead and dying."

"Claudio isn't dying and often there's someone in greater need than myself. I won't hold Douglas back because we're married. I'm not some helpless damsel who needs a man beside her all the time."

"No, you'd rather have one below or on top of you." Alexander threw a piece of wood onto the fire.

Magdalene laughed, and when she started, she couldn't stop. Alexander turned to her with alarm as her laughter grew hysterical.

Douglas ran into the room. "What's going on?"

She continued to laugh without being able to offer an explanation. Douglas took Georgiana from her and looked at Alexander by the fire. "Is there a safe location we can place Georgiana in the house until I can get out to the stable to build a coffin?"

"What can be so important about that bastard child that you forgo all the anger I know you have for me to seek a resting spot for her?"

"She's my goddaughter and I promised to care for her, but that's not why I refuse to keep battling you. This last act in your father's den showed how spiritually lost you are. You're either so overcome with demons that you don't care or you're afflicted by madness."

"Like your Magdalene there? I can telegram the nearest asylum when the storm clears and have them come for her."

Magdalene looked at Alexander and giggled.

"A resting place for Georgiana, and then I'll see to Maggie."

"Give her to me and I'll lay her in my bed." Alexander stood before Douglas and held out his arms. "I speak of the baby, not your wife."

Magdalene tried to catch her breath, but the last remark started her back to maniacal laughter. Alexander took the body of his half-sister from Douglas and left the room.

Douglas pulled Magdalene to her feet. "What's going on with you?"

"Alexander tried to be biting with his remarks about you always leaving me." Magdalene started giggling and placed a hand on his arm to steady herself. "I told him I didn't need a man beside me all the time. And he—" She could no longer speak for laughing.

"Maggie, pull yourself together." Douglas took her by the shoulders and shook.

She laughed more. Alexander returned. With a swift movement, he slapped her across the face. Douglas turned on Alexander with a fist at the ready.

"If you can't see she needed that, you should open your eyes," Alexander said.

Magdalene, shocked to sobriety, had a hand on her cheek where she still felt the sting. "I'm sorry, Douglas. I meant no disrespect. It was only that Alexander—"

"I said she didn't need a man beside her because she'd rather have one below or on top of her." Alexander plopped down in his seat by the fire, straight-faced.

Magdalene started giggling and Douglas shook his head.

"That does sound like our *posseduta*." Claudio's voice was quiet but clear.

Magdalene squealed like a little girl and dropped to her knees beside him. His eyes were still closed, but she reached under the blanket for his hand. "You're back!" She rested her head on the blanket and squeezed his hand that was on top of his warm stomach under the cover. "Douglas, go tell Lydia he's awake."

Claudio gripped her hand in return before he loosened his hold. "Magdalene, it would be best if you took your hands from under the blanket. It is not proper, especially when it feels like I'm only in my under clothes."

"You are," Alexander said from his chair, "and one guess who helped you undress."

Claudio blinked at Magdalene's smiling face before him. "Tell me he jests."

"You were soaked and Alexander and Douglas were exhausted from carrying you back. I took off your shoes and shirt and toweled you off, but Douglas stopped me at your pants. I thought nothing of your exquisite lines at the time. And see?" She folded back the blanket and moved his hand to the cross. "I gave you your stole and crucifix."

"And then she kissed you several times, including your lips." Alexander smirked.

"Is it confession time for all misunderstood actions or can we include the blatant ones as well?" she asked.

Douglas came back during the stare down between his wife and Alexander. He looked between them and then at Claudio before speaking. "Lydia's gone, as are her clothes and boots."

"At least something went well tonight, though I lost five dollars." Alexander gave Magdalene a harsh stare. "Even if she doesn't make it out there, I would have killed her in here."

Magdalene crossed her arms. "A hurricane looks good from my view as well."

"Hearing you argue like children makes one wish to lose consciousness again." Claudio leaned forward and felt the back of his head.

"Can you feel and move your feet?" Douglas asked him.

He could and did. As the two went over his movements, checking for injuries, Magdalene paced the room. The lack of the swirl of skirts was odd when she turned about and she fingered the rolled waistband.

"You should have thought to grab my belts when you tossed everything else downstairs." Alexander scowled at her as she pivoted in front of the mantel.

Magdalene rolled her eyes. "You're just jealous I look better in your clothes than you do."

"Don't bother giving them back because you'll have stretched the seams with your hips and chest."

"You say that like it's bad when half an hour ago you couldn't keep your hands off those very things."

"Enough!" Douglas roared. "I think I preferred it when you two flirted."

Claudio, now sitting up, managed to laugh. "I see I have missed a lot, but also not so much while I was sleeping. If Lydia is gone, where is the child?"

Magdalene turned serious. "She died not long ago. Lydia put her in my care to see to her burial because she wanted to flee to a town where people didn't know her shame."

Douglas stopped Magdalene when she tried to walk past. He wrapped his arms around her and snuggled into the space between her neck and shoulder. "I'll see to Georgiana as soon as I can."

Magdalene went limp in his arms, exhaustion setting in. Douglas walked her to the small settee. "You need to sleep, Maggie."

"But Claudio needs to eat and drink."

"I'll see to that."

Magdalene sat down. "I won't be comfortable unless I have your shoulder to sleep on."

Douglas kissed her forehead. "I'll be with you as soon as I'm done. I'm going to check on Uncle Simon and bring down some decent pillows, if that's okay with Alexander."

"Why start asking now?" He threw his hands in the air. "Bring the whole upstairs down if you want. I'm not cleaning when this is over."

Douglas ascended the stairs as the mantel clock struck twelve. The remaining three stared at each other after the chimes quieted, listening to the raging storm outside.

"Alexander," Claudio said as he hung his crucifix around his neck, "come help me over by the fire so *posseduta* can stretch out."

Alexander held out an arm for Claudio to grip and walked him across the rug to his mother's chair by the fire. With Claudio seated, he dragged the full-sized settee perpendicular to the chairs so it was across from the fireplace, blocking Magdalene on the far side of the arrangement.

"There, no use for us all to be spread about the room when our numbers are few. I'll walk you over." Alexander came around to Magdalene. She stared at his offered hand as if it were an opossum about to scratch her for the last bite of food. "Don't be stubborn, Magdalene. I'm done with you. I might tease and torment you verbally, but as Claudio is my witness, I'll stay clear no matter how beautiful you look in my clothes. My body can't take a beating, even if I deserve it. Your husband's aim is true and his strength great."

"Is that what you tell yourself so you can sleep at night?"

"My nose is swollen and it hurts to breathe."

Magdalene was in his face, swaying slightly from standing too quickly. "Don't give me your sad, pleading eyes routine. I believe you're scared of Douglas as much as I believe you'll live in joy and peace in your current state. You're scared of yourself—of what you did and what you think yourself capable of. You're scared of the monster you realize is within you."

In a swift movement, Alexander planted a hard, quick kiss on her lips. "I love you for seeing the real me, but it could never work for us because of that very thing. My soul is raw before you." The fire in his eyes shifted from smoldering to scorching. "I feel it inside me, seeking for a way to destroy you."

"Magdalene, my bag," Claudio said.

Momentarily transfixed by Alexander's fiery stare, Magdalene blinked to clear her vision and dashed to the chair by the potted palm. She snatched the bag's handles and was almost to Claudio when Alexander grabbed her arm.

"You're back to being a pawn of the priest." Alexander spat the words at her. "Where's the woman who thought she could best me with her own cunning?"

Magdalene dropped the bag just behind the large settee and turned to him, driving him back a few steps with the intensity of her gaze. "Right here, and with my own wits about me. Not in some snare in which you made me forget who I am."

"They make me do it," he whined. "I don't want to hurt you, I never did. I only wanted to love you, like I loved my queen."

His hands came toward her, and she felt impressed to take one of them into her own. Her other hand went to his forehead before she thought better of it, recalling the firm words which she'd heard Douglas and Claudio speak on numerous occasions. "In the name of the Father, and of the Son, and of the Holy Spirit, I command you, demon, to leave this man alone!"

With each word Alexander weakened, until she had to help him lower to the floor. Next to her, Claudio dropped to his knees, placing a hand on her shoulder.

"Well done, Magdalene. He will need much more, but this is a good start." He placed the purple stole across Alexander's chest, along with a Saint Benedict's crucifix. "I cannot lift the bag. Would you bring it to me?"

Magdalene did and then kneeled on the opposite side of Alexander from the priest, hands clasped in prayer.

Claudio chanted the Rites in Latin, sometimes muttering phrases in Italian to himself as he went along. Douglas returned with an armful of pillows and blankets, which he placed on the settee, and then kneeled beside Magdalene, looking over Alexander with concern. Magdalene clutched her hands around Douglas's and laid her head on his shoulder.

***

Morning wasn't so different from the night with the exception of gray rather than black skies and the wind blowing from the east as the hurricane continued its northerly course. Magdalene woke curled on her side, her head facing the fireplace on top a pillow on Douglas's lap and a crocheted afghan over her legs.

Claudio stood at the window, staring at the driving rain. Alexander slumped to the side in his father's wingback chair, a pillow wedged between him and the armrest, eyes closed. The fireplace was dark and smoky, hissing softly from rain that found its way into the flue. Though in a room with those she knew best, Magdalene felt alone. She stretched her legs the length of the settee.

Douglas's warm hand rubbed her arm and he bent over her face, kissing her temple. "I love you more today than yesterday," he whispered.

His beard tickled her ear and she rolled onto her back and smiled up at him. The clarity of his blue eyes was striking in the dim light. Knowing the gleam behind them—as well as the smile on his lips—were for her caused an aching that plummeted her heart to her stomach. She was the source of considerable heartache in the past few days and didn't feel worthy of his devotion. It pained her to see his fidelity as she had been quick to toss it away.

"Don't be sad." He stroked her cheek. "We survived to see the light of another day."

She turned back toward the fireplace, but not soon enough. Douglas reached around her, tugging her into his lap as he cradled under her knees with his left arm and her head resting in the crook of his right arm atop the bandage—another reminder of her follies.

Kissing away the tear, he nuzzled against her neck. "What is it, Maggie?"

"I feel isolated, like I'm locked in a glass room unable to feel anything beyond my own misery." She went limp in his arms and stared at the dark ceiling. "My mistakes are too grievous to merit your forgiveness or anyone else's. I'm destined to live my life within these walls, surrounded by those dearest to me without the benefit of communion with them."

"I'm here and I love you. I forgive everything. Most of what goes on in this house isn't your fault, not in your control."

He kissed her face, her lips. She felt the motions, the pressure, but not the passion behind it. Nor were her own emotions stirred.

You're as dead as Georgiana. Accept that I've won you.

Magdalene began trembling.

"It's here for me!" she shrieked before her body convulsed and everything went black.

Thirty

Magdalene lay supine on the Oriental rug in the parlor, her body fenced in by the settee and chairs as Douglas, Alexander, and Claudio stared down at her from in front of the fireplace. They looked like an odd assortment of guards trying to figure out what to do with a prisoner who attempted escape.

"At least she's no longer jerking about like a freak," Alexander remarked.

"*Sí*, and she did not hurt herself." Claudio put a hand on Douglas's shoulder, which he shrugged off. "You did well by putting her on the ground so she would not fall."

"What can I do now?" Douglas, with a mournful face, looked to the others. "She was so despondent not even my kiss could reach her."

Alexander snorted. "That doesn't say much. Shall I try?"

Claudio put a hand before him. "I witnessed you promise to stay away from her."

"That was before she drove the demon from me. I must try to repay the favor." He pushed Claudio's arm aside but Douglas grabbed him by the shoulder.

"If you value your life, don't touch her."

"Then what are we going to do, stand around holding hands?" Alexander stomped to the other side of the room and opened his brandy decanter, only to find it empty. He dropped the bottle on the rug but the thick, crystal-cut glass held together. After rummaging through the bottom cabinet, he pulled out a half-filled bottle. "There's still some gin!"

"Can you at least wait until after breakfast?" Claudio asked.

Alexander set the bottle heavily on the side table. "Then give me something to do."

Claudio looked at him calmly. "Pray, check on Mr. Campbell, make coffee, or fix breakfast. There is plenty to choose from."

"But only half are feasible for me." Alexander came to the edge of the settee and looked at Magdalene. "She knew what a worthless creature I was from the beginning. She saw right through my bluster to all that I fell short of, yet some part of her still yearned for me."

"The one plagued by a demon." Douglas sneered from the other side of Magdalene.

"I thought that too, but she told me that not even the demon could make my father appealing to her. There has to be a base desire for the oppression to work. That means the time I had with her in the den last night proves she still has some attraction to me. Allow me a chance to awaken her with a kiss."

"This isn't a fairy tale and you're no charming prince." Douglas's knuckles turned white and he ground his teeth. "And if you'd stop with your 'she loves me more' notions, you might actually be helpful now that you aren't oppressed. Will you see to my uncle or not?"

The mantel clock ticked the seconds as the two glowered at each other.

"No," Alexander finally replied.

Claudio moved for his bag. "Then pray, Alex. Get down on your knees and beg for her deliverance."

"You might want to put in a few prayers of forgiveness for your own sins while you're down there," Douglas said on his way out.

"Can he not hold his tongue?" Alexander asked Claudio as the other collected supplies from his bag.

"The same could be asked of you. What do you expect when you speak of kissing his wife? And what happened in the den while I was not functioning?"

"She was glorious, Claudio! If you only knew what she wears under those clothes…" Alexander's sly smile turned to embarrassment before the priest. He pushed his flaxen hair off his forehead and cleared his throat.

"Is it confession time, Alexander?"

"I'm beyond confession." He sighed and went to his knees between Magdalene and the dead fire.

"Try it and see if it does not lift a weight off your shoulders." Claudio sat cross-legged at Magdalene's head and laid the stole across her chest.

Alexander watched the rise and fall of the purple fabric several times before closing his eyes and holding his hand to Claudio. "Pass me a rosary. I can't look upon her without sinning."

"She makes it difficult, but through no fault of her own. You must learn to see her as Douglas's wife rather than a woman."

"I don't know Douglas. I only know Magdalene, the time we shared, and the dream that haunted me all these months. I ache for her, Claudio. I haven't felt like this since Lucy, and I never thought I'd feel anything like that again." He squeezed the rosary until the wooden cross bit into his palm. "None of the women in Newport held a candle to that vision of Magdalene in my dream. I waltzed women across marble floors, gazed at their reflections in gilded mirrors, but all I could think of was Magdalene Jones, daughter of a blacksmith and lady's companion to my mother. She has bewitched me and momentarily eclipsed Lucy in the process."

"You have to let her go, for your own sake as well as hers. She's moving on from here with her husband and you have your own wedding to think of."

"If Beatrice knew I preferred the chauffeur's wife, she'd have my head. They met the day you received your orders and she despised her from the moment she saw her leaning on the automobile in the yard." Alexander groaned. "Magdalene was like Eve eating an apple in the garden, so sensual and carefree. I would have partaken right there if she'd offered, but instead she kissed her husband and tossed me a smirk. And those ridiculous driving goggles. She was ravishing even in those."

"Douglas and I gave them to her for doing so well with her driving lessons. She does make a striking figure behind the wheel." Claudio briefly hung his head. "I see your dilemma."

"I know Beatrice saw me watching Magdalene Sunday. What do I tell her on our wedding night when she sees my scars?"

Claudio placed a small cross on Magdalene's forehead and looked to his friend. "Your scars?"

"You slept through everything, De Fiore!" Alexander wrapped the rosary beads between his fingers and undid the top of his shirt. "From my final night here, before I wrote the letter asking you to safeguard Magdalene and my mother. I'm not as skilled at speaking scriptures or uttering prayers like you and Magdalene. I tried to free myself through physical force so I wouldn't hurt her."

Claudio sucked in his breath and murmured in his native tongue before speaking to Alexander. "You do care for her."

"Yes, but no one believes me! They all think me mad with desires, but there's more than lust coursing through my veins. God help me, she reminds me of my Lucy. You understand me now, don't you, Claudio?"

"*Sì.*"

"And I almost had Magdalene convinced last night in the den. I wanted her to help me heal. At least that's what I told myself, though I know it was wrong." Alexander kissed the rosary. "I could never understand how something that feels so good can be wrong."

Claudio's smile was bittersweet. "It is good—a blessing—but only within the bond of marriage. The devil would have us misuse those emotions and sensations to make us servants of the flesh rather than co-creators with God. Did you learn nothing from what happened with Lucy?"

"I'm too stubborn. Tell me how to honor my feelings when I am to marry another."

Claudio looked upon Magdalene, his hand hovering over her lips before he pulled back and grasped his crucifix. "You give your feelings to the Lord. Only he can help you through the anguish when you have to leave your love behind or she is taken from you."

"My Lucy and your Eliza." Alexander breathed his sister's name, laced with pained memories. "I'm sorry for being cruel to you."

"Think nothing of it." Claudio adjusted the cross on Magdalene's forehead.

"But I was most foul to you that night of the dedication, accusing you of tainting Magdalene and telling you my sister didn't love you, though I knew that was a lie."

Claudio met Alexander's gaze above Magdalene's body.

"Eliza told me she was running away with you. She confessed her love and fear over our parents ever knowing who she had shared herself with the past few months while she was engaged to Sean. Yet to wound you, I lied. Her passion for you was steadily stronger until it was all love and no common sense. She had the perfect match with Sean but you were what she waited for—her muse, the great romantic love affair she'd searched years to find."

A tear fell from Claudio onto Magdalene's cheek. He quickly wiped it with his thumb and sat back. "Thank you for telling me. I often thought she only used me to escape your parents because Sean would not move away."

<hr>

"She showed me her sketchbook of your passionate times and made me promise to destroy it after she left." Alexander rubbed the wooden beads in his hand.

"You had the sketchbook?" Claudio stood over Alexander. "Do you know what trouble those cursed pages caused?"

Alexander's eyes were wide as he looked at the dark figure above him. "No, but I've been racked with guilt ever since because I left that promise undone. It wasn't where she left it when I got back. Part of me blamed you for Eliza's death and wanted your liaisons known. I half hoped someone would find it so Mother would know that her perfect deacon was nothing but a sinner like me. Like Father."

"I did blame myself for her death. Many times I came close to confessing to *signora*, but I never could. It was Magdalene who convinced me to confess to Father Angelo. That placed me on the road to healing. But that book, Alex, it infested Magdalene's bathroom! She was tormented by the demon, and when Douglas found it—"

"What was he doing in her bath?" Alexander's voice was hard.

"He helped me exorcise the house to save Magdalene from further possession. That cursed book distressed me to see and ripped my pain anew. My sins—even my very flesh—were made known in detail. Because of you, Magdalene saw me as a man. She yearned to see and touch me for herself so she could draw me. She stole pictures from the fire and obsessed over them for weeks. She fell more in love with Douglas but the demon used those pages to fuel a lust for me. Douglas and I fought several times over her within these walls, but it was nothing to the battle going on in her heart. In not destroying the sketchbook, you nearly ruined her."

"Must I ruin all the women I love?" Alexander fell forward, his face on Magdalene's arm as he wept.

"And you and your diabolical dreams!" Claudio continued, practically spitting the words. "She woke up screaming from that dream you shared across the miles. You left her with fear and oppression because of your broken promises and eagerness to serve the flesh."

"God forgive me!" Alexander cried out as he grasped Magdalene's hand. "It was I who first sinned within these walls, not my father. Lucy and I shared everything that winter day."

He lowered his head until it rested on Magdalen's shoulder and cried more.

Douglas ran in from the hall and stopped short upon seeing Alexander weeping over Magdalene. Claudio raised a hand to prevent him from advancing and sprinkled water from the aspergillum over the two on the floor while he prayed. Slipping into the wingback chair by the fireplace, Douglas muttered his own prayers to protect his wife as the one who'd tormented her most cried over her stagnant figure.

After half an hour of prayers, Magdalene took a deep breath and her body shivered. Claudio, still praying in his native tongue, stood and brought Alexander with him. The priest sat his friend in the chair opposite Douglas and the two men stared at each other for several seconds.

"My humble apologies," Alexander said as he wiped his face. "I did not understand the full implications of my actions. I'm grieved and mortified over what pain I have caused to befall Magdalene. My weakness was wanting to love her, but the demon did not think that best and used me to damage her."

Upon seeing Douglas's lack of violence toward Alexander, Claudio turned his attentions back to Magdalene. He kneeled and placed his hands upon her head.

Thirty-One

Magdalene felt the hands upon her head and heard Claudio's whispered prayers, but she knew they were not alone. Beyond the priest, she sensed healing powers reaching to her from multiple sources. And further than the silent prayers, an absence of evil while the storm continued to blow outside. No anxiety, no fear. She opened her eyes to the love that flowed through the space.

"Welcome back, *posseduta*." Claudio removed the cross from her forehead and kissed her where it had been.

She looked up at Claudio, his face upside down to her but she could tell he'd been crying. Her gaze took in the others. Alexander was red-eyed as well. Douglas's face, though softened with a smile, appeared to have aged and he was in his own clothes rather than Alexander's ill-fitting ones.

"Will no one help me up?" she asked.

Claudio patted her shoulder. "Rest a few minutes. There is no hurry. You have been in a dark place, but are now safe."

Magdalene closed her eyes. "How long was I gone?"

"About an hour." Douglas sat beside her and brought her right hand to his lips. It was then that Magdalene felt the dampness of her sleeve, though no other part of her seemed to be affected. He smoothed her flyaway hair and kissed her hand once more. "You woke up melancholy and then were screaming that it was here for you before convulsions set in. You scared us all."

"But I feel so light now, like I could float away."

"Not in this weather, Maggie. You would blow off course." Douglas squeezed her hand. "May I make you some tea?"

"Yes, please."

Douglas stood and looked toward the others. "Tea or coffee?"

Claudio asked for tea and Alexander coffee, and then Douglas was gone.

"Help me up, please, Alexander." She tilted her head to the right and watched him as he came to her, noticing his hesitant steps and a humble air about his countenance. There was a light in his eyes but it did not burn as it had before. On bended knee, he offered his hands as Claudio stepped away.

As her body rose from the floor, so did her heart. Magdalene flung her arms around Alexander's neck and fell against him. "Why was it you who wept for me and not Douglas?"

He pulled back, keeping his hands at his sides. "How did you—"

"I can smell you on my damp arm and it's written across your face." She brought a hand to his alabaster cheek. "Douglas was frightened, but you…you were broken."

"No one knows me like you do." His arms went about her waist and he rested against her like he'd found his solace.

"Alexander!" A sharp edge of warning punctuated Claudio's voice.

He continued as though he heard nothing from the priest. "You've always seen the real me. I'm here before you, my sins washed clean. I confessed all and collapsed before the Lord. Now I must seek your forgiveness for my trespasses. All of what befell you here was my fault and it will take time for me to forgive myself. I understand if you can't come to peace with me today."

She ran her fingers through his hair.

"Alexander," she breathed. "Do you feel it? The pull of what might have been if we had found each other someplace other than Seacliff Cottage. This is the attraction with no oppression." Her hands went to his chest. "Just as Douglas's refusal to lie with me before marriage showed his devotion, your scars are testament of your true feelings for me."

"I didn't want to hurt you. I've carried the pain from hurting someone else I love and didn't wish to wound again. The power over me was too strong but I did what I could to protect you when I was able. I'm sorry for everything." His straight brows hooded the pain overflowing from his eyes before he buried his head in her unkempt hair.

"Don't be. Not all our time together was damaging. There are moments I'll always cherish."

"I was upset with myself when I wasn't within these walls. I turned a cold shoulder to you." Alexander spoke into her neck. "I didn't know how you would take to me without the dominating hunger that coursed through me when we were together here. I was afraid to approach you without that, but I always cared for you. I thought of you every day when I was gone, and not just because of the scars."

The tears flowed from her without shame as Claudio backed out of the room. "I forgive you, Alexander, but you're not entirely to blame. Several times I wanted you as much as you wanted me. But now, here we are. Married and engaged to separate people, and I'm happy with where I am."

"I know he loves you, Magdalene. I've seen him these past days being a man I could never be. Douglas will care for you, I just pray he always remembers how special you are."

Her smile broke through her teared-streaked face. "Feel free to remind him, tactfully of course. And you enjoy that society bride. She'll keep you the envy of the men's club and every lady will wish she was Beatrice Melling, I'm sure. But don't let it go to your head."

He laughed and then turned serious. "And what do I tell her of my scars?"

"The truth. Tell her Eliza's death was hard on you as well as your mother. Tell her you went through a dark period in the spring but the summer with her helped you heal. Tell her you're ready to start this life with her and hold nothing back. Then bring her to your wedding bed and forget me."

Alexander looked her straight in the face. "I'll never forget you, but I'll learn to put you to the side. Promise me, if we both find ourselves widowed or alone for whatever reason, you'll consider me a reasonable alternative to lonesomeness. I would care for you and anyone else in your family all the remainder of my days."

A lump of salty tears swelled in her throat until she couldn't help but to choke back a sob. She nodded, lower lip trembling.

"I know it's not proper, but there's a priest ready to hear confessions, and I have to ask while we're both in our right minds. Magdalene, may I share a final kiss with you? One that I know you give freely to me. I'll ask for nothing more."

Magdalene hesitated only a second before placing his hands on her waistband, which he grasped instinctively and pulled her against him. She ran her fingers around his narrow shoulders as they kissed. His lips were soft and warm but the absence of Douglas's tickly beard kept her aware of her immoral choice. When she pulled away, her hand lingered on his smooth cheek while she gazed into his icy blue eyes.

Alexander kissed her once more and offered his arm to help her to the settee. "You give me hope. That's all I can wish for in my wretched state."

She grabbed his hand and brought it to her lips. "Allow yourself to heal. You deserve a happy life."

With a sad smile, Alexander stepped to the doorway. "Come, Claudio. You need not hide from us, though the privacy made it somewhat easier to say goodbye."

"No one else is leaving during the hurricane." Claudio sat beside Magdalene.

"No, but we needed to clarify a few things." Alexander stood before the priest. "Confession time. We kissed at my instigation and I stole another afterward, but there will be nothing more as long as either of us is married."

Claudio huffed in defeat. "After my time in Seacliff Cottage, any parish will seem tame. You have trained me for all situations. Magdalene, you must tell Douglas of this."

She nodded. "I knew I would have to as soon as I agreed to it. I'll go to him now."

Douglas worked at transferring drinks to a tray as the two entered the kitchen. Claudio removed Magdalene's and Douglas's cups and took the remaining three for himself, Alexander, and Uncle Simon on the tray. "Sit and have tea with your wife."

With a quizzical brow, Douglas saw Magdalene to the nearest seat and then carried their cups to the small kitchen table. "Why does my heart feel heavy?" he asked.

"Because I've disappointed you once again."

He reached a hand to her cheek. "I left you for ten minutes, Maggie. What mischief is about now?"

"Alexander and I were both free from oppression for one of the few times that we've known each other."

Douglas crossed his arms and leaned back in his chair.

"We had a good conversation about where we were before, where we stand, and he apologized for everything he's done. Then, as closure, he asked if I'd kiss him of my own freewill."

Douglas gave Magdalene a harsh stare. "Must you continue to tempt the devil?"

"It was wrong and I'm sorry for hurting you. It'll never happen again, of that I'm sure." Magdalene nudged his leg with her foot under the table. "I thought of you the whole time, missing your beard and wishing for you to pull me into you with your strong arms."

"That's supposed to make me feel better?"

"I'm not certain of anything, but it's there for you to know. I keep nothing from you, no matter the price I'll pay. Put me away, call that asylum if you must, I'll take whatever repercussions you deem fit to place upon me."

"Punishing you won't make me happy." Douglas took her hand in his and squeezed. "It's my heartache you see and hear, not vengeance."

She dropped her head to their clasped hands, nearly upsetting her teacup. "I'll do all I can to help you heal the pain."

"Drink your tea, Maggie."

When Douglas and Magdalene returned from the kitchen, Alexander made an apology to Douglas, which was met with a stiff nod and tightened fists. After that, he kept silent in his claimed chair or standing at the front window, seeming to be deep in thought.

The next few hours saw the height of the hurricane. Wind ripped down more trees as the rain continued to soften the ground. Mid-morning, the rain bands weakened as the eye of the storm moved northwest. Claudio, Douglas, and Magdalene helped each other with household responsibilities. They checked on Uncle Simon and rehung the crucifixes around the house, but Douglas persisted on holding Magdalene at arm's length. Just before noon, when the storm had noticeably lessened, Magdalene and Claudio went to the kitchen to see to dinner.

"I knew he would be angry," Claudio said as Magdalene rummaged through the pantry. "That is one of the reasons I could not stay in the room with you and Alexander this morning. I did not want to be part of what would tear your marriage asunder."

"I'm sorry, but for good or ill it had to be done. I've never felt freer within this house. I feel guilt for hurting my husband yet I'm at peace with where I am. This too shall pass, right?"

Claudio shook his head. "I do not know anymore. You have shaken things within my soul I did not know were moveable. It is difficult to judge your actions because I am not an impartial jury. I will continue to strive to be more righteous each day I live."

"That's all any of us can do." Magdalene sighed. "Will you speak to Douglas on my behalf?"

"This is something you must work out yourself. I would only complicate things because I am too close to the situation. Do you not recall what I did when you woke up from your possession this morning?”

With her arms full of canned salmon, she stared at Claudio, trying to recall what had happened. When she remembered, a smile crept to her lips. “You removed the cross from my head and kissed me in welcome.”

“*Sí*. I am afraid Douglas thinks of me as another man who wants to kiss his wife. One of many, I am sure.”

Magdalene laughed. “We make the most unlikely of groups, don’t we? Lydia was the smartest for running away. We’re all liable to self-destruct if left here much longer.”

***

After a dinner of salmon cakes and canned green beans, Douglas coolly thanked Magdalene and Claudio for their work and left to check on Uncle Simon.

“May I slap him?” Alexander asked Claudio as they cleared the dining table.

Claudio looked first to Alexander and then to Magdalene. “Your action toward Magdalene this morning was an emotional slap, as was her return of affection. Give him time.”

“It’s been hours!” Alexander tossed the plates into a stack. “He’s too harsh with her!”

Magdalene shook her head. “He’s justified. If he had kissed someone, I would be stomping around the house for days, if not longer, and probably throwing things at him, too.”

“I bet you have good aim.” Alexander eyed her.

“Like any good country girl, I play a fine game of horseshoes.” She smiled at him as she gathered the four glasses from the table.

Alexander followed her to the kitchen with the stack of plates. “I’d like to see you play sometime.”

“Not likely to happen, Alexander. Hurry back for the other dishes, please.”

“You don’t want to be alone with me?”

“It’s not because I don’t trust you, because I do. But it doesn’t look right. I don’t want to do anything that might cause Douglas pause on his road to forgiving me.”

"He's a fool, Magdalene. Anyone could see where your heart lies. You've been nothing but honest with him and he spurns you for it."

"He rejects my sin, not me." She took the plates from Alexander. "Yes, it hurts that he doesn't look me in the eye or touch me, but my pain can't be any worse than his in knowing I strayed from my wedding vows."

"I shouldn't have asked for the kiss." Alexander hung his head.

"But you did, and it was my choice to accept it. Now we live with the consequences."

"I'm glad you understand, Maggie." Douglas came through the hall door with the load of serving platters they expected Claudio to bring and set them on the counter. "I'm sorry, but I stopped to listen to your conversation before making myself known."

"You have every right to be where I am, to hear what I speak to another man." She held her chin high. "I don't seek to undermine our relationship. My choice this morning was about locking the past away so you and I could traverse the future unbidden by my previous actions."

"I understand how you see it that way, but today you erred willingly even though you felt you did it for us."

Magdalene reached for her husband and smiled when he didn't turn her away. She laced her fingers through his and held his gaze. "I won't repeat this mistake again."

"You need to cleave to her, Douglas, now and always." Alexander stepped toward them. "As she has no father or brothers to look after her welfare, I will come to her aide if you ever mistreat her. She deserves a life of love and passion, to be cared for by one who loves her. Cherish her always. You won't find another woman like Magdalene as long as you live."

Douglas hugged her to his chest. "She's the world to me, and as such, it smarts more when I'm let down."

"I make mistakes, Douglas. I'm human." She nuzzled against the curve of his shoulder.

"Gloriously human."

Alexander stood beside them, a hand on each of their shoulders. "You two were meant for each other. Forgive me, once again, for all I've done to wreck your happiness. Excuse me while I help Claudio with another round of blessings within these walls. My house is yours. I don't expect you two to camp out in the parlor with us another night, if you know what I mean."

Douglas smirked at Alexander. "You're not half bad when you put your demons aside."

"What can I say? Your Maggie makes me want to be a better man."

"Good enough to help with the dishes?" Magdalene teased.

"I'll leave that for you and your lucky husband."

Alexander left the kitchen with a smile and Douglas hugged Magdalene once more. "I'd be happy to help you, Maggie."

They rolled up their sleeves and tackled the wash together, their wet hands playfully working while Douglas stood behind her, reaching under her arms to help while watching over her shoulder. They were like that when Claudio, in full vestments, and Alexander returned.

Alexander whistled. "Maybe I should have signed up for dish duty."

"The position has been filled," Douglas said as he scooped a clump of bubbles and placed them on Magdalene's nose.

She wiped the suds on the sleeve of her shirt and laughed.

"It is good to see joy instead of pain on your faces," Claudio remarked before continuing his prayers.

Douglas rinsed his hands and set to drying the pile of clean dishes while Claudio and Alexander went about the room. Magdalene listened to the words she couldn't understand but felt overpowering peace and joy. Outside the kitchen window, the yard was a giant puddle and a steady rain continued to fall.

After the others moved up the back stairs, Magdalene turned to Douglas. "Should we stay here another night or try to make it home?"

He resumed his spot behind Magdalene, reaching into the water to locate something to help wash but only finding her hands. "I don't relish getting Uncle Simon across that swamp, and it's safe for us here. Alexander offered us our own space, so we could claim the attic one more time." Douglas tasted an earlobe and kissed down her neck to the top of the blue shirt.

Magdalene turned toward him, her hands leaving wet prints across the chest of his shirt as she grasped for a firm hold on him. He pulled his hands from the sink and did likewise across her body.

"Maggie, you're still wearing those underclothes. They can't possibly be comfortable." His hand went under her shirt as though searching for fasteners.

"I've had worse on me, thanks to a certain lady." Her hands followed his to bring them back out. "It's fine until we—until we decide it's time to get undressed."

Douglas smiled and kissed her cheek. "I scrubbed the mud off your dress when I went up to change last night. Your under things are dry, too."

"Thank you. I'd like to get back into my own clothes soon."

"And I'd like you in them as well. It's unnerving to see you about in Alexander's, though you do look ravishing in trousers and a straight shirt, Mrs. Campbell. It allows your body to speak for itself, and it's loud and sultry."

"There's something that needs to be seen to before we go further. Georgiana needs a resting place so Alexander can have his bedroom back."

"There's an umbrella in the front hall. I could dash to the stable to work on a coffin."

Magdalene looked out the window. "I could come, too."

"We both know I wouldn't get any work done." He fingered her cheek and she blushed under his intense gaze, which made him laugh and pull her close. "Maggie, my love, my heart. Never stray from me."

***

Magdalene read to Uncle Simon from one of Mrs. Melling's books in the guest room. Alexander found her there, watching from the doorway as she finished an Edgar Allan Poe poem about a lady named Annabel Lee.

Magdalene lowered her feet from being propped on the corner of the bed and sat up. "Yes?"

"May I speak with you in the hall for a moment?"

Magdalene patted Uncle Simon's shoulder. "I'll be right back."

"Take your time, Maggie. I'm not going anywhere."

Douglas had been in the stable the past hour, and Claudio off in prayer. When she passed into the hall, she smiled fully at Alexander. "It's nice to see your eyes clear. Beatrice will think you a new man. If she doesn't appreciate the change, she's a fool."

"Keep your flattery to a minimum. I could be easily swayed to my old ways."

"Yesterday is considered old?"

"When it feels like I've been reborn—yes, it was a lifetime ago. There's much I want to do to help wounds heal and I want your opinion on one thing."

Magdalene nodded.

"Douglas builds the coffin for Georgiana, but I'd like to make it comfortable for my half-sister. I was thinking of offering one of my pillows and finding one of your dresses or even Eliza's to further pad the box so there is something from all of us with her."

"I think that's perfect, Alexander."

"Will you call me Alex? The way you say my full name stirs my feelings toward romance. Alex is short and sharp. I can hear you joking with me as Alex rather than whispering my name with longing."

Magdalene took his hand and squeezed. "Of course, Alex. And I may yet begin to tease you as casually as I do Claudio. You may call me Maggie if you'd like."

He squeezed her hand before releasing it. "Thank you for your confidence, Maggie. Would you help me find the right fabrics?"

"Yes, but with another as chaperone, for Douglas's sake." She went to the top of the stairs. "Claudio, we need your assistance!"

He appeared at the bottom of the stairs wearing his black robe and a look of feigned annoyance on his placid face. "Like a dog, I come when called."

Magdalene laughed. "Like a good dog, you even wear a collar. We're on errand for Georgiana and need your chaperoning in the attic."

Claudio stopped to scoop some of the loose clothes still on the floor at the base of the stairs before climbing. "Tell me again when we are to part ways. I know I will treasure being called a dog by you at some future point, but today is not the day."

Magdalene poked his upper arm when he reached the landing. "Do I need to remind you that you started it?" Then eyeing the armload of laundry, she spied the cream and black gown she'd worn yesterday and pointed to it. "I don't think that needs to go to Alex's room."

"And what am I to do with all the other things? Stand around with them like a human wardrobe?" Claudio narrowed his eyes at her.

"Toss them in the corner of my room," Alexander said. "Rosemary or someone else will deal with them."

Magdalene turned to Alexander. "That someone could be you."

"You speak as though I know the first thing about laundry."

"And you speak as though you have no brains or capable hands." She stared mercilessly at him for several seconds before both laughed.

Claudio tossed the clothing into the bedroom and then clapped Alexander on the back. "Welcome to the club, Alexander. Magdalene only jests with her friends."

Thirty-Two

Magdalene spent her time before supper hand sewing one of Eliza's petticoats into a cover for Alexander's pillow. Then she cut and cinched the top of one of the pastel lace tea gowns Mrs. Melling had bought her into a simple gown for Georgiana. She worked near the fire in the parlor with the gaslights on high against the evening gloom outside the windows. Claudio sat across from her, reading aloud from the holy Bible, struggling with the King James English in the book of Saint Luke.

When she heard the phrase, "Mary called Magdalene, out of whom went seven devils," she looked up from the pink dress.

"Have you cast the demon out of me seven times?"

"I have lost count, but between Douglas and me, you have kept us busy."

"All part of good training, for a priest or a dog."

Claudio laughed. "You came here when I was at my darkest and gave me hope. Hope that I could help someone from making the same mistakes I did and hope in utilizing the atonement to cleanse my grievous sins. We have had our share of intense moments, Magdalene, but you have been a great friend."

"As you have been for me." Magdalene smiled mischievously. "We're more alike than anyone else here."

"Why do you say that?"

"Ruled by passion in such a way that we're willing to give all against reason or morality for the one we love. Impulsive and fiery and easily consumed with guilt when those impulses get us into trouble."

"*Sí*. You would make a good Italian—or Catholic." He laughed, then closed his eyes and leaned his head against the chair. "I pray to stay strong when I leave. Louisiana seems a long way from here."

"The people in Monroe will be blessed to have you, just as we've been blessed to know you." She sighed. "But saying farewell is always difficult."

Magdalene worked on in silence. Even when she pricked her finger with the needle she did not cry out. She worked through the pain while Claudio rested. Alexander came in as she finished the final hem of the gown.

She pointed to the covered pillow on the settee. "You can see how that fits in the coffin."

"It looks fine, Maggie. Thank you," Alexander said as he picked it up. "Cooking, sewing, drawing, flirting. Is there anything you can't do?"

"Hold my temper."

Claudio laughed. "Very true!"

Alexander smiled as he brought the pillow to the pine coffin which rested on top of the coffee table outside of their seating arrangement. "It's just right, Maggie. Eliza's mausoleum has empty space, doesn't it? Did either of you see inside when it was under construction?"

"There were spaces for three on each side, though Mrs. Melling never spoke of placing anyone else there." Magdalene pursed her lips. "Eliza's stone was mortared in the center space on the right, but the others appeared sealed as well."

"I'll ask Douglas about it, but if there's a way to open one easily, I think we should place Georgiana inside rather than placing her in an unmarked grave somewhere."

Douglas strode into the parlor. "Supper's ready."

Alexander showed Douglas the cushion and told him his idea for the Georgiana's resting place. Claudio, who'd remained silent on the topic, finally spoke.

"If you want to attempt it, I would suggest going on the opposite side. You do not want to do something that might damage Eliza's resting place. One wrong placed chisel could crack the slab and then it would be known someone tampered with it."

"We'll look in the morning," Alexander said. "The rain should be over by then. If the mausoleum is too much trouble, there will be suitable place in the clearing."

"*Sí*, if we can see to it in the morning, that would be good." Claudio stood. "Even though this has been a stimulating experience with you all, I need to get back to the church and see to the rest of my travel plans, even if my departure is delayed."

Magdalene trimmed the final thread from the gown and looked to Douglas. "How do you think Captain Walker fared through all this? Do you think he'll come for us tomorrow?"

He shook his head. "There's no telling what might have happened to him or his fleet. We'll just have to wait and see. Come, everyone, let's eat."

Douglas helped Magdalene from the chair and brought her to the coffin where she laid the tiny gown while the other two left the room. "You did a fine job, Maggie. It makes me want to pack all those dresses you despise so you can have the fabric to make over into dresses for any girls we might be blessed with in the future."

"The heartache in losing one so small…I don't know if I could handle it."

With a tender kiss, he wrapped his arms around her. "Don't be scared to open your heart by anticipating pain. There's much joy to be had in life if we let it in."

She embraced him in return. "You've brought me more joy than I thought possible."

After supper, Claudio and Alexander saw to the dishes while Douglas and Magdalene went to the second floor to check on Uncle Simon. Douglas helped his uncle to the bathroom and Magdalene saw to the infant. Her hands began to shake as she went to pull the gown over Georgiana's head. Sitting on the bed beside the body, Magdalene sobbed.

Douglas rushed in at the sound of her anguish and joined her on the edge of the bed.

"I can't do it. I'm afraid I'll hurt her."

"Maggie, she feels no pain." Douglas stroked her hair, trying to soothe her.

"I've never dressed a baby before. I don't know what to do, how to hold the head properly. Nothing! If she had lived and Lydia died, I surely would have injured the poor girl with my ignorance. I'm not fit for this!"

"You're doing well, my love. You just need to calm down." Douglas wiped her tears. "Here, I'll do it, and if you feel up to it, watch. But if you don't, there will be plenty of other opportunities to learn. Don't be so hard on yourself."

Douglas walked her through each step, from unpinning the towel from Georgiana's bottom, to supporting the infant's head while pulling the gown on. When he was done, they stared down at the small figure on the white sheet in quiet reverence.

"The pink was a good choice, Maggie." He took her hand. "It brings a little rosiness to her face. Now, would you like to carry her down or shall I?"

"You, please. Lydia trusted you to make sure I didn't muddle things."

With Georgiana's body safely in her husband's arms, Magdalene stripped the bed of all sheets and put the pile of laundry into the hallway.

"Are you intentionally tearing apart Alexander's room bit by bit?"

Magdalene's smile was sad. "I'm only trying to help. I want to make things as easy as possible for him. You can't deny the change in him."

"Aye, he's different, decent. Someone I might have called a friend, but there's too much he did that I can't forget even if I do forgive."

The others were still in the kitchen, so Douglas gently laid Georgiana's body into the homemade coffin. Then he and Magdalene clung to each other, awaiting Claudio and Alexander. When the men arrived, Claudio put on his vestments and prayed over the child.

Alexander paced the parlor. "We must do something more!"

"Like what?" Douglas asked.

"We sing," Magdalene whispered. She cleared her throat and started "Nearer, My God, to Thee" with a soft soprano.

Douglas joined in with a rich bass and Alexander started in with the tenor part for the second verse. He eyed Magdalene with a look that let her know that she had known what he needed.

The silence that filled the room afterward was peaceful. Magdalene retrieved the coffin lid and handed it to Douglas, not wanting to be the one to cover the baby. When it was done, Claudio stood and prayed once more, sprinkling holy water upon the box. Magdalene rested her head on Douglas's shoulder.

As Claudio removed his vestments, Alexander thanked him and then approached Magdalene and Douglas. "Thanks to Douglas for his skills in building and you, Maggie, for your sewing and singing. The three of us sounded good together."

Magdalene brought her hand toward Alexander, and after a brief look at Douglas—who nodded—she embraced him. "I'm sorry that your sisters keep getting taken from you. Even though you wanted nothing to do with Georgiana, I know it still hurts. Thank you for giving her a place to rest. Your part was just as important."

Alexander hugged her back and then stepped away, wiping a tear from his eye before he turned to the alcohol. "Gin or wine, anyone?" his voice was strained.

"I'm going to say goodnight," Magdalene told the others. She kissed both Claudio and Alexander on the cheek and then whispered to Douglas, "I'm going to shower and go to the attic. I'll be there for you when you're ready."

On her way up the stairs, Magdalene collected the remainder of Alexander's clothes and added them to the pile Claudio had thrown into his bedroom. She said goodnight to Uncle Simon and retreated into the bathroom, not locking the door for the first time in six months.

***

Sunrise found Magdalene and Douglas in each other's arms in the attic bed. Magdalene's stretching grazed her body against his, awakening her desire for his touch, which she satisfied by bringing one of his hands to the curve of her waist.

"Mm, Maggie." He reached his other hand to her and tugged her against him. "I love you more today than yesterday."

"And I love you."

"Do you hear that?" Douglas whispered as he fingered her lips.

Magdalene strained her ears toward the one window they'd left open and to the stair door. "No, nothing."

"Exactly. There's no rain, no birds. It's a bit unnerving." He rubbed the gooseflesh that sprouted on her arms and kissed her. "Let's see what it looks like."

Magdalene wrapped the purple silk around her and went with Douglas to the open window. The sky was as blue as his eyes, the air cool and fresh, but the forest looked like a field after harvest, so bare were the branches of the trees remaining upright.

She pulled the sheet around Douglas and clung to his side. "I've never been this close to the coast during a hurricane. It's humbling."

"Aye, I've never seen anything like it. The yard was covered in debris yesterday, but it was difficult to tell how severe it was with the rain still falling. Truly, we're blessed to be spared."

Magdalene walked them back toward the pallet bed. "I'm blessed to have you."

Douglas smiled down at her when she lay back on the bed, and then he knelt beside her. With caressing hands and a smile, she urged him to join her.

Afterward, Douglas studied Magdalene as she buttoned her dress. "Nothing has been more worth the wait than you. As I've said before, it's even more difficult to stand beside you without wanting more."

"I'll not complain if you fail to stay idle."

His grin dazzled against his ginger beard. Seeing his nose crinkle from the vastness of his smile created a flutter in her stomach. She grasped his shirt as he pulled them together for a kiss that lifted her off her feet. When he set her back down, he smoothed her striped dress and closed the final three buttons for her.

"Tonight," she whispered. "In your bed?"

He kissed her. "Tonight, in *our* bed, Mrs. Campbell. Whether it's in the carriage house or on Dauphin Island."

They went downstairs and found Uncle Simon sitting up in bed, drinking a cup of coffee.

"Claudio beat you to it this morning," he said. "I think he's eager to be on his way."

"I wonder if the road to Daphne will be passable," Douglas said. "There are a lot of trees down out there."

"Only one way to find out. And if the road is blocked, you men can help clear the way for others." Uncle Simon shifted his position. "Stay with me a few minutes. I'll be ready to go down shortly."

Magdalene patted the old man's shoulder and kissed Douglas on the cheek. "I'll go on to the kitchen and see what I can do to help."

Claudio and Alexander sat at the table drinking coffee and sharing a pack of oyster crackers.

"It is about time, *posseduta*. There is much to do today, no time for sleeping in."

Alexander looked Magdalene over and smirked. "Oh, they weren't sleeping, priest. Look at how—ouch!"

Magdalene punched him on the upper arm. "Get some muscles and that won't hurt."

Claudio laughed. "I was trying to be polite, something you should try sometime."

"If Maggie weren't so short tempered—"

"Oh, no, you don't! You had it coming." Magdalene fixed her tea and joined them at the table. "Have either of you been outside?"

"We're waiting for your mighty Scot to come with us in case we need his muscles. I obviously haven't the required strength for post-hurricane clean-up or Maggie defense." Alexander winked at her.

She laughed. "Don't be a cad, Alex."

Claudio grabbed one of each of their hands across the small table and brought them to his heart. "I will miss you all terribly, but it is good to see you on friendly terms. The bonds formed within Seacliff Cottage shall be stronger than the forces that tried to tear us down."

"Now that's something to toast!" Alexander raised his cup. "To friendship unfeigned!"

"And Maggie, who unites us all, through the good and the bad." Claudio raised his cup.

"You could have left that last part off." Magdalene frowned.

He smiled. "Then how about to black eyes and bloody noses!"

The three were all laughing when Douglas came down the back stairs with Uncle Simon. "Morning, everyone," he said as he grabbed a towel off the counter. "Uncle Simon wants to sit on the back porch. I'll dry off the seats."

When he opened the door, a cooling breeze flooded the room with renewed life.

Alexander ran for the window. "I'll open every window and door in this house to continue to feel that air!"

Claudio and Magdalene saw to clearing the table and then she poured a cup of coffee for her husband.

"How do you want it today?" she asked with a teasing smile when he came in from the porch.

He cozied up beside her and nibbled her ear. "You decide."

"Red pepper it is." She turned her face to his and gave him a hard kiss as he pressed further against her side.

Claudio cleared his throat. "You realize you are not alone, no?"

Douglas backed away from Magdalene and turned to his friend. "Sorry, Claudio. I'll be ready to work as soon as I get my coffee. Join me outside and we can make a plan."

When he'd stepped out back, Magdalene grated part of a cinnamon stick into his drink and then added a dash of sugar. She stirred it and then brought it to him where he leaned against a gazebo post—the lattice and wisteria no longer there.

"Thanks, Maggie." He playfully grabbed for her hand and squeezed it before she sat on the swing he'd dried off for her. His eyebrows rose when he held the cup under his nose, but he took a tentative sip and then another. "Sweet and spicy, just like you. I love it."

Alexander, having completed his task of airing the house, joined them. "What's this?"

"Much ado over a cup of coffee, it would appear." Claudio straightened. "We need to see to the sepulcher first. Or possibly walk the perimeter of the houses to see if there is any structural damage to the living quarters."

"Houses first," Alexander agreed.

"We'll all need work boots," Douglas said. "I can get mine and round up a pair for both of you."

"Take mine," Uncle Simon said, "and there should to be a pair of Wellingtons in the stable."

Douglas rolled up his pant legs and crossed through the puddles to the carriage house. A few minutes later he emerged in his work boots and set another pair on the porch before walking around the building. He circled the barn before going in and came back to the porch with two pairs of boots and his report.

"Just a few scratches on the house and there's a tree against the back of the stable, but it didn't break through. And some shingles off the roofs, of course."

Alexander pulled on the Wellington boots over his loafers and saw to Seacliff Cottage himself. Aside from the gazebo trim, the only damages were a few missing roof tiles and the den window Douglas had smashed to rescue Magdalene. Then Alexander, Claudio, and Douglas tromped to the forest, leaving Magdalene and Uncle Simon behind.

Thirty-Three

Magdalene paced the length of the porch, frowning. While she wanted the men to return, she knew it meant that it might be the last time she saw Claudio.

"They're fine, Maggie." Uncle Simon leaned forward as she passed him for the twentieth time. "They're merely seeking the damages."

"I feel like something's wrong, like something bad will befall them. But it might be Claudio's leaving and not knowing if Captain Walker is coming today or not. There's too much uncertainty."

"Uncertainty never killed anyone and worry will just wear you out. It's going to be a long day and you'll need your energy."

She sat on the swing and kicked her feet to distill her anxiety.

Douglas, Claudio, and Alexander were gone over an hour before they finally emerged from the forest. She watched the three men cross the yard, focusing on the one whose lines had captivated her much of the summer—fortifying his image in her mind.

"We had to pick our way there and back and move a few trees, but the mausoleum is out of the question." Douglas took the space next to Magdalene on the swing. "We don't have the correct tools to open one of the vaults. Alex offered to dig a grave while I drive Claudio to town. The location is already blessed, so we can handle the rest ourselves."

She placed her hand on her heart. "Manual labor? Alex, I'm shocked."

"I might as well try to build up my muscles. I've heard they're lacking."

"Have you ever used a shovel?"

"Maybe when I was a boy. The metal end goes down, right?" Even Uncle Simon laughed at that.

Douglas took Magdalene's hand into his. "We went to the cliff to survey the beach. There are trees down in the cypress grove and the pier is mostly gone, but a dinghy could be rowed from ship to shore. We should be fine for whenever Captain Walker comes for us.”

“As much as I hate to leave this party,” Claudio said as he removed the borrowed boots, “I need to go.” He went inside and came back several minutes later in his collar and robe, carrying his bag. The sight of him caused Magdalene to tear up.

“I wish you could go to the island with us.” She threw her arms around him.

“Our paths might cross someday, but in the meantime, I will write you and Douglas.”

“Yes, please.” Her tears left wet spots on his shoulder. “Do you remember when we met on Ecor Rouge? I thought you were a madman set on throwing me off the cliff.”

He laughed. “You thought that of me, *posseduta*? You were my *signorina* then, but I thought you were Eliza at first, that I remember.”

“You had a wild look in your eyes and you grabbed my wrist. Then you spoke of passion and fell to the ground, crying and muttering in Italian.”

“He does that a lot,” Alexander remarked.

Magdalene smiled through the tears. “And I love him for it. Don’t change, Claudio. You’ll always be Deacon De Fiore to me, one of my dearest friends, even if you wear a fancy robe and title. Thank you for all your help these past months. You’ve meant more to me than you’ll ever know.”

He kissed both of her wet cheeks and hugged her to him. “I do know. I have felt the stirrings. I have fallen into sin in your presence and have been delivered by you and your husband. We are all bound together in the events of Seacliff Cottage. Bound together in friendship and love.”

Magdalene nodded and pulled away. Douglas filled the void by handing her a handkerchief from his pocket.

Claudio put both his hands on Douglas’s shoulders. “Treat her well, protect her, and love her all your days or I will come for you, *amico*.”

“You’ll have to get in line. I already have first dibs if he harms Maggie,” Alexander said.

“I could take on either of you, but it would be safer for me to behave myself.”

“Then do so,” the priest said. “There is too much at stake if you turn your back on your Maggie.” Then with a hand atop each of the couple's heads, Claudio offered a prayer in Italian and then turned to Alexander. "Allow me to bless you as well."

His dark hands on Alexander's blond hair as the words flowed from Claudio caused fresh tears to fall from Magdalene's eyes. Douglas put an arm around her shoulder and kissed her cheek.

Claudio stepped toward the door and placed a hand on the wall. "Stay free from evil," he commanded the house. "Be a happy place for this family and all who enter."

Douglas leaned to Magdalene's ear. "Stay alert. I'll be home as soon as I can, but it could take hours to navigate the roads. You're not allowed to worry about me until suppertime."

She kissed and hugged him once more before fingering the bandage on his arm she'd rewrapped the night before. "Try not to break it open."

"I'll do my best, Maggie." He looked to his uncle. "Keep an eye on her. And him." He motioned over his shoulder.

Alexander scoffed. "I'll be digging, maybe until after you get back. I'm not sure what I got myself into, but the ground should be soft at least."

With a final hug to Magdalene from Claudio, he and Douglas drove away in the Great Arrow.

Magdalene looked to Alexander. "Be sure to bring something to drink with you. And come back for dinner. You don't want to lose steam if it takes too long."

"I planned on bringing a flask. Would that work?"

She crossed her arms. "Only if you want to dig while tipsy."

Alexander laughed. "I've done worse while drunk."

"That doesn't surprise me."

"You'll do good to switch to these other boots, Master Melling." Uncle Simon pointed to his pair that Claudio had used. "They'll be sturdier on your ankles and less likely to slip on the shovel. And you better get going. The day could heat up to be a scorcher."

Magdalene braced for Alex's backlash from being bossed around by the former help, but he merely sat and began to pull off the Wellingtons.

"Thanks, Campbell. Any help is appreciated. I fear I'll make a fool of myself with this job and Douglas will laugh at me."

"Don't worry about Douglas," Magdalene said. "He knows you mean well and will put in a good effort."

"But will it be enough?" His sharp eyes seemed to stare through to her soul as he looked up at her.

She touched his shoulder. "The Lord will provide the rest."

Alexander swept her hand into his and quickly kissed the back of it. "So He shall."

***

Magdalene and Uncle Simon spent an hour on the back porch before he grew restless.

"Walk with me to the house, Maggie. I'd like to pack the rest of my things on the off chance the captain makes it here today."

"You don't think he will?"

He shook his head. "Storms like this one bring havoc to the coast. Wipe out whole fleets, destroy entire towns."

"Then what will we do?"

"Live in the carriage house out of our bags until we get word. The Mellings won't kick us out, but we'll need to buy more groceries soon."

Magdalene helped him into the extra boots and hooked her arm through his as they started across the muddy yard. She remembered to hold her skirt up and they walked slowly to keep the splashing to a minimum. When they reached the front stoop, Uncle Simon went in and got a pitcher of water for Magdalene to rinse her feet.

"Let me get dinner cooked today. I can throw together a soup of some kind. You straighten up or do whatever you want, Maggie, just don't fret over what you can't control."

Reflecting on their last day there—how she ran into the rain and Douglas chased her—Magdalene went to collect their clothes from the bathroom where she'd put them to dry. While she swept the loft, she remembered they left their coats in the kitchen at Seacliff Cottage. She tied on her old boots and climbed back down the ladder.

"I need to get our coats from the other house, Uncle Simon." She paused at the front door. "I'll be back in a few minutes."

He waved to her from the stove and she jumped off the stoop onto a puddle-free patch of spongy earth. She picked her way across the yard, from the driest patch of mud to the next in her own game of hopscotch. Feeling childish, she jumped onto the gate and swung back and forth a few times before shooting for the driest patch of grass within the fenced yard. Then she skipped to the back porch.

Magdalene left her boots by the swing and slipped into the kitchen through the screen door. The house felt as if nothing had been blessed, nothing was sacred, nothing safe. Evil had returned. Grabbing the coats off the backs of the chairs, she darted for the door but wasn't fast enough. The hall door swung open and the imposing figure of George Melling in a black three-piece business suit stepped into the kitchen.

"I'm here to collect my son." His gaze pored over her like she was goods in a store window. Magdalene, frozen with fear, clutched the coats to her chest and stared as he made his way across the room. "His mother and bride are most distressed over his absence and want him back in the city. I went through considerable trouble to get to the docks and secure a captain with an able ship willing to bring me across the bay this morning. Upon seeing that our pier is damaged, they had to row me to shore, costing me more money. Now where's Alex?" His hand struck the prep counter between them with a bang.

"He's out, working," her voice quivered. She was against the sink and knew she had to run or fight, though her body wouldn't cooperate.

"Working?" Mr. Melling laughed. "The only thing he would be working around here is you. I know he came here for one reason, and it wasn't peace and solitude before his wedding. Did he get a final taste of you? Is that why the parlor is in shambles with pillows and blankets all about? Did he take you in each room?"

The remembrance of Alexander laying her on the chaise in the den flashed through her mind, followed by scenes of what they had done. Alexander's soft touches, their kisses, her lingerie…

"I see it in your eyes!" He reached for her arms holding the coats but she flinched away. "And what of that rough husband of yours? Have you put him away to become mistress to my boy?"

"No!" she shouted. He blocked the back door, but she dropped the coats and ran for the front hall.

Mr. Melling had Magdalene by the braid before she could reach the exit. Flinging her into the parlor, he vied to trap her. Rather than cower in the corner, Magdalene boldly placed her hands on top of the tiny coffin on the coffee table in the middle of the room and met his stare.

His eyes flicked between the wooden box and her face. "And what's that?"

"This is what remains of your affair with Lydia. Her name was Georgiana and she lived ten days."

"How dare you bring that bastard child into my house!" He raised his arm to strike but was attacked from behind.

Alexander, sweat soaked and muddied, yanked his father's raised arm behind his back and swung his other arm around his neck. "Never raise your hand to her!"

Mr. Melling easily shook him off and turned to his son with a sneer, allowing Magdalene to circle to the other side of the room. "What's the first rule I taught you when you became a man? Never become emotionally involved with your playthings!"

"Maggie's not a plaything, she's my friend!" His nostrils flared as he stared up at his father. "And I'll no longer be taking your advice on anything other than legal matters, and even those will be sparingly. I've seen some of the deals you've done and I want no part in disreputable business."

With an accusing finger raised, Mr. Melling approached Alexander. "You stand to inherit the law firm your grandfather established. If you think I'm going to let you drop clients or claims because they don't meet some level of your expectations, you have much to learn. You don't want to end up like—"

"What?" Alex glowered at him. "Like Eliza, whose murderess you slept with? That sounds like emotional involvement to me, even if you casually toss aside your own daughters!"

"That," he shouted as he pointed to the coffin, "is not my daughter! As for Eliza, Lydia informed me she'd been messing around with the deacon. I thought it better for things to be kept quiet. How could you allow your sister to be defiled by one of your friends while she was engaged to another?"

Alexander's face turned red. "At least they loved each other, which is more than I can say for you and your affairs! Are not the women you chase someone's daughters and sisters? There's no honor in your double standards!"

He took his father's slap stoically and then threw back a fist in a way that reminded Magdalene of Douglas.

Mr. Melling easily deflected the blow, but the look on his face showed his fury. He pointed across the room at Magdalene. "This one's ruined you! Lucille Easton has nothing on this mess."

"You're not worthy to speak her name!"

Mr. Melling laughed. "First it was the society tramp you ruined, then you couldn't conquer Magdalene, and now it appears she's turned you against me."

"Your own despicable actions did that!" Alexander spit on his father's shoes and turned toward Magdalene. Mr. Melling shoved him head first over the edge of the settee.

Magdalene was quick to Alexander's side, helping him up so he could defend himself.

"Go, Maggie! Douglas will never forgive me if you don't leave."

She clasped his hand in hers. "I'll stay with you. We'll reason with him."

"You can't reason with a devil, Maggie! Run!" He nudged her toward the side of the room as his father came through the space between his chair and the settee, but she kept her hand in his and pulled him along with her.

"A Melling doesn't allow a woman to lead him like a witless sheep. You're no son of mine!"

"And a Melling man is never loved, only feared." Alexander tucked Magdalene behind him, the coffin and settee now between them and his father. "Excuse me as I attempt to carve a better life for myself than the dark one you've shrouded me in all these years. My summer away showed me what a glorious world there is out there, away from those who only seek my friendship in hopes of getting on your good side. If I hadn't promised Mother I'd return, I would have stayed north with Beatrice."

"And miss your conquests with dear Miss Jones?"

"It's Mrs. Campbell now, and though there's been some good in returning, I'd give them up if it would keep her safe from your filthy hands."

"There is no dirt on me, son. But look at yourself, tramping mud through the house and looking like you're nothing but a ditch digger."

"The dirt is your sins and the blood of Eliza and Georgiana!" Alexander broke free from Magdalene and removed the coffin's lid. "Look upon what you might have saved if you had honorably cared for the woman you impregnated and provided for her care. Look! She's just like Eliza, a helpless victim of your selfishness!"

"She's nothing to me!" Mr. Melling roared and stepped around the furniture. He swept the coffin aside, spilling Georgiana's body onto the floor.

Magdalene shrieked but her legs wouldn't move as the towering man grabbed Alexander and threw him against the wall. Her teary gaze went from Alexander slumped against the doorway, to Georgiana's tiny body half sticking out from under toppled coffin, and finally to Mr. Melling's advancing figure.

"I'm tired of you taking what's mine," he said as he stood before her. "You shifted the spirit in the house before to torment me and now you take my son's heart."

"Isn't that what you wanted?" As much as her legs tremored under her skirt, she made herself stand tall and feign bravery. "Why be angry when we've formed a bond?"

"Dominance! That's what he was supposed to experience, not this blind devotion. This nauseating display of romanticized chivalry." Mr. Melling fingered a loose strand of Magdalene's hair before she slapped him away. "No matter how pretty you are, there's no excuse for his weakness. It's like Lucille all over again. I raised him to be better than this!"

"Yet in spite of your dark ways he's managed to see the good in the world and wish to change his path. He's more of a man than you'll ever be." Magdalene stepped to her right, toward the coffin.

He mirrored her steps. "You only say that because you haven't been with me. That will change today."

"You'll do no such thing if you value your life." Her voice held volumes of coldness that caused Mr. Melling to hesitate. His pause allowed her to right the coffin, but then he blocked her from picking up Georgiana.

"I'm in control here. You think because you've escaped me before you can get away without blemish this time. Wrong, Miss Jones! Today is my day."

She straightened and glared back at him. "I thought today was all about fetching Alexander for the women in Mobile. You have the boat waiting in the bay to take you home. Go! Carry him to the boat so he may return to his mother and bride."

"The boat can wait!"

"Surely they'll grow tired of waiting for you to return."

"They'll stay as long as I need them to. I own them for the day and soon I will own you for the hour." He grabbed her upper arms and dragged her toward his den, Magdalene kicking and screaming as his grip tightened.

Mr. Melling slammed her against his door as he turned the knob with his left hand. When the door gave way, Magdalene stumbled in, his right hand still holding her arm.

He looked at the white rocking chair on the floor, the torn drapes, broken window, and the water damaged walls and floor. "What happened in here?"

"There was a hurricane," Magdalene said as she yanked her arm free and shoved passed him.

She ran for the front door but he pushed her to the floor, landing face down beside Alexander in the entry. Grasping his hand, she cried out, "Alex, please help!"

Mr. Melling yanked her hair. Magdalene kept hold of Alexander's hand. The movement tugged him from the wall until he fell onto the hall runner when she had to let go. Jerked awake, Alexander looked up, dazed.

Mr. Melling pulled Magdalene by the hair. On the third step up, she started fighting back, willing to take her chances with falling down the stairs rather than being brought into Mr. Melling's bedroom.

"Maggie!" Alexander shouted as he tried to stand.

Magdalene watched him struggle as she tried to free herself from Mr. Melling's grasp. The hem of Alexander's untucked shirt began to ripple, and then he stood quickly. He placed a hand on the newel post. As he looked up, a cool breeze rustled her skirt.

"Father, forgive me, but I must have her." Alexander's voice was deep and rasping, the look in his eyes one Magdalene knew all too well.

Mr. Melling turned on the stairs and looked down at him. "I see that you're ready." He let go and Magdalene fell on the steps between father and son.

Alexander reached to help her, his touch colder than the air churning around him. "Come, Magdalene. It's finally our time. Father is here to make sure of it."

"Alex, please." She shut her eyes against his touch, fingers trailing over her cheek and down her neck to undo her top button.

"You know my touch is soft. You needn't fear."

He stood on the stair below hers, eye level with her lips. She thought about pushing him backward, but she'd still be trapped between the two. Unless Alexander was knocked unconscious, she'd never get away. It needed to be a battle of faith to escape the

Mellings. With a silent prayer for guidance, she placed her free hand on his shoulder and smiled.

He put his right foot on her step and leaned into her. "My room, Magdalene."

Magdalene couldn't remember if he had a crucifix in his bedroom. Douglas replaced all the crosses upstairs, but her mind could not sort out all the details with her body awash with fear. She bit her lower lip and shook her head. "Take me somewhere Douglas hasn't had me. We can make it our own."

Alexander smiled, opened the second button, and kissed her neck.

"You don't need to seduce her," Mr. Melling barked. "Take her to my room and be done with it."

"This isn't about your father," she whispered in Alexander's ear as she wrapped her arms about his neck. "This is about you and me, and finally getting what you've wanted. Build me a fire in the parlor, lay me on the dining table, or bring me to my old room. There are many places to choose from."

"You deserve the comforts of a bed." Alexander took her hand.

Mr. Melling put a firm hand out to stop Magdalene. "If you do anything to prevent this from playing out with him, I'll deal with you myself."

She shoved his arm aside and continued. "Alex can handle me just fine."

Alexander led Magdalene to her old room.

"There's no lock on that door. I'll be in to check your progress," Mr. Melling called out.

Magdalene slammed the door behind them, and then leaned against it breathlessly. "Are you man enough to take me without your father watching?"

His hands were on her buttons as his mouth drew closer to her. "Yes."

"Then push the wardrobe in front of the door so we can have our privacy and take our time."

He looked from the seven-foot-tall piece of furniture to Magdalene and back again.

She started undoing his shirt. "Come on, Alex. You've built up your muscles this morning digging. I know you can move that wardrobe. Don't you want me all to yourself?" Magdalene ran her hands over his scars and around his ribs until he sucked in his breath from the sensitive motions. "You don't need to share me, Alex. You're master here."

With a surge of vigor, Alexander set to accomplish the task like a gladiator proving his strength. It took three shoves, but he got the wardrobe in front of the door. Still riding his wave of power, he carried her to the bed.

Magdalene, gazing heavenward for the first time, saw the empty nail above the massive headboard. Her heart stopped beating.

"We've been here before," he said as he gently laid her on the soft coverlet, "but this time is different."

Magdalene forced a smile and fingered his arm propped beside her. "How's that?"

"We know all your tricks, Magdalene." He straightened, pulled off his belt with a fluid movement, and tossed it onto the pillows by her head.

"Alex!" Panic surged in her voice as she struggled to sit up. "We're friends! You call me Maggie now."

He knelt on the bed before straddling her torso, his damp pants leaving muddy streaks on the pale blanket. With his hands on either side of her head, he leaned within inches of her face, a leering smile on his lips and a wintry stare from in his hollow eyes.

"It's a silly name for one as glorious as you, Magdalene." He pulled open the top of her dress that he'd unbuttoned, momentarily reveling in the simplicity of her chemise. "No corset, no shapewear. Just Magdalene."

"No, Alex!"

"Maggie didn't meet with me in the night, that was Magdalene. Maggie didn't wear a midnight blue gown with the grace of a swan, that was Magdalene. Maggie didn't cause me to rip my flesh, that was Magdalene. Maggie isn't who we want, it's Magdalene—the virginal woman who came to Seacliff Cottage in hopes of finding a new family. And you did. You belong to us now."

"No! I belong to Douglas! I've taken his name and gave him my innocence."

Alexander's kiss chilled in its hardness on her mouth. "You were never innocent. Innocent young women don't drink in the parlor unchaperoned. They don't welcome a man into their chamber at all hours of the day and night. They don't hide naughty pictures of a naked deacon. Do you wish I was Claudio, Magdalene? Would he put you at ease? Is he more your taste than me? Do I come in third?"

He licked her tear-stained cheek and set to binding her hands
with the belt while she struggled to push him off. Magdalene
grappled for freedom but Alexander seemed enhanced with vitality as
he flipped her over. She was face down, his knee in her back while he
bound her arms with the belt when she heard the most bittersweet
sound in the world—the Great Arrow pulling into the yard outside
the open window. Before, her only thought was to block Mr. Melling
out, but now she knew in doing so she prevented Douglas from
being able to save her.

Thirty-Four

Magdalene's shrill scream carried through the still air.

"Maggie!" Douglas bellowed from the yard.

Mr. Melling tried in vain to open the door from the hallway. "Curse you two!" he yelled.

Alexander's laugh vibrated through Magdalene like an earthquake as he raked his fingers through her hair to undo the rest of her messy braid. "Your plan was splendid, Magdalene. No one can reach us."

He climbed off the bed to remove his muddied clothing. His dirt-stained hands turned her around and yanked the soiled bedspread out from under her, tossing it to the floor.

"Alex, don't let the demon win. Just this morning we joked around the kitchen table and you gave your time in service to Georgiana."

"Don't speak to me of such things unless you want to be gagged."

"What are you doing here?" Douglas's rage was clear in his voice.

"This is my house, I should ask you that!" Mr. Melling roared in return. The sound of a scuffle and the door pounding against the wardrobe sent waves of despair through Magdalene.

"I almost wish I could watch that fight, but I'd rather be here with you." Alexander's hand played down her neck, until his fingertips caressed her collar bones and then continued to the lace edge of her chemise. "You're gorgeous, Magdalene."

Alexander dropped fully on her, kissing her with frenzied desire. Kicking and squirming, Magdalene did the only thing she could think of—she bit his tongue, tasting his blood before he pulled away. He spit to the side of the bed and turned back to her, blood trickling from the corner of his lips as a cold tempest swirled through the room.

"You're tenacious. Turn that passion to me and this could be beautiful for both of us."

In the hall, the clash between Mr. Melling and Douglas continued—the wall shuddering beneath the weight of the men striking against it.

Magdalene kicked, trying to knock Alexander off balance.

"Surrender to me and I'll be gentle. If you keep fighting, it will make it vulgar when what we have together is magnificent." His gaze softened as he stroked her cheek, wiping away the fresh tears. "I never wanted to hurt you."

"You're hurting me, Alex, physically and emotionally." She puffed the words out as she shoved him with her feet. "We shared a real kiss yesterday and promised we'd seek the other out should either of us end up alone. You even told your father we're friends and fought him for me. If you go through with this now, that will all be lies."

Alexander crumpled between her knees. "I'm not strong enough, not good enough."

She scooched toward the top of the bed to get away from him and knocked something hard against the wooden headboard. Feeling under the pillows with her bound hands, her fingers clutched a familiar shape and pulled it free.

Alexander began to mumble as he rocked back and forth in his self-made cocoon. "I didn't mean to hurt you. I didn't want to do it!"

From the hall, what sounded like a head being repeatedly slammed against the wall shook the room like thunder. Magdalene slid off the edge of the bed, still clutching the crucifix in her hand behind her back, and tottered toward the door.

"Douglas!" she cried out, afraid to either hear his reply or silence because she knew he was either being thrashed or beating Mr. Melling to death.

Something hit the floor and then the wardrobe began to shake from the door shoving against it.

"Maggie!"

The wardrobe had been pushed a few inches, but Douglas could only get his bloodied fingers through.

"Maggie, are you okay?"

"Yes. I'll try to help push. Tell me when you're ready." Magdalene, without the full use of her arms, put her back to the side of the wardrobe and bent her knees so she could leverage it with her lower body muscles.

Douglas counted to three and then they worked together, opening the door enough for Magdalene to slip out.

"Maggie, my love." Douglas kissed her in spite of his split lip and bleeding cut over his blackening eye. Then he undid the belt around her arms and rubbed them gently before buttoning her top, wincing from the movement of his bloodied knuckles. "What did they do to you?"

"Alex needs your help. Don't be mad at him. He came back from digging and fought his father off me. Mr. Melling slammed him against the wall, and when he woke up, he became oppressed. Mr. Melling was dragging me to his room. As awful as it looks and sounds, Alex did save me." Douglas held Magdalene close, burying his head in the hair hanging over her shoulder. "I wasn't thinking about you coming back, I was trying to keep Mr. Melling out. I'm sorry."

"No, Maggie." He kissed her again. "You did well. You kept yourself as safe as possible in the midst of hell."

Magdalene glanced to the ground where Mr. Melling slumped against the wall.

"Don't concern yourself with him. He's not going anywhere."

"Is he—"

"It doesn't matter, but if he does wake, he'll wish he was dead."

"Come help Alex. There's a boat on the beach waiting to take them back to Mobile." Magdalene urged Douglas into the room. He winced at seeing the state of the bed and Alexander in nothing but his under drawers collapsed on his side.

"He didn't get to me, Douglas. He was himself longer than he wasn't. He fought for me honorably before we came in here."

"I've failed her, Douglas. I failed you both. Please put me out of my misery."

"I'll do no such thing," he answered.

Magdalene approached Alexander—crucifix outstretched. Douglas retreated to the fireplace but kept watch. She carefully placed the cross in Alexander's open palm. "Redemption is within your grasp, Alex. You were a hero until you slipped into the darkness, but you're back."

"I'm sorry for failing you," Alex whispered.

"You, Alexander Melling, came in like a lion and protected me as long as you could. And from the looks of your clothes and boots, you dug Georgiana a terrific resting place before that."

"It's as tall as me, even if the bottom has a foot of water in it. I hope Douglas won't have to fix it. I wish I could stay to see it to the end, but I know you need me and my father gone."

Magdalene placed her hand on his cheek. "Your mother and bride await your safe return. Beatrice will be overjoyed to see you. Cleave to her."

"I'll keep our promise tucked right here." He pointed to his heart with the crucifix and squeezed her hand with his free one.

Douglas stepped between the two. "Let's get clean clothes for you, Alex."

Alexander handed Magdalene the crucifix and followed Douglas from the room. Magdalene climbed atop the bed and rehung it in its rightful place before going to meet the others. She stopped in the doorway to stare at Mr. Melling's swollen and bleeding face. His arm resting across his chest began to twitch and reached out, striking the paneling on the lower half of the wall.

"I can smell you, Miss Jones. I sense the passion that draws Alex to you." He heaved himself off the floor by gripping the molding, and briefly rested face-first against the wall, his blood smearing against the deep red of the wallpaper. "Now it's my turn."

He turned and tried to fall upon her, but she screamed and jumped toward the back stairs.

Douglas rushed into the hall, pushing past the man to get to Magdalene.

Half-dressed in clean pants and an unbuttoned shirt, Alexander grabbed his father from behind. Fury seared across his face as he hoisted the large man over his head. Mr. Melling struck the chandelier with a shattering crash of glass. A sickening hiss filled the space as his clothing caught fire on the exposed gas flames.

"Alexander!" Mr. Melling yelled. "You're the death of me! Put me down!"

"I told you not to touch her!" Alexander threw his father against the wall. The stench of burned flesh filled the stuffy hall as smoke rose from Mr. Melling's suit jacket. "You couldn't leave Maggie alone, you allowed Eliza to die without justice, and…my Lucy!"

He kicked his father before Douglas could wrap Alexander in a bear hug.

"Get a hold of yourself, Alex! Look over at Maggie. See, she's fine."

Magdalene tried to fight back the memory of her own father's burning flesh, but the smell was too much for her to repress. She shuddered and retched into the open doorway of the bathroom.

Alexander couldn't shake Douglas loose, so he kicked at his father. "It should have been me fighting him, but I was too weak! I'll always be too weak—my scars prove it."

Alexander stopped struggling and Douglas relaxed his grip.

Magdalene, tears running down her face, looked to Alexander. "You're a lion, Alex."

Alexander shoved Douglas toward Magdalene. "Run! Take her and go! This is the only way to save her, to save all of us!" Fervor burned in his ice blue eyes as he yanked his shirt off and threw it into the open flames of the chandelier above his head.

Douglas shielded Magdalene as Alexander dropped the burning shirt upon his father, the flames quickly spreading up the glossy paneling.

"Go!" Alexander yelled. "I must see this finished!"

"Alex!" Magdalene shrieked and clawed at the doorframe when Douglas tried to take her down the back stairs. "Alex, don't leave me!"

"I'll be part of his sin no more and won't live a lie. Remember, I'm not scared of fire."

Douglas threw Magdalene over his shoulder and ran down the stairs.

Uncle Simon looked into the kitchen from the porch.

"Open the door!" Douglas yelled at him. He stepped to the side so his nephew could run out with Magdalene.

"Go get him!" Magdalene screamed as she pummeled Douglas's back. "Save him!"

He placed her on the ground at the white fence. "He'd never forgive me, even if I could. It's too late, Maggie. You know it's too late."

She fell back against the fence. "Georgiana! I tried to help her but couldn't before he was after me. I promised Lydia! Don't take that away from me. Too much is already lost!"

As Magdalene buried her face in her hands, Douglas ran for the house.

"My God, Seacliff Cottage is burning!" Uncle Simon shouted as he looked at the flames coming out of the window in Magdalene's old room. "Where's Master Melling?"

Magdalene lifted her head. "Inside, with his father."

"Douglas told me not to come in, so I waited. Could I have helped?"

She shook her head and continued to cry.

Douglas returned carrying the small coffin in his arms. "Come to the stable yard in case the house goes down."

Magdalene made no effort to move, even when Uncle Simon offered his hand. She stared at the flames that selfishly took one of the men she loved. Douglas saw the coffin and his uncle to their front stoop and returned, gathering Magdalene into his arms.

"Can you hear me, Maggie?"

She nodded—or thought she did—in her numbness.

He carried her toward their house. "I need to speak with the captain of the boat Mr. Melling hired."

Magdalene, seeing her husband clearly for the first time since Alexander charged at his father, fingered his broken face and motioned to his bloody knuckles. "You're in no shape to be doing that. I need to tend your wounds."

"The fact that you're alive and we've survived another battle within those walls is what's powering me right now. I can't stop until this tragedy is seen to, and that won't happen until word of the fire reaches the rest of the family."

"He didn't need to do it!" She cried on Douglas's shoulder, causing him to stop before the front step.

"Alex did what he felt was best to protect you. He loved you, Maggie. He gave his life to save you." Douglas sat her down on the little porch and went for the beach.

A short time later, he returned with the captain and two deckhands. They stood by the picket fence and watched the flames devour the interior of the house until the saturated exterior walls folded in. Magdalene sat beside the coffin on the front step of the carriage house, one hand on the lid, with Uncle Simon in the rocker behind her. When Seacliff Cottage was a smoldering island in the middle of the saturated lawn, the captain and his workers returned to the beach.

Douglas's measured steps brought him back to his family.

"I asked the captain if he'd heard reports from Dauphin Island or Captain Walker. He knows he's alive and at least one of his boats is serviceable, but he's not sure about the rest of his fleet. I asked him to pass along that we're here when he's ready and able, but I'm sure it will be several days before he gets to us."

"No trouble there." Uncle Simon pushed himself up from the rocker with the aid of the chair arms. "We just need more food."

"I bought a box of canned goods at the store in Daphne with just that in mind. It's in the automobile."

"You two take fine care of an old man, but I did say I'd see to dinner today. Looks like it will be more like supper. I'll get back to it."

"I'm not hungry," Magdalene whispered.

Douglas placed his hand on her shoulder and looked at his uncle. "We're going to see to Georgiana and then we'll be home. Let's try for some closure, Maggie."

Magdalene and Douglas set off into the forest. It took time to navigate the cluttered paths with his load and her distracted state. When they made it to the clearing, they were met by an impressive mountain of wet, crimson dirt beside the gravesite.

"Alex did well," Douglas said as he lay on the damp ground and lowered the coffin into the hole.

"He was scared he'd disappoint you," Magdalene whispered.

Douglas stood and took the shovel. "He worried too much what other people think. If he hadn't—"

"Don't you dare say it!"

He hung his head. "I don't mean it, Maggie. I'm sorry."

Magdalene walked to the sepulcher while Douglas shoveled dirt on top of the coffin. She wandered between the two places, watching his progress. When the hole in the earth was half filled, the chasm in her heart widened. Alexander Melling, the man she'd had her first experiences with as a woman, was no more. The man who claimed his passion for her consumed him to self-injury proved the truth by burning himself alive to save her. She collapsed on the marble steps, wracked with sobs.

Douglas was beside her, holding her to his chest. "I know it hurts, but it wasn't your fault."

"I'm not innocent!" The words Alexander had spoken to her in the bedroom came back with sickening clarity. "He knew I desired him. I drank with him in the parlor and gave him entrance to my room several times. God help me, I even yearned for Claudio! I'm not fit for you, not fit to live."

Douglas smoothed the hair off her face.

"I loved him! I didn't know how much until now. I feel myself slipping away. He's pulling me with him."

"He sacrificed himself to save you. Don't go into the darkness or it will be in vain." The tremors began in her body like when she convulsed in the parlor the day before. Magdalene lingered in cold darkness. "Don't leave me, Maggie. I need your love."

She opened her eyes when his salty tears fell upon her face. "Is there love for me here?"

"My heart is yours. I'll never stop loving you." His breath was hot on her cheek as he kissed her.

She put her hands over his and brought them to her lips. Douglas's knuckles seeped with fresh blood. "Help me up and give me the shovel."

"No, you rest."

"Your body needs to heal from the fight." Magdalene lifted her skirt, tore off the ruffled hem of her chemise, and took Douglas's right hand into her own to wrap his knuckles. When she tied it closed, she kissed the back of his hand. "Give me the shovel and I'll finish."

Epilogue

The island air was cool with a hint of salt as the late
winter wind blew in from the mainland. Douglas, with his bag
thrown over his shoulder, jogged up the path toward the shingled
house on the edge of the village. Through the palmettos and oaks, he
heard the O'Farrells' goats in the next lot and smiled because it
reminded him of the sheep on the Highlands back home. The past
five months of living on Dauphin Island were easily his happiest days
on earth. His job on the water was fulfilling, but it wasn't until he
stepped through the door of his little house that he truly felt alive.

"Maggie, supper smells wonderful," he called.

Uncle Simon peered around the kitchen doorway, a grin on
his wrinkled face. "Thank you kindly, son. The gumbo will be ready
in another half hour."

With a laugh, Douglas set his bag and cap on the rocking
chair in the front room. "Where is she?"

"Went out to see Mrs. Walker for some advice, but she
should be here soon."

Not wanting to wait to see his wife, Douglas hastened up the
lane. When he cut under the branches of a sprawling oak to get to the
next street, he came out from under the canopy right in front of
Magdalene in her new, loose-fitting cobalt dress.

"Maggie!" He took her into his arms right there in the road
and kissed her like he'd been gone for weeks rather than the day. She
smelled of cinnamon like his morning coffee, tasted of sweet cream
butter, and possessed that faraway look in her eyes that descended
whenever a letter came from Claudio. "Was there mail today?"

"How'd you know?" She smiled as they stepped under the
tree.

He took hold of a tendril of her rich brown hair that had
come undone from the braid and tucked it behind her ear as he

kissed her rosy cheek. "You have the Seacliff gaze in your eyes. How's Claudio doing?"

"The senior priest finally retired so the parish is his. He's worried, of course. Some of the older members think him too vivacious to be taken seriously. But he's concerned about Mrs. Melling. She's visiting cousins in New Orleans now, so he's going to visit her there next week." Magdalene's chest heaved as she sighed, calling attention to the way her breasts were developing. "When there's news about her, I can't help but think about Alexander and Georgiana. Then I worry about losing our baby. I went to speak to Claire to see if there's anything else I can do to help prevent a miscarriage."

Douglas went to his knees, gently placing his hands on her rounded belly. He knew the town already talked of his and Magdalene's uninhibited ways—how they kissed and hugged in the street and at the docks no matter who watched—so he didn't mind if someone spied him under the oak caressing his wife's curves that held their growing baby.

"Maggie, this little Campbell is strong. I've seen you gasp from the movements and the babe is only half grown." He cupped his hands around his mouth and pressed them to her belly. "You're a strong, glorious baby. Keep growing until you make your mother miserable this summer with the weight and kicking."

Douglas flattened his palms around her middle and waited as her laughter died away. And then he felt it. He stared, mouth gaping, as the first prickle of movement traveled from his hands to his heart, causing a chill to encompass him as the reality of his impending fatherhood wafted over his being.

Not wanting to break contact, he looked through a veil of unshed tears and saw Magdalene's radiant smile. "I love you both more today than yesterday."

Magdalene tugged his arm. "Come on, before someone sees us."

"Only if you promise I can play with the baby tonight, my hands on the bare swell of your body."

"If the baby's as stubborn as me, you'll be hard-pressed for a response when you want one."

He stood and placed his hands on her hips, walking her backward with him until he was against the trunk of the oak. "I'll try every night until I see our baby in your arms. Remember that day the hurricane started?"

"How could I forget?"

"When we were in the loft together with Georgiana, you said you had an image you couldn't shake from your mind until you saw it fulfilled and I said I had the same thing."

Magdalene leaned sideways against his chest. "Yes, and I said they both had to wait because we had a houseful of people."

"Mine was to see you holding our child. After seeing you with Georgiana, I wanted nothing more than to see you gaze in wonder at a baby we created together." He placed a hand low on her belly and the other around her back. "The day grows steadily closer for mine to be fulfilled. What's yours?"

"Nothing so noble, but it's already happened."

"You promised to tell me everything."

Magdalene blushed. "That morning, when the rain started, I let it pour over me as I felt your face and we kissed. When we got back on the porch—"

"Your white blouse!"

"Yes, and when you finally got me to go in to change, you said if we were alone, you'd make love to me in the rain. That's all I could think of for a while."

"That first week of work here, I forgot my bag on the boat one afternoon and you insisted on walking with me to get it, but not until after supper. I never could understand why you didn't want me to run back right away and save you the trouble of coming along." Douglas smiled and raised his left eyebrow.

"Don't give me that look! The rain clouds were building and it needed to be dark."

"And when it started pouring, I tried to get you into the cabin but you pulled me onto the deck. You started kissing me while unbuttoning my clothes." He smoothed his bushy beard and furrowed his brow.

"All part of seeing my vision fulfilled, but don't look at me like that! You know what it does to me." She playfully knocked him on the arm.

Douglas leaned his wooly, red chin against her head so he could inhale her scent as he thought of the way the rain had run down her skin and made for a new experience. "And was it everything you expected, everything you wanted?"

"You remember how I was. What do you think?" She brought a hand up his chest and ran her fingers around his side.

"I think I need to take my spicy Maggie home before the neighbors see more than necessary."

***

On a Saturday night in May, the windows open to allow the slight breeze to cool the house as drizzle ran off the roof and trees, Douglas sat cross-legged on the bed in his under drawers. He stared at Magdalene lying on her side next to him, her belly exposed.

"There!" he nearly shouted. "That was a foot!"

Magdalene groaned. "And now the offending foot is pushing against my ribs. You need to start doing this in the morning instead of bedtime."

"You want the baby used to getting up by four to see Papa off to work?"

"Yes, and I'll show the child how to make your coffee with just the right amount of cinnamon so I can sleep in."

"But you won't even tell me your recipe."

She looked up at him with a teasing smile. "That's because I want you to need me every morning."

"Like you need me every night?" He fingered her lips and she took a spirited nip at him.

"Those were the days—and nights."

"Yes, Maggie, but we still have quality even if the quantity has changed. Do you remember what I told you in the stable the first afternoon we met?"

"You thanked me because I helped with Janus."

He laughed. "Besides that, or because of it. I told you we make a good team. Over a year later, we still do. Better than I expected." He leaned in for a kiss that turned to touching, which led to baby acrobatics.

Magdalene held her round abdomen, and looked like she felt nauseous.

Douglas put his lips to her belly. "Little Campbell, Mum says it's time for bed."

A foot or hand thrust out in response, prodding Douglas's jowl.

He rubbed his chin, covered in a week's worth of red growth. "Feisty, like Mum."

"Or Uncle Claudio. If the baby is a boy, Claude would be a fine name."

"Is that what he fills his letters with these days, petitions for the baby to be named after him? I don't suppose he's suggested Claudette, has he?"

Magdalene laughed and then shifted to try to get comfortable. "No, but he reminded me his sister's name was Gabriella."

"At least that has a pretty ring to it." Douglas shut off the flame on the oil lamp and settled next to his wife, caressing her arm from shoulder to fingers. "Have you handled enough babies now to not be frightened at the thought of caring for one?"

"Thanks to you I can't walk anywhere without a lady handing off her child to me. Word travels fast here, faster than in Seven Hills because everyone lives closer on an island."

He chuckled and rubbed a hand over her belly. "Anything to help my Maggie."

***

Douglas ran from the docks, his sweat soaked shirt no worse for the jog as he'd been working since before sunup that Wednesday in the September heat. He got a few scowls from the men as he was one of the few husbands on the island who returned home eagerly each day rather than gathering for drinks or swapping tales while smoking. He'd been warned his attitude would change with a screaming baby in the mix of home life, but he continued to race home to see his wife, son, and uncle.

"Maggie, my bride!" he shouted as soon as he reached the yard.

She met him on the porch with a smile and their two-month-old in her arms, a sight that never ceased to make his heart soar.

"Happy anniversary, Maggie." He dropped a small crate and his bag on the floor and passed her a paper-wrapped bunch of red roses from the city. "Shall I wear my kilt to supper?"

She smiled and leaned to him for a kiss. "Please do. And the flowers are gorgeous."

"Pass me Kade so you can find a place for them."

She shook her head. "Your shirt's soaked. I don't want him catching a chill."

Douglas undid the top few buttons and pulled his shirt over his head, dropping it on Uncle Simon's rocking chair. "My son, please."

"Kade Gabriel Campbell, if you're half the man your father is, you'll be set for life." She kissed his sparse, dark hair and placed him in Douglas's eager arms, taking a moment to run her fingers over her husband's muscles.

"Aye, I love you too, Maggie." He took the cooing baby to the swing he'd built for Magdalene's birthday on the end of the porch and laid his son in his lap so he could make sure everything about him still worked properly. Fingers, toes, smiles, and giggles. Then he held him to his chest and sang ditties from his childhood.

Magdalene returned from seeing to the flowers and pointed to the crate. "What's that about?"

"Came on the mail boat addressed to both of us. Not sure what it is, but I thought it'd be fun to open it together since it's our special day. It's postmarked from Louisiana."

Magdalene brought it to the swing and took Kade from Douglas so he could use his pocket knife to leverage open the small crate. A mess of pine shavings and another box were within.

She caught her breath when Douglas removed the bottle of amber liquid. "It's like seeing a ghost."

Douglas pulled out an unsigned note from the box and passed it to Magdalene.

For the happy couple who only have a taste for Scotch and each other. Enjoy sharing it.

He kissed her cheek. "I happily accept the gift and hope you'll allow me to share some with you after supper."

"We have no fancy parlor or the proper drinking glasses."

"And does that bother you?" He trailed a finger down her rosy cheek.

With softness in her brown eyes, she smiled. "Not in the least, because I have you."

THE END

Bonus

"Grace Shadowed"

The Possession Chronicles #3.5

John Woodslow walked into the back parlor of the Aethelwulf Club, eyes on the graying man amid the dark paneled walls.

Dr. Stephen Moore stood and extended his hand, his bulk towering over the younger man. "Dr. Woodslow, it's a pleasure to meet with you."

"Thank you for arranging the time, Dr. Moore." John firmly shook the offered hand. As soon as they were settled in matching leather wing chairs, a butler poured them each a snifter of brandy. Dr. Moore offered a cigar. John accepted, pleased the older doctor didn't hold back his hospitality before the subject at hand was broached. "Thank you."

When the room cleared of all but a gentleman reading The Daily Register under the corner lamp—newspaper concealing his face—Dr. Moore smiled.

"Well, John, I'm sure you've guessed why I wanted to meet with you. I know word is out that I'm seeking a partner in my practice."

"Yes, Dr. Moore. And I'm honored you thought of me."

"You come highly recommended, having graduated top of your class and doing well in your early years at the hospital, but I have reservations. That's why I wished to meet in an informal setting with you first. I don't want you to get your hopes up too high, young man."

At twenty-six, John was hardly inexperienced, though he knew a doctor over forty would see him as green. "I'm happy to put any of your concerns to rest, Dr. Moore."

"I'm pleased to hear your willingness, but I'm afraid the matters at hand could sully your reputation in the medical field if they prove to be true."

John felt the color drain from his face and glanced nervously at the hidden man in the corner. "I can't think what you might have heard that would sour you toward me."

"Mystics of Dardenne membership for one." Dr. Moore's grin shone more amused than disappointed.

The butler came into the doorway. "Telephone call for you, Dr. Moore."

"I know you understand what life as a doctor is like, but you must excuse me, John. I'll return as soon as possible." Dr. Moore stood and took his hand with the Dardenne handshake.

John stared after the doctor as he left.

Across the room, the newspaper lowered to reveal a smirking Rupert Lyons. "Gave you the old handshake, did he?"

"How did you know?"

Rupert laughed. "You look as though you've seen a ghost and my stint as secretary of the society afforded me the opportunity to peruse the books. I'm happy to report Dr. Moore's years as a member gave a grand showing, even given our record as most debauched. He was head Dardenne in eighty-one when—"

The butler returned to top off the brandy glasses on the side table between the doctors' chairs. Rupert raised his own tumbler and the man saw to it before leaving.

"Then why is he no longer a member if he never married?" John asked.

"Not many Dardennes hold membership for longer than half a dozen years. Those who don't marry tend to step down or are run out well before they turn thirty. We'll get our letters of resignation after this carnival season, with or without a bride to walk down the aisle."

John sucked on the cigar and blew smoke rings as he took a mental tally of the eligible debutantes in the city. Grace Anne Marley always seemed brighter than her peers. Unfortunately, he'd heard too much about her loose ways from other Dardennes to take her seriously.

"Now that my purchase of the Mellings' law firm has been finalized, I'll be staking my claim by New Year's Eve," Rupert warned. "The hurricane in September seems to have all the men in the city on the move. Better choose fast if you want prime pickings. Study the ladies at the Stuarts' Christmas party tomorrow and call dibs before Sean or one of the others step up."

Rupert raised the newspaper as Dr. Moore returned.

"Sorry to keep you waiting, John." He took his former seat and swallowed a shot. "Now, as I was saying, you're at the age of settling down if you wish to remain respectable in society. In order to keep the esteem of my patients, I can only bring in a partner who's in good standing socially. If you'd like to entertain an offer, I insist you revoke your membership and find a respectable wife. There seems to be too many scandals hanging over the Dardennes and debutantes these days, but maybe that's more to do with that gossip magazine than an influx in wanton behavior. That Kate Stuart…" The doctor took another swig. "Whoever chains himself to that firecracker will be in for a treat."

***

"Grace Anne!"

Sadie's shrill voice carried up the stairs to where Grace Anne sat as she fixed her hair at the dressing table. She turned as her sister careened to a stop in the bedroom.

"Grace Anne, you have to help me! It's a matter of life and death!" Anything and everything was a dramatic episode to the twelve-year-old.

She put a hand on Sadie's quaking shoulder. "It can't be all bad."

"But it is! Come to the back porch and see for yourself. Alice and I had to rescue it from her brothers."

Grace Anne groaned. If the Beauchamp boys were involved, there was no telling what mess her sister had gotten herself into. "Judith is picking me up in thirty minutes and I still need to powder my nose."

"You know I wouldn't bother you on a party night if it wasn't important. And we need to move fast before Cook or Nanny notices and tells Mama and Papa when they get home."

She sighed, but followed her sister's blonde pigtails down the front staircase. At times like these, Grace Anne resented being the oldest and having a nine year gap between her and Sadie. Esther, the sister between them, took ill in the yellow fever epidemic nearly a decade prior and didn't survive. Sadie was too young to remember but their parents took years to recover from the loss. Five-year-old Marie wasn't born until 1901, four years after Esther passed away. The three remaining sisters were too spread age wise to be bosom friends and Grace Anne felt more like an aunt than a sister to them.

They exited the house through the dining room and met Alice Beauchamp on the patio. The solemn-faced girl held a rope attached to a mangy brown dog that was knee-high to her. Its matted fur had an odor of the sewer from ten feet away.

"Alice's brothers were tormenting him."

"Of course they were! That beast isn't fit for human companionship." Grace Anne thought of her beloved dog, Flora, who disappeared after she was sent out of town when Esther took ill. She returned to a home devoid of her dear sister and collie.

"It's not his fault he's dirty!" Sadie said with indignation. "Those boys were pulling him through the alleys like he was a tin can on a string. We had to save him, but Alice can't keep him with her brothers around. If you could hide him in your roo—"

"Absolutely not!" Grace Anne crossed her arms over her blue gown. "I don't have time for a filthy mutt, especially with Carnival season upon us."

"But if we get him clean, we could give him to Marie for Christmas. Mama wouldn't say no to a present, especially one so cute."

"He's hideous!"

"He's not so bad. And once he's washed and brushed he'll be even sweeter. We've never asked for a dog before, so Mama never told us no. It'll be the first—"

Grace Anne's chin went up. "I had a gorgeous dog with silky fur. She was the smartest thing this side of Government Street. Esther and I played with her every afternoon and she slept at the foot of my bed each night. There can never be another dog like Flora in this house."

"Please, Grace Anne," Alice said with pleading brown eyes. "I can't hide him from Nanny in my room and if we let him go Richard will kill him."

"That brother of yours is a hooligan, but not a murderer, Alice." Both girls continued to stare at Grace Anne—the dog joining in with sad eyes. "I won't let you bring him inside in his current state."

"We'll wash him out here and brush him real good. We'll work fast before Nanny brings Marie down for supper. I only need to keep him in your room until Mama comes home and it's too late for her to say no. Please, Grace!"

"If he soils *anything* in my room—"

"He'll be good as gold," Sadie promised with a smile. "Come on, boy."

The two girls led the dog toward the garden spigot, the poor thing limping behind them.

"That dog's lame," Grace Anne called after them.

"He's just tired is all," Alice said. "My brothers wore him out."

The mantel clock chimed through the open door and Grace Anne hurried back to her room to finish preparations for the Stuarts' Christmas party. She wanted to be sure to look appealing enough to catch the eye of one of the handsome bachelors—preferably Dr. Woodslow.

***

John trudged up the front walk of the Victorian monstrosity on Government Street and handed his hat and coat to the help as soon as he was in the door. After the obligatory greeting to Mr. and Mrs. Stuart, he journeyed through the evergreen swags for the sitting room where the younger crowd gathered and forced a smile for the host's daughter.

"It's always good to have a doctor in the house," Kate Stuart simpered as she took in the fit of his black tuxedo. "You are looking especially well tonight, Dr. Woodslow."

"Thank you, Miss Stuart." Unable to find something to compliment her on—other than her well-endowed chest beneath the tight gown—he stopped his greeting at that.

When he tried to continue into the room, she put a hand on his arm. "We seem to have more ladies than gentlemen in attendance tonight. Would you be a dear and spend a little extra time dancing so none of our guests go without?"

"Of course, Miss Stuart."

"It would, after all, be beneficial to you as well. I know Dr. Moore is set on partnering with a family man."

The hurricane might have put an end to *Snitch*, but magazine or not, Kate was still on top of the gossip game. John nodded to her, hoping she'd release him from her clutches soon. "We're all approaching the settling years."

"Just don't settle for anything short of the best, Dr. Woodslow." She angled toward his ear. "I assure you there are plenty of virginal ladies within these walls tonight. There's no need to be a Davenport with your choice."

"Well said, Miss Stuart." John smirked at the thought of Alexander Melling's ex-fiancée now joined with the most respectable man of their age group in the city. As he helped himself to a glass of eggnog, John wondered if it were possible to find a debutante whom a Mystics of Dardenne member hadn't deflowered. He didn't want to sink himself so low as to court a first year deb, but which lady in the room hadn't felt the groping hands of a Dardenne at a masquerade or entertained more? Probably only Kate Stuart herself as no man would dare attempt anything on that predator.

Thomas and Sean waved him over to the corner. Sipping his drink, he ignored their attempts at conversation as his eyes roamed the sea of colorful gowns across the room. Grace Anne Marley's hour-glass figure filled her royal blue dress perfectly, her golden hair framing her heart-shaped face like a halo. Her nose was a little too sharp, but those lips made up for it. If it weren't for the fact that Sean and several others had boasted about kissing her, he would have declared himself to her when they danced at The Point Clear Hotel the weekend before the hurricane.

Rupert joined them.

"Did you do it?" Sean asked.

"I have her father's permission." Rupert grinned.

Sean slugged Rupert and laughed. "I don't envy you that prize, Lyons."

"What?" John looked between the two.

"Did you not hear anything we were talking about?" Sean gave him a scowl before continuing. "Rupert asked Mr. Stuart's permission to court Kate."

John choked on the eggnog, sputtering until Thomas slapped him on the back—which, thanks to Thomas's boxing hobby, nearly sent him face-first onto the Oriental rug.

Rupert leaned closer once the coughing subsided. "She may be a frigid bitch, but I know where to get what I want. Even though Consuela left town this autumn, there are plenty more to choose from. And what better way is there to avoid being gossiped about than by marrying the source of the chatter? Kate is all about saving face. She'd never speak ill of me to anyone."

Though impressed with Rupert's business plan for marriage, John couldn't get over the idea of marrying a woman he had no desire for. Life was too short for that. He wanted respectability *and* love. He'd be too busy with work to see to a woman at home and then seek release elsewhere. It was already rare he entered the red light district outside of carnival season. His lack of time and energy was to blame because—unlike his lawyer friends—his job was physically demanding and took more hours from his day.

A few minutes later, a string quartet began playing across the hall. Rupert offered his arm to Kate and they led a procession to the ballroom. As couples paired off, John ditched his tumbler on the credenza and approached Grace Anne.

He bowed before her. "Would you do me the honor of this dance, Miss Marley?"

With a beguiling smile, she dipped into a curtsy that showcased her décolletage. "It would be my pleasure, Dr. Woodslow."

Keeping his hands in respectable locations as they waltzed, John couldn't help but stare at Grace Anne's perfectly bowed pink lips. At least they weren't red from use like they often were at gatherings. Maybe tonight he'd be the one to bring color to those succulent petals.

"Have you had a pleasant December thus far, Miss Marley?"

"Yes, though my hands are full at the moment. My parents are in Birmingham for a week and my younger sisters always manage to court trouble, especially the middle one as she's old enough to go about without Nanny."

John smiled down at her, happy to hear she wasn't overly strained with the care of rambunctious children—for he wanted a few of his own one day. "Nothing too troubling, I hope."

"She brought a mangy dog home," Grace Anne blurted, showcasing her manners weren't as refined as some of the other ladies.

John laughed and enjoyed the way her eyebrows pinched together as she flashed a quick frown.

"It's not only that," she continued. "Sadie expects me to keep the dog hidden in my room until Christmas. She wants to give it to Marie, our youngest sisters, so our parents can't turn it out."

"Would they turn out a helpless puppy?"

"It's not a puppy, Dr. Woodslow. It's a dog. A filthy little beast it looked too." Grace Anne's cheeks turned rosy.

"Do you not like dogs?"

"I have nothing against them. I had my own as a girl." Grace Anne shuddered and a shadow crossed her face.

John instinctively held her closer. "What is it, Miss Marley?"

Her eyes widened and she appeared to blink back tears. "Nothing, Dr. Woodslow. But that creature was not fit for proper living in the state it was in."

The song came to an end and he took her by the elbow, not wanting to let her go. "May I escort you to the refreshment table?"

"No, thank you. You've been most kind."

He reluctantly watched her leave. Heading for a tray of wine being brought around the ballroom, John found himself reaching for a glass at the same time as Dr. Moore.

"While it's good to see you dancing with an eligible young lady, please keep in mind that one's father has had his fortune less than a decade and she was unfortunately linked with Lucille Easton as recently as two years ago."

John felt his cheeks go red and smoothed a hand over his slicked back hair in desperate need of a trim. "Miss Marley was on a European tour with her family when the scandal happened. I hardly see how that impugns her character."

"Those young ladies were dearest friends, were they not?"

"I cannot say." John kept his gaze on the doctor's. "I haven't a younger sister or connection to either of them other than through Edmund Easton, who was just as shocked as the rest of us over the fall of his sister."

The knowing look in the older doctor's eyes was one of amusement as he patted John's back. "Choose wisely, Dr. Woodslow."

***

Grace Anne stood with a chattering Judith McGowan—her companion for the night—but all she could think about was the feeling of being in John's arms. It had been three months since she'd spoken to him. The previous time was a September night across the bay during the celebration for Alexander Melling and his Yankee fiancée, Beatrice Kirkpatrick. The New Yorker was elegant, but no match for how he and Lucy must have looked together. Having missed her best friend's first relationship and its aftermath, Grace Anne resented her European travels. If she had been home, she could have kept Lucy from losing her head over a smooth talker like Alexander. But she was pleased to know her dearest friend was now settled with a gentleman. Frederick Davenport had always been kind to Grace Anne when she was playing at the Eastons'—even before her father's lumber business took off during the Spanish-American War.

Kate joined the group emanating a surprising glow.

Hoping to keep Kate focused on her own affairs rather than sniffing out news about Grace Anne's dance partner, she focused the conversation on her. "Do you find Mr. Lyons to be a good dancer, Kate?"

"Of course he is." She checked the time on the pocket watch on her necklace, as though down-playing the excitement in her voice.

"He's nowhere near as fine as Alexander Melling was," Judith said. "He was a scoundrel, but the best dancer in town, though Frederick Davenport is light on his feet as well. Is he here tonight?"

Kate snorted back a laugh. "My parents wouldn't invite that trollop he married into our home. Becoming Mrs. Davenport doesn't make a lady out of a fallen woman. Poor F.L.D. will turn into a hermit from lack of invitations this Mardi Gras season."

"Still," Judith said, "Mr. Lyons isn't as good a dancer as Mr. Davenport."

"He's a thousand times more functional on the dance floor—and other places I bet—than the ancient man you keep making eyes at. And he asked me to call him Rupert." Kate turned away from Judith with a sneer.

"Mr. Smith is a seasoned businessman," Judith retorted. "What's a twenty-year difference anyway? If he doesn't last long, at least his money will. Rupert Lyons is nothing but an upstart lawyer with well-connected relatives."

Kate turned back, her watch lifting from her chest with the quick motion. "Haven't you heard, Judith? Rupert bought the newly renamed *Lyons*, Melling, and Associates. He now owns one of the longest established law firms in the city."

Judith's torso hardly moved within her tightly strung corset, but Grace Anne could tell she huffed for breath. "But he's still a crooked nose cad like the rest of his friends."

Rolling her eyes, Kate went for the hall.

"Have you danced with Rupert Lyons?" Judith asked Grace Anne.

"Unfortunately."

"See! He's nothing to get worked up over, especially compared to a man like Frederick Davenport. Kate can say what she wants about Lucille Easton, but that girl has to have something we don't to land a man like that with her reputation."

Grace Anne held her tongue, refusing to speak of her former best friend though she knew Frederick had loved Lucy since childhood. He was the type of man to remain loyal, no matter what.

"But that Dr. Woodslow," Judith continued. "He's nearly as fine to look at and seems smitten with you tonight, Grace Anne."

"Do you think so?" She cursed the eager tone in her voice when Judith responded with a toothy smile. "I mean, he is handsome, but I—"

"He's coming this way."

Grace Anne felt the blood leave her face and forgot how to breathe as John came to a stop beside her.

"Are you all right, Miss Marley?"

Managing to nod, she gazed up at John, focusing on his strong jaw as she wondered what it would feel like to kiss him.

"She does look pale, doesn't she?" Judith took a step away. "Why don't you take her to get some air, Dr. Woodslow? The veranda can be reached through the dining room."

Judith winked at Grace Anne as John led her toward the hall. The brisk night air kept the party indoors, but Grace Anne was no stranger to dark locations. She'd often gone off with dance partners to show them the kissing skills she'd perfected from her time toying with chauffeurs and the brothers of her friends.

John stopped beside a trailing bougainvillea, the white railing and columns behind him a striking contrast to his black tuxedo and the dark vine. His touch lowered from her elbow, caressing her white gloves until he held her hand. "Are you well, Miss Marley?"

If it wasn't so chilly, she would have melted at the sound of the concern in his voice. "I'm only worried about that stupid dog and what mess might await me at home."

His grin was charming even in the dim space. "I'm afraid I can't help you much with that."

Still holding her hand, she half wished he'd steal a kiss like his friends always did—but the other half was glad he didn't if it meant he respected her. Or maybe he had no interest, though Judith was seldom wrong when it came to what men wanted. Testing her sway over him, Grace Anne tilted her head and pursed her lips ever so slightly.

John squeezed her hand. "Has anyone told you that you're a beguiling figure, Miss Marley?"

"No, Dr. Woodslow," she whispered.

"But surely they must have, with all the men—"

Grace Anne yanked her hand free and stepped back. "Just what do you mean by that?"

"I didn't—"

"Surely you don't think me dim-witted enough to believe there's no accusation when a man referrers to *all the men* in regards to a lady? Just what do you think all these men are doing?"

"Kissing you, Miss Marley," he said with shame. "What man could resist your perfect lips?"

"Surely you can, Dr. Woodslow. We've been acquainted several years now and you've yet to do more than dance a few times with me. Are you morally stronger than the other suitors you accuse me of being fresh with or am I beneath your appeal?" Her hands were on her hips now.

Cheeks ruddy, John met her glare with a soft gaze. "Neither of those things. Please forgive my poor word choices."

She shook her head, not wishing to think about John knowing all of her exploits—however innocent they seemed at the time. "Please excuse me, Dr. Woodslow."

***

The next morning, John stood between Rupert and Sean on the cathedral portico. The three bowed to the widow in black when Mrs. Melling walked by, but soon returned to their whispered conversation.

"And you didn't even kiss her?" Sean looked incredulous.

John shook his head.

"There's definitely something wrong with your approach if you didn't get any action from Grace Anne," Rupert smirked. "The only deb more willing than her is Judith, though she's mellowed a bit now that she's working the older crowd. Mark my words—Judith will be on the arm of a rich widower before Fat Tuesday."

Sean laughed. "And she'll be back on the market within a decade. As long as she keeps those measurements, she'll have no problem scoring another pay day."

"Excuse me, gentlemen." Rupert straightened his tie and descended the steps, offering his arm to Kate when she entered the churchyard with her family.

John cleared his throat and looked at his friend. "How far have you gone with Miss Marley?"

"It's been two years, but it's not something to forget." Sean laughed and slapped John on the back. "Relax, Woodslow. She's not like my Eliza. She's more than willing to kiss, but she's no pushover. I know for a fact she's slapped Thomas and a few others who went for a feel though they'll deny it and claim they won the prize."

He smiled as the woman herself entered the gate. The three Marley sisters with their varying shades of blonde hair were a bright spot amid the Sunday crowd. Grace Anne held the hand of the youngest tucked into her own and the middle sister—the one causing her trouble—followed behind them. On the portico, they paused as Grace Anne removed their mantillas from her reticule. Watching the motherly sight of her pinning the head coverings on the girls spurred John to action.

Reaching the door nearest them, John held it open for Grace Anne with a bow. "Good morning, Miss Marley."

"Good morning, Dr. Woodslow." She gave a shallow nod and went through the door without a smile, though the middle sister turned to stare at him.

Sean came to his side. "What *did* happen between the two of you last night?"

"I fear I made a muddle of things when I alluded to all the men she might—"

Sean laughed. "I knew you weren't as smooth as Easton, but of all the things to say to a woman, that's the worst!"

"Think she'll ever forgive me?"

With a hand clapped on his shoulder, Sean led him into the cathedral. "What girl could resist a Dardenne? Give her time."

But did he have time with Dr. Moore seeking to fill the role of a partner? And would Grace Anne be acceptable in the older doctor's eyes?

***

After Sunday supper, Grace Anne came to terms with what she hoped to avoid. Staring at the chocolate brown dog that followed her around whenever she was in her room, she could no longer pretend its limp wasn't increasing. A whine even accompanied it every few steps. Seeking to provide a bit of relief for the creature, she sat at her desk. The dog immediately settled at Grace Anne's feet.

Reluctantly, she reached down and rubbed behind its ears. Her hand then trailed down to the dog's back, fingers threading through the long fur that was softer than she expected.

After hearing Nanny bring Marie down the hall from the bathroom to the nursery, Grace Anne slipped out of her room to the telephone in her father's study on the main floor. She waited while the operator looked up the number and connected her to the other extension.

"Dr. Woodslow's residence," the voice of a housekeeper or cook came across the line.

"Is the doctor available?" Grace Anne asked.

"Yes, ma'am. May I ask who's calling?"

"Grace Anne Marley."

She twisted a finger around the cord of the earpiece as she waited.

"Miss Marley?"

"I'm sorry to bother you, Dr. Woodslow, but there's a medical issue in my house. I was wondering if you would be able to examine the patient."

"I'd be delighted to, Miss Marley. Is half an hour soon enough?"

"That would be perfect. Thank you. I'll leave the front door unlocked. You may let yourself in so my sisters aren't unnecessarily disturbed. I'll wait for you in the parlor, just to the left upon entering."

"I'll be there as quick as possible, Miss Marley."

Grace Anne said goodnight to Marie and made sure Sadie was settled in her room with a book before collecting the dog. She bundled it in a blanket to carry the poor thing downstairs so no fur would mar the front of her red Sunday dress. After putting the blanket in the corner, she sat in one of the armchairs. Grace Anne was pleased her coldness to the doctor at the cathedral that morning didn't affect his willingness to help.

Five minutes later, John silently stepped into the parlor carrying a black bag.

"The door, please, Dr. Woodslow." When he closed it, she stood. "Thank you for coming so promptly."

He grinned and smoothed a hand over his dark-blond hair that showcased a schedule too busy to visit the barber as often as his friends. "I'm happy to be of service, Miss Marley. I do hope you'll forgive my fumbling words."

Her cheeks heated at him bringing up the unladylike behaviors he alluded to the night before. "Let us speak no more of it, Dr. Woodslow. Are you ready to see the patient?"

"Of course. Which sister is ill? They both looked to be in the peak of health at Mass this morning." He turned for the door. "Or is it one of the help?"

Grace Anne crossed the room to him, the dog jumping from its blanket to follow. "Here, Dr. Woodslow. See how he limps?"

John watched the dog for a few seconds before staring at Grace Anne in disbelief.

"Sadie thought he was simply tired from being strung about by the Beauchamp boys, but it's only gotten worse." She pointed to the floor. "The dog, Dr. Woodslow, or have I grown a second nose that I'm not aware of?"

"I am no veterinarian, Miss Marley. I have been schooled and trained to work exclusively with humans, not animals." His handsome face set in a grimace of indignation.

"Then I suppose I should have called Dr. Hughes. I remember he always gave Flora a checkup when he came to examine me or Esther."

John's face softened before a chuckle escaped. "I'll have to remember that if I move from the hospital to doing regular house calls. Kindness to an animal would be the best way to the heart of an uncooperative child."

It was Grace Anne's turn to take a defiant stance. "First a wanton and now an uncooperative child. Never in all my life have I been subject to such uncouth accusations!"

"You misunderstand me once again." He set his bag on the nearest chair and moved toward her.

She crossed her arms and sidestepped. "Don't try to take it back. I know perfectly well when I'm being insulted."

"I'd never wish to insult or harm you, Miss Marley." His hand settled on her shoulder. "I'm forever saying the wrong things because you make me feel like a school boy before your beauty. My brain runs through a heap of jealous thoughts and my heart beats quicker than my mouth can run. Forgive me for falling under your spell."

A smile of relief found her lips. "You don't think ill of me?"

"Never, Miss Marley."

With a flood of relief, Grace Anne's arms were about his neck, hands playing in the hair that grew over his stiff collar as she angled for his mouth. Pleased John could be bold, she reveled in his taste as his arms encircled her waist. She pressed against him and enjoyed the surge of delight their bodies together brought her.

As though taking her motion as an invitation for more, John's hands roamed her back until they settled on her hips with a kneading motion that made Grace Anne's body tingle with passion. The kisses turned ardent and he worked his lips to the red ruffle at her throat.

She gasped. "Dr. Woods—"

"Call me John, Gracie." He kissed his way back to her lips, planting one there before pulling back enough to look her in the eyes as he ran a thumb across her cheek.

***

Maybe he did wrong by calling her by a pet name before Grace Anne even asked for him to call her by her given one, but it fell from his lips as natural as azaleas blooming in March.

"John," her red lips curved prettily as she whispered, "I don't know what you've heard, but please know I've never allowed a man to hold me like this."

He shushed her with a finger on her mouth—which urged him to lean in for another taste of her sweetness. "As long as I'm the only one you give your kisses to from now on."

Her hug was tight and the feeling of her bosom pressed against him was nearly too much. "I've had my eyes on you a long time, John Woodslow. Every time I practiced kissing, I imagined it was you. I hope I didn't disappoint."

"Let's not start in on that again." He laughed and stroked her arm in an attempt to erase all the stories he'd heard about her. "But you're wonderful, Gracie. And I've been watching you as well."

At their feet, the dog shifted and whined.

"Oh, the poor dear!" Grace Anne bent to retrieve the dog.

"It appears you've taken a liking to him since you cared enough to phone a doctor. Or was that a ruse to get me here for a kiss?" He winked as she blushed.

"He's really much better looking since Sadie and Alice cleaned him up. I believe he has a bit of terrier in him. Of course he doesn't compare to my old girl. Flora was twice this size and her coat was long and silky."

"Set him down a moment so I can see how he stands." John stood back and noticed the way the dog favored its front right paw. He motioned to the blanket. "Is it all right to use it to examine him on?"

Grace Anne quickly spread it over the settee and knelt on the floor beside the dog she'd placed on the blanket.

John got his bag and joined Grace Anne, retrieving the necessary supplies from the case before angling the side table lamp to shine on his four legged patient. Slipping the metal band for his head mirror over his hair, he adjusted the disc so he could see perfectly through the center hole with his left eye. He chanced a look at Grace Anne—the brightness of the reflected light making her creamy complexion glow. He wished the dog wasn't in pain, for he wanted nothing more than to hold her once more, but he silently blessed the mutt for bringing them together.

"Hold him steady, Gracie."

She leaned over the dog with one arm, its affected paw tight in her other grip. John angled closer and the gleam of the mirror immediately caught something in its light. Carefully spreading the fur between the pads of the paw, he licked his lips and held his breath before gingerly touching the object. The dog whined and tried to wince, but Grace Anne held him firm.

"What is it?" she whispered.

"Looks like a piece of glass." He took the scissors in hand. "Let me trim some of these hairs and get a better look."

Trimming done, John turned to Grace Anne. "Would you like to see it through my head mirror?"

"No." She shuddered and buried her face in the dog's coat. "Please hurry and get it out."

"I assume you had no romantic notions of nursing if you can't even bear a bit of glass in a dog."

"No, never. I tend to faint at the sight of blood."

"And yet you've set your sights on a doctor," John teased.

"I might change my mind," she said as she took a coquettish glance at him.

He filched a kiss from her before she could protest. "Don't you dare, Gracie. You're even more amusing than I imagined."

"I shall add amusing to the ever growing list of insults you're unintentionally labeling me with."

"Will I forever be sticking my foot in my mouth around you?"

"I hope so, for it would mean I'll see you again."

John returned her smile before focusing on the task of removing the inch long piece of glass with a steady hand.

"I need alcohol," he said upon removal as he held a clean cloth to the paw. "I've got him."

Grace Anne hurried across the room to a decanter set and returned with two glasses. "Do you always celebrate after a successful operation?"

John laughed so hard he dropped his hold on the cloth. Grace Anne set the drinks on the coffee table and paled at the sight of the bloody linen. Turning to her, John took the nearest tumbler and brought it to her lips. "Drink it quick, my dear. It'll set you to rights."

She downed the whiskey and coughed. John continued to chuckle as he held her upright with a loving arm.

"How old are you, Gracie?"

"Twenty-one last September." Her cheeks were now rosy with health.

"Forgive me for adding another vulgarity to my ever growing list, but how did you manage to make it to twenty-one when you're delightfully naïve about so many things?"

Rather than watch the spark of anger in her eyes, John turned his attention back to the dog. After pouring the contents of his glass over the wound and applying pressure for another minute, he wrapped the paw with fresh bandages from his bag.

"There." He sat back on his heels. "I can honestly say that's the finest paw I've ever tended. Now, do you think I could get a drink I'll be able to enjoy this time?"

After his Monday morning rounds in the hospital, a visitor waited for John in the doctor's lounge.

Dr. Moore snuffed his cigarette in the nearest ashtray. "Did I not make myself clear, Dr. Woodslow?"

"Sir?" John closed the door behind him and prayed no one would enter until the conversation was over.

"About that Marley girl not being the right sort of doctor's wife for my partner. I was leaving a house call at the Powells' across the street after ten o'clock last night and saw her accompany you out onto her porch. I know her parents are out of town and—"

Indignation over the reproachful tone regarding the woman he loved surged through John. "I may be on staff at the hospital, Dr. Moore, but I have been known to take house calls when the need arises. I'll have you know Miss Grace Anne Marley assisted me in a medical procedure for someone in her household. She bravely sat with the patient to offer comfort while I removed a glass splinter from a limb. Then she helped with the sanitation of the wound afterward. If that doesn't sound like a doctor's wife, I don't know what actions would."

"Well…" Dr. Moore puffed his cheeks with a flustered exhalation. "There's still the issue of her friendship with Lucille Easton."

"Perhaps you don't know because you weren't the physician who attended the families, but Miss Marley lost a sister during the yellow fever epidemic of ninety-seven along with the Eastons' three children, all close in age to Lucille. The two bonded in their grief, Dr. Moore, because they both had heartaches not many other children could relate to." John was pleased to have learned that information himself the previous night during a quiet chat over coffee while the dog convalesced on the sofa. "They shared books and daydreams like well-bred girls do in their tender years. They never went about wantonly on the town or any such nonsense you seem determined to believe of Miss Marley because of her childhood friendship with another girl in mourning."

Dr. Moore smoothed his suit jacket as he stood. "It seems you've taken this all to heart, Dr. Woodslow. I'm happy to see you're thinking things through, but do remember the citizens of Mobile don't always know the intricacies of a person's personal life. They only know what they've seen and heard. When they choose a doctor they want respectability."

"As you've said yourself," John said with a smile, "I'm doing well at the hospital. Patients who find themselves within these walls are often too far gone to care what the gossip was about a physician or his wife from years back. They only care that the hands are capable. And the board of directors will see the statistics of those cared for and medical achievements when selecting a head surgeon."

The older doctor laughed. "You're intelligent to the end, Dr. Woodslow. I wish you the best."

"Thank you, Dr. Moore." He offered his hand.

"And she's a vivacious young lady. Just the type to satisfy a Mystics of Dardenne member."

"Was there no one sprightly enough in your day, Dr. Moore?"

"Only one," Dr. Moore said with a smile. "Another Dardenne may have taken Ruth down the aisle, but I got to her first."

***

Grace Anne entered the parlor Monday night, her shadow directly behind the train of her tea gown. While she carried the dog up and down the stairs when it needed to go out, Shadow made fine progress for short trips around her room that day. Settled into the corner of the settee, the shaggy dog curled on the rug beside her.

John let himself in a few minutes later. His grin lit the room and Grace Anne found herself rising to meet him. The dog came directly behind her and John dropped to a knee to look him over.

"If I'm going to come in second to patients, Dr. Woodslow, I'll have to rethink allowing you to court me."

"Well Miss Marley," he said with his drawling charm as he looked up at her, "I'd say seeing our patient is doing well is a cause for celebration. We make a good team, you and I. Another dose of alcohol is just what the doctor orders if all is well, but first I need to inspect the wound."

She motioned to the folded towel on the settee with an air of superiority.

Standing, he took her by the waist and kissed her hard. "And today someone had the nerve to tell me you wouldn't make a proper doctor's wife."

"Yet another insult!" She tried to squirm away, but he held fast.

His warm lips were at her neck, breath in her ear before he whispered. "You may be certain, Gracie dear, that I praised your bravery and comforting abilities when you worked diligently beside me. I hope you'll do as well tonight and we're able to enjoy another conversation afterward."

Feeling completely adored within his arms, Grace Anne pressed her mouth to his and threaded her fingers through his unruly hair.

"Is my sister paying for house calls with affections?" Sadie asked from the doorway.

Grace Anne turned to the door. "Of all the—"

"Come now, Miss Sadie. You know better," John said as he approached the girl in her nightdress. "Your sister and I have a connection deeper than the dog. I respect her too much to accept payment for tending to someone within these walls—human or otherwise."

"Grace Anne said Shadow's better. Is he truly?"

"Shadow is it?" He smiled and looked from Grace Anne to the dog at her feet. "So they've both taken a liking to each other enough to earn a fitting name. The only way to know for sure is to check the wound. Miss Sadie, would you care to be my assistant when I remove the bandage?"

"Yes, please!" Sadie took the doctor's hand.

"But only if you promise to go straight back to bed as soon as Shadow's tended," Grace Anne added.

"Yes, yes. Anything!"

John motioned them toward the settee and set about arranging his supplies. He pulled a bottle of clear alcohol from his bag. "So I'm not accused of using up your daddy's good whiskey on a dog."

Grace Anne placed Shadow in her lap and allowed Sadie to hold the affected paw over the towel so her sister had full view of the happenings instead of her.

"No sign of infection and the swelling is significantly less than it was yesterday," John declared. "It appears your big sister is a better nurse than she expected."

Sadie giggled and then John poured the alcohol over the wound. The dog whined but held still until the paw was wrapped once more. Then Shadow licked John's face before jumping down and lying at Grace Anne's feet.

"Go on to bed now, Sadie," Grace Anne said gently.

The girl stopped beside John as he repacked his medical bag. "Will you have to see Shadow again? Our parents come home tomorrow and he's supposed to be a secret."

"I most certainly will make inquiries over my patient. I've grown rather fond of Shadow and wish to speak to your father about bringing him to my house in the future."

"But I wanted to give him to Marie for Christmas!"

"That dog has chosen your big sister, Sadie. Don't give Shadow to anyone else because I aim to take care of them both."

Sadie caught on with a blush and giggled. "Yes, Dr. Woodslow. Goodnight, and thank you for helping Shadow."

Once they were alone, Grace Anne extended her hand to him. "Do you really mean it, John?"

He pressed his lips to each knuckle. "With all my heart, Miss Marley. I'll declare my intentions to your father tomorrow evening and ask permission to escort you to Christmas Mass and Order of Mayhem's New Year's Eve ball so all of Mobile will know the best kisser in the city is off the market."

"Will you ever learn to pay me a compliment without shaming?"

"I'll keep trying, Gracie, if you can keep on forgiving me."

"I'll do my best, but you better pray Shadow's sore foot is the only wound you'll need to heal between us." She tugged him to the settee beside her. Their kiss broke when Shadow jumped into Grace Anne's lap. She rubbed the dog's ears and looked to John with a playful smile. "You may keep company with some scoundrel friends, but Shadow will protect me. He'll not stand by and allow my heart to be broken."

His arms were about her waist, a smolder in his eyes that promised a lifetime of passion. "You could do no better in life than with a faithful dog and loving husband. And you'll always possess my heart with your enticing ways. Though please remember, I am good with stitching if the need arises."

THE END

Author's Note

As the third book in the series, the list of people to thank is about the same as the others—be sure to check out those acknowledgements for more details. My understanding children and spouse are still forgiving when I'm consumed with writing and editing. The same goes for my extended family—thanks for your support.

A special shout-out to my critique group. Write Club/Dial-a-Nerd is the best for all things critiques, grammar, and support in this emotionally demanding profession. I love you all, even if I don't hug you often.

And last, but not least, two more special thanks. Jennifer Lamont joined my inner circle as a beta reader—thanks for loving these characters as much as me. And to the members of Dalby's Darklings, my Facebook readers group: it's beyond amazing to have a group of core readers and friends to help me out with everything from silly to serious in regards to *The Possession Chronicles* and all my other endeavors. No matter if you're Team Alex, Team Douglas, Team Freddy, Team Claudio, or those renegade Team Opal readers (you know who you are), the interaction is always a pleasure.

About the Author

While experiencing the typical adventures of growing up, Carrie Dalby called several places in California home, but she's lived on the Alabama Gulf Coast since 1996. Serving two terms as president of Mobile Writers' Guild and five years as the Mobile area Local Liaison for the Society of Children's Book Writers and Illustrators are two of the writing-related volunteer positions she's held. When Carrie isn't reading, writing, browsing bookstores/libraries, or homeschooling her children, she can often be found knitting or attending concerts.

Carrie writes for both teens and adults. *Fortitude* is listed as a Best History Book for Kids by Grateful American Foundation. She has also published *Corroded*, a contemporary teen novel about friendship and autism, several short stories that can be found in different anthologies, as well as a multitude of Southern Gothic novels for adults.

For more information, visit Carrie Dalby's website:

carriedalby.com

9 781957 892160